SENSUAL HEALING

Me[illegible]mp nearest the front do[illegible] cast enough light for he[illegible]llows behind his back an[illegible]at he wasn't wearing an[illegible]ve more than enough light to see that his hair was tousled and he looked handsome and somehow vulnerable and still sexier than any man she knew, and she knew all the way to her toes that she'd made a mistake in coming to his room. She also knew she couldn't retreat to save her life . . . or her heart.

With the remote he shut off the television and just looked at her.

"I come in peace," she said, aiming for teasing and failing. Taking a deep breath, she forced herself over the threshold and to the bedside table, where she set down each gift as she spoke. "Ice for your knee. Chocolate because it makes everything feel better. Coke to wash the chocolate down. And"—she dug in the pocket of her robe—"an antiinflammatory for whatever ails you."

He looked from the offerings to her, his expression unchanging. "I don't like chocolate," he said at last, "and I'm not really thirsty, and little blue pills aren't going to do a damn thing for the part of me that's most inflamed . . . but I appreciate the thought."

She felt like crying, and didn't know why. With a lump growing in her throat, she nodded brightly, then turned to go back to her room. She'd made it as far as the door when he spoke again.

"Melina . . ." His voice was husky, the tone intense. "You didn't ask what would make me feel better."

She tried to speak, cleared her throat, then tried again. "What—what would make you feel better?"

"You." His gaze seared her. "Just you."

Praise for the novels of Marilyn Pappano

GETTING LUCKY

"[A] warm and charming tale of a small town has guardian angels that just may be the real thing. . . . Pappano's sparkling writing makes for a cozy, heavenly tale."
—*BookPage*

"Bethlehem is a town touched by angels, and gifted author Pappano continues to populate her stories with wonderfully rich and complex people."
—*Romantic Times*

FIRST KISS

"A warmhearted and compassionate story."
—*Romantic Times*

"Ms. Pappano can keep writing stories about Bethlehem forever and I will read every one. What a story!"
—*Rendezvous*

FATHER TO BE

"Heartwarming, funny, and memorable."
—Debbie Macomber

"Stirring and poignant." —*Romantic Times*

SOME ENCHANTED SEASON

"This is a four-hanky book, not to be missed. Deserves more than 4 hearts."
—*The Philadelphia Inquirer*

"This uplifting tale is for anyone who believes in love."
—*Publishers Weekly*

Also by Marilyn Pappano

SOME ENCHANTED SEASON

FATHER TO BE

FIRST KISS

GETTING LUCKY

HEAVEN ON EARTH

Marilyn Pappano

A DELL BOOK

Published by
Dell Publishing
a division of
Random House, Inc.
1540 Broadway
New York, New York 10036

ISBN: 0-440-23714-9

Printed in the United States of America
Published simultaneously in Canada

January 2002

10 9 8 7 6 5 4 3 2 1
OPM

List of Characters

Nathan and Emilie Dalton Bishop,
New York City detective turned small-town cop and assistant manager at the local inn
Michael, *son*
Alanna, Josie, and Brendan Dalton,
Emilie's nieces and nephew

Berry Dalton,
the Dalton children's drug-addicted mother

Corinna Winchester Humphries & Agatha Winchester Grayson, *Bethlehem's grand dames and matchmakers extraordinaire*

Ross and Maggie McKinney,
CEO of McKinney Industries and wife/mother
Rachel, *daughter*

J. D. and Kelsey Grayson,
psychiatrist and social worker
Trey, *J.D.'s son*
Caleb, Jacob, Noah, and Gracie Brown-Grayson,
adopted children
Bud, *J.D.'s father and newly wed to Agatha Winchester Grayson*

Gabe and Noelle Rawlins,
engineer at McKinney Industries and angel-turned human

Sophy, Gloria and Norma,
guardian angels; Noelle's replacements

Tom and Holly McBride Flynn,
second in charge at McKinney Industries and owner of McBride Inn

Ben and Lynda Barone Foster,
carpenter and top executive at McKinney Industries
Alanna Dalton,
Ben's daughter

Melina Dimitris,
private investigator from Buffalo

Sebastian Knight, *carpenter*
Chrissy, *daughter*

Julie Bujold,
Alanna's homeless friend and caretaker

Bree Aiken,
Holly McBride Flynn's half sister

Alex and Melissa Thomas,
lawyer and plant nursery owner

Mitch and Shelly Walker,
chief of police and wife/mother

Harry Winslow and Maeve Carter,
owner and waitress at Harry's Diner

Chapter One

THE DOUGHNUTS SHE'D BOUGHT THE NIGHT before were stale, the coffee in the thermos was lukewarm and bitter, and every bone in Melina Dimitris's body ached from spending ten hours in the cramped seat of an eighties vintage Mustang. She was definitely too old for these all-nighters, she thought as she rubbed her gritty eyes. She wasn't a two-bit P.I. trying to make ends meet. She owned the biggest and best investigations firm in all of Buffalo, so what was she doing hunkered down outside a sleazy motel watching the room where her client's sleazy husband was holed up with his girlfriend of the week? Why wasn't one of her employees doing this while she spent a lovely, comfortable night in her lovely, comfortable condo?

One of her employees had been doing it, honesty forced her to acknowledge, until she'd shown up in the wee hours of morning, unable to sleep and in need of a distraction, and had sent him home. She couldn't keep doing it, though. She wasn't as young as she used to be, and her body didn't bounce back the way it used to. Just because Sebastian Knight had broken her heart, the rat bastard, didn't mean she had to let him break her body and spirit. Instead of moping around like some lovesick schoolgirl, she would deal with him properly, starting today. She would finish up here, shower, then go to her folks' house for the weekly Dimitris family get-together, and there she was going to ask her brother Nikos to set her up with one of his friends. Greek, Italian, or hell, maybe even plain old white-bread American—she didn't care, as long as he wasn't six feet five, incredibly broad-shouldered, ruggedly handsome, and didn't have intense hazel eyes and amazingly strong, gentle hands.

As long as he wasn't someone she could fall for. That falling was tough business, especially when you landed. She'd done it twice now, and she wasn't inclined at the moment to do it ever again. If she wanted that kind of pain, she could just shoot herself and recover a whole lot faster.

Movement at the motel drew her attention across the street. The door to Room 16 opened, and the sleaze stepped out. She raised the camera with its telephoto lens and snapped off several pictures as Miss June appeared in the doorway, showing an incredible amount of tanned skin, and examined the rat's tonsils with her tongue.

Now all Melina had to do was follow him home, where he would tell his wife all about his weekend business trip to Chicago—the difficult client and the lousy hotel that left him badly in need of an afternoon's sleep. Then she would be free to tend to her own business. Meeting family obligations. Finding a new guy. Getting Sebastian the pig out of her system.

The sleaze pulled onto the street, and after a moment, she followed. She was thinking about her client, who'd trusted this man enough to make him the father of her children, and about what an amazing risk love and marriage were for any woman, when too late she realized she'd been spotted. Instead of trying to lose her, though, the bastard slammed to a stop, his car angled across the quiet residential street, and he jumped out, grabbed a baseball bat from the backseat, and ran toward her.

"What the hell are you doing following me?" he shouted, his face mottled. "Did my wife hire you? Do you really think I'm stupid enough to let you give her evidence against me so that bitch can divorce me and take everything I have?" He smashed the bat against the Mustang's driver's door, rocking the entire car, then leaned in the open window, forcing her back in the seat and making a grab for the camera.

His fingers were knotted around the camera strap when Melina brought her weapon up and pressed the barrel against his temple. The Sig Sauer was warm and hard, and it made his eyes practically pop out of their sockets. "Go ahead," she said softly. "Give me a reason. Threaten me with a bat. Steal my camera. Breathe too loudly."

He froze, and beads of sweat broke out along his forehead. She could smell his fear, along with Miss June's perfume, a hint of Cool Water cologne, and the stink of sex. "I—I—"

"Let go of my camera."

He did.

"Drop the bat."

He did that, too, and it landed with a clatter before rolling to a stop.

"Now back away. Slowly." Keeping the gun aimed at him, she grabbed her cell phone, then got out of the car. The door panel was crumpled from top to bottom, side to side, and was so flat at the point of impact that odds were, the window was shattered, too.

As she dialed 911, she gestured with the pistol. "Get on the ground. Facedown." Under different circumstances, she might have let the bastard go, or at least get his wife's opinion before she had him hauled off to jail, but if he was angry enough to take a bat to a stranger's car, who knew what he might do to his wife given the chance? Besides, she was nursing a healthy dislike for anyone with testosterone this morning. He'd be lucky if she didn't shoot him before the cops arrived.

The officer arrived within minutes, a female cop whom Melina knew and had tried on several occasions to hire away from the department. Faced with two women with guns, the sleaze stayed sullen and silent. Once he was handcuffed in the backseat of the patrol car and a wrecker arrived to hook up his car, the officer approached Melina. "Still stirring up men wherever you go, huh?"

"All men are bastards."

"Ain't that the truth. But like the saying says, we can't live with 'em and we can't live without 'em."

"I thought the saying was we can't live with 'em and we can't just shoot 'em." They both laughed, then Melina went on. "Speak for yourself. I intend to live a long, happy life without 'em. Except," she added wickedly, "on occasion."

"Tell me, Melina, you ever wonder what you're doing in a job where people come after you with a baseball bat?"

"The thought has crossed my mind a time or two." Or twenty. She spent more time with sad people and lowlifes than anyone ever should. She'd been shot at, threatened, punched a few times, and run off the road. She'd feared for her life and had fought against becoming overly cynical. And she loved her job. How was that for weird?

"You know the routine," the cop said. "I'll need a written complaint from you to attach to my report, then it'll go to the DA tomorrow."

"Who will look at it and say 'Felony assault with a baseball bat on a woman? Throw the book at him. Oh, wait, it was Dimitris. She probably provoked him. Give him a better weapon and her home address, and let him go.' "

Again they laughed. Though she got along well with most Buffalo cops, her relationship with District Attorney Milligan was less than congenial. She blamed several factors—his distrust of private investigators in general, his dislike of capable, independent women, and, most importantly, the fact that she had gathered evidence for his ex-wife to use in their much-publicized divorce a few years earlier. He'd gotten caught with his pants down, and he'd hated Melina for it ever since.

"If you ever decide you want better hours, a better salary, and much cooler weapons, give me a call," Melina said as she gingerly opened the banged-up door, then slid behind the wheel.

"I'll keep that in mind."

Once the wrecker had driven away, Melina returned to the high-rise that housed Dimitris Investigations, typed a quick report, left instructions to get an estimate on the Mustang, then headed home. Within two hours of the crack of the baseball bat against her door, she was walking into her mother's house, greeting relatives and exchanging hugs for kisses as she went. Anyone coming from a normal background could be forgiven for thinking it must be a special occasion to bring fifty or sixty relatives together for dinner, but the Dimitrises weren't a normal family. They were Greek, which pretty much explained everything.

The closer she got to the kitchen, the more amazing the aromas became. Nobody could cook like a good Greek mother, and at the moment, there were about ten of them in her mother's kitchen, putting together a feast. It was a good thing the dress she wore fitted too snugly to accommodate one single excess pound. It was the only way she knew to keep from growing as round as the other women in the family.

As if reading her mind, one aunt shook her finger as she passed. "I wouldn't allow my Mona to wear such a dress in public."

"Aw, Aunt Saba, you'd wear it yourself if Uncle Gene would let you out of the house."

"Tell me one thing," Aunt Olympia requested. "Where do you hide your gun with a dress like that?"

"You'd be surprised." Melina gave her a wink and a smile. "Yaya Rosa!" Bending, she kissed her grandmother's cheeks. There had been a time when Rosa had cooked for a crowd this size single-handedly, but these days, she supervised from a comfortable chair at the kitchen table. She was about eighty years old, frail in body but not in mind, and was most definitely the matriarch of the Dimitris family.

Rosa peered up at her through thick lenses. "How many criminals have you locked up since last we saw you?"

"Only one. But we caught four cheating husbands—five, counting this morning's loser—and two deadbeat dads."

"Good for you, *koretsi mou.*" Rosa applauded. "With a busy week like that, have you had time to meet any men?"

Every time Melina saw her grandmother—or her mother, any of her aunts, or most of her female cousins—she got the same question, but it usually didn't stir a twinge of pain in her gut. This time, as an image of Sebastian formed in her mind, it did. She'd had such hopes for him—such silly, romantic fantasies—and he'd destroyed them. "Nope," she lied. "You have to remember, the people I run into at work aren't exactly the sort I'd consider settling down with."

"Not the crooks, cheating husbands, or deadbeat dads," her cousin Antonia agreed. "But surely there's a petty thief or two. A white-collar criminal. Maybe an industrial spy?"

Melina gave her a phony smile as she circled the island to reach her mother. Antonia was a year older than she, had gotten married right out of high school, and had three kids by the time Melina had graduated from college. She'd added three more in the years since and was the accomplishment Olympia lorded over Melina's mother most often. As if producing a daughter who could breed like a rabbit was something to be proud of, Livia Dimitris groused. Deep in her heart, though, Livia was longing for grandbabies of her own, and none of her three children showed any sign of providing them just yet.

Truth was, Melina was longing for them, too. At thirty-four, she still had plenty of time, but she'd always hoped to have a few years to settle into a committed, permanent, happily-ever-after marriage before she started a family. With that in mind, time was about to get short.

She kissed her mother's cheek, then bent to inhale deeply of the fabulous aromas coming from the pan Livia was stirring on the stovetop.

"You look hungry," Livia said. "Eat."

Obediently Melina scooped up a triangle of baklava from a nearby tray. The flaky phyllo dough was golden brown and buttery, the layers filled with nuts and redolent with honey. Like everything else that came out of this kitchen, it was incredible.

"How was your week?" Livia asked.

"Busy." It wasn't entirely a lie. She'd spent a good part of Sunday, Monday, Tuesday, and Wednesday making wild, passionate love with Sebastian. Then he'd dumped her. No excuses, no explanations, just a heartlessly cold kiss-off.

No, that wasn't exactly true, either. There'd been an explanation—the wedding band he'd been wearing for the kiss-off. She'd thought he was divorced. It was common knowledge in Bethlehem that he'd been alone since his wife left him four years ago. At the moment, though, she neither knew nor cared about the status of his marriage. She hated him, and that was all that mattered.

"I called your office Tuesday and they said you were out of town. On business?"

"Everything in my life is business, Mama."

"More's the pity. How are you sleeping? You look tired. Are you getting enough rest?"

"I'm fine. Is there anything I can do?"

Just as Livia opened her mouth, the cell phone in Melina's handbag trilled. "You can get the phone," Livia suggested. "I think we have enough cooks in the kitchen today."

"I'll be right back." Melina hugged her mother, then fished out the phone as she headed for the back door and a bit of quiet. Only a bit, though, since all the cousins under twelve were playing in the backyard. Taking a seat on the top step, she pressed the phone to her ear. "This is Melina."

"Hi. Are you busy?" It was Lynda Barone, her best friend since their first day of college, and she sounded about as down as Melina felt. She was having man problems, too, except hers were vastly different. Ben Foster was handsome, charming, and sexy as hell, and he clearly loved her, but she'd chosen to punish him for being selfishly human thirteen years ago. Melina had to admit, she found it a lot easier to see Ben's side of things than Lynda's. So he'd gotten a girlfriend pregnant when he was a kid. So he'd broken up with her rather than accept the responsibilities of fatherhood. It was a long time ago, and he'd grown up and was trying to make things right.

Of course, having been recently dumped herself, it was easier to relate to another dumpee rather than the dumper.

"I'm at my folks' house. We're about to sit down to enough souvlaki, tyropitta, and kadaifi to feed a small country. What's up?"

"You remember I told you that Ben has a daughter who lives with her aunt and uncle here?"

"Uh-huh."

A grim note came into Lynda's voice. "She ran away this morning. Two other children are also missing. One is a good friend of Alanna's, and the other apparently chose to tag along. The authorities have been notified, but of course their parents are worried sick, and Ben— We want you to look for them, Melina, please."

She gazed across the backyard where a dozen or so kids played. What would it be like to have a child of your own, then lose him? Like losing the better part of yourself, she imagined. "All right. Do you think your boss would have one of his pilots pick me up?" It was a five-hour drive from Buffalo to Bethlehem, and she'd rather not waste all that time.

"Not a problem."

"I'll get a suitcase at home, then head for the airport. Set up a meeting with the parents. Ask them to bring recent photographs of their kids. If they have any idea where the kids went or why, I want to know. I'll also need lists of their friends and relatives, both in town and out, and the best guess they can make at what the kids took with them—clothing, a toy, any photographs or money that's missing, everything. If they left notes, I want to see them. Any clue where they're headed?"

"Providence. Alanna left a note saying she's gone to see her mother, and that's where Berry lives."

"Providence . . . I'll see if I know anyone who works there." She paused and softened her voice. "Is Ben okay?"

"He's really worried, and he's blaming himself. Apparently, Alanna found out that he's her father, and she was upset. Melina, if anything happens to her—"

"Nothing will," Melina promised, though she was far from sure. "What about you? Are you okay?"

"Sure. Just worried about the kids and Ben." Lynda made an obvious effort to lighten up. "Hey, he asked me to marry him, or maybe I asked him. I don't remember. Anyway, we're getting married. He loves me, Melina. Can you believe that?"

The wonder and awe in her voice brought a sheen to Melina's eyes. That was how she'd felt with Sebastian. She'd thought she was the luckiest woman around. Turned out, she was merely the biggest sucker around.

She swallowed the lump in her throat and forced an excited whoop. "Of course he loves you, darlin'. The only one who doubted it was you. Congratulations! After we find the kids, we'll celebrate properly. Now I've got to go and pack before I turn pea-green with envy. I'll see you in a few hours."

After disconnecting, she sat motionless on the stoop. *She* was the one who'd announced not long ago that she wanted to settle down, get married, and have kids, and Lynda had been cynical. They were modern women. They had careers, money, travel, and excitement to keep them happy. They didn't need men or marriage. Now the cynic was getting married and would probably be pregnant before she could say "impending motherhood," and the wanna-be bride was further from commitment than she'd ever been.

Life just wasn't fair.

But if it was, she would be out of a job that paid very well and supported her in the way she wanted to be supported. After all, it was the schemers and deceivers who kept her in business.

As she reentered the kitchen, Livia looked up, subjecting her to a moment of study before her full mouth flattened. "Something's come up, and you don't even have time for a bite of food with your family. What is it this time? Another straying husband? A bad-check artist? Someone stealing from wealthy old women?"

"Three missing kids." She knew that would silence any

complaints from Livia. Though her mother adored Lynda, Melina also knew not to tell her about the engagement. She found a man in that burgh where she lives? Livia would complain. *And you can't find one in the entire city of Buffalo? That's all it takes, you know. Just one.* "I'm going to head out the back. Make my apologies to Papa and everyone, will you?"

"You be careful. And keep in touch with your mother, you hear?"

"I will, Mama. Love you." Slipping out the back door, Melina made her way around the house and down the street, where her Bug fit right in with the secondhand cars that surrounded it. It was a classic car, older than Melina, a convertible, and in better shape than most people its age. Though she could afford virtually any car on the market, the Bug had been a sixteenth-birthday present, and she loved it dearly.

Above her, the sun went behind a cloud, cooling the air briefly. That was why she felt a shiver down her spine, Melina told herself. Not because this new case involved children, and kids-in-danger cases were always tough. Not because it involved Ben's kid, and she adored Ben and would have married him herself if Lynda hadn't accepted his proposal. And certainly not because she was going back to Bethlehem, where she could conceivably run into Sebastian long before she was emotionally ready to face him again.

But she *wasn't* going to run into Sebastian. He was pretty much a loner, and his only daughter was too young to be a friend of Alanna Dalton's, and surely, after his behavior last week, he would be no more eager to see her than she was to see him. The rest of her life might be filled with surprises and unexpected events, but she was pretty sure it was never going to be filled with Sebastian again. He didn't want her.

He'd made that painfully clear.

"TELL ME SOMETHING, ALANNA," CALEB BROWN SAID sarcastically. "How did you manage to find out what time Miss Agatha's cousins were leaving to go home without finding out that they weren't going home?"

The muscles in Alanna Dalton's jaw tightened as she ignored him. She'd thought she had a perfect plan for getting out of Bethlehem—hide in the travel trailer belonging to guests of the Winchester sisters, Miss Agatha and Miss Corinna, go along for the ride to Utica, then sneak out and catch the bus or the train to Providence. It would have worked, too . . . if Miss Agatha's cousins had gone home to Utica like they were supposed to.

But it would still work. It had to.

"Do you have *any* idea where we are?"

She'd seen a few highway signs, but nothing was familiar. For all she knew, they could be anywhere, and with the sun high overhead, traveling in any direction. She was hoping they were headed south or east. The closer Miss Agatha's cousins got them to Providence, the better.

"What do you think they're doing now?"

Caleb had asked that question before, and she hoped he didn't ask it again. She didn't want to think about their families and how worried they were. She remembered what it was like when Caleb ran away the summer before because he'd caused so much trouble for his foster father, Dr. J.D.—how scared she'd been, how hard she'd prayed. She didn't want to put Aunt Emilie and Uncle Nathan through that.

"Are you hungry?" she asked, sliding to her feet and going to the tiny kitchen. The refrigerator held only bottled water and some cans of protein drink for old people, but in the cabinets, she found crackers and peanut butter. She was looking for a knife when a loud thump made her freeze.

Caleb jumped up from the bench and came to stand beside her. "What was that?"

"Maybe we hit a bump."

"Where did it come from?"

With a trembling hand, she pointed toward the closet. There couldn't be anyone in the bedroom, 'cause they'd hidden back there until they'd gotten on the road, and they'd both been in the bathroom, too. The only place in the entire trailer that they *hadn't* been was the closet.

Caleb was walking that way when a crash came from the closet. She saw the door rattle, as if something had hit it from the inside, and could feel her knees knocking. Maybe one of the neighborhood dogs or cats had wandered inside while Miss Agatha's cousins were loading their suitcases this morning, or maybe it was a—a—

Trying to look brave, Caleb wrapped his hand around the doorknob, looked back at Alanna, then jerked it open. She clamped her hands over her mouth so the scream in her throat wouldn't escape, then he immediately slammed the door again.

"I don't believe this! Of all the rotten luck . . . That little snot-nosed brat . . . !" He jerked the door open again, and this time a box tumbled out, followed by a mussed and sleepy-looking Chrissy Knight. She wore a backpack over one shoulder and clutched a pink stuffed cat with her other arm.

"S'prise!" Grinning broadly, she looked from Caleb to Alanna, then headed straight for the table and the crackers. "I didn't mean to fall asleep in there, but I was up late last night 'cause of the party, and then I was excited about today so I didn't sleep good, and—"

Alanna wasn't sure if she'd stopped talking or if the cracker she'd stuffed in her mouth blocked the words. She glanced at Caleb, who was looking both mad and mean.

"What is she doing here?" he demanded.

"I don't know! I didn't ask her to come."

"Well, I sure didn't. I see enough of her when she comes over to play with Gracie." He ran his hand through his hair. "Great. This is just what we need."

It took Chrissy a moment to swallow the food in her mouth and clear her throat. Alanna got her a bottle of water from the refrigerator, and she drank half of it before wiping her mouth with the back of her hand and grinning. "Are we almost there yet?"

"What are you doing here, Chrissy?"

"I'm goin' with you to find your mama so's we can find mine, too. I haven't seen my mama in a long, long time. I don't even hardly r'member her at all. Daddy gived me a picture of her to keep by my bed, but I really want to see her."

As Caleb sat down again, Alanna slid in next to Chrissy. "Where is your mom?"

"In the special place. With yours and his."

He gave her that mean look again. "My only mother that matters is back home in Bethlehem worrying about us. I don't know where my other mother is, and I don't care."

"She's with Lannie's mom and mine," Chrissy said,

looking real serious. "My grandma said. She told my aunt Shauna there's a special place for mamas like mine and yours and Lannie's. She said, and my grandma don't lie."

"Yeah, but it ain't Providence," Caleb said. "That special place she was talking about is—"

Alanna kicked him under the table, warning him to be quiet the way she did with her little sister, Josie, sometimes. "Chrissy, I don't think your mother is in Providence. I think you'd better go back home and talk to your daddy, and let him take you to wherever she is." If he even knew. She'd heard the grown-ups talking sometimes when she wasn't supposed to, and she didn't think anyone knew where Chrissy's mother had gone. Just like Caleb's mom, she'd disappeared one day and never come back.

"I can't talk to my daddy about my mama. It makes him sad and real quiet. And my grandma doesn't like to talk about her, either, and my other grandma just wants to talk about when she was a kid." Chrissy's brown eyes looked big enough to fill her face. "Ever' kid I know has a mama somewhere. Even you got your aunt, and ol' mean Caleb's got his new mother, but all I got is my mama I don't r'member. I just want to see her and tell her I love her and ask her why she left us, and I want to bring her back home so her and Daddy and me can be a family again."

Alanna knew how she felt. Josie had big dreams about living with their mom and being a family again, even if everyone else knew it wasn't ever going to happen. Chrissy had big dreams, too.

"You don't understand, Chrissy," she said. Reaching into her pocket, she pulled out a crumpled envelope and laid it on the table in front of them. "This is a letter from my mom. See? It's got her name and address in Providence. That's how I know she's there. Not because all bad mothers go there."

Chrissy stroked the envelope as if it were special. "My mama's not bad. She just needed a change. Grandma said."

Yeah, the same kind of change Berry and Caleb's mom had wanted—not taking care of her family, being selfish, doing only what *she* wanted without having to care about anyone else. Because they were bad mothers and bad people.

"I never had a letter from my mama. Will you read me yours?"

Alanna didn't need to open the letter to remember what it said. It was full of excuses, like always. The visit Berry had promised wasn't going to happen after all, because she had to find a new place to live. But if she hadn't been moving, it would have been something else. She would have spent her travel money on booze or drugs, or she would have been arrested and not allowed to leave the state, or locked up again in another rehab clinic or jail. She had more excuses than Alanna could count.

"Maybe later," she said, putting the envelope back in her pocket.

"How do you plan on finding your mom?" Caleb asked. "Do you have an address?"

Clearly unconcerned, Chrissy shrugged. "I'll ask someone."

"In a city the size of Providence? Oh, yeah, like that's gonna work. Especially since she's probably not even there. Not that it matters. As soon as we get out of this trailer, you're going back to Bethlehem. We'll turn you over to the police."

"Will not!"

"Will, too!"

"If you do, I'll cry and tell 'em you kidnapped me and stole my money."

She would, too, Alanna thought. Even Miss Corinna and Miss Agatha said Chrissy was too spoiled, and they believed all kids should be spoiled at least some. She was used to getting her way, and she was a tattletale.

"Then we'll just put you on the bus back to Bethlehem."

Chrissy's brown eyes got huge. "All by myself? I'm just a little kid!"

"She's right, Caleb," Alanna said. "We can't turn her over to the police or put her on the bus alone."

"How about we just leave her on the street and run the other way?"

Alanna kicked him again. "We have to take her with us. It's the only way to keep her safe and not get caught ourselves. But, Chrissy, you've gotta be good, and you've gotta do what Caleb and I tell you without whining or asking questions. Okay?"

She nodded, and she looked as if she really, truly meant it, but Alanna knew better than to believe it.

Caleb leaned back on the bench, mumbling, "Like any bad guy would want her, or she's got anything worth stealing."

"I do, too." Chrissy swung her backpack onto the table, then began digging inside it. Grinning triumphantly, she came up with a handful of twenty-dollar bills.

Alanna looked at the money, then at Caleb, who shrugged. It wasn't like the money made a difference. Even if she didn't have a penny, they didn't have any choice but to take her with them. But since they *had* to take her along, a hundred and twenty dollars or more would help.

Chrissy leaned across the table, stuck out her tongue at Caleb, and in a prissy voice said, "So there, Caleb Brown-Grayson!" When he moved as if to grab her, she squealed.

Alanna rolled her eyes. The money would help.

But, she was afraid, not enough.

Chapter Two

Sebastian Knight had had his share of tough times. Until this warm June Sunday, the toughest had been walking into his house one evening four years ago to find his wife, his daughter, and everything they'd owned of any value missing. He'd found Chrissy, thank God, at his mother's house, but he'd never heard from Diana again. Once he'd scraped together enough money—she'd cleaned out their bank accounts, too—he'd hired a private detective, but by then the trail had gone cold. If anyone had had a clue where Diana had gone, they weren't talking.

But the panic and fear he'd felt that night were nothing compared to what he was feeling now. His little girl—his reason for living—was gone, disappeared without a trace, and this time her fleeing mother hadn't dropped her off with a relative for safekeeping.

He stood at a window in a courthouse conference room, hands knotted on the sill, gaze fixed sightlessly on the town square below. One of Chrissy's favorite treats was a Sunday-afternoon cone from the ice-cream shop across the street, eaten in the cool shade on the square's bandstand steps. That was where they should be at that very moment, just the two of them. He shouldn't be alone there, helping to organize a search for her, and she shouldn't be wherever the hell those kids had taken her. She belonged right there with him, and when he got her back . . . please, God, when he got her back, he was never letting her go again.

There was quite a crowd in the conference room and in the lobby outside. His parents and Diana's mother were somewhere behind him. So were Alanna Dalton's aunt and uncle and J.D. and Kelsey Grayson, Caleb's adoptive parents. Ben Foster and Lynda Barone were there, too, as well as Corinna Winchester Humphries, town matriarch along with her sister Agatha. Miss Agatha would have been present, too, if she hadn't left for her honeymoon the night before. The kids' brothers and sisters and friends waited outside with concerned neighbors and extended families. Sebastian's own three brothers and his sister were out there, with all their kids safely in sight. He envied them that, and was ashamed of himself for it.

All were waiting anxiously for Melina to arrive. Hiring a private investigator had been the police chief's idea, one that everyone else had instantly agreed with. Cops had plenty of problems to deal with; three runaways couldn't have a hundred percent of their attention. If they had to pay someone to get that hundred percent, not a problem. He just wished they'd hired someone else. He wasn't on Melina's list of favorite people. Who knew whether that would affect how she handled this case? On top of that, he wasn't ready to see her again. It was too soon. He felt too guilty.

On the street below, a patrol car pulled into a parking space in front of the courthouse. He watched as Melina slid out of the front seat, all long legs and curly black hair and sensuous movements. She was one of the most beautiful women he'd ever met. She had a great body and dressed to show it, and she liked men and showed that, too. When he'd first met her at the Starlite Lounge, he'd thought she was easy, or whatever the modern-day equivalent of a tramp was. He'd thought she was perfect for his purposes—a night or two of hot sex, *So long,* and *I'll call you,* which he never would have done.

She hadn't cooperated, though. Oh, she'd been easy, all right. She'd given him the hot sex, and a whole lot more. They'd spent four days and nights together, and she'd crawled under his skin. He'd been a fool, thinking he could use her, then walk away. He'd been playing with fire, and they'd both gotten burned.

Now his best chance at finding his little girl was a woman who despised him and would sooner shoot him than look at him.

She disappeared from sight as she approached the building. He could imagine her walking in the double doors, climbing the stairs to the second floor, dazzling the officer escorting her and anyone else who caught a glimpse of her. She would come into the conference room any minute now and take command.

Or maybe see him, realize he was one of her clients, and walk right back out.

The hushed conversations in the room quieted as the door was closed behind her. He listened to her footsteps—heels on polished oak planks—and followed her movements to the table without looking. She went to Lynda and Ben first. Sebastian recognized the soft murmurs of their voices. A moment later she introduced herself to Police Chief Mitch Walker and Sheriff Charles Ingles. Finally she faced the group as a whole. "Hello. I'm Melina Dimitris, and I'm the best damn private investigator in this state. I'm sorry we have to meet under these circumstances, but I want to tell you right up front that if anyone can find your children, it's me."

She didn't lack for confidence, Sebastian thought with a thin smile. The night they'd met, she had picked him out of the crowd, introduced herself, announced her desire to dance with him and her intent to have a good time. She had, too, for a few days. Had the fun lasted a few days too long? Or a lifetime too short?

"Did you bring the photographs as I asked?"

"They're in this folder," Mitch Walker said, apparently handing it to her.

There was a soft rustle as she opened the file and thumbed through its contents. "What I'd like to do first is talk with each set of parents. If we could have one end of this table—"

Her words ended abruptly, as if the switch that powered her voice had been flipped to off. Sebastian continued to stare outside even as he became aware of her intense gaze riveted on his back. Slowly, with a deep breath, he turned to face her. She stared, and he stared back.

She should have been told before she'd traveled all the way from Buffalo. She should have been given the option of refusing the case, which she surely would have done had she known he was involved. But Ben and Lynda had apparently kept that fact to themselves. They'd wanted the best and had been willing to hold back the truth to get it. He didn't blame them at all.

An eight-by-ten-inch glossy of Chrissy dangled from Melina's limp grasp. For one moment he let his gaze slide to the upside-down image of his little girl. His mother had insisted on the portrait after her seventh birthday three months ago. The photographer had shown up at the farm one sunny afternoon and posed Chrissy on the creek bank, wearing a red-gingham shirt and faded overalls with the legs rolled halfway to her knees. Her feet were bare, and her long dark hair hung in a heavy braid, and she looked like exactly what she was—a healthy, active, country-raised tomboy. It was Sebastian's favorite picture of her.

Suddenly a wave of fear washed over him so strong that he felt sick with it. He couldn't stand knowing she was out there somewhere, that she could be lost, hungry, afraid, in danger. She was his life, and he wanted her back *now.*

Looking away from him, Melina straightened the photograph so he couldn't see it anymore. She lined up the items inside the folder, then closed it and tapped it nervously on the table. "I, uh . . . I need to . . ."

Sebastian saw that everyone was looking at her curiously, except Lynda and Ben. They knew what he'd done to her. He doubted Mitch Walker had a clue, but he stepped in anyway.

"Let's all clear out from this end of the conference table. Emilie, Nathan, why don't you start? Come on down here and have a seat."

While everyone shuffled to new positions, Ben and Lynda came to stand with Sebastian. He'd worked with Ben for about a week, had known him a little longer.

Though Lynda had lived in Bethlehem over eighteen months, he didn't know her at all. She worked a lot. He kept to himself a lot. At least, until he'd met Melina.

"You should have told her," he remarked as he leaned back against the windowsill.

Lynda brushed her hair back in an awkward gesture. "I should have, but I didn't want her to turn me down."

Sebastian didn't believe that would have happened. Melina loved Lynda better than a sister, and there was nothing she wouldn't do for the people she loved. For a short time—a few hours, maybe even a few days—she'd thought she loved *him*. He'd known she didn't, but watching her think so had been . . . sweet. Other than Chrissy, there wasn't much that was sweet in his life, and hadn't been for a long time.

If he didn't get her back again safely, there would never be again.

SHE CARRIED A GUN. SHE HAD A BLACK BELT IN tae kwon do and excelled at full-contact sparring. There was an illegal canister of ten-percent pepper spray tucked in an inside pocket of her purse, and if all else failed, she wasn't averse to kicking, jabbing, scratching, and punching her way out of a situation. In short, she could give as good as she got.

Melina was going to enjoy giving someone what they deserved for the dirty trick that had just been played on her.

She pretended to review the notes she'd made while talking to the Bishops and the Graysons—anything to keep that empty chair across from her empty a while longer. She could tell the police chief she had all the information she needed. After all, how many times did she have to hear a parent relate the discovery that his child was missing? What did it matter what clothing Chrissy Knight had taken with her? What could Sebastian possibly add that might be of any importance?

And what would everyone think if she didn't take a few minutes to hear his version of events?

When she looked up, her gaze went straight to him, as if she'd known he would be standing across the room from where she'd last seen him. He looked worried and restless, as if he might bolt out the door to find his daughter himself. The only thing holding him back, she knew, was the fact that he didn't have a clue where to look. He felt helpless and impotent—a condition she might happily wish on him once this was all over and she could go back to hating him again—and in spite of herself, she wanted to wrap her arms around him and assure him that Chrissy would be all right.

Not that the rat bastard deserved either the hug or the assurances.

Deliberately she shifted her attention to the police chief. "Could you get Chrissy's father, please?"

A moment later Sebastian slid into the chair across from her. She was no fragile flower—she was five nine and nicely muscled—but he was big enough to make her feel like one. Six five, broad shoulders, slender hips, a nice butt, long legs, and his hands . . . She had a thing about men's hands, and his were big, strong, and callused. His nails were blunt cut, his fingers marked with small scars, and he could do thoroughly amazing things with them.

"Hello, Melina," he said quietly, his voice deep and low and recalling dark nights, feverish need, and husky cries.

Reminding herself that she hated him, she called on every bit of the professionalism she'd acquired in the past twelve years, smashed down every ounce of vulnerability, then glanced up and smiled. It wasn't a nice smile, not a pleasant, reassuring put-the-client-at-ease smile like she'd given the other parents. This was purely a spurned-woman gesture. "Bet you never guessed last Wednesday evening when you dumped me that a few short days later, your best hope of getting your daughter back would be me, did you? If you'd known, it probably would have changed things, wouldn't it?"

His only response was a flicker of guilt across his features. Did he feel bad about the way he'd treated her? Good. He should. He should feel at least as bad as she did, if not worse. Her preference was much, much worse.

She flipped to a clean page on the legal pad. "What is Chrissy's full name?"

"Christina Diana Knight."

"And she's seven?"

He nodded.

"When did you discover she was gone?"

"I didn't. She went to church this morning with my parents. They called me when the service was over and she was nowhere to be found."

"When was the last time you saw her?"

"Last night at Miss Agatha's wedding reception. She wanted to go home with my folks, and I let her."

"Are your parents here?"

Another nod.

"So . . . I really don't need to waste my time with you, do I?" *Oops. Too late for that.* "You can go now."

A flush turned the taut skin across his high cheekbones a deep crimson. Embarrassment at how easily she dismissed him? She doubted it. More likely anger. She didn't care either way. He hadn't hired her. The way she looked at it, she was there to find Ben's daughter. The other kids were freebies.

She glanced around the room, scanning the people she hadn't yet met, and found the likeliest candidates for Sebastian's parents at the far end of the room—an attractive blonde who was as trim as her own mother was round and a silver-haired, handsomer version of Sebastian. "Mr. and Mrs. Knight? Would you please come over here?"

Their son ignored her dismissal, and she ignored him. Once the elder Knights were seated, she asked the same questions the other parents had already answered. Chrissy had left no note, she'd taken her backpack, clothing, and a stuffed cat that went everywhere with her, and they didn't have any idea why she would run away. Or so they said.

Melina wasn't buying that. Happy, well-adjusted kids just didn't hit the road for no reason. Alanna Dalton had gone to find her absentee mother, and Caleb Brown-Grayson had gone along to look out for her. Why had Chrissy joined them? "Did your granddaughter get in trouble last night?"

Both elder Knights shook their heads.

"You hadn't punished her for something? Gotten cross with her? Lost your temper?"

"No, not at all," Mr. Knight said.

"Was she good friends with Alanna and Caleb?"

The Knights looked to their son to answer. Reluctantly, Melina did, too. He shrugged. "She knows them, of course. The Graysons live down the road from us. She goes to church and to school with them and the

Daltons. She plays with the younger kids, but . . . Alanna and Caleb are five and six years older than Chrissy."

At their ages, that was a big difference. Nikos was five years older than she, and though it hadn't mattered since college, as kids it had been important. He hadn't wanted her tagging along anywhere with him and his friends, just as she hadn't wanted five-years-younger Stavros tagging along with her friends. "Then why would she run away with them? Would they force her to for some reason?"

"No." The answer came from all three of them at once, then Mrs. Knight continued. "Chrissy had no reason to run off. She's having a good summer. She's been learning to swim and going fishing with her grandpa. She's taking part in the summer reading program at the library, and next weekend she's supposed to go camping with the Brownies. She's looking forward to Vacation Bible School next month, and she loves the Fourth of July. She's a normal, happy, well-adjusted child who wants for absolutely nothing but—"

Melina, Sebastian, and his father all looked at her, waiting for her to go on. When she didn't, Melina gently prodded her. "But what, Mrs. Knight?"

The woman looked at her husband, then gave her son an apologetic look. "A mother. Chrissy misses her mother."

"Where does Chrissy's mother live?" Melina asked Mrs. Knight. Call her overly sensitive, but this wasn't the time to be discussing Sebastian's wife, or ex-wife, with him.

Mrs. Knight's mouth thinned, and her eyes took on a disapproving look. "We don't know. Chrissy doesn't, either."

So a little girl who missed her mother overheard

another young girl making plans to find her own mother. In the convoluted thinking of a seven-year-old, she somehow believed that wherever Alanna's mother was, her own might be, too, and so she'd tagged along. It was a stretch, but kids' minds worked in strange ways.

"Thank you, Mrs. Knight, Mr. Knight."

The couple both rose and had walked a half-dozen feet away when she turned back. "Oh, Ms. Dimitris, Chrissy also took the money from my purse—about two hundred dollars, as far as I can figure."

So the angelic-looking child was a resourceful little thief. At least they wouldn't go hungry—provided they didn't get mugged. People had been killed for less. But not *these* people. She fully intended to bring all three kids home safe and sound. How deeply in her debt would that put Sebastian? she wondered. How guilty would it make him feel for the way he'd used her?

"What are you going to do now?" he asked.

As she pushed back her chair, she looked at him as if she'd forgotten he was there. "I'm going to find these kids."

He caught her wrist. "How?"

She stared at his hand. She'd been with him four days and nights—hardly a blink of the eye in the context of a lifetime—but his touch was familiar. Intimate. It created both pleasure and pain, arousal and revulsion. For four days he'd been everything she'd ever wanted in her life, and then she'd found out it was all an illusion. She'd lived in a wonderful little fantasy world for ninety-six hours, and then he'd dragged her into the real world.

Once again he flushed under her narrow-eyed stare, and he withdrew his hand. Pointedly she turned away, taking a few minutes to talk with the police chief and the sheriff, then found Ben alone at the window. When she slid her arm around his waist, he gave her a sickly smile. "Where's Lyn?" she asked.

"She got a call from her mother. She's taking it outside."

"You okay?"

"Yeah." He didn't sound very convincing.

"It's not your fault."

"If I'd stayed in Georgia . . ."

"You wouldn't have met Lynda. More importantly"—with a flutter of lashes, she switched into a bad Southern accent—"you wouldn't have met me."

"And that would have been a loss?" he teased weakly.

"Lyn told me you're getting married. I would've married you myself, darlin', if you'd given me the chance."

"Nah, I'm not your type."

She gave him a chastising look. "You're male, and you're breathing. Those are my only two requirements for a prospective mate. Anyway"—rising onto her toes, she pressed a kiss to his cheek—"welcome to the family. And make no mistake about it. I *am* part of the family."

"I'm well aware of that, darlin'." He returned the kiss to her forehead, then looked past her. "Sorry about Sebastian. We didn't mean to spring him on you without warning."

The *pffft* Melina spat out sounded rude and nicely coarse. "Why, Ben, I do believe I'm insulted. It takes a hell of a better man than Sebastian Knight to get me down. I was just using him for sex, you know. I couldn't care less about seeing him again."

It was a bald-faced lie, and Ben was one of the few

people who knew it. When she'd drowned her post-dumping sorrows in too much wine, beer, and scotch, it was Ben who'd carried her into Lynda's living room and tucked the covers around her on the sofa. But for the sake of her ego, he pretended to believe her disclaimer, and she loved him for it.

"I'm going to find your daughter," she said suddenly, fiercely. "It may take a few days, but I swear to you, Ben, I'll find her."

BY THE TIME THE MEETING BROKE UP, SEBASTIAN had a headache, a case of heartburn that could take down a weaker man, and a sense of bitter helplessness. There was nothing more they could do, the police chief had announced, and slowly the families were leaving. He hadn't moved from his position against the wall. Was he supposed to go home? Pretend it was a normal day? Act as if Chrissy weren't in danger? He couldn't do it.

"Come over to the house with us," his mother said, reaching up to brush his hair back the way she'd done when he was a kid himself.

"Not right now."

"You can't just camp out here at the courthouse."

No, he couldn't. But what could he do? Half the town had already driven up and down every road in the county, looking for any sign of the kids. Police officers and deputies had questioned everyone else in town. They'd notified authorities all across the state. Bus stations and train stations had all been alerted, and the Providence police were keeping an eye out for them at that end. Everything that could be done was being done. All he could do was wait.

"You guys go on. I'm going to hang around here a while." Ben and Lynda were seated at the table again with Melina, Mitch, and Sheriff Ingles, devising a plan, he assumed. He intended to sit in on it.

"You really should—"

His father tugged his mother's arm, making her break off. "He wants to stay here, Hildy. Come on. Let him be."

"If you need anything, you call," she said as she was led away. "Anything at all."

He waited until they were gone to move to the table. Melina sat at the end, spine straight, long legs crossed. She'd introduced herself as the best damn private investigator in the state, and he assumed she was, or McKinney Industries wouldn't be one of her best clients. Ross McKinney hadn't made billions for himself and others by settling for less than the best.

She certainly didn't look the part, though. Her black hair spun in wild curls halfway down her back, and her sleeveless black dress clung snugly to every curve and ended high on the thigh. Her skin was the same sweet-scented olive shade all over, her features were perfect, and her brown eyes literally sparkled with life. She looked more like every man's midnight fantasy than a hotshot P.I.

She didn't even glance his way as he slid into the empty chair next to Ben. Mitch was talking, detailing what action had already been taken. ". . . sent out an endangered-child broadcast once we were certain the kids were gone, and they've been entered into NCIC. That's the computer network run by the FBI," he explained. "Miss Corinna and Kelsey are putting together a list of all the wedding guests, and the Providence police are trying to locate Berry Dalton. Apparently, she's moved from the last address the Bishops had for her."

"You think someone here for the wedding took them?" Sebastian asked.

"No. But it's possible that someone saw them this morning, or that the kids might have stowed away in someone's vehicle."

"How could they not notice that they're leaving town with three kids they didn't have when they arrived?" Ben asked.

"It would be tough," Mitch agreed. "But if someone was driving a pickup with a camper or an RV . . . We have to check all the possibilities."

Lynda laid her hand over Melina's. "What are you going to do now?"

"First, we need flyers with the kids' pictures on them."

"Our computer services people at McKinney Industries can take care of that," Lynda offered.

Melina started to hand over the file with the photos, but the sheriff stopped her. "We've already scanned the pictures. If you'll stop by my office downstairs, Ms. Barone, Reggie will give them to you on a diskette."

With a nod, Melina went on. "While we wait for the list of wedding guests, I want to talk to the kids' siblings and friends. The Graysons said they would meet me at the Bishops' house, and they're rounding up the best friends, so I'll conduct the interviews there. I also want to go to McBride Inn and talk to the staff on duty last night."

"I'll call Holly Flynn, the owner, and have her get them all together," Mitch volunteered.

"Sounds good." Melina stood up, gathered her notes

and files, and took two steps before stopping. "I forgot I flew in. I'll need a ride."

Everyone started to offer at once, but Sebastian cut them all off. "I'll take you."

She gave him a cool, cutting look. "No, thanks."

He shrugged as if her refusal didn't sting. "I can take you, or I can follow you. Either way, I'm going along."

"I don't—"

"This is my little girl. I have to do something."

After a moment, *she* shrugged and started toward the door. "Suit yourself."

Just don't expect civility. That was okay. As long as she did her best to find Chrissy, he didn't care how she behaved toward him.

He followed her out of the conference room and down the stairs. When he would have opened the door for her, she pushed ahead. She spotted his pickup in the lot at the side of the courthouse and headed in that direction without so much as a glance toward him.

"I—I appreciate what you're doing, and I'll pay whatever it costs . . ."

She waited until they were inside the truck, seat belts buckled, to respond. "I'm not working for you."

"I know you're doing it for Ben, but at least let me contribute—"

"No."

His mouth tightened, and he didn't say anything else for the remaining few blocks to the Bishop house. The Graysons' cars were already parked out front, along with several others. He pulled to the curb, and Melina was out of the truck before the engine quieted.

It was a somber group that awaited them inside. Kids

were everywhere, it seemed—the Bishops' three, the Graysons' five, others that he knew from church and Chrissy's school. Some of the younger kids were sniffly. They all looked bewildered, and all were unusually quiet.

Melina made herself comfortable at the kitchen table. Though she scowled at him as if his mere presence tested her patience, she didn't say anything when he chose to lean against the counter across the room. She called Gracie Brown-Grayson in first. J.D. brought her in and sat down at the table with her.

Settling on her knees in the chair, Gracie leaned across the table toward Melina. "Are you gonna bring Caleb home so's you can take 'im away again?"

"I'm sure gonna try to bring him home, but no one will take him away again."

Gracie plopped down on her butt. "Last time he runned away 'cause he was in trouble. Is he in trouble now?"

"I don't think so." Judging from her lack of reaction, Sebastian assumed Melina already knew the story. After being placed in J.D.'s foster care a year earlier, Caleb had been obstructive and rebellious, and when a gang of kids had beaten him up, he'd seen the chance to get himself and his siblings removed from J.D.'s care by blaming his injuries on him. The kids *had* been removed from the home, J.D. had been charged, and Caleb's lies had quickly grown out of control. So he'd done the only thing that had seemed logical at the time—he'd run away.

"Did Caleb say anything to you about running away this time?" Melina asked.

Gracie shook her head.

"You're friends with Chrissy Knight, right?"

"Uh-huh. She's the only girl 'cept my baby sister who lives by us, and my sister's too young to play."

"Did you see her at the party last night?"

"Yeah. At least, until Kenny was mean to her."

That grabbed Sebastian's attention. He unfolded his arms from across his chest and gripped the rounded edge of the counter instead. "How was Kenny mean to her?"

Gracie glanced at him, slowly tilting her head back to see all the way up to his face, then scooted closer to J.D. "He was teasing her," she said warily.

"About what, Gracie?" J.D. asked.

She slid over onto his lap and wrapped one arm around his neck. "He said everyone has a mama 'cept Chrissy, and she said uh-huh, she did, and he said huh-uh, and then he said if she had a mama, then she didn't love her or she wouldn't have run off. Is that true, Daddy? Did my other mama leave 'cause she didn't love us?"

"No, it's not true," J.D. said.

But apparently it was of Diana, Sebastian thought bitterly. He hadn't had a clue she was unhappy. Her leaving was the last thing on his mind. They'd just celebrated her birthday and their anniversary a few weeks before. They'd left Chrissy with his mother and gone into the city for a long weekend. They'd seen some Broadway shows and eaten in expensive restaurants, and they'd made love every night and had even talked about having another baby. She'd never hinted she was unhappy, and he hadn't seen any difference in the way she acted or the way she said I love you. Then, two weeks later, she'd abandoned them both. No note, no drop dead, no goodbye. She'd taken everything worth taking and had left only her wedding ring as an explanation.

He'd missed her so much for so long that it had become a way of life . . . until he'd met Melina.

"So Kenny teased Chrissy about her mother," Melina said. "Did it upset her?"

Gracie nodded. "She tried to hit him and he pushed her and she felled, and the boys laughed at her, and that made her mad. I told her nobody cares what ol' dumb Kenny says, and she said go away, so I did."

"Did you see her again?"

Gracie rubbed the back of her hand over her nose. "Just when she left with her grandma. She was laughin' then."

She had been, Sebastian remembered. He'd carried her to his parents' car on his shoulders, and when he'd swung her down, she'd giggled and shrieked. He hadn't guessed that a short time earlier, she'd been upset and teary-eyed. Had her mood improved so much, or was he just unobservant as hell?

"Okay, Gracie, thank you very much. Can I talk to your father for a minute?"

She nodded and skipped out of the room when J.D. lowered her to the floor. He looked from her to Sebastian, then back, waiting expectantly.

"How street-smart are these kids?"

"Chrissy, not at all. Alanna and Caleb . . . they've both been on their own a lot more than kids their age should have been. They're both smart and resourceful. Caleb took care of his brothers and sister when his father disappeared, and Alanna's done much of the raising of her brother and sister."

"If they find themselves in a strange place, will they know to ask for directions? Will they be able to figure out where they are and how to get where they're going? Will they know to budget their money and to be careful who they trust?"

"I have no doubt about it. And they'll keep Chrissy safe." J.D. directed that last to Sebastian. "They're both born caretakers. It comes naturally to them."

It didn't make Sebastian feel much better. He was grateful his daughter wasn't out there by herself, but damn it, he wished she was with someone a lot more grown-up. Better still, he wished she was home where she belonged, with him.

Melina tapped her pen on the legal pad. "Okay, thanks. Can you ask Trey to come in?"

While they waited, Melina doodled on the pad. Sebastian watched her, her apparent nonchalance making his nerves stretch tighter until he couldn't stand it anymore. Crossing the room in three long strides, he pulled the pen from her hand and dropped it onto the table. "Are you planning to interview all those people?" he demanded, gesturing to the list on the pad.

"Yes."

"Why? They're all going to tell you the same thing. Why waste all that time when you could be out there doing something to actually find the kids?"

"All I *know* is that three children are missing. They could be on their way to California or Mexico or Kathmandu, and left the note about Providence to throw us off their trail. They might be going *anywhere* . . . and they might have confided in a friend."

"You *have* Alanna's note. She *says* she's going to Providence to see her mother."

"And people always do what they say they will. Is that

it?" She made an obscene sound. "So last week when you *said* you would meet me at the inn for dinner . . . Were you really there and I just somehow overlooked you? Or did I miss the message where you canceled the date? Or maybe, possibly, conceivably, you lied. Maybe you had no intention of showing up. Maybe you preferred the coward's way out."

He stared at her, his face suddenly hot. Before he could think of a response, though, Trey Grayson cleared his throat in the doorway. "I, uh . . . I can come back later if you want."

Melina stared back, disdain in her eyes. Then she looked at the boy and smiled, and all hint of anger was gone. "No, please, come on in. This will just take a few minutes. I'm Melina Dimitris."

She offered her hand, and he shook it. "Trey Grayson."

"You're Caleb's stepbrother."

"Just brother. Our family's complicated enough, so we dropped the *step*'s and the *half*'s."

"Makes sense. I have just a few questions."

Sebastian turned away, going to stare out the window. She was right about the coward bit. He'd thought he was getting into a casual, short-term affair, and when it had turned out to be so much more, he'd panicked. He had wanted out, and the easier it was for him, the better. If Melina got hurt . . . well, better her than him.

God will get you for that, his younger sister had often jokingly threatened whenever she'd caught him or their brothers up to no good. Maybe it hadn't been such an empty threat. After all those years, maybe his sins had caught up with him, or maybe his last sin had been of such magnitude that now he was having to pay for it.

That was fine by him. He'd screwed up, and he was more than willing to pay the price. But Chrissy . . . she'd never hurt anyone. The cruelest thing she'd ever done was be selfish with her new toys at Christmas. She didn't deserve to suffer because he was a fool.

Please, God, don't let her suffer.

Because if she did, he would never survive.

Chapter Three

After what seemed to Alanna like forever, the trailer left the interstate and pulled into a gas station. The instant Miss Agatha's cousin went inside to pay, Caleb opened the trailer door, jumped down, then lifted Chrissy to the ground. Alanna jumped down, too, and was turning to close the trailer door when the cousin came around the back of the trailer. He came to a sudden stop, then his face got all red and he yelled, "You kids get away from there! What do you think you're doing trying to sneak into my trailer? Get out of here before I call the police!"

Caleb grabbed Alanna's and Chrissy's hands and backed away, pulling them with him. "We weren't doing anything, and we're leaving now. There's no need to call the cops."

"Thieving little punks," the man muttered as he slammed the trailer door. "Can't even walk thirty feet to pay for a tank of gas without someone trying to rob you blind."

Caleb pulled the girls across the parking lot and around some bushes, out of sight of the trailer, then took a deep breath. He looked as nervous as Alanna felt. She had kind of an empty place in her stomach that made her want to go home. Maybe this wasn't such a great idea. Maybe—

"I gotta pee."

Alanna and Caleb both turned to stare at Chrissy. "We just spent all morning five feet from a bathroom and you've got to go *now*?"

"I didn't have to go then. I do now."

"Let's go to McDonald's," Alanna suggested. "She can use the bathroom, and we can find out where we are, and maybe have some lunch."

Caleb agreed, and they crossed the parking lot. Alanna felt funny when they walked into the restaurant, like everyone was watching them. She'd been in Harry's Diner back home without a grown-up plenty of times, but she knew Maeve and Harry and everyone else who went there. She belonged there. She didn't belong here.

Caleb bought lunch while she took Chrissy to the bathroom. When they sat down at the table with him, he slid a piece of paper across the table. It had been torn from the yellow pages of a phone book. At the top he pointed out the address for the bus station. "We're in Syracuse."

"Syracuse? It can't be. That's the wrong direction."

"Tell that to Miss Agatha's cousins."

"It's not even that far from Bethlehem." Just three or four hours, and in the wrong direction. All that time in the stupid trailer, and now they would have to go back the way they'd just come, where people were looking for them. They would probably get caught, and it would all be her fault—and Miss Agatha's cousins'.

"So now what do we do?"

Alanna picked at her lunch. She hadn't counted on anything going wrong. She'd thought they would get a ride to Utica, magically find the bus station and buy tickets, then sit back and leave the rest to the bus driver. Easy.

"It's not too late for us to call home. My dad and your uncle could be here in no time."

She scowled at Caleb. She had a dad now, too—Ben Foster. He talked with a Southern accent, seemed like a nice enough guy, and lied as easily as her mom did. Everything he'd told her had been a lie—every smile and every word. He hadn't wanted her for twelve years, and she didn't want him now. It didn't matter if he was a nice enough guy. She didn't care if she never saw him again.

"Okay," Caleb said without waiting for her to answer. "You wait here with Chrissy, and I'll go back to the station and get a map. I'll ask the clerk to show me where the bus station is."

After he left, Chrissy said, "I want to go out and play."

Alanna glanced at the playground outside. No one would notice kids alone out there, so it was as good a place as any to wait. She threw away their trash, then followed Chrissy out the door.

Besides the toys, there was one picnic table with benches attached. Alanna sat down at the end and sighed. The sound made the girl at the other end look up. She didn't say anything—just looked at Alanna, then went back to reading her book. It was wrapped in clear plastic like a library book, and it crinkled when she moved.

Chrissy was going the wrong way on the slide when Caleb came back. He sat down beside Alanna and unfolded the map. "Here's the address," he said, giving her the yellow page again. "The clerk was busy, so we gotta figure it out ourselves."

Alanna stared at the map. There were about a thousand streets, and the writing was so small she could barely read it. "How are we supposed to find anything on here?"

"I don't know. Maybe we could ask—"

A shadow fell over the map. "You look like you could use a course in Cartography 101." It was the girl. She was thin, but not very tall, and wore jeans that were ripped in both knees and tattered at the hem, and her tank top was almost too little. Her hair was mostly black, and it was shaggy and kind of crooked, the way Alanna's used to be when her mom had cut it for her. She looked okay, but Alanna still felt queasy. She didn't want to talk to *anyone*.

"You know how to read a map?" The girl waited, but when neither of them answered, she pulled the map away and turned it over. "That's the index of streets. You look up your street here—what is it?" She glanced at the address. "Okay, here it is. J-12. Now, back over here . . ." The paper rustled as she flipped it again. "See the letters across the top and the numbers down the side? You find J and 12 and go to the block where they meet. Your street's in that square. Where are you going?"

Alanna hesitated, sure they shouldn't trust the girl, then murmured, "The bus station."

She stared at them a long time, then said, "Huh." Like that was more than she'd wanted to know or something. Then she pointed. "It's right about here. And we're right here. It's only about five miles. It shouldn't take you more than two hours to walk it, maybe three with the little one."

Two or three hours . . . Alanna didn't even want to think about walking so long, especially with Chrissy. She wished she was home. She would be unpacking her stuff in her new room in their new house, and her best friend Susan would be helping, and they would laugh and giggle and have a good time.

Walking all that way with Chrissy was *not* going to be a good time.

The girl looked at them, like maybe they had some more questions, then shrugged and went back to sit down with her book.

Alanna stared at the blocks between the two places the girl had pointed out, memorizing street names, then glanced at Caleb. He looked as if he wanted to go home, too. If it was his choice, he would be on the phone to Dr. J.D. in a flash. But it wasn't his choice. "We'd better go. Come on, Chrissy."

THE GIRL WATCHED THEM GO, HEADING DOWN THE street with Chrissy in the middle. There wasn't a sidewalk there, so they walked in grass that needed mowing and, for a few yards, in a ditch. They were just kids, awfully young—

"—to be out on their own," a voice completed the thought.

She jerked her gaze back to see an older woman with a broom and one of those metal boxes on a stick used for sweeping up. She was way too old to be working at a fast-food place—grayish-brown hair stuck out around her visor—but she had kind eyes and a nice smile.

"Headed to the bus station, are they? Those are tough neighborhoods they'll be walking through. A charitable person with a car would offer them a ride to make sure they get there safely."

"So why don't you do that?"

The question prompted a big laugh that sounded like chimes on a windy spring day. "*Me?* Behind the wheel of a car? Oh, the good Lord in heaven would frown on that! I'm many things, but a driver of automobiles isn't one of them." She stuck out her hand. "I'm Gloria."

"I'm . . ." She hesitated. She'd been trying on names for days. Every new town deserved a new name, didn't it? She'd narrowed it down to three favorites—China, Skye, and Blue. But the name that came out had never been in the running. It reminded her too much of home and happier times. It hurt even to think it, much less say it. "I'm Cheyenne."

"Pretty name. At least, it's different. Betcha never had another Cheyenne in your classes at school." Almost immediately Gloria turned back to the kids. "Seems a shame to let them walk into trouble when you could prevent it."

"What makes you think I have a car?"

With a chastening expression, Gloria looked straight at the Cavalier that had been a present, used, for Cheyenne's sixteenth birthday. Since her seventeenth birthday, it had been home.

"Just a ride to the bus station. What could it cost you?"

About half the gas left in the tank, and she was almost flat broke. Wherever she ran out of gas this time, she would have to stay, at least until she got some money. Not that it really mattered. It wasn't like there was anyplace she had to be.

"Guess I'd better get back to work. Nice meeting you, Cheyenne." Humming to herself, Gloria swept off around the corner.

Cheyenne looked down the street and could just barely make out the three kids. They *were* way too young to be out on their own, and naïve, too. She knew naïve. She'd been the princess of naïve until her mother's new husband had moved in with the family three years ago. She might be only seventeen, but some days she felt about seventy, and some days she just felt dead.

She tried to start the next chapter of her book, but it was no good. She kept thinking about the kids, about the same ages as her own brothers and sister back home. If they'd run away together and someone could keep them from maybe getting into trouble, she would want them to do it. And so what if she used the rest of her gas? There were Help Wanted signs all over town. She could find a couple of jobs real easy and make enough money to move on before long.

Closing her book, she dug her car keys from her pocket and headed for the car. The engine was slow to turn over, but she whispered encouragement and patted the dash gratefully when it sputtered to life. After fastening her seat belt, she looked over her shoulder to back out and saw Gloria, smiling and waving as if they were the best of friends. Nosy woman, but at least she cared. Cheyenne knew from experience how few people she could say that about.

When she got close to the kids, she pulled to the curb a few yards ahead of them and leaned across to roll down the window. "Hey. My name's Cheyenne. Come on and I'll give you a ride to the bus station."

The little one made a beeline for the backseat, but the boy yanked her back before she had a chance to climb in. "No, thanks."

"Hey, it's just a ride in the middle of the day. It's all right."

"We appreciate the offer, but . . . we don't know you," the older girl said politely.

"I wanna ride," the kid whined. "My feet hurt and I'm tired and hot, and this is gonna take forever. Please, Lannie, let's ride."

"She's a stranger, Chrissy."

"She's not a stranger. Her name is Cheyenne, and she's nice and pretty."

Cheyenne smiled. "Thank you, Chrissy. You're nice and pretty, too."

Chrissy turned a wheedling smile on Lannie. "Please . . . If we was in Bethlehem, we'd go with her."

Cheyenne didn't have a clue where Bethlehem was and didn't ask. She simply watched Lannie and the boy trying to decide. Finally he nodded. The two girls got in the backseat, and he climbed in front, keeping plenty of room between him and her. She waited until they were strapped in, then pulled back onto the street.

She wanted to talk to them, but she'd spent so much time alone lately that she couldn't think of anything to say. Before she realized it, they were at the bus station. She expected the kids to jump out and disappear inside. When they didn't move, she looked around and saw a police officer standing beside his car out front. "Are the police looking for you?"

It was the boy who answered. "We haven't done nothin' wrong."

"You've run away from home, haven't you? That's wrong."

"We're going to see my mom," Lannie said. "That's all."

"You live with your dad?"

"*No,* and I never will! He's a liar and can't be trusted."

So welcome to the real world, Cheyenne thought. "Who do you live with?"

"My aunt and uncle."

"And you forgot to tell them you're going to see your mom."

"S-sort of."

"Do you have reservations on the bus?"

"No."

"Do you know what time it leaves?"

Lannie's answer was softer, less hostile this time. "No."

"Tell me where you're going and I'll go in and find out. You can't hang out with the cops here."

While Lannie was considering it, Chrissy blurted out, "We're going to Providence. It's a special place for moms like ours."

"Okay, you guys wait here. Stay quiet and don't act suspicious."

There was another officer inside. Ignoring him, she walked up to the window like she didn't have a care and leaned on the counter. "Hi. Can you tell me when the next bus to Providence leaves?"

She watched while the clerk checked the schedules—at least, until she saw the flyer on the counter. She read as much as she could upside down in the moment it took him to come up with an itinerary and departure time. Smiling brightly, she thanked him, then forced herself to walk normally back out to the car. Ignoring the kids' questions, she started the engine and headed back the way they'd come, turning at the next corner and parking on the side street.

"You can't take the bus. They've got your pictures in there. If you show up, they're just gonna turn you over to the police."

"I don't believe you," the boy said, his dark gaze narrowed.

"Oh, you don't, Caleb Brown-Grayson? Alanna Marie Dalton? And Christina Diana Knight?" She watched the surprise cross their faces. "There's no way you're gonna make it to Providence by bus. But there might be another way."

"What?" Lannie—or Alanna, she knew now—asked grudgingly.

"If you've got money for gas . . . with me."

They stared at her. She stared back, probably as surprised as they were. "You'd take us all that way?" Caleb asked suspiciously. "Why?"

Good question. Too bad she didn't have a good answer. The idea had just popped out on its own. But instead of taking it back the way she should, she shrugged. "I don't have anything else to do. You got gas money?"

Reluctantly he nodded.

"Then you've got a ride."

And Cheyenne had a couple of days, depending on where the hell Providence was, to decide when she'd gone crazy.

MELINA WAS FEELING THE EFFECTS OF SLEEPLESS nights and skipped meals when she and Sebastian walked out of the McBride Inn after interviewing Holly McBride Flynn and the staff who'd worked at the previous night's wedding reception. Her head was aching, her stomach was about to start some very unladylike growling, and she'd had enough of Sebastian to last a lifetime, but she wasn't ready to ask for a ride to Lynda's house just yet.

"Now where?" he asked as she fastened her seat belt.

She glanced at him, but kept it brief. Even just looking at him stirred a pang deep inside her. She knew from her experience with Rico the rat—former partner in Dimitris Investigations and former fiancé—that it would be a long time before she got past the overwhelming heartache, and longer still before hurt and regret turned to indifference. God help her, if she survived this go-around, she wasn't risking it again. The next time she met a man who started her thinking about love, marriage, and forever, she was going to save herself the trouble and just shoot him. After all, three strikes, and you're out.

Or was it third time's the charm?

Stubbornly, she shook any hint of hopefulness out of her mind and focused narrowly on the case at hand. "Where does your wife live?"

Taut lines formed at the corner of his mouth. "My mother told you we don't know where my *ex*-wife is. Didn't you believe her?"

"I believe *she* doesn't know. I also believe men have a tendency to keep certain things from their mothers." Like tawdry affairs with easy women in town visiting a friend. Like callously tossing said easy woman away when he was finished with her.

"I don't know where Diana is. I've neither seen nor heard from her since the day she left four years ago."

"Then how did you divorce her?"

He shrugged, his broad shoulders stretching the fabric of his shirt. His work was arduous, and it showed in his amazing body. "It can be done."

She knew that, of course. It was a relatively simple matter of making a legitimate effort to locate the missing spouse, advertising the intent to file for divorce in various legal newspapers, and waiting until the deadline for a response. Even if the spouse never saw the announcements, the divorce was legal and binding.

"Does Diana have family here?"

"Her mother, a couple of cousins, an aunt and uncle."

"Have they had any contact with her?"

He shrugged again. "Her mother blamed me for her leaving. She wouldn't tell me anything if her life depended on it."

"What if her granddaughter's life depended on it?" Melina regretted her words as soon as they were out. They brought Sebastian's gaze sharply to her—dark eyes. Wounded, frightened eyes. They made her want to squeeze his hand, pat his arm, or envelop him in a comforting embrace—not good things when she hated the rat bastard.

"Let's go by your mother-in-law's—pardon me. Your *ex*-mother-in-law's house."

She hadn't known Bethlehem had a poorer part of town, but the neighborhood of Edgewood was apparently it. The wrought-iron arch at the entrance was rusted and missing a few pieces, and the brick columns supporting it looked none too stable. The lots were smaller than elsewhere in town, the houses cheaper and closer together. Still, if this was as bad as it got, Bethlehem was way ahead of cities like Buffalo, where their worst neighborhoods were dangerous, shabby no-man's-lands.

Sebastian parked at a house halfway down the main street of the subdivision. The house was a duplex, painted beige with dark brown trim. One half was more neatly maintained than the other, where a '68 Mustang was up on blocks in the driveway, with a group of rowdy-looking young men gathered around it.

Melina slid to the ground and felt the men's attention turn her way a second before a sharp wolf whistle split the air. She smiled at them, thinking how easily she could break any one of them in half, then sauntered across the grass to the tiny stoop and door.

Scowling fiercely, Sebastian rang the bell. Not happy to see his ex-mother-in-law? Or maybe just the slightest bit jealous?

She didn't have a chance to decide before the door was opened.

The woman on the other side of the screen was in her late fifties, Melina guessed, and looked as if every single year had been difficult. Her hair was more salt than pepper, her face generously wrinkled, her expression set on permanent displeasure. Melina thought she detected a few signs of concern for her granddaughter, but it was hard to say with all that hostility.

"Ramona Franks, Melina Dimitris," Sebastian mumbled ungraciously. "Melina's the private investigator who's trying to find the kids."

"They're not here."

"Of course they're not." Melina smiled politely. "Can we come in and talk with you? It'll just take a few minutes."

"I haven't seen Christina in two weeks. I wasn't at the wedding party last night. There's nothing I can tell you."

When she started to close the door, Melina blocked it.

"I don't want to talk to you about Chrissy—Christina. I'd like to ask a few questions about your daughter."

Ramona stiffened, shifted her gaze to Sebastian for a moment, then unlatched the screen and stepped back.

Melina followed her into the living room, taking a seat at the opposite end of the sofa. Sebastian stopped just inside the door, hands behind his back, looking uncomfortable.

"What do you want to know about Di?"

"Do you know where she's living?"

"No. I haven't seen her since *he* run her off."

"You haven't spoken to her? Gotten a birthday card or a letter from her?"

"Not a word."

"Were you surprised when she left?"

Ramona scoffed. "Only that she left Christina behind. Of course, that was his doing, too. No one was surprised. The whole town knew how miserable he made her. She was just waiting for the chance to escape him."

That wasn't the story Melina had heard, courtesy of Lynda, but she wasn't surprised. She'd learned long ago that few people ever saw the same situation the same way. For whatever reason, it was easier for Ramona Franks to believe Diana had had no other choice—that she'd been forced against her will to abandon her husband and child and flee.

In most situations, it wasn't the choices that were missing. Just the willingness to accept responsibility for the choice made.

"What about Diana's father? Has she been in touch with him?"

Ramona looked as if she didn't know whether to be

insulted at the suggestion that her daughter would contact someone else but not her, or bereaved at the mention of Diana's father. "My husband died twelve years ago, bless his heart. Cancer of the liver. It was awfully hard on poor Di."

And none too easy on her father, Melina thought unkindly. She wasn't taking Sebastian's side against anyone, but truth was, Ramona Franks gave her a creepy feeling. The woman was too hard, too unforgiving—not someone she would want in her life on a regular basis. But wasn't it likely life had *made* her hard and unforgiving? She'd lost her husband, then her daughter and, to some degree, her granddaughter. Considering her undisguised venom for Sebastian, Melina couldn't imagine him—or any father, to be fair—making much effort to include her in his daughter's life.

She asked a few more questions, got nowhere, and stood up. "I appreciate your time, Mrs. Franks. If you think of anything at all that could help us locate Christina, would you please give me a call?" She offered her business card, but when the woman didn't take it, instead she laid it on the television. A framed photograph there caught her attention. "Is this Diana?"

"Yes, that's my baby." Ramona's smile softened her face and eased the wrinkles around her eyes. "Isn't she a beauty?"

She was, Melina admitted grudgingly. Blond-haired, blue-eyed, tanned, with a beauty-pageant smile. She wore a cheerleader's uniform in the teenaged photo and looked like every popular girl Melina had envied in her high school years. Disliking her for no more reason than that, she murmured something appropriate, then walked out the door.

The young mechanics next door whistled again, and one called out, "Hey, baby!" She absentmindedly smiled and waved as she climbed into the truck.

"What was the point of that?" Sebastian asked sourly as they drove away.

"I was just being—" She was about to say *friendly* when she realized he was talking about the interview with Ramona Franks, not the boys next door. "Thorough," she substituted. "As far as we can guess, Chrissy tagged along with the other kids in the hopes of finding her own mother. I wanted to be sure that she doesn't know something about Diana that we don't."

"How could she possibly know—You think Ramona might have lied about not knowing where Diana is."

Melina nodded. "I thought she might have let it slip to Chrissy."

"Chrissy would have told me."

"Maybe. Or her grandmother might have convinced her to keep it secret."

"So what do you think now?"

"I think Ramona Franks is a sad woman whose life hasn't turned out at all the way she'd planned. She lost her husband and was abandoned by her daughter and feels that she's lost Chrissy, too."

Sebastian turned onto Main Street and headed downtown. Twice he started to speak, then stopped. After pulling into a parking space, he turned to face her. "Her husband didn't die of liver cancer. He drank until his liver gave out on him, and he was a mean drunk. He tore things up, verbally abused both Ramona and Diana, and shoved around anyone who got in his way. Diana begged her mother to divorce him, but Ramona would never do it. She believed his apologies and his promises to change, and she nursed him right up to the time he died, when she rewrote history and turned him into the best husband and father ever." His voice turned cynical. "Ramona does that a lot—rewrite history."

"We all have to find ways to live with what we do." And he was no different from the rest of the world. Somehow, he'd justified dumping her, to himself if no one else. He'd found some logic, shaky or not, to prove that he hadn't done anything wrong.

Realizing they were sitting in front of Harry's Café, she frowned. "Why are we here?"

"You haven't eaten."

True, but she hadn't planned to do so at a table with *him*. The idea zapped her appetite cold. "I'm not hungry," she lied, but her stomach chose that moment to contradict her.

His level gaze didn't waver, but his voice lost all hint of emotion. "Is that your way of saying you don't want to have dinner with me?"

A flush heated her cheeks, and she let the slamming of the pickup door behind her pass as her answer. She was halfway inside the diner before she heard the slam of his own door.

Harry's was open until eight P.M., seven days a week, but late Sunday afternoons were rarely busy. Melina had her pick of booths. She automatically chose one at the front, where any number of distractions were available outside the plate-glass window. It wasn't until she was seated that she realized it was the same booth she'd shared with Lynda and Ben on another Sunday not too long ago, notable because it had been the first time she'd seen Sebastian. At the time, she'd paid him little mind—she'd been too concerned about the animosity her best friend had been trading with the handsome, green-eyed stranger she was now planning to marry. If only Melina had known then what she knew now . . .

Sebastian slid onto the bench across from her as the waitress, a redhead named Maeve, approached with menus and a coffeepot. She murmured his name, patted his shoulder, and said something about prayers before greeting Melina with a halfhearted smile. "Do you need a minute to look at the menu?"

"I'll have the special." Melina didn't have a clue what it was, but it smelled fantastic. Besides, all the food at Harry's was fantastic.

Sebastian ordered the same, then stared down at his coffee long after Maeve left. Melina was wondering if they were going to sit in awkward silence through the entire meal when he spoke.

"About what happened between us . . ."

Her foot twitched with the need to stomp her three-inch heel on his instep, but she didn't follow through. He made it sound so innocent, so blameless. *What happened.* Not *What I did to you.* Bottom-feeding bastard.

Finally he looked at her, head-on. "I'm sorry. I handled things really badly. My only excuse is . . ." With a self-mocking smile, he shook his head. "Excuses don't matter. But I am sorry."

He looked sincere—but he'd looked sincere when he'd told her she was the most beautiful woman he'd known. He'd looked damn sincere every time he'd told her how much he wanted her, and when they'd made love . . . A man couldn't get any more sincere than that.

Or so she'd thought.

She straightened her spine, lifted her chin a notch, and coolly said, "Don't worry, Sebastian. If your daughter is with Alanna Dalton, I'll find her. You don't have to try to get on my good side to ensure my cooperation."

"I'm not—I just wanted—" Muttering a curse, he scowled at the street outside.

A part of her wished she hadn't said anything. After all, any conversation was better than this stiff, almost-like-strangers silence. Another part wished she'd spoken *and* stomped his foot. He was good at inflicting pain. Was he equally good at enduring it?

That last thought stirred her guilt. He'd been both father and mother to Chrissy for more than half her life, and now she was missing. She couldn't imagine much that was more terrifying, or more painful, for a parent to endure than that. But she *would* find Chrissy and the others, and she *would* bring them home, safe and unharmed.

Let Sebastian deal with that.

Chapter Four

For the first time in her life, Corinna Winchester Humphries felt every one of her seven decades and then some as she puttered around the kitchen. It was Monday morning, she had a house full of people, with coffee to make and baking to finish, and all she wanted to do was stare out the window into the backyard and worry about the children.

Where were they? Where had they slept the previous night? Were they safe? Had they eaten? Were they homesick?

Too many questions. Not enough answers.

"Miss Corinna? Are you all right?"

Startled, she turned to find Kelsey Grayson removing a pan of sticky buns from the oven. Years of experience told her by smell alone that the buns were burned but still edible. When was the last time she'd burned a pan of buns? Probably right after her dear Henry had died.

Her smile was faint and weary. "Just woolgathering, dear. What can I do for you?"

"J.D. and I think it's time we notified Miss Agatha and Bud that the kids are gone."

Corinna nodded. She hated to disrupt her sister's honeymoon, but the newlyweds would never forgive them if something terrible happened and they weren't present to deal with it.

"Do you want to call them?" Kelsey asked.

"You handle it, dear, will you?" She wasn't up to breaking the news herself, not yet.

"Sure." Kelsey hugged her tightly before leaving the kitchen.

Almost immediately the private investigator from Buffalo came in. Hers was hardly a profession for a young lady, though if she could locate the children, Corinna would change her opinion in a hurry. "Miss Corinna, can you take a look at this guest list and tell me who lives here and which out-of-town guests have left and when?"

"Of course, dear." She took the lengthy list of Agatha's wedding guests, got an ink pen from a drawer, and set to work. She'd put the list together herself the day before when she'd desperately needed something to keep her mind busy—had helped Agatha compile it originally when they were planning the wedding. Poor Agatha, with her honeymoon ending in such a way. Perhaps, once the children were home again, she and Bud could try again.

She worked in silence, handing each page to Melina as she finished with it. When she was finished, approximately three-fourths of the names were marked as having left after the party Saturday night or on Sunday. "What will you do with that?"

"First we'll rule out everyone who left Saturday night. I'll contact the others to find out if they saw any sign of the kids Sunday morning. We know they didn't buy bus tickets, and they certainly didn't borrow a car and drive, but somehow they made it out of town without anyone seeing them."

"I don't believe any of our guests would have picked up three juvenile hitchhikers. They're much too sensible for that."

"I'm sure they are. But maybe they saw someone else picking up the kids. Maybe the kids stowed away in someone's vehicle. Maybe—" Melina shrugged as if she'd run out of possibilities, but her confident smile suggested otherwise. "Kids can be amazingly resourceful. I understand when Caleb ran away last year, he made it all the way to Binghamton."

"Yes, he did. And Alanna's a bright, capable child."

"Had she mentioned to you that she wanted to see her mother?"

"Oh, no. To the contrary, in fact. She told me not long ago that she didn't care if she never saw her mother again. Of course, that was before she found out that Ben Foster was her father." Corinna sighed. She liked what little she knew of the young man, and she sincerely hoped—for Alanna's sake as well as his own—that it wasn't too late to undo the mistakes of the past. If he truly regretted his actions, if he was truly sincere in wanting to know his daughter now . . .

"Alanna was growing more resentful of Berry as time passed," she went on. "She understands that her mother has problems—drugs and alcohol, you know—and she's always made allowances for her, but lately . . . I suppose it has to do with growing up. All children need to believe that their parents love them dearly, and young girls need their mothers. The fact that Berry put her own selfish needs ahead of her own children's welfare was becoming harder for Alanna to accept and impossible to forgive." She gave a sorrowful shake of her head as she turned to the bread dough rising on the counter. "What is it about mothers these days?"

THE SCREEN DOOR CREAKED AS SOMEONE CAME OUT of the Winchester house, but Sebastian didn't look up from his seat on the steps. He'd been inside earlier, listening to talk, questions, and theories, none of which seemed to bring them any closer to finding his little girl. Filled with all the caffeine, assurances, and sympathy he could bear, he'd finally come outside.

Usually on a sunny summer day there were kids and dogs everywhere, but this morning the street was quiet. It was eerie in a way, but just as well. At the moment he didn't want to be around other people's kids, playing happily as if nothing had happened.

Ben sat down at the opposite end of the steps. "Hell."

Sebastian's smile was weak. That one word said a lot. In fact, it described the last twenty-four hours perfectly.

For a long time, neither of them said anything. Sebastian was comfortable with silence most of the time. He and Ben could work for hours in the same room without speaking more than a dozen times, and he liked that. Or they could talk—like normal people, his sister Shauna said. He liked that, too.

He didn't have many friends. There was Shauna and his three brothers, a few cousins, and a couple of neighbors like J. D. Grayson, but as far as friends—guys from high school, people he shared common interests with—there weren't any. Not since Diana left. When she'd left, he'd been so . . . that he'd turned his back on everyone but family, and he'd tried his best to shut them out, too. He'd lost all his friends and hadn't cared.

So what? The missing word nagged at him. Angry? Hurt? Bewildered? All that and more. Frightened. Confused. Ashamed. So ashamed. Four years later he still felt all those things and tried to minimize the chance of feeling them all over again by refusing to let anyone get too close. Like Melina.

Wishing he had some obnoxious habit like smoking or drinking to distract him, he glanced at Ben. "You ever do something you regret but you don't know how to fix it?"

Ben's laugh was rusty and bitter. "My daughter ran off because she found out that she *is* my daughter, and she took your daughter with her. Do I really need to answer that?"

"I didn't know Chrissy missed her mother. She doesn't even remember Diana, and she never asks about her—at least, not to me. I thought she was perfectly happy with it being just her and me. I should have known . . ." That she would be curious. That someday she would need to know about her mother.

That handling Melina the way he had was going to come back to bite him.

The screen door opened again, and Melina came out, passing between them. She was wearing jeans today with a plain white T-shirt. Too many washings had leached the color from the denim and made it soft enough to cling to her thighs and hips and narrow waist, and the shirt was tucked in, stretching snugly across her breasts. With her well-worn tennis shoes and her long black hair curling wildly, she looked about sixteen. A very sexy sixteen.

She took the steps two at a time, then turned to face them—well, Ben, actually. She didn't acknowledge that Sebastian was there. "Hey, handsome."

She liked men and herself, was a flirt, a tease, a self-described woman of easy virtue. She was beautiful, sensuous, and sultry, and had experienced more things with more men than Sebastian could begin to guess at. He'd learned that much about her in the first thirty minutes he'd known her.

In the next thirty hours, he'd learned that she was also amazingly generous, both in bed and out. Sweet. Surprisingly contemplative. Fiercely loyal. She loved her family and her friends, and for a few days, she'd thought she loved him. And she was delicate. Vulnerable. She could be had, and she could be hurt.

He'd managed both.

"What's on the schedule now?" Ben asked.

"I've got phone calls to make." She waved a sheaf of papers that contained the information she'd requested on the out-of-town wedding guests. "Chief Walker has offered me the use of an interrogation room and telephone at the police station. I'm heading that way now. Want to give me a ride?"

"Sure." Ben started to stand up, then he sat down again. "I'd better wait for Lynda. We left her car at home. Sebastian, do you mind?"

He watched the hostility creep into Melina's dark eyes. In their short time together, he'd commented once on her passionate nature, and she'd shrugged languorously and said *I'm Greek,* as if that explained everything. And since they'd been naked in bed at the time, and he'd been about to explode inside her, he hadn't pursued it. Later she'd added that Greeks embraced life with fervor. When they loved it was with a stunning intensity, and they hated the same way.

Now he believed it.

He started to rise from the step when she sarcastically said, "No, thank you. I'd rather walk."

He could have argued. Hell, no bigger than she was, he could have easily thrown her over his shoulder and carried her off to his truck. Instead he sat down again. "Suit yourself."

He doubted there was much he could do that would surprise her. She already expected the worst from him. But that did. She blinked once, twice, before sliding dark glasses over her eyes. Then she made a huffy turn and headed toward the street.

Ben's rebuke was mildly voiced. "I offer you a chance to spend a little time alone with her, and you don't even take it?"

"What good would it do? She's seriously pissed with me."

"With good reason. And she's not going to get over it without equally good reason."

"I can't worry about it now," Sebastian lied. "I've got more important things on my mind."

"You don't start dealing with it now, son, when you get around to it, it might be too late."

Sebastian watched Ben go back into the house, then scowled. The situation was different for him. Yes, his daughter was missing, but he hardly knew Alanna. He hadn't warmed her bottles, changed her diapers, calmed her fears, or dried her tears. He'd never lived with her, and probably never would. And he'd never done anything to deliberately hurt Lynda.

With a weary sigh, he pushed himself to his feet. On a normal Monday morning, he would be in his workshop, making a dent in the backlog of orders that had necessitated hiring Ben to help out. He was a cabinetmaker by trade, though cabinets were his least favorite of all the pieces he produced. They were so standard, each one put together in the same general manner as the hundreds that had gone before. Oh, the door fronts varied, as well as the hinges, the woods, and the quality of the drawers, but in the end they were basically the same.

He preferred the work that allowed him creative license—the rockers, the chairs, the highboys, that he could inlay, carve, and experiment with. That particular Monday, though, whatever creative energy he possessed had been drained right out of him. He doubted he could even apply a set of European hinges properly at the moment. Picking up a carving knife would only lead to disaster.

So when he backed his truck out of Miss Corinna's driveway, he didn't head for Main Street and the highway that would take him home. Instead, he took Hawthorne downtown and pulled into the courthouse parking lot. When he got out of the truck, his glance skimmed across the baby shop across the street where his mother had bought frilly dresses, ruffled socks, and pink slippers for Chrissy to wear to church. Her dentist's office was just down the block, the ice-cream shop she loved on the opposite side of the square. In between was the bandstand, where they'd attended Christmas services and concerts every year since she was tiny. Everywhere he looked, he saw something to remind him of her.

Clamping his jaw tightly, he went inside the courthouse and into the police department on the first floor. Sadie, the dispatcher, offered her sympathies and prayers along with directions to a small room at the back. He thanked her, then lowered his gaze to avoid the pitying looks from officers and clerks.

Melina sat in a wooden chair, telephone braced between her ear and shoulder, feet propped on another chair, and a clipboard on her lap. If not for the pen tapping frenetically on the table, she would have looked lazy and at ease. "So you didn't see any children at all yesterday morning other than the ones who were also guests at the inn? . . . No, thank you, Mrs. Barrett, but it'll be easier for me to call your cousin and your daughter. I've got their numbers. Thank you."

With one finger, she disconnected the call, then fixed a blank look on him. As he slid into the chair across from her, he searched but couldn't find even the slightest hint of emotion on her features. "What do you want?"

He replied with the obvious. "My daughter."

"Hanging around disturbing me isn't going to make that happen any quicker."

"I won't disturb you."

She mumbled something that sounded like, "Yeah, right," as she dialed the next number on her list. "Hi, could I speak to Mr. or Mrs. Browning? . . . Mrs. Browning, my name is Melina Dimitris, and I'm a private investigator. Corinna Humphries gave me your name and said you were in Bethlehem Saturday for Miss Agatha's wedding. . . . No, no, Corinna and Agatha are fine. The reason I'm calling is, several children ran away from Bethlehem on Sunday, and I wanted to find out whether you'd seen anything that might help us find them."

She had her spiel down pat, Sebastian thought. Of course, she did this for a living, and they weren't her kids. In fact, she hadn't even met Alanna and Caleb, and he'd limited her exposure to Chrissy to a couple of hellos and goodbyes. He hadn't wanted his daughter to know that he was seeing someone, hadn't wanted to risk her getting attached to someone who would only be around a few days.

Which was a few days longer than any woman he'd been with since Diana left. Though he'd never had a one-night stand in his life before then, he'd gotten pretty good at them since. One night hadn't been enough with Melina, though. Neither had four. That was part of the reason he'd stopped seeing her—because he'd begun to wonder how many nights would be enough.

He listened as she made call after call, asking questions. *What time did you leave? What kind of vehicle do you drive? Did you meet the children? Did you hear anything? See anything?* She explained who she was time and again—sometimes in the same call—and her calm, friendly tone never wavered. Once he left to get her a Diet Coke from the machine outside. Once he slid her a note: *Lunch from Harry's?* She slid it back with a request for a chicken salad sandwich, but when he returned with it, along with another for himself, she took a few bites, turned green, and pushed it away.

Too much going on? he wondered, then remembered the way she kept looking at him. Probably not. She thrived on work and challenges, and kept a schedule that would wear out most people. Most likely, there was a much simpler explanation for her queasiness.

Too much of *him*.

IT WAS LATE MONDAY AFTERNOON, AND CALEB AND Chrissy were asleep in the backseat. They'd spent Sunday night in some tiny town, parked behind an abandoned grocery store. They'd rolled the windows partway down to let in some cool air, but it had also let in the stink from the Dumpster nearby, and there had been lots of noises that kept Alanna awake. She'd wanted to be at home in her bed so bad she'd almost cried, but she'd kept the tears inside. Once she talked to her mom, though, she would never run away again.

Ever since the others had gone to sleep, Cheyenne had turned on the radio and was singing along with it. Reaching across, Alanna turned down the sound, then asked, "What's your real name?"

"I told you—Cheyenne."

"Nobody names their kid Cheyenne."

"Frank Zappa named his kid Moon Unit."

"Who's Frank Zappa?"

"Just a guy."

"So your honest-to-God real name is Cheyenne."

She grinned and shrugged, but she didn't actually say yes. Just like Alanna thought. It wasn't her name at all.

"What's your last name?"

"Don't have one."

"Everyone has one."

"What about Madonna? And Cher?"

"Madonna's got a last name even if she doesn't use it. And who's Cher?"

Cheyenne gave her a funny look. "Just how old are you?"

"Twelve."

Cheyenne's hair swung when she shook her head. "You're so young."

"Yeah, like you're so old. How old are you?"

"Seventeen . . . but I'm a lot older than that." Kind of a sad look came across her face then, making her look about Chrissy's age, and Alanna wondered again why she didn't go home. Maybe she didn't have a home to go to. Maybe her mom was like Berry, only she didn't have an aunt to take care of her. Maybe her parents were dead, or maybe they just didn't want her.

"What're you doing in New York if your mom is in Providence?" Cheyenne asked.

"Me and my sister and brother live with our aunt and uncle in Bethlehem."

"Why?"

"My mom—" Alanna stopped. All her life she'd been making excuses for her mother, repeating the same lies Berry told. But not anymore. "She's a doper and a drunk, and she doesn't want to live with us."

"Then why are you draggin' those two all the way to another state to see her?"

For a long time, Alanna stared at the road ahead. They weren't taking the interstate because the car's top speed was only about forty miles an hour, and because it overheated all the time and they had to stop to let it cool down, and Cheyenne thought they'd get less attention. So far, she'd been right. No one had even looked twice at them.

Finally she sighed. "I met my dad for the first time a

couple of weeks ago, and I've got some questions I want to ask her."

"What kind of questions?"

"Like why didn't she tell me about him and why didn't I know his name and what did she do to make him stay away all these years. Like why we have to live with Aunt Emilie and why she don't love us enough to get better and why she's so selfish and why we can't have a better mama."

"Don't bother. She'll just tell you what she thinks you want to hear. If she doesn't want you, she doesn't want you. Period. You oughta just go back to Aunt Emilie right now and forget all about your mom."

"Does your mom not want you, either?"

For a moment Cheyenne looked as if she might cry, then she got a hard look on her face and shrugged. "She does, but she wants my stepdad more. What about *them*? Why are they with you?"

Alanna looked into the backseat. Caleb was sitting sideways in the seat with his legs sprawled to the other side of the car, and Chrissy was stretched across him, her head on his shoulder, his arm around her middle. Chrissy'd better wake up first, 'cause if Caleb did, he'd act like he was mad at her for climbing up and snuggling with him.

"Caleb's just makin' sure I'm okay."

"And Chrissy?"

"She thinks her mom is with mine. She's not—my mom don't know anyone in Bethlehem but us. But Chrissy hid in the trailer until it was too late, and she said if we tried to turn her in, she'd tell on us. We can't just run off and leave her, so we have to bring her along."

It got quiet again for a while, and Alanna started thinking about how upset Emilie and Nathan and the kids probably were, and Caleb's and Chrissy's families, too. She wondered if Ben Foster knew it was his fault and hoped he felt bad about it, and she hoped no one told Miss Agatha and Grandpa Bud and ruined their honeymoon. Since thinking like that just made her want to go home even more, she started talking again. "Where are you from?"

"Nowhere," Cheyenne said fast enough that Alanna knew it was a lie.

"Where are you going?"

"Besides Providence? Nowhere."

Alanna watched her for a moment or two, then quietly said, "Kids like us who leave on purpose are runaways, but kids who have to leave 'cause no one wants 'em are called throwaways. That's what you are, aren't you?"

Cheyenne slammed on the brake, pulled to the side of the road, jumped out, and headed into the woods. Alanna listened to all the squeaks and grumbles the car made, like it was slow to realize it had stopped, then Chrissy's snoring in the backseat got louder. She didn't know whether to go after Cheyenne or wake Caleb or just do nothing. She'd finally decided to wake Caleb when a rustling in the weeds made her look that way.

Cheyenne was coming back, frowning real hard. She got in and fastened her seat belt, then pulled onto the road again. After a while, she said, kind of tough like, "I had to pee."

Though they'd made a couple of roadside bathroom stops, Alanna didn't believe her. For one thing, she'd forgotten to take the toilet paper stuck between the seats. For another, her eyes were red and kind of shiny and she kept sniffling, and for another, there was makeup on the sleeve of her T-shirt. Alanna had made her cry, and she felt real bad about it, but as long as Cheyenne didn't admit it, she couldn't apologize for it.

All she could do was promise herself she wouldn't let it happen again.

MELINA TOOK A BREAK TO STAND AND STRETCH, then walk to the window. She couldn't remember the last time she'd spent so much time on the phone—in Buffalo she had staff to handle calls—and she was tired and more than a little ready to go back to Lynda's house, take a nap, and maybe get something to eat. But just the thought of food was enough to make her stomach muscles clench, and there were only a dozen names left on the list, and then she could call it a day.

Gazing at a mother with a toddler in the square, she spoke to Sebastian for the first time in several hours. "Are you always this patient?"

He grunted a response that she figured could mean anything she wanted. Sitting quietly for hours watching someone else work was beyond her capabilities . . . well, most of the time. There had been an evening—oh, a week or so ago—when she'd sat in his workshop, wearing nothing but a denim shirt sized for his broad shoulders, and watched him carve an intricate pattern into the doors of a massive armoire. He'd worked freehand with chisels and knives, and she'd alternated between watching the rippling muscles across his back and the finely controlled movements of his hands. He'd carved for hours, and neither of them had said a word, and then she'd been overcome by an incredible need to feel his hands on *her.* She'd slipped out of his shirt and he'd put down his tools, and they'd—

She gave a soft sigh and wished the chief would lower the thermostat a few degrees. It had become much too warm in the small room for her taste.

"Don't you have work to do?" she asked, then immediately wished she hadn't. The image of his hands at work merely made her hotter.

"Pardon me if I find it difficult to concentrate on cabinets at the moment," he said dryly.

She turned but avoided meeting his gaze. "For what it's worth . . . I'm sorry Chrissy's missing."

"I know."

"I have a few more calls to make, then I'm calling it a night. Can you give me a ride to Lyn's?" She hated to ask, but Lynda's house was quite a bit more than the few blocks from Miss Corinna's to the courthouse, much of it uphill. She preferred to save her energy for work, not proving how obstinate she could be.

"Sure."

With a curt nod, she sat down again and dialed the next number. A man answered—a hard-of-hearing man, apparently, for he spoke loudly enough to make her wince. "Is this Mr. Stuart?"

"Yes, ma'am, it is," he all but shouted. "What can I do for you?"

"Mr. Stuart, my name is Melina Dimitris, and I'm a private investigator. Corinna Humphries gave me your number . . ." She ran through the usual lines, learning the timing for when to pull the phone away from her ear for his answer and when to bring it back. She expected the call to be another strikeout, but she asked all the questions anyway.

Finally she prepared to cross his name off her list and made her final comment before hanging up. "So you didn't see anything at all yesterday—nothing unusual or strange, no kids."

He would yell no, she would thank him, hang up, then try again, and before long—

"Well, come to think of it . . . It wasn't in Bethlehem, but . . . well, it was unusual."

The tiny hairs on the back of her neck stood on end. "What wasn't in Bethlehem, Mr. Stuart?"

"My wife and I left Sunday morning, planning to go straight home. We live in Utica, you know. Of course you do, since you called here. Anyway, we'd just left Bethlehem when Cornelia—that's my wife—suggested that we drop in on our youngest boy over in Syracuse. He wasn't able to get to the wedding—he doesn't really know his cousin Agatha that well, anyway, and his wife had to work Saturday until six, so there's no way they could have gotten there on time."

Melina seized the opportunity and jumped in when he breathed. "And what happened, Mr. Stuart?"

"Well, we went to Syracuse—had a nice drive through the countryside since no one was expecting us—and when we got there, we stopped to get gas. I filled up the tank and went to pay for it, and when I came back, I caught three kids at the trailer."

"Trailer? I thought you were driving a pickup."

"Yeah, we were, but we were towing our travel trailer behind in case Corinna needed some extra beds. It's handy for get-togethers like that. So, anyway, I was coming back from paying for the gas, and I came around the back of the trailer, and there was these kids—a boy and two girls—and they were standing there and the door to the trailer was open. I yelled at 'em to get away before I called the police, and the boy said there was no reason to call the cops, and then he grabbed both girls' hands and they took off. I thought they were trying to sneak in and rob us, but after hearing what you said, I have to wonder if maybe these are your kids and they were sneaking *out* of the trailer rather than in."

"Can you describe them?" Melina asked. Across the table, Sebastian had perked up and was leaning toward her as if to hear everything.

"Well, I didn't pay a lot of attention. The boy was fourteen, maybe fifteen, and had dark hair. The little girl had dark hair, too, kinda long, and the other girl was blond. She was probably about the boy's age. I really didn't pay 'em much mind. They took off, and I made sure nothing was missing from the trailer, and then we went on."

"Do you have access to a fax machine, Mr. Stuart? I'd like to send you pictures of our missing kids."

"Sure do, over at my son-in-law's office. But if *you* have access to a computer, it would be quicker if you send 'em by e-mail. Can you do that?"

"Yes, I can." She smiled faintly. She knew it was age discrimination or something, but she was always surprised to find a cyber-savvy senior citizen. Why, her older relatives wouldn't have a computer in their houses, not even for the ease of e-mailing relatives back in Greece.

She asked a few more questions, double-checked his

e-mail address, then hung up. Before saying anything to Sebastian, she tapped the glass pane in the door to get Mitch Walker's attention and waved him inside. Nathan Bishop came with him.

"I think we've got a lead." She always got a kind of tight, excited feeling in her stomach when she was on the right track, and she had it at the moment . . . unless it was the chicken salad sandwich again. Tamping it down, she related her conversation with Mr. Stuart.

"That would explain how they got out of town without anyone seeing them," Mitch said. "I'll get in touch with the Syracuse police and give them a heads-up."

"Tell whoever you talk to that I'll be in town in the morning. I'll canvass the area, put up flyers, and see if I can find out where they went from there. In the meantime, we need to e-mail the kids' photos to Mr. Stuart for a positive ID—here's his address—and I'll go ahead and call the remaining names on the list to see if they can add anything."

Nathan took the paper with the e-mail address and left the room, going straight to one of the computers in the squad room. Mitch leaned against the table. "Your job doesn't seem to be much different from ours. Occasional moments of excitement interspersed with hours of tedious routine."

"Yesterday a guy came after me with a baseball bat." She grinned. "Routine's not so bad."

"A wayward husband who didn't like having his dalliances recorded for posterity—and divorce court?"

"Bingo."

"What'd you do?"

"Showed him my weapon and politely asked him to

back off. It's amazing how fast looking down the barrel of a forty-caliber Sig Sauer can change a man's attitude."

With a laugh, Mitch left the room, and Melina picked up the phone for the thousandth time that day, or so it seemed. She wouldn't be surprised if she sprained her ear before the day was over.

Across the table Sebastian was watching with an odd expression on his face. Was he bothered by the fact that she could joke about pulling a gun on someone? Did he think investigative work should be left to the big, strong men? She'd never made any effort to hide what she did from him or anyone else—well, except her parents and Yaya Rosa, but she'd given that up years ago. And he certainly hadn't cared when he was yanking off her clothes last week.

She finished the last of the calls, learning nothing, then gathered her papers. She was stuffing everything into the slim shoulder bag she used for a briefcase when Mitch and Nathan came back.

"Mr. Stuart positively identified the kids," Nathan announced.

Melina smiled. She loved it when she got her first solid lead in a case. It gave her a sense of accomplishment and whetted her appetite for more.

"I called Syracuse and talked to Detective Norris in the Juvenile Division," Mitch added. "He'll be looking into it on their end. He's expecting a call from you tomorrow."

Melina took the paper he offered, containing the officer's name and phone number, and slid it into her bag, too. "Well, guys, I'm heading out. Thank you for the use of your facilities. I'll check in with you tomorrow and let you know what's going on."

She managed to make it out of the department and the building before Sebastian spoke. "I'm going to Syracuse with you."

It wasn't the first time a client had wanted to be part of an investigation. Some thought that footing the bills put them in a decision-making position, some didn't trust her to do the job right without supervision, and some were truly distraught and needed to do *something.* The reason didn't matter, though. Her answer was always the same. This being Sebastian, it was doubly the same. "No, thanks. I don't need the company."

He caught her arm, pulling her around to face him. "Damn it, Melina—"

Her gaze locked with his for a moment before slowly, pointedly sliding down to where his fingers circled her forearm. A lesser man not only would have let go, but would have backed away about ten feet for good measure. Sebastian, though, didn't uncurl one single finger.

"Look, I know you hate me, and I'd be sorry about it if I had any emotion to spare, but I don't. Chrissy's my daughter. She's seven years old, and she's all I've got. I can't stay here and do nothing to get her back. I *need* to go with you."

"The only way you can help is by staying out of my way."

"I can do that just as well in Syracuse as here."

Except that if he stayed here, then she wouldn't have to look at him, speak to him, or think about him. Alone in Syracuse, she could keep so busy that treacherous memories like that one of making love late at night in his workshop couldn't weasel their way out of their dark corner. Alone in Syracuse, she could do her best to concentrate on the case, to forget that he was Chrissy's father—hell, to forget him completely.

Yeah, right. Rat bastards weren't so easily forgotten. Desire for Rico had continued long past the point where she'd been ashamed to admit it. Though she'd known him months longer than Sebastian, she had this niggling worry that he'd merely been practice for Sebastian.

"I can drive, run errands, make sure you have what you need. The rest of the time, I'll stay out of your way. I swear. You won't even know I'm there."

She fixed her narrowed gaze on the house across the street. She'd worked with partners before—Rico, employees at the agency, a time or two with a Buffalo cop. It wasn't so bad, as long as everyone clearly understood who was in charge. And while she didn't object to doing her own driving—she loved roaring down the highway with the wind in her hair—she wouldn't mind having someone provide meals or anticipate her frequent need for a Diet Coke. And since runaways didn't hang out in the better parts of town, this investigation was likely to lead her into some pretty rough areas. Though she was an expert shot, so well versed in self-defense tactics she could teach classes, and never went anywhere without her weapon and her pepper spray, she wasn't ever going to intimidate somebody with nothing more than her appearance. At six feet five, with broad shoulders and amazing muscles, Sebastian could.

She scowled at the For Rent sign in the small patch of grass that fronted the house. Was she really considering letting him go along? Considering, hell. It sounded as if she'd already made up her mind. Was she crazy? Delirious from lack of food? Masochistic?

Maybe all of the above. Or maybe she was just looking

for some pathetic excuse to prolong her time with Sebastian. Maybe her pride and dignity had seeped out through her broken heart, because damned if she didn't give him a sidelong glance and woodenly say, "Fine. We'll leave as soon as I get my bags from Lyn's house."

Chapter Five

THE SUN WAS SETTING, THE TEMPERATURE DROPPING, the tires humming at high speed on the pavement. Sebastian lifted one hand from the steering wheel, flexed fingers that had been gripping too long, then turned down the air conditioner a notch. According to the highway sign a few minutes back, they were only thirty miles from Syracuse, and hopefully one big step closer to finding his daughter. He had a sick, empty feeling in his stomach that wasn't going to go away until Chrissy was in his arms again.

Never mind the fact that part of the emptiness had been there before she'd disappeared.

He glanced at Melina, sitting with spine straight and legs crossed, but still managing to look at ease. They'd gone from the courthouse to Lynda's house, then stopped at his place on the way out of the valley. He'd invited her inside. She'd bluntly said no. It was just as well. Her presence in his house was slowly starting to fade. It had taken three washings to get her scent out of his sheets. He wasn't sure how to scrub away the memories of her lying in his bed, sitting at his kitchen table, lifted against the workshop wall.

He cleared his throat. She didn't seem to hear. "Syracuse isn't on the way to Providence."

For a time she sat so still that he wondered if she'd dozed off behind her dark glasses. Then she glanced toward him. "No. Presumably, the kids thought they were stowing away to Utica, or maybe they didn't care *where* the Stuarts were going, as long as it was away from Bethlehem. Wherever they wound up, they probably intended to take the bus or the train, or maybe even fly—none of which they could do without getting out of Bethlehem first."

"Wouldn't they try the same thing in Syracuse?"

"More than likely, unless one of them realized they would be walking into a trap. They might still be in the city or . . ."

"Or?"

"They might have started walking or hitched a ride."

The thought sent a shiver through him. What kind of person would pick up three little kids hitchhiking without turning them over to the cops? The kind he didn't want his daughter anywhere near.

Mile after mile passed while he worked to get the uneasiness rumbling through him back under control. Finally he could take a breath without his chest aching. He could think without the muscles in his stomach spasming. When he was pretty sure he could speak without yelling out his frustration, he changed the subject. "Why did some guy come after you with a baseball bat yesterday?"

"Instead of going to Chicago on business, as he'd told his wife, he'd spent the weekend with his latest girlfriend at a motel in Buffalo, and I had the pictures to prove it. Not surprisingly, he didn't want me to give them to the missus."

"Would you have shot him?"

"He did more damage to the car I was driving than the damn thing's worth. He tried to steal a thousand-dollar camera, and he threatened me. Yes, if he'd made it necessary, I would have shot him." Her voice turned silky sweet. "But I wouldn't have killed him. I just would have hurt him. *Very* badly." Then it returned to normal, with more than a hint of belligerence. "Does that bother you?"

It shouldn't. He'd had his chance with her, and he'd blown it. He'd destroyed whatever was between them, made her hate him, and had hurt her in the process. He'd cut her out of his life, and now nothing about her life—beyond finding Chrissy—concerned him. But . . . "Yeah. It bothers me."

She turned one of those if-looks-could-kill looks on him. "You think he has a right to sleep around on his wife? To lie to her and their children with every breath he takes? You think he's got the right to waltz out of his marriage without being held accountable for the damage he's done to it? To leave his wife and kids with nothing while he goes on living his sleazy, worthless life in comfort?"

Her accusing tone crawled under his skin and made his temper flare. He wasn't the most honorable man in the world, particularly where she was concerned, but he deserved more credit than that. He knew firsthand what it was like to be lied to and left with nothing. He didn't know if there had been another man involved in Diana's leaving, but he didn't think it could have hurt any worse if there was.

Scowling, he responded in the same hostile tone she'd used. "I think if he could do that much damage to your car, he could have killed you. All the pictures in the world aren't worth dying for."

She stared at him a long time—long enough to make him squirm in the seat. Then slowly, coolly, she smiled. "Better watch out, Sebastian. Keep making remarks like that, and I might start to think you're human."

He was all too human—weak, foolish, prone to stupid mistakes. He'd been unable to save his marriage, too thickheaded to even realize it was at risk, and not up to the job of putting his life back together once it was over. He hadn't even tried, instead withdrawing from everyone but Chrissy and occasional, meaningless one-night—or four-night—stands. If he'd tried, maybe Chrissy wouldn't have run away. Maybe she would have felt she could come to him about her mother.

So all this was his fault. No surprise. According to Ramona, it was his fault Diana had run away, too, and he was certainly the one responsible for shoving Melina away. He would take all the blame, all the guilt, if he could just have his little girl back safely.

His nerves taut, he gestured to the city spreading around them. "Where to?"

She thumbed through her notes, then glanced up in time to read an exit sign. "Take the next exit. The gas station's there, and we can look for a motel and a restaurant in the area."

At the next exit, there were motels on either side of the interstate, as well as several fast-food places and chain restaurants. Given a choice, he would have gone to the gas station first to ask for information about the kids, but she directed him into a restaurant parking lot. "We can get rooms at that motel," she said with a wave toward the back of the lot. "But right now I need food."

The restaurant catered to travelers, truckers, and families with noisy kids, and Sebastian was pretty sure there wasn't a male in the place who failed to look when Melina walked past. He knew how they felt. The first few times he'd seen her, he'd hardly noticed her—but then, he'd been known to walk right past his own parents without realizing it. But ten days ago, when she'd walked up to his table in the Starlite Lounge, he'd been instantly addlepated, as his grandmother used to say. They'd been halfway through their first dance before he'd spoken, and even then, whatever he'd said had surely been lame. He'd been too dazzled to think. In her short, tight red dress and matching barely there stiletto heels, she'd been a sight to drive every rational thought from a man's mind.

He'd thought that night what incredible luck occasionally struck. He'd married the prettiest girl in high school, had the sweetest daughter in all of Bethlehem, and had just been picked out of a crowd by the most beautiful woman in the entire state.

She shouldn't have wasted her time.

The hostess seated them at a table for two against the plate-glass window. When he sat down, Sebastian's knees bumped hers, and when they both moved in response, his feet tangled with hers. Finally as comfortable as he was going to get, he glanced at the menu, then laid it aside. "What's the plan?"

"I'll call Detective Norris in the morning. After dinner, I'll walk over to the gas station and McDonald's and see if anyone there recognizes the kids' pictures. More than likely, though, the people working tonight weren't working early yesterday afternoon. And then"—she broke off to cover a delicate yawn with one hand—"I'm going to bed. I could use about ten hours of sound sleep."

He wanted to ask what they would do the next morning and the next afternoon and that night. What if someone did recognize the kids? How would that help them figure out where they'd gone? What if this lead led to a dead end? Unless one of the kids had carelessly announced their plans, how could it not?

But the waitress came, and Melina was in the process of ordering enough food for two or three people, and he didn't want to annoy her by asking questions she might not be able to answer. So he kept his mouth shut except to order a hamburger, fries, and Coke.

She ate ravenously, polishing off her meal as well as a salad, a handful of his fries, and a piece of pie. Finally, long after he'd finished his burger, she leaned back in her chair and gave a great sigh. For the first time all day, there was some color in her cheeks and a bit of sparkle in her eyes. "Why don't you get us two rooms at the motel, and I'll run across the street to the station."

"Why don't I—" He broke off as the waitress brought the tab. Without thinking, he pulled some bills from his wallet to cover it.

"Keep the receipt," Melina said. "For my expense report, so you can get reimbursed."

"I don't need to be reimbursed." He would gladly pay

her entire damn fee if she would let him. He didn't care about a few meals and motel rooms.

Once they reached his truck, he finished what he'd been about to say earlier. "Why don't I go across the street with you?"

In the dim glow of the truck's dome light and the nearby street lamps, her gaze narrowed dangerously. "You know, Sebastian, I've been doing this job a long time, and I haven't yet needed help from an amateur. I know the questions to ask. I know how to get people to talk."

"I know that. It's just . . ." He should have forgotten what he'd started to say, or simply agreed with her suggestion. Instead, he dragged his hands through his hair and scowled. "It's late, we're in a strange city, and I'm pretty sure this area doesn't make the tourism office's top ten list of Syracuse sights they'd like you to see."

She stared at him incredulously. For a moment he thought she might burst out laughing, but she didn't. "I appreciate your concern," she said, though clearly she didn't. "But I'm more than capable of taking care of myself. I'd like a nonsmoking room, something away from the highway if possible. I'll meet you outside the lobby when I'm done."

He watched her stride across the parking lot, hesitate at the street for a moment, then run across and inside the brightly lit gas station. Of course she could take care of herself. That wasn't the point.

And what was the point? That she was a woman? He didn't worry about every woman he knew. That she was a woman he'd slept with? He barely knew the names of the few women he'd been with since Diana. The point was . . .

Hell. He'd figure it out later.

IT WAS RAINING TUESDAY MORNING WHEN MELINA and Sebastian met outside their adjacent rooms for breakfast, but the cool showers couldn't hide the fact that it was going to be a hot day. She didn't mind heat—she was Greek, after all—and she liked rain, though sometimes it made surveillance or tailing a subject more difficult than it needed to be. But she wasn't running away and didn't have to be exposed to the elements enough to be more than slightly inconvenienced. She'd had a motel room to sleep in, with all the conveniences kids took for granted—dry shelter, heat and air-conditioning, running water.

"I wonder where the kids slept last night." Sebastian was standing next to her under the motel's porte cochere, watching the rain and the gray sky.

"Hopefully, out in this mess," she said cheerfully. "Let's get some breakfast." She'd gone a dozen feet before realizing he wasn't following. Turning, she found him staring, just as she'd expected. With an impatient sigh, she explained. "Kids like these think of running away as an adventure. They have a little fun and excitement, and when they go home, everyone's ecstatic to see them. Let them face a little hardship—going hungry, sleeping outside in the rain, blistered feet, and so on—and they'll want to go home a lot quicker. Sheesh, didn't you ever run away from home?"

He shook his head.

"I did, when I was five. I couldn't bear to leave anything behind, so I packed virtually everything I owned in Mama's biggest suitcase. Of course, the bag was so heavy I could barely lift it. I carried it twenty feet—I didn't dare drag it and scuff the leather any more than it already was—and rested, then carried it another twenty feet. I got as far as Yaya Rosa's three blocks over and let her stuff me with dolmathes and baklava while she talked me into giving Mama and Papa another chance to prove they still loved me best."

"And what did they do to make you doubt it in the first place?"

"They brought a stinky, noisy baby boy named Stavros to live with us." She grinned at the memory. "I'd already explained to them that it would be best all around if they just left him at the hospital. Nikos and I were quite happy being the only son and daughter in the family. Bringing in another child of either gender would merely upset the delicate balance we'd achieved."

He almost smiled, and she felt as if she'd come close to accomplishing an impossible task. He wasn't a man who smiled a lot, and she was certain he was due for one any day now.

"I assume Stavros stayed."

"He did. It actually turned out to be a good thing. Nikos and I had someone to blame all our adventures on—and still do. Stavros turned twenty-nine two months ago, and we can still get him in trouble today." She started toward the restaurant again, and within a few seconds, he'd caught up with her. "You've got brothers and sisters?"

"Three brothers, one sister. I'm the oldest, and Shauna's the baby."

It was difficult to imagine him ever having been a baby. If present-day Sebastian was anything to judge by, he'd probably weighed ten or twelve pounds at birth and had come out scowling, keeping everyone at a distance except for little necessities like meals and diaper changes. Of course, she admitted, the baby image conjured by present-day Melina would have hit the ground running, looking for excitement and making passes at all the little boys in the nursery, when in fact, she'd been the perfect sweet little baby girl, according to Yaya Rosa.

The restaurant was crowded with travelers heading out on the road again and a large number of locals who apparently came to smoke and indulge their appreciation for an endless supply of strong coffee. After putting her name on a waiting list, Melina accepted an old lady's offer to share a narrow bench with her and her friends. Picking up a front section of newspaper someone had left behind, Sebastian leaned against the wall nearby and started to read.

She tried to forget about him and concentrate on the other diners waiting in the small lobby, but it wasn't easy, particularly when she noticed that the four young women sitting opposite her were talking about him in animated whispers behind their cupped hands. Based on her own experience with friends who didn't know the meaning of the word *subtle,* she figured three of them were encouraging the fourth to approach him. It made her regret that she'd dressed in jeans and a T-shirt again this morning, because she'd been wrong when she'd said she couldn't intimidate anyone with her mere presence. In the right dress and shoes, she could intimidate the hell out of most women, if she so chose.

"Those women over there appear to be interested in

your young man," the elderly woman beside her commented quietly.

It was on the tip of Melina's tongue to insist that he wasn't *her* young man and she couldn't care less if the four tramps entertained themselves with him all day. After all, it would keep him out of her way while she worked. But it wasn't true. For reasons she was in no mood to examine, if any one of the women made a move on him, Melina would have to snatch her bald. And if he showed any interest in them, she would hurt him, too—badly.

"Yes," she agreed evenly. "They do."

"Women used to look at my Max that way. He was a fine man—handsome as an angel and wicked as the devil. Why, I once had to push a woman in the swimming pool to get her off him. It was easier than getting a bucket of water to throw on her." The woman looked past her to Sebastian, and her faded gaze brightened with appreciation. "You know . . . with those jeans so nicely filled out, if you take away that shirt, he'd look just fine on the cover of a romance novel. You know the kind of book I'm talking about—the beautiful woman spilling out of her clothes, the man big, handsome, all broad chest and bulging . . . muscles."

She sighed wistfully, then became aware of Melina's at-a-loss-for-words stare. With a laugh, she patted her arm. "Don't look so surprised, dear. As my friends are fond of saying, I'm old, not dead. If he were twenty years older, I'd give you a run for your money."

If he were twenty years older, Melina thought, he'd still be a good twenty years younger than the woman. Obviously, the same thought occurred to *her,* because she smiled wickedly. "What can I say? I like 'em young enough to have some stamina. When I leave 'em as limp as a wrung-out dishcloth, I want them to recuperate . . . eventually."

After a moment, Melina burst into stunned laughter. Sebastian's gaze flickered her way, curiosity in his hazel eyes. He didn't speak, though, but returned almost immediately to his newspaper. "You are a dirty old woman," she teased.

"Oh, darlin', I do my best. My name's Elsa. How about you?"

"Melina. Are you from around here?"

"Nope. My friends and I are from—" Abruptly her gaze narrowed. "You're not a police officer, are you?"

Melina shook her head and lowered her voice to the same conspiratorial tone. "You're not a wanted woman, are you?"

"Somewhere, I hope!" Elsa's throaty laugh came again. "Actually, my friends and I are . . . hmm, how can I say this so it doesn't sound totally foolish? Runaways."

Leaning forward, Melina looked at each of the three women. Elsa was probably the youngest, and if she was a day under seventy-five, it didn't show. The other two appeared to be somewhere between eighty and a hundred and ten, though they also appeared as spry and lively as Elsa. "Runaways from what?"

"The home. Our children forced us into a retirement prison where our every move can be monitored twenty-four hours a day. For my own good, my son said. Ha! For *his* convenience, is what he meant. So when he reneged *again* on a promise to take me to the Grand Canyon, I invited Imogene and Susie to go with me instead. After all, I'm not getting any younger. I don't have time to wait for him to get his schedule under control. The man is sixty years old. If he hasn't managed yet . . ." With pursed lips, she gave a shake of her head. "Do you two have children?"

"No," Melina replied, feeling a twinge of regret cloaked in biological-clock panic. "We aren't married."

"Why, darlin', marriage isn't what causes that!" Elsa said with a great laugh. She paused as the hostess called her name. "Watch out for the barracudas over there. And if the coppers come bustin' in here lookin' to take us in, all I ask is that you slow 'em down long enough for us to get out the back door."

"It would be an honor," Melina said, restraining a grin.

Imogene and Susie went straight to the hostess stand, but Elsa detoured by Sebastian, looking him over from head to toe with blatant appreciation. "She's a lovely girl. You make an honest woman of her, and she'll make a happy man of you." She gave him a big, lascivious wink, then sashayed after her friends.

When no one else claimed the bench vacated by the women, Sebastian sat down. "What were you two talking about?"

"Sex. Old age. Bulging muscles. The Grand Canyon." Though her answer didn't help make Elsa's remarks any clearer for him, she smiled. "I'm gonna be just like her when I get older."

He looked confused. "Well, there's a questionable goal."

"She's about eighty years old. She appears to be in good health, she's mentally sharp, she still enjoys sex, and she's got the spirit to run away from the retirement home her son forced her into to do something *she* wants. Would it make more sense to you if I aimed for being feeble in body and mind or, hey, how about dead?"

"Their families must be crazy with worry."

"Their families should have paid more attention to them."

"You think I didn't pay enough attention to Chrissy?"

Melina stared at him. "Who brought Chrissy into this discussion?"

"You said those women ran away because their families were neglecting them."

"News flash, Sebastian—people run away for a lot of reasons, and the reasons of three very mature old ladies have nothing to do with the reasons of one seven-year-old child. Elsa, Imogene, and Susie are competent to make their own decisions, but because people in this country don't value the wisdom and experience of the elderly, they've been forced into a reversal of roles where their children get to parent them. They're rebelling—exercising their rights. Chrissy, on the other hand, is an immature, inexperienced young child who believes in magical thinking. She's not allowed to rebel, and she doesn't have any rights."

Though she knew her last dismissive remark wasn't totally correct, it was a good ending to her rant. Besides, kids' rights were sufficiently restricted that if he was foolish enough to contradict her, she would be happy to respond. After all, to a hot-blooded Greek, there was little entertainment better than a heated discussion.

But he didn't argue. He simply gave her a flat, blank look and repeated, "Susie?"

She laughed. "Before long we'll have our first generation of grandmothers who answer to Brittney and Stephanie." *And Chrissy.*

Just as one of the barracudas stood up and took a few steps their way, the hostess called Melina's name. She gave the woman a cool, smug, warning smile as she and Sebastian also stood up, and thought she heard the distinctive last sounds of the word *bitch* as she passed. Damn right, she thought. Not that she cared whether some other woman came on to him, or if he took her up on whatever she was offering. It was just incredibly rude to do it when he was obviously with someone else. Melina knew that firsthand from all the times she'd done it herself.

And Sebastian was oblivious to it all. Once they were seated, he returned to the conversation with such ease that she honestly doubted whether he'd noticed the four women in the lobby. It was an amazing thing for a rat bastard. Rico would have been inventorying their assets within thirty seconds of walking through the door.

"What are your grandmothers' names?" he asked.

"My grandmother Emanuelides was named Thalia, after the Muses. She died when I was a little girl, so I don't remember much about her. Yaya Dimitris is Rosa. She's about eighty and still lives in the first house she and Papous—my grandfather—bought when they emigrated to the United States. It's Greek tradition to name the first daughter after the father's mother, so I'm Rosa Melina." She smiled dryly. "Sounds like some kind of pasta, doesn't it? What about your grandmothers?"

"My mother's named after her mother. Gran is Hildred, and Mom goes by Hildy. My dad's mother is Sara. They're both still alive, still in Bethlehem. I don't see them as often as I should, but Mom makes sure Chrissy does."

"I see most of my family every week I'm in town—not just my parents and brothers, but Yaya Rosa, my aunts, uncles, cousins. There's usually fifty or more of us for Sunday dinner, and for something special, like Easter or a saint's day, there'll be easily more than a hundred."

Suddenly struck by the ease of the conversation, she blinked and pretended to focus on the menu. They'd done a lot of talking in their time together, but they hadn't learned much about each other—just that she'd wanted to spend the rest of her life with him. All the nitty-gritty getting-to-know-you . . . she'd figured they would take care of that over the next forty years.

And he'd figured he would get laid enough times to take the edge off months of unfulfilled need, then never see her again.

After they placed their orders, he settled back in the chair, stretched out his legs, and bumped hers. A shiver ran through her as they both automatically withdrew. Within an hour of meeting, they'd been having hot, intense sex somewhere between his driveway and his front door. Now they couldn't accidentally touch without both of them reacting guiltily. Life was funny . . . not.

"What did you mean back there about Chrissy believing in magical thinking? You mean like wishes and witches and angels?"

"No, of course not," she began, but the waitress interrupted as she filled their coffee cups.

"Now don't be discounting the presence of angels," the older woman said with a broad smile. "They're everywhere. Why, here in Rochester we're big believers in angels and miracles."

"We're in Syracuse," Melina politely corrected her. Her forehead wrinkled as she studied the woman—middle-aged, brown and gray hair, an ill-fitting polyester top in brown and beige stripes, brown pants, and jack-o'-lantern orange socks. She had the vague sense that she knew the woman, though from where she hadn't a clue. There was just something oddly familiar about her.

"Syracuse, Rochester—same difference. Both cities in New York," the waitress said with a careless shrug, "and they've both got their share of angels. Keep your senses attuned while you're here and you might even meet one. Are you in town on business or pleasure?"

"Business." Melina reached into her bag for a flyer. "We're looking for three runaways."

The waitress's eyes opened wide. "You're not after Ilsa and her friends, are you?"

"No. I hope the ladies have a marvelous time at the Grand Canyon." Melina laid the flyer on the table, pictures right side up for the woman. "We know the kids were in this area Sunday. Have you seen them?"

Moment after moment slipped past while the waitress studied the photographs. Finally, with a gentle smile, she looked at Sebastian. "The little one's your girl."

He nodded.

"And yours, too," she added to Melina.

"No, I'm not—" Melina wasn't sure what to say. *I'm not her mother, I'm not married to him, I'm not connected to any of the kids.* Before she had a chance to decide, the woman went on.

"Of course you're not. But you know, you don't have to give birth to a child to love her as if you did." She nodded her graying head confidently.

Love Chrissy? She hardly knew the kid. She hadn't spent more than an hour at a time in her company last week, and even that had been awkward. Chrissy was accustomed to being the only female in the Knight house, and the sole focus of her father's attention. She hadn't been thrilled about sharing him. Only regular bribes involving Sebastian's parents had kept them all happy.

Deliberately she redirected the woman's attention to the photographs. "Do you remember seeing them at all? Maybe they came in to eat or you saw them on the street."

"They definitely didn't come in here. I would've remembered three kids all alone. Have you tried over at McDonald's?"

"We plan to after breakfast. Do you think your manager would let us post this flyer at the door?"

The waitress grinned as if at an inside joke that couldn't be shared. "*My* manager would let you paper the city with it, but I'll ask the restaurant manager."

"Do you always talk to strangers like this?" Sebastian asked once the woman left.

Perceiving an edge of criticism to his voice, Melina stiffened her spine. "It's part of the job." Though it was true that, in the investigations business, information was power, the bottom line was she was a friendly person who liked people. She liked finding out utterly useless stuff about them, and offering tidbits about herself. She liked gaining a stranger's trust and peeling away all the layers to uncover the person behind the façade. It was part of what made her job so satisfying—along with the good money, being her own boss, catching a few criminals, standing up for the underdog, and relieving people's worries.

"If I hadn't been so friendly, you never would have gotten to first base with me," she pointed out. She wouldn't say he was shy—more of a loner, she supposed. But if the first move had been left to him that Saturday night at the Starlite Lounge, there never would have been a second. "Guess that makes it my fault, huh?"

The guilt flashed through his eyes again, and he opened his mouth, but instead of an apology or excuse, he asked another question. "Why were you? Friendly, I mean."

She could come up with a ton of answers. She liked sex. Liked men. Had been alone much longer than usual. She'd been working hard, and what better way to let off steam than with hot, passionate, energetic sex? His big, rugged, macho *everything* had appealed to her. He was so large he'd made her feel delicate in comparison. His hands had intrigued her. Her hormones had betrayed her.

Her heart had betrayed her. She had approached Sebastian that night solely with the intention of enjoying a dance with him. But somewhere between the booth he'd shared with Ben and the dimly lit corner of the dance floor where they'd finally wound up, she'd gotten sucker-punched. Maybe it had happened when he'd taken her in his arms and she'd been overwhelmed by the feeling of belonging. Maybe it had been his first kiss, as innocent as a kiss between a man and a woman could be—and also as intense, compelling, and intimate. Maybe it had had something to do with the way he'd touched her face so tenderly, or the way he'd spoken her name. A whisper, a plea, a promise.

Whatever the excuse, she'd fallen in love with him before they'd left the bar. Maybe not real love—commitment love, happily-ever-after love—but more real than anything she'd ever known before.

And damned if she was going to tell him that.

She shrugged nonchalantly. "Being friendly to men is what I do for entertainment. Some people read. Some play golf. I have sex. Now," she went on without a pause. "About this magical thinking . . ."

AS THEY WAITED FOR A LULL IN TRAFFIC SO THEY could cross the street, Sebastian decided that magical thinking held a certain appeal. Not the taking-blame part Melina had talked about—that if a child wished something bad on someone else and, by coincidence, it happened, often the kid believed his wish was the cause. But the truly magical part—the if-I-only-believe-hard-enough or want-it-bad-enough part . . . He could put that to good use. He would wish Chrissy back where she belonged, Diana out of their lives and their minds for good, and Melina . . .

What wish would he make regarding Melina? That she would go back to Buffalo and stay there? That their four days and four nights had never happened? Or that they'd never ended?

He didn't know, and told himself he didn't have the energy to figure it out. Not until Chrissy was back. Until then, nothing else—no one else—mattered.

The gas station clerk was a kid, maybe eighteen or twenty, with bad skin, a gold stud through one nostril, and a silver one through his tongue, which didn't slow his vigorous gum chewing and popping at all. He admitted to working Sunday at the time the Stuarts were gassing up their truck, dismissed the pictures of the girls with hardly a glance, then studied Caleb's picture. "Yeah, I remember him," he remarked. "He came in, bought somethin', wanted to know about somethin', then left."

"What did he buy?" Melina asked.

"Don't remember."

"What did he want to know?"

"I dunno. Directions or somethin'."

"Directions where?"

The kid shrugged, waited on a customer, then came back.

"To the bus station? Maybe to a shelter?"

"Yeah. Maybe."

She gestured toward the glowing light of a camera mounted above the counter. "Do you suppose we could look at the security tapes from Sunday afternoon?"

"Ain't any. Camera broke a while back and hasn't been fixed. Owner says as long as people *think* they're being taped, it serves its purpose."

Melina smiled sweetly and wrangled permission to post flyers on each door and at the pumps, then headed for McDonald's once that was done. There she spoke to the manager and a handful of employees without learning anything and left a bunch of flyers. They were about to walk out the door when she stopped short, causing Sebastian to sidestep to avoid running into her. An employee outside in the play area had caught her attention. The woman was leisurely picking up trash as if it weren't pouring down rain, and she appeared to be talking, or possibly singing, to herself. With a shrug, Melina changed directions, and Sebastian automatically followed her.

She stopped just outside the door, staying in the narrow strip along the building kept dry by the overhang of the roof. Sebastian stood a short distance away. "Excuse me. Could we talk to you for a minute?"

The employee turned and greeted them with a bright smile. "Isn't it a beautiful morning?"

The uniform was different, and the hood of her navy blue slicker covered all but a few damp wisps of hair, but the face, the voice— It was the waitress who'd served them breakfast across the street not twenty minutes ago.

Melina's smile was slow, sly. "What are you—Super Waitress? You help out at all the restaurants around here?"

The woman smiled, too. "I told you—we're everywhere."

No, she hadn't, Sebastian thought. She'd said *angels* were everywhere. Maybe it was true—he was too grounded in reality to consider his opinion valid—but he was pretty sure celestial beings, if they existed, didn't hang out in fast-food restaurants stuck between truck stops and cheap motels.

As if he'd spoken his doubts aloud, the woman fixed her clear gaze on him. "*Every*where," she repeated softly. "I'm Gloria."

Melina looked startled, as if the name meant something to her but she couldn't quite figure out what. "I'm Melina Dimitris, and this is Sebastian Knight."

"Pleased to meet you . . . again." Gloria's eyes twinkled. "Are you going to show me the pictures of your missing kids?"

"Why?" Melina challenged. "You already said you hadn't seen them."

"No, I *said* they didn't come in the other restaurant. I told you to ask at McDonald's."

"Well, we asked, and no one remembers them."

"You didn't ask me."

"I did ask and you said—"

"Come now, it's too lovely a morning to quibble over words. Let me see the pictures again, please."

With a wary look in her dark eyes, Melina pulled out a flyer, and the woman studied it for a moment. "I do remember them," she said at last. "They had lunch here—well, inside. Then the boy went to the station to buy a map of the city, and the girls came out here. This one—Alanna—sat right here at this table while the little one played."

"Do you know where they were planning to go?"

"To the bus station."

"Were they able to find it on the map?"

"They needed a little help from the other girl—the one sitting right down there. Her name is . . ." She closed her eyes as if it helped her to think, then shrugged. "Something Anne. Lee Anne? Dee Anne? Dianne?"

Sebastian's stomach knotted painfully. Sweet hell, what if it wasn't magical thinking on Chrissy's part? What if she'd been in touch with her mother—most likely through Diana's mother—and they'd planned this whole adventure together? If she'd run off not to *find* her mother but to *be* with her? Would he ever get her back?

He forced himself to stop grinding his jaw long enough to ask, "How old was this girl?"

"Dianne? It's hard to say. You know, girls don't look like they used to. There was a time when a fourteen-year-old girl looked fourteen, but these days, most fourteen-year-olds could pass for twenty or twenty-five. But if I had to hazard a guess, it would be . . . oh, sixteen. No older than eighteen."

Relief swept through Sebastian, making him feel strangely weak.

"So this girl gave them directions," Melina said.

"She showed 'em how to read the map. Then she gave 'em a ride." That all-encompassing ain't-life-grand smile stretched across Gloria's face again. "That was my idea. There's some tough places between here and the bus station, and that little one didn't look like she was gonna make it that far. They started out walking, but I told Dianne—"

"Dee Anne," Sebastian interrupted.

"Lee Anne," Melina substituted.

"I told that Anne girl that any charitable person with a car would offer them a ride, and she did."

And where had she taken them? With their pictures all over every bus station, there was no way they could have managed to take the bus without getting caught. Had she dropped them off at the station and left them on their own again? Or had she taken them someplace else, like out into the country where it would be easy enough to get rid of three little kids and claim their money for her own? Had she—

Strong fingers closed around his, grasping tightly enough to stop the trembling he hadn't even noticed until it was gone. Melina wasn't looking at him, but she continued to hold his hand, steady, controlled. "Do you know this Anne girl?"

The waitress got a curious look, as if the question required some thought. "Yes and no. Sunday was the first time I'd met her, but I'd heard about her."

"From whom?"

Her hands fluttered. "Oh, here and there. She moves around a bit, and I've got friends everywhere."

"She's a runaway?"

"Oh, no. Better to say she's homeless."

"Have you seen her since Sunday?"

"No."

"Have you seen the kids since then?"

Gloria shook her head.

"Do you have any idea where Anne stays?"

"I told you, she's homeless. Homeless people tend to stay in shelters or abandoned buildings, in alleys or cars—wherever they can find some measure of shelter. For some time Anne's been living in her car—and before you ask, I don't know what kind it is other than white."

"Great," Melina murmured. "Do you have any idea how many white cars there are on the road today?"

"No, I don't. I don't drive myself. I never quite got the hang of working both the steering wheel and the foot pedals at the same time."

Melina asked a few more questions, including one for a detailed description of Anne, made some notes, then offered her hand to Gloria. "Thank you for your help."

"You're welcome."

"Are we going to run into you at any other restaurants around here?"

"You never know. But if you do, most likely you won't remember me."

"I'm very good at remembering people," Melina said.

"But I'm very good at being forgotten." With a grin, Gloria strolled back into the rain, picked up a few sodden burger wrappers, then disappeared around the corner.

"I think it's time to call Detective Norris," Melina announced. "Someone he works with may know this girl or might have filled out an FI card on her."

"What's—"

"Field interview. Someone's acting a little suspicious, maybe loitering, doing something to catch a cop's attention that he doesn't necessarily want to arrest 'em for, he does a field interview—date and time, name, address, reason for being in the area, a description of the vehicle if there is one, tag number, and so forth. Then, if something pops up later—say, a burglary or an assault—they check the FI cards for that area." She glanced at the rain, falling with enough force to splash halfway up their jeans. "Let's get back inside where it's dry."

It took her ten minutes to connect with the detective on the cell phone, another twenty for him to show up at the restaurant. He was probably in his early forties, and he wore a wedding ring, but it didn't stop him from giving Melina the once-, twice-, and thrice-over. She accepted his shameless interest as her due and extended him no more friendliness than the dopey kid at the gas station—hell, no more than she gave Sebastian himself—but he still felt an unaccustomed twinge of jealousy.

Jeez, it had been a long time since he'd been jealous. He'd experienced bouts of pure envy from time to time—when Nathan Bishop had found a ready-made family with Emilie and the Dalton kids, or when J.D. had gone from being alone and lonely to making a home with his new wife, five kids, his father, and a baby on the way, all in less than a summer. He'd wondered at those times what they'd done to be so blessed, and what he'd done to be so cursed, and he'd grown bitter that all he'd ever wanted was Diana and all he'd had was nothing.

But to be jealous of the way a woman looked at another man, smiled at him, offered her hand, and said "I'm glad to meet you, Detective" . . . Not since high school. Hell, not even then, because he and Diana had been kids then, playing at falling in love.

There was nothing the least bit playful about the dark emotion tightening inside him.

They'd been sitting at a table for two when the cop arrived. After introductions, they moved to the nearest booth, and Sebastian innocently—deliberately—cut off the detective when he would have slid into the cramped space beside Melina. Norris gave him a speculative look as he took the opposite bench. Sebastian kept his expression blank as he gazed back.

Melina told Norris everything they knew, and he agreed to provide them with an introduction to someone within the police department who could help. He also offered introductions to several of his "girls"—prostitutes, Melina explained, who provided information to the police in exchange for cash or preferential treatment. Drug dealers, hookers, homeless kids—they all tended to wind up in the same neighborhoods. If anyone in the city was likely to know the mysterious Anne, it was them.

The thought of Chrissy in that environment was enough to make Sebastian ill.

"Before we go to the station, how about we run by the bus station?" Norris suggested. "Then, after the rain stops, we'll track down my girls and see if they can help."

"Sounds good."

As they stood up, the detective gave Sebastian a cagey look. "Uh, you know, Melina, I don't mind helping you out, especially when the request came from Chief Walker back there in Bethlehem, but . . . my lieutenant's not gonna be happy about having the father of one of the runaway kids poking around in our business. No offense, pal," he said to Sebastian.

Maybe he had a valid point. Sebastian was smart enough to know that cooperation between law enforcement agencies was often restricted, cooperation between cops and a private investigator even more so. But he'd be willing to bet the farm that Detective Norris's primary motive was to get Melina to himself. He wanted to protest, to flatly say "I'm going with you," and leave it at that.

But he had no claim on her time or her attention. Moreover, he'd promised to stay out of her way, and he was pretty sure she wouldn't consider pissing off a cop whose help they needed as staying out of her way.

Ignoring Norris, he fixed his gaze on Melina. "I'll go back to the motel. Do you want the truck?"

"Not necessary," Norris said smoothly. "I'll take you wherever you need to go."

A taut smile curved the corners of her mouth. "That's kind of you, Detective."

"Call me Adam."

She slipped a business card into Sebastian's hand. "Here's my cell phone number. Call me if anything comes up."

They'd walked a few feet away when Norris turned back. His expression was tinged with triumph. "You don't need a ride to the motel, do you?" he asked in a tone that made it clear he was asking only for Melina's benefit.

"I think I can walk," Sebastian replied sarcastically. He watched them leave, then sat back down in the booth and studied the business card. She'd given him one the day after they met, with exactly the same message but an entirely different meaning. He'd accepted it at that time, knowing he would never use it. Knowing he would see her again in an hour or so, would make love to her again and again, and then it would end, and he would never call her, never see her. It would be best for both of them. Her home was in Buffalo, and his was in Bethlehem. She was looking for love. He'd given up on it. The best part of her life was ahead of her, and his best was over and done. He'd been so certain that there was no other possible outcome for their affair that he'd hardly noticed how bad it hurt.

This time . . . maybe it would be different.

Chapter Six

"ARE WE ALMOST THERE YET?"

Figuring Chrissy had asked that question at least once every fifty miles, Cheyenne rolled her eyes. "No."

"And we're never gonna get there," Caleb retorted. "That car is a piece of junk. We oughta just leave it here and walk the rest of the way."

"The car's fine."

That came from Alanna. She was the peacemaker of the bunch. Chrissy was the whiner, and Caleb . . . Cheyenne didn't have a handle on him yet. He seemed to be permanently in a bad mood, though she suspected it was more than that. He saw himself as the girls' protector—a role he took very seriously. She didn't expect him to relax until they were all safely back home.

Cheyenne leaned back on her palms and tilted her face up to the sky. They'd driven out of the rain about an hour ago, which was good, since the Cavalier had a cracked carburetor and the car stopped running when dampness seeped inside. After the rain, they'd found this park for an early lunch picnic. It wasn't much of a picnic—or much of a park. There were no tables, no bathrooms, no playground toys, and the grass hadn't seen a mower in weeks.

But that was okay. The sun was shining, there were some bright yellow flowers growing wild, and the butterflies that fluttered around them didn't care about everything the park lacked. They were happy enough with what it had. She tried to be that way, too. She didn't have much, but crying over it wouldn't give her more.

But, oh, there were times when she missed it all so much. Her bedroom with the posters on the wall and the closet full of clothes. Fighting with her brothers and sister over the bathroom. Fixing Alli's hair in a fancy French braid. Taking Matt and Dex trick-or-treating on Halloween. Having enough food and a warm bed and not being scared all the time.

Because she thought she just might cry, she closed her eyes and smiled instead. She willed the lump in her throat to go away and breathed slowly until the tightness in her chest eased. She was all right. She would survive.

Abruptly a warm, heavy weight settled on her lap. "What're you thinkin' about?" Chrissy whispered.

"Home," Cheyenne whispered back without thinking.

Chrissy wriggled this way and that until she couldn't get any closer. It seemed wrong to not put her arm around the kid, so Cheyenne did. "I wish I was at home." The words were little more than a breath, like she was afraid to say them out loud. "Wanna hear about my house?"

Opening her eyes, Cheyenne smiled. "Sure."

"My daddy and I live on a farm that's been in our family for gen—gen'rations. What's a gen'ration?"

"A long time."

"Grandma Hildy and Grandpa James used to live there before I was born, but now they got a house in town, and Mama used to live there, too, but not anymore. Daddy and me've got a dog named Sundance. She's an Irish'etter, and she's real big, and she likes to sleep on top of my feet at night." She giggled, then rubbed her nose. "I got a room all by myself, and it's pink, 'cause that's my favorite color, and my daddy made the bed and dresser and table and chairs and bookcases all just for me. And my grandpa takes me fishing, and he puts the worms on my hook, and me and Gracie—that's Caleb's sister—" she stuck her tongue out at him—"play house in the little tiny house my daddy built out back. We don't let the boys come in there, 'cause we don't like boys."

For a moment everyone was quiet, then Chrissy gave a big sigh. "Where is your home?"

"Right there." Cheyenne pointed to the car.

"Where're you gonna live when it falls apart?"

"It's not gonna fall apart."

"Caleb says—"

Because she knew Caleb was right and the idea scared her silly, Cheyenne answered in a sharper voice than she meant to. "It's *not* gonna fall apart. Come on now. Let's go."

She boosted Chrissy to her feet, then began gathering leftovers from lunch. She'd stuffed everything into a paper bag, then wadded it when an approaching engine caught her attention. When she saw a sheriff's car turn into the park entrance, her stomach tied itself in knots. "Okay, guys, let me do the talking, okay? Get our stuff and get in the car, but don't rush."

As they obeyed, she brushed her hands on her jeans, removed her ball cap and combed her fingers through her hair before putting it on again. When the car stopped behind hers, she took a few steps in that direction, stopping when the deputy got out.

He was about her dad's age, tall and skinny like him, too. Just thinking of her dad made her stomach hurt, but she smiled anyway. "Hi."

"Having a picnic?"

"Yeah. I hope it's okay."

"It's a public park. You from around here?"

"No. No, sir," she hastily added. "My sister and I are taking our cousins back home. They were staying with us while their mom had another baby. A girl. Named her Britney after that girl singer."

"Where's home?"

"Providence. I mean, Syracuse." Her laugh sounded fake and nervous to her. To him, too? "My sister and I live in Syracuse, and our cousins live in Providence. That's where we're going."

"Can I see your license and registration?"

"Sure." She hurried over to the car, leaned over Alanna, and rooted through the glove box until she found them. Going back to the cop, she gave him her license. It was a little over a year old, the picture taken when she was still blond, when she lived in Ohio. She looked like a baby.

The cop studied the license for a moment, looking from it to her, then back again. Finally he asked, "How long have you lived in Syracuse?"

"A few weeks. We moved as soon as school was out."

"State law says you have thirty days after you move here to get a New York license. You'd better get it taken care of as soon as you get home."

She took the license and registration when he offered them, then folded her arms over her chest, hands tucked under. "I will, sir."

"And make sure those kids use their seat belts."

"Oh, we do, sir. All the time."

"Have a safe trip."

She watched as he climbed into his car, backed out, then left the way he'd come. When he turned onto the road, she gave a great sigh of relief. Quickly she hurried back to the car, coaxing the engine to start. She wanted to get on the road before he had second thoughts and came back.

"I thought that policeman was gonna take us to jail," Chrissy said, leaning over the backseat to speak right into Cheyenne's ear.

"So did I." Not that the kids would have gone to jail. The cop would've just called their parents. But he probably would have charged her with kidnapping or something. "Sit down and get your seat belt on, Chrissy. You, too, Alanna, Caleb." She fastened her own seat belt, then turned out of the park in the opposite direction of the cop.

As they tooled along just barely above the minimum speed, the clammy fear seeped away. The rain had stopped, the car was running, and she wasn't on her way to jail. Any way she looked at it, that made it a pretty good day.

DETECTIVE NORRIS—"CALL ME ADAM," HE'D SAID twice more in five miles—pulled into the parking lot that flanked the bus station, then parked in the space nearest the door. "Wait a minute, and I'll come around."

Because she had no desire to get soaked, Melina waited for him to open the car door, a black umbrella raised to shelter them from the rain. It was so small that they had to huddle together, but as soon as she stepped through the door, she moved away. While he folded the umbrella and shook out the rain, she crossed to the counter, going straight to the window where a gray-haired man was idly watching an all-news channel on a small TV.

"What can I do for you?" he asked without raising his gaze from the screen.

She introduced herself and handed across a business card. "I'm looking for—"

"Let me handle it, Melina." The detective's credentials appeared in front of her as he smoothly interrupted her. "Syracuse PD. We're looking for some runaways—a boy and two girls—who might've been in here Sunday afternoon." He pulled a flyer from his jacket pocket, smoothed the creases, and slapped it on the counter in front of the clerk. "You seen 'em?"

The old man studied it a moment, scratched his jaw, then said, "Yeah, as a matter of fact, I have."

Her excitement was short-lived, though. The clerk rooted around in the papers on the desk, then pulled out the flyer the Bethlehem Police Department had sent out before she'd arrived Sunday. "Same kids, huh?"

"Yeah, same kids. You seen 'em?" Norris asked.

"Nope."

"You sold any tickets to Providence since Sunday?"

It took him a moment to check, then he shook his head.

"Okay, thanks." Norris looked at Melina. "We knew it was a long shot, right? Come on, let's head back out."

"Had a girl ask about Providence," the old man called as they turned away. When they both spun back around, he went on. "Not either of those girls. She was older—maybe sixteen, maybe twenty. Scrawny. Black hair. From a bottle."

"What did she want to know?" Melina asked.

"She just asked what time the next bus for Providence would be leaving. I told her, and she smiled real bright and said thanks and left. That's why I remember her. Most kids aren't polite like that. Well, that, plus the dyed hair. Reminded me of my mother."

"And she was alone?"

"If there was anyone with her, they was waiting outside."

Melina thanked him, then she and Norris left. Once they were in the car, he headed toward the police station. "How did a Buffalo P.I. snag a case in a little place like Bethlehem?"

"I have connections to the town."

"So you've known Knight a while."

"A while," she agreed, figuring the intensity and intimacy of their affair made up for the brevity.

"Anything between you besides work?"

She didn't bother to point out that she wasn't working for Sebastian—or that it was none of Norris's business. Instead, she answered with her own question. "Why do you ask that?"

"Just curious. Why don't you answer?"

"I don't discuss my clients or my personal life with strangers."

He smiled charmingly. "I'm not a stranger. The whole Syracuse PD will vouch for me. I'm harmless . . . except to the bad guys."

"And will your wife vouch for you, too?"

He raised one brow, and she gestured toward the wedding ring on his left hand. He laughed. "Oh, that. Habit. The marriage lasted eight years. The divorce is going strong in its third month."

She wasn't sure whether she believed him. She *was* sure she didn't care.

She gazed out the side window at the rain-washed city. The night Sebastian had dumped her, he'd been wearing his wedding ring for the first time in their brief acquaintance. Habit? Or had he put it on not expecting to see her again? Was he divorced and over Diana, still married and in love with his wife, or some variation of the above? Suddenly she wanted to know. Not that it would make a difference. He was still a self-centered, callous bastard who didn't deserve her. She just liked to know things.

At the station, Norris introduced her to his lieutenant, and then she tagged along while he talked to a half-dozen cops about Dianne-Diana-Lee Anne. He checked the FI cards—computerized, thankfully; Melina had worked with a department or two where they weren't—for reference to a teenage girl with black hair and every variation of the name Anne they could come up with.

"Presumably this Anne is a runaway," Norris said when every effort had come up empty-handed.

"The woman who gave us her name was very clear that she's homeless but not a runaway."

"Teenage girls don't generally wind up homeless by themselves. If a family gets evicted, they *all* get evicted. Unless her folks threw her out."

Though she knew such things happened, Melina could hardly imagine it. There was nothing in the world she or her brothers could do to make their parents throw them out—no sin that couldn't be forgiven, no wrong that couldn't be made right. The Emanuelides/Dimitris families tended to take kids in, not boot them out. Whatever flaws any of her relatives might have, they took their family obligations seriously.

"How are the shelters around here about cooperating?"

Norris shrugged. "Pretty good. We can swing by 'em while we're looking for my girls."

Melina was sure there were tougher propositions than finding a bunch of prostitutes on a steamy, rainy day, but she would be hard put to make a guess what they were. By the time Norris returned her to the motel that evening, she was tired, her head ached, and she wanted nothing more than to find some diversion to occupy her evening. A delicious dinner would make a good start, followed by a night of dancing and wild, passionate sex. If she'd been reading the detective right—and in all the years since she'd turned sixteen, she'd misread only two men—she could have all three just for the asking.

She didn't ask, and when he did, she felt a moment's regret. Regret that he'd asked so she had to turn him down? Or that she *wanted* to turn him down?

"How about dinner?"

"Thanks, but I've got reports to prepare, some phone calls to make, some decisions to consider." She smiled weakly. "A P.I.'s work is never done. But thank you for all your help."

"When will you be leaving town?"

"That's one of those decisions I have to consider." She had a gut feeling that Anne was the key. Find her, and they would find the kids—and that made her job tougher. A teenage homeless girl who'd never been arrested or even

FI'ed and who apparently had kept her distance from the shelters, the hookers, and the drug addicts had some pretty damn good survival skills. Good for the kids. Not so good for Melina.

"Give me a call before you go."

"I will." Though for no other reason than to see if he'd found out anything. "Thanks again, Detec—" At his chastening look, she smiled. "Adam."

Gripping her room key tightly, she got out of the car and dashed the few yards to her door. There she looked back once and waved, then she stepped inside as Norris drove off. The room was cool and shadowy. The lights were off and the drapes were pulled, and for a moment she considered leaving things just that way and sinking onto the bed and napping until her headache went away.

But when she switched on the bedside lamp, she saw that her headache wasn't going anywhere. All six feet five inches of it was stretched out on her bed, sound asleep. A glance showed that the door connecting her room to Sebastian's—closed and locked when she'd left that morning—was now open. Easy enough to accomplish, she supposed, since he'd paid for both rooms.

Her first impulse was to awaken him by slamming the door or throwing her shoulder bag onto his back as if unaware he was there. The second, and stronger, was to stand there silently and remember the last time they'd shared a bed. She'd been indulging in the sappiest of daydreams—she, the toughest and best P.I. in the state of New York, love-'em-and-lose-'em Melina. Taking him home to meet her family—preparing him for that would have required some effort, she thought with a faint smile. Getting married. Having babies. Living just a few miles from Lynda and Ben and their babies. Embracing the life—marriage, husband, home, and family—her mother and grandmothers had always dreamed of for her. Being well and truly happy, not just for the time being, but for forever.

A few hours later, when she'd seen him again after being stood up for dinner, he'd looked so guilty, so uneasy and ashamed. But that hadn't stopped him from breaking her heart.

She went into his room, sat on the bed with the pillows stuffed behind her back, and called Lynda's house. Her friend answered on the second ring. She gave her a rundown of everything she'd done and what little they'd learned and asked her to pass it on to Ben, Chief Walker, and the rest of the families.

"You sound tired," Lynda said.

"I am."

"Everything okay with Sebastian?"

"What constitutes okay?" she asked dryly. Not hating him? Not wanting him? Not hurting—or hurting him—every time she looked at him?

"Well, under the circumstances, if you haven't shot him yet, I'd say you're way ahead of okay."

She smiled faintly. "No, I haven't drawn my gun. However, I've been tempted to reach for the pepper spray a time or two. You know, if I shot him, Detective Norris would come and take me away in handcuffs."

"Based on what little you've told me about the handsome detective, he would do that anyway if you'd let him."

Melina winced melodramatically. "Jeez, Lyn, you hook up with a bona fide Southern bad boy, and suddenly you get kinky."

"Oh, yeah, that's me—wild, wicked, and wonderful."

"That used to be me," Melina said, feigning wistfulness. "Now you're the one having all the fun, and I'm the one turning down dates with handsome cops. What's wrong with this picture?"

"It'll get better. Either you'll get over Sebastian or he'll come to his senses."

"I vote for the first. And then I'm instituting a new policy. Great sex is going to be my only use for men from now on."

"Except for the occasional aberrant emotional connection, great sex has *always* been your only use for men," Lynda dryly reminded her.

"Yeah, and it was *fun*." Melina rubbed her eyes with one hand, then yawned. "Hey, I'm going to let you spread the word, and I'm going to get back to work. Give my love to Ben, and I'll talk to you tomorrow."

After hanging up, she sat there a moment, eyes closed, thinking how easily she could fall asleep. Then she swung her feet to the floor, stood up, and opened her eyes . . . to find Sebastian standing in the doorway watching her, looking too comfortable to have just arrived.

He looked as if he'd slept, but neither well nor long. His shirt was wrinkled, pillow lines creased his cheek, and there were shadows under his eyes. His dark hair was tousled, and the stubble of a darker beard covered his jaw. He looked cranky. Adorable. Way too appealing for her own good.

Stifling the urge to lean close and comb her fingers through his hair, then give him a big, greedy kiss while she was so close, she approached the doorway, waited pointedly for him to move, then returned to her room. As he continued to watch, she turned on every light in the place, dug an aspirin bottle from her bag, and washed down a couple tablets with a cup of water from the bathroom sink before finally speaking to him. "You just missed my report to Lynda," she said, plopping down on the bed, still warm with his body heat, and using the remote to turn on the television. "We didn't find out—"

"Detective Norris asked you out?"

She'd thought he looked as if he'd been there more than a few seconds. She couldn't recall saying anything that might come back to embarrass her, though if she did, it was his fault. He shouldn't have fallen asleep in her room, and should have had the courtesy to stay there once he realized she was on the phone.

"Just to dinner," she said in response to his question. Not that it was any of his business.

"Did he manage to provide any help at all in between trying to liven up his social life?"

Because she really wanted to throw something at him, she smiled brightly. "Why, thank you for thinking I can liven up his life. Maybe when this case is done, I'll come back here and do just that before I return to Buffalo."

A muscle in his jaw twitched, and his hazel eyes turned icy. "This isn't *a case.* It's my child, and Ben's and the Bishops' and the Graysons'."

She wanted to disagree with him, to make him think that finding these kids was no more important to her than catching a straying husband or tracking down a long-lost relative. She couldn't do it, though—couldn't sound so coldhearted and callous. Instead, she quietly asked, "Aren't you curious about what we learned?"

"I know you didn't get a lead on the kids or you would have told me."

Deep inside she was annoyed that he sounded so damn sure of her. Deeper, it pleased her. He didn't want her, didn't love her, and apparently didn't even much like her, but he trusted her. It wasn't a lot, but she appreciated it.

After kicking her shoes off, she settled comfortably on the bed and gestured for him to sit, too. Rather than join her on the bed—an idea that would both panic and please her—he brought a chair from the table near the window and situated it at the foot of the bed. "We learned that a girl matching Anne's description asked at the bus station Sunday afternoon about tickets to Providence. The clerk remembers her so well because she was polite and thanked him."

"What about the kids?"

"He didn't see them. Too bad, too, because he had a flyer with their photographs right in front of him. So . . . from Gloria we know the kids were going to the bus station and Anne gave them a ride. Presumably, one of them was smart enough to realize that the bus stations had probably been alerted about them, so they stayed outside in the car while she checked it out inside. She might have seen the flyer or found out they didn't have enough money, and so she went back out and . . ."

"And what?" Sebastian asked.

Melina shrugged. "She went back out to the car, and they . . . disappeared."

THE VERY INSTANT BUD BROUGHT THE CAR TO A STOP in the driveway, Agatha Winchester Grayson launched herself out of the passenger seat and up the steps to the porch of the house where she'd lived her entire life. Inside, her sister was sitting in her favorite chair, the one where she usually did her needlework, but that Tuesday evening, she was simply staring into the distance. "Corinna! Have you heard anything?"

Corinna looked up, and Agatha saw that she'd been weeping. That was so unlike her sister that she feared the worst, and clutching one hand to her throat, she sank into the nearest chair. "Oh, merciful heavens!"

As Bud came through the door, Corinna gently admonished her. "Don't go expecting the worst. There hasn't been any news worth crying over. I was just . . . feeling my age. Bud." She presented her cheek for his kiss, then got up to hug Agatha. "I'm so sorry your honeymoon was ruined. I understand Kelsey and J.D. had a bit of trouble locating you."

"We made a few unscheduled stops," Agatha replied, careful not to look at Bud, for if she did, she would surely blush. "And it wasn't ruined—merely postponed. We both would have been very upset if we hadn't been told."

"What's being done to find the kids?" Bud asked. Bless him, he'd been so worried—not only for the children themselves, but for their families and the children left behind. He was so tenderhearted, and he loved his grandchildren dearly—both the ones of his blood and the adopted ones, as well.

"The police are doing what they can, of course," Corinna answered, "and Ben Foster has hired a private investigator. Everyone who knows her says she's the best. I just had an update from Emilie a short while ago. She's tracked the children as far as Syracuse. I assume from there, she'll go to Providence."

Agatha's mouth tightened. "I cannot believe those three babies are traveling alone to another state to find that undeserving mother of Alanna's. If anything happens to them—"

Bud patted her arm comfortingly. "Nothing will happen."

"We should have been expecting this. Alanna's feelings toward her mother have been in turmoil for months. We should have been prepared—"

Corinna smiled faintly. "And what would we have done? Kept all the children on a short leash?"

"It's something to think about," Agatha declared, even as the foolishness of such an idea made her smile, too. Young Brendan Dalton, a timid little boy, was probably the only child in all of Bethlehem who wouldn't object to such restraints, particularly if his favorite bear Earnest was tethered with him. All the other children were wild and free, and she wouldn't have them any other way.

"We can't protect them from everything," Corinna said. "All we can do is teach them well and pray. Caleb's a good boy. He'll look out for the girls."

"And Alanna's a bright girl. She'll look out for him," Agatha added.

"So . . . tell me about Niagara Falls."

When Agatha and Bud had first announced they intended to honeymoon at Niagara Falls, they'd taken some ribbing from their younger friends. Granted, the falls weren't the honeymoon hot spot they'd been half a century ago. Perhaps, she mused, that was why they'd chosen them. Corinna and her Henry had gone there oh, so many years ago. Virtually all of Agatha's friends had honeymooned there, and she liked to think that if she and Bud had married back then, they would have followed the tradition.

And so they had. Just fifty years late.

"Oh, they were wonderful," she said with a smile for Bud. "Of course I've seen them before but . . . it was different this time. We had a wonderful time. Just wonderful."

"So your two-day honeymoon was . . . shall we say, wonderful?" Corinna asked dryly.

Agatha couldn't take offense at her sister's gentle teasing. Anyone who knew her knew she rarely repeated herself and was even less rarely at a loss for words. Being in love, she'd discovered, could do that to a woman.

"I hate to impose, Corinna, but seeing as we're back early and Bud has a surprise up his sleeve about where we'll be living that he still won't share with me, could we spend the night here?" Agatha was so certain of her sister's answer that she rose from the sofa and turned toward the hall before Corinna stopped her.

"Actually, Agatha, it really is quite an imposition. I've grown accustomed to being alone lately. I think it would be best if you shook Bud's sleeve and see what falls out."

Agatha turned back, staring impolitely. Her sister had never been rude to anyone in her entire life, and she had certainly never turned away family before. But before she could react, she caught sight of the grin that was making the corners of Bud's lips twitch. She scowled from him to Corinna, then back again. "All right, what's going on?"

He came to her, sliding his arm around her waist as naturally as if they'd been married for years instead of mere hours. "It's a beautiful evening, my bride. Let's go for a walk."

"But . . ." It was late. She was tired. They'd had a busy few days, and the last thing she wanted to do was take a walk. On the other hand, a walk in the moonlight with her husband just might be the thing she needed most. "Would you like to come with us, Corinna?"

"No, thank you. I've got a few things to do."

When they left the house, Bud turned her to the right.

"Just once around the block, and then we'll find a place to tuck us in."

They couldn't have had a lovelier evening for a walk if they'd ordered one specially. The temperature was perfect, the breeze warm and sweetly scented. The sky stretched overhead like the softest black velvet, with stars shimmering everywhere. Even the sounds of the night—birds, an occasional barking dog, distant traffic—were just the right touch.

"What are you thinking about?" Bud asked as they reached the end of the block and turned right onto Fifth Street.

"What an incredibly blessed life I've led." It was true. When Samuel Thomas, the first man she'd loved, hadn't come home from World War II, she'd thought she'd lost the better part of herself. Without Sam, there would be no marriage. She would be no one's wife, no one's mother, and she would die an unfulfilled old maid. Then, when she'd least expected it, she'd met Bud and discovered how sweet love could be the second time around. She was *his* wife, J.D. already called her Mom, and his children called her Grandma. Dreams she'd given up on forever had come true, and she was happier than she'd ever thought possible.

"Where are we going to live?" she asked as they turned the third corner, and Bud laughed heartily.

"You've lived a blessed life, but you're afraid you're going to have to bed down in the backseat of the car?" he teased.

"I'm not afraid at all," she replied indignantly. "I'm a bit old for backseats, but I could do it and enjoy it if need be."

"I'm sure you could. In fact, I don't think there's *any-*

thing you can't do, Agatha Grayson, if you put your mind to it. But living in a car isn't going to be necessary. I planned a little bit better than that."

"I don't care where we live as long as we're together and as long . . ." She felt the heat of a blush but forged ahead. "As long as we've got some privacy."

With another of those laughs she loved so dearly, Bud swept her into his arms and danced her in swoops and swirls to the end of the block, where he stopped in the light of a street lamp and gazed down at her. "Privacy is a must, my love, and I'm thinking we need it soon. But first there's something we have to take care of."

"And what would that be?" she asked, but he refused to answer.

They were practically back to her and Corinna's house when he stopped her in the middle of the sidewalk. "Notice anything?"

She glanced around. The block was fairly quiet, with lights on in every house . . . including the big Victorian next door to theirs. Except for the few weeks that Emilie and the children had "borrowed" it when they'd first arrived in town, it had stood empty for ten years, but tonight there were lights on in the windows, cars in the drive, and three children's bicycles were neatly lined up on the porch.

"We have neighbors!" she exclaimed. "Oh, how wonderful! And they have children. Oh, that big old house needs a family with children to make it come alive. Let's go say hello and introduce ourselves."

She was halfway up the sidewalk before a few other minor details registered. Such as the fact that one of the vehicles in the driveway was Nathan Bishop's police department Blazer, and the other was Emilie's car. And those three bicycles on the porch spent almost as much time in her yard as anywhere else. And the new neighbors who weren't really new at all were standing in the driveway with Corinna, watching her expectantly.

Brendan pulled away from his uncle and ran to her, wrapping his arms around her middle and pressing his face to her. "I missed you," he whispered.

"I missed you, too, honey," she said, and bent so he could give her a kiss. When she straightened again, she kept her arm around his thin shoulders and gave his family a curious look. "All right. I admit it. I'm bewildered. Josie, would you offer an explanation, please?"

"Well . . ." Self-importantly, the girl moved forward into a circle of light cast from the porch light. Suddenly Agatha was struck by how much she'd grown in the past three years. She was still thin, and her short blond hair still curled wildly around her head, but she was taller and so much less a little girl. She was growing up.

"Now that you and Grandpa Bud are married, you need a place to live, but not as much as we needed one, on account of we've got too many people living in our house 'cross the street. So Grandpa Bud bought this house, only you don't need all them bedrooms 'cause it's not like you're gonna have any babies or anything, but Uncle Nathan and Aunt Emilie pro'bly are, and someday my mama—"

Her blue eyes widening, Josie looked back at Emilie and Nathan as if she feared she'd done the wrong thing in mentioning her mother. When Emilie murmured, "It's okay," Josie went on with a relieved look.

"Anyway, Grandpa Bud bought this house, and then he sold it to us, and so now we're moved into our new house, which is really our old house, except it wasn't ours then, so I guess it is a new house, and you—" She paused to drag in a deep breath, and eased the tightness in Agatha's own lungs. "You and Grandpa Bud are gonna live in our old house. So we'll still be neighbors, Miss Agatha. Ain't that great?"

As she gazed at the blue house across the street, the schoolteacher in Agatha absently corrected her. "*Isn't* that great?"

"It sure is," Josie agreed.

Two hours later, with Bud snoring softly beside her, Agatha lay awake, smiling foolishly in the dark night. A new husband, a new life, and now a home of her own, one with her sister and the Bishops and Daltons—her family—right across the street. She had only one thing to say.

"Ain't that great?"

Chapter Seven

"Canvassing the area," Sebastian discovered after breakfast Wednesday morning, was nothing but a fancy way of saying doing a lot of walking, repeating the same questions a hundred times, and hearing the same answers as often. It was tedious and depressing, especially since *nobody* had seen the kids.

"How can three kids be so unnoticeable?" he asked when he and Melina took a break for lunch in one of the restaurants.

"People are lousy observers. They don't pay attention to most other people, and when they do, they generally don't notice details with any degree of accuracy. Take yourself, for example. The first time I ever saw you was in Harry's Café a few weeks ago. I was with Lynda and Ben. You were alone. It was a Sunday evening, and there were seven of us in there, not counting the waitress and Harry. I had a turkey sandwich on fresh-baked wheat bread, with a side of the creamiest potato salad I've ever had. We sat in the third booth from the door, and you were at a table for two against the wall. The other diners sat at a table near the counter—a man, a woman, and a teenage boy. They all had the special—roast beef with the trimmings. Ben had that, too, and Lynda had a turkey sandwich, hold the mayo, hold the potato salad. You wore a white shirt and jeans, you'd already finished dinner and had nothing in front of you but a cup of coffee. With cream." She smiled smugly. "And what do you remember about that night?"

Not nearly as much as she did. It wasn't unusual for him to go to Harry's on Sundays, to sit there alone and brood while his parents took Chrissy to church. Usually he tried to go with her—church had always been a family thing when he was growing up, and he'd wanted his daughter to have the same experience—but sometimes he was too angry or bitter. Sometimes he felt like such a fraud that he couldn't bring himself to walk through the church doors.

"Ask me about another night," he said at last. "Ask me about that Saturday night at the Starlite."

She shook her head. "That night was significant. You'd damn well better remember it. But we're not talking about remembering significant things. We're talking about how three kids could have gone into a restaurant or walked through a neighborhood without anyone remembering them. What little contact anyone had with them was insignificant. The kids didn't steal anything. They didn't demand attention. They didn't cause trouble. For all practical purposes, they were invisible. Most of us usually are."

Sebastian couldn't imagine the situation in which

Melina could ever be invisible. She was so damn beautiful, and everywhere she went, she drew attention whether she wanted it or not.

But he'd been oblivious to her at Harry's that Sunday evening.

That wasn't ever going to happen again. Now she was with him even when she wasn't. Her image nagged him, kept him on edge, kept him hungry.

Deliberately he changed the subject. "What are we going to do after lunch?"

"I plan to walk from here to the bus station and put out flyers along the way. I want to talk to anyone I see along the route—see if they remember the kids or Anne."

Gloria's voice echoed in his head—*There's some tough places between here and the bus station.* "What about Norris?"

"What about him?"

"Is he meeting you?"

"No. This may surprise you, Sebastian, but I usually work alone, and I still manage to get the job done."

"Then I'll go with you."

She looked as if she wanted to argue. Her dark eyes grew even darker, and her mouth flattened in a grim line. Then suddenly she shrugged. "Suit yourself. After that, I'll check in with Norris and see if he has anything new to offer."

"Can he send a description of this girl's car to the state police so they can be looking for her between here and Providence?"

She gave him a level look. "We don't *have* a description of her car."

"We know it's white—"

"Along with about a million other cars on the road."

He scowled. "And it's got our kids in it."

"Sorry, Sebastian, no police department is going to put out a broadcast on a car with no make, no model, no year, no license number, no nothing. It would be pointless. So . . . if Norris hasn't found out anything, then we're outta here. We'll head to Providence this evening."

"And there you'll . . . ?"

"Ask questions. Track down Berry Dalton's last known address. Try to find her current address. Check with the local cops and the shelters. Talk to the kids on the street—the hookers, the runaways."

"It sounds like finding a needle in a haystack."

She shook her head. "We know the address the kids have for Berry. We also know she was planning to move, and we hope she stayed in Providence. If the kids can find her, so can we. And if we're in the same neighborhoods, looking for the same person, odds are, sooner or later, we're going to cross paths."

Sooner or later. Dismay weighting his shoulders, he shook his head. "This is the longest I've ever been apart from Chrissy in her life. Even the times Diana and I left her with our folks for a weekend, we left Saturday morning and picked her up Sunday evening. Now I haven't seen her since Saturday. My mom bought her a new dress for Miss Agatha's wedding—all ruffly and lacy, the sort of thing she would normally never wear. I think Mom bribed her to get her into it. She looked so different. Not like the tomboy she's always been."

Swallowing over the lump that had suddenly formed in his throat was difficult. So was breathing, with the chill that had formed in his chest. Chrissy was a beautiful little girl, and such terrible things could happen to little girls out there alone. If anyone hurt her . . .

"Don't go borrowing trouble," Melina said, her voice damn near cheerful. "Apparently, they're in good hands with Anne."

"Excuse me for not being thrilled that my seven-year-old daughter is roaming the country with a teenage girl none of us know and the best we can say about her is she's good enough at what she does that she hasn't been caught."

Melina stood up and slung her bag over one shoulder. "Has it never occurred to you that maybe Anne hasn't gotten caught because she hasn't done anything wrong? That maybe she's just a nice, decent kid who found herself out on the street through no fault of her own, with no one to turn to and no place to go? That maybe she's just Chrissy, only ten years older?"

He left enough money to cover the tab and the tip, then caught up with Melina at the door. "Chrissy will never be out on the street with no place to go. She'll *always* have a home in Bethlehem."

"She's on the street right now," Melina pointed out.

After holding his gaze for a moment, she slid a pair of dark glasses into place, then started off in the direction of the bus station. He considered returning to the motel and letting her go off by herself, but the previous day pacing an empty room had been one day too many. Besides, if he let her go alone and something went wrong . . .

Once more he caught up with her. "You don't like me much, do you?"

She didn't glance at him. "Nope."

Under the circumstances, it was a stupid thing to point out, but he did it anyway. "You didn't have any problem with me a week ago."

"I didn't know you were a rat bastard a week ago."

Great. Now he was not only a bastard, but he'd sunk to the level of Rico, the poorest excuse for a man she'd ever met. He'd had to ask, hadn't he? "Look, Melina—"

"I don't want to have any conversation that starts with 'Look, Melina.' It means you're either going to make excuses or explain things in terms simple enough for my feeble little female brain to understand. I'm not interested in your excuses, and I'd put my IQ up against yours any time, so . . . well, hell, I've already said it—I'm not interested."

She started off again, and though he followed, this time he let her go in silence.

Once they got a few blocks away from the interstate, the businesses on the street became more sparse and more rundown. Boarded-up buildings and vacant lots dominated the blocks ahead, with an occasional house or apartment building tossed in for good measure. Melina handed him a stapler and a roll of tape and sent him across the street to post flyers on telephone poles and dusty plate-glass windows. The sun was hot overhead, the day still humid from yesterday's long rain. Before they'd gone six blocks, sweat was trickling down his spine and his feet seemed to absorb the pavement's heat right through the thick soles of his tennis shoes. He found himself wishing he was back home, working in his air-conditioned shop or stretched out in the shade on the creek bank while his fishing line bobbed in the water. Chrissy would be playing nearby, or maybe down the road at the Graysons' house, or maybe she would be at her grandparents' house in town and Melina . . .

Melina wouldn't give him the time of day if she wasn't being paid to find his kid, and he had no right to resent that. Hadn't he fully intended to never see her again when he'd stood her up last week? Hadn't he taken what he wanted from her, then dumped her without a thought about how it would make her feel? He *was* on a par with Rico. He deserved every bit of her loathing and then some.

Though he couldn't honestly say if he could go back and do it again, he would do it any differently. He'd *needed* her—the sex, her passion, her vitality, her life. He'd been alone so long, barely living for so long, functioning poorly as a father and not at all as a man, and he'd needed every bit of warmth, energy, and emotion he could absorb from her. But four days was three more than he'd intended to offer. It was more than he'd been able to deal with—more sex. More emotion. More connection.

Voices distracted him from his thoughts, drawing his attention across the street. Melina had stopped in front of an apartment building, three stories built of brick with a patch of dirt out front to pass for a yard. Open windows on each of the floors suggested no air-conditioning. Broken glass, torn screens, and crumbling brick suggested no maintenance.

A woman sat on the steps, hot, tired, defeat easy to read on her thin face. Playing in the dirt were two kids, about two and three, one wearing only a diaper, the other a pair of cotton pants, against the heat. It was impossible to tell whether they were boys or girls.

He leaned against a street lamp, the broken glass of its bulb crunching under his feet, and watched Melina. "We're looking for these kids," she said, giving the woman a flyer. "We know they were in this area on Sunday afternoon, headed for the bus station. Did you see them?"

The woman looked at the pictures, shook her head,

and handed the flyer back. "But if you don't find 'em, I've got a couple here you can have to replace them."

Sebastian's temper flared. He was well aware the woman was joking, but it hit him the wrong way. If her kids had ever gone missing, if she'd had to spend one endless night wondering where the hell they were, if they were all right, if they were *alive,* she wouldn't find such a comment the least bit amusing. Gritting his teeth to keep from telling her so, he walked to the end of the block, out of earshot, and waited.

A few moments later, Melina caught up, and they continued their silent journey. He estimated they were past the halfway point to the bus station when they reached a series of underpasses where the freeway and its exit and on ramps crossed the street. The expanse of shaded concrete was about ten degrees cooler than the surrounding area, and it was the first place they ran into trouble.

The boy looked about sixteen or eighteen and stepped into Melina's path from behind a massive concrete column. His clothes were baggy, his ball cap worn backward. "Whatcha got there?"

She stopped instantly, as much distance between her and him as possible, and so did Sebastian. Though she appeared totally relaxed, he could tell she was alert, balanced on the balls of her feet, and already considering her options. He knew she had several things in her favor—she was armed with both a pistol and pepper spray, she was accustomed to talking her way out of trouble, she was fast on her feet, and she could, she had informed him, break any bone in the human body with a well-placed chop or kick. And knowing all that, he couldn't help feeling pissed and protective that some punk thought he could hassle her because she was a delicate woman who appeared unable to defend herself.

"I'm looking for some missing kids—a boy and two girls," she said, her voice level, showing no hint of concern.

"I'm a boy. If I had two girls, maybe I wouldn't want to be found." He grinned expansively. "Lemme see the pictures."

She slowly approached him and offered a flyer. When he took it, she rested her hand on her waist, her fingertips right at the opening of her jeans pocket, where she kept the canister of pepper spray.

"Ain't seen 'em."

"Too bad. What about a homeless girl named something-Anne? Dianne, Diana? Has black hair and drives a white car?"

At a gesture from the punk, several more boys stepped out from behind the columns—one to Melina's right, two behind her. "Do I look homeless?" he snapped.

She glanced at the other kids as if they didn't matter. "No. But you look like someone who knows what's going on in his neighborhood."

He puffed up at her observation. "Damn straight I do." He jerked his head in Sebastian's direction. "He with you?"

She glanced at him as if he didn't matter, either. "Yes, he is."

"He your protection?"

She glanced across the street again, then smiled. "He's big enough to be, isn't he? But I don't need protection. I can take care of myself."

The kid studied her a moment, the skepticism in his expression fading bit by bit as he reached the same conclusion Sebastian did—she was too calm, too cool, to be bluffing. Maybe the encounter with the punks had gotten her adrenaline flowing, but it hadn't scared her. She had zero doubt about her ability to take all four of them down.

The kid stepped aside. "Ain't seen the kids, and don't know nothin' 'bout no homeless girl named Anne."

"Well, thanks for your help." Melina smiled cheerfully, then walked away.

Sebastian didn't take his gaze from the boys until she was well out of their range. Finally he moved on, too. His stomach slowly settled, and the chill inside him gave way to the day's heat again. Maybe she enjoyed this sort of thing, but he didn't. He wasn't cut out for any of it—the tedium, the potential danger, the doggedness. Even being in the city this long was wearing on him. He kept to himself on his farm in the country for a reason, because he liked the quiet and the security.

But he could endure it for Chrissy. There was nothing he wouldn't do to find his daughter. He glanced at Melina, talking now to a gas station attendant, and silently emphasized his vow.

Nothing.

BY THE TIME THEY REACHED THE BUS STATION, THEN caught a cab back to the motel, all Melina wanted was a shower, food, and possibly one hour where she didn't have to say the words *looking, missing kids,* or *a boy and two girls* to anyone. Though Sebastian was ready to check out of the motel and head off to Providence, she'd decided their departure could wait until the next morning.

Instead, she'd showered and dressed in a short red dress and sandals, pulled her hair back from her face, and told him through the closed connecting door to meet her in front of the office at six-thirty for dinner. She wanted Greek food but knew better than to trust just any restaurant that called itself Greek, so she'd settled on Italian instead. The desk clerk had given her directions to what he considered the best Italian in town and advised her to try the ensalata caprese. Already the thought of fresh, soft mozzarella was making her mouth water.

And she was waiting for Sebastian.

Six-thirty ticked past. Six-thirty-five. Six-forty.

Exactly a week ago she'd waited in vain for him to appear. She and Lynda had been seated on the terrace at the McBride Inn restaurant, the most romantic setting for a date in all of Bethlehem, and she had announced to Lynda while they waited that she was going to marry Sebastian. She'd been so certain that he was the man she'd been looking for, that she wanted to spend the rest of her life with him, that she was in love with him.

They had waited, and talked, and neither Ben nor Sebastian had ever shown up. At least Ben had had a reason, having been picked up by the local cops.

Sebastian had had a reason, too, she reminded herself with an ache inside. He'd never intended to show. He'd been a coward. He'd wanted to end their affair with the least bit of inconvenience to himself.

He hadn't wanted her.

It was amazing how much it still hurt. She hated him now—or, at least, despised him, honesty forced her to admit—but it still hurt deep inside that she'd fallen in love with him when all he'd ever wanted was sex. She'd been planning a future, and another woman would have suited him just as well. She'd been the first woman to approach him that night, and that had been his only reason for choosing her. If some other fool had been ten seconds ahead of her, he would have broken *her* heart instead.

Damn, it hurt.

"Melina."

Swallowing hard, she put her sunglasses on before turning to face him. "You're late." Her voice sounded unsteady to her, but he didn't appear to notice. She loaded on the sarcasm as she continued. "Guess I should be grateful you showed up at all, shouldn't I? Last Wednesday night I wasn't so lucky."

A muscle twitched in his jaw, and his eyes chilled. "My mother called as I was walking out the door. I had to talk to her."

"Yeah, sure. Let's go." She started across the parking lot toward his truck, and he kept pace. She tried not to notice that he smelled of soap and earthy cologne, or that his black T-shirt stretched tautly over broad shoulders and chest and clung to a hard belly before disappearing into snug-fitting faded jeans. She didn't pay attention to the fact that the black played well against his bronzed skin, or that his hair was a bit damp and tousled as if a lover had combed it with her fingers. She certainly didn't notice the tingle deep in her belly when he opened the pickup door for her.

Or so she insisted.

She gave him directions to the restaurant, a small family-owned place located on the corner of a block in an older neighborhood. Parking was on the street, and they had to park nearly a block away—a good sign, she hoped.

After a brief wait, they were shown to a table in a

distant corner. A red-checked cloth covered the table, and an empty wine bottle in a woven basket held a flickering candle, as well as the wax dripped from dozens of candles before it. The aromas were fabulous, the ambiance romantic.

Maybe she should have opted for burgers and fries.

As soon as they got settled, the waiter brought a loaf of crusty ciabatta and a dish of olive oil and balsamic vinegar. She tore off a hunk of bread, dipped it in the dressing, then savored the rich flavors, eyes closed and a smile on her mouth. "I love good food. If I ever give up P.I. work, I'm going to open a restaurant."

"I wouldn't have thought you could cook."

She gave Sebastian a curious look. "Why?"

"You have a career. You're single. You like to be around people."

"I'm Greek," she said with a shrug.

"So automatically you can cook?"

She thought about it a moment while she ate another piece of bread. "Yes," she decided. "All Greeks have a fine appreciation for food. It's in our blood. If you visit a Greek home, you won't get out the door without being offered, at the very least, coffee and pastries or bread drizzled with olive oil and herbs. If you visit a Greek home at mealtime, you'll be invited to share, always. And there's always enough food for unexpected guests." She smiled faintly. "Our culture is very food-intensive. We're always having celebrations of some sort, and our celebrations always involve feasts, so we have to know how to cook. I learned from my mother, my grandmother, and my aunts, and when I have a daughter, we'll all teach her, too."

When she had a daughter . . . First, though, she

needed a man. A husband would be nice—would certainly please her parents and Yaya Rosa—but wasn't necessary. She wanted it all—husband, kids, home—but damned if she was going to settle for nothing just because she couldn't find Mr. Right.

Sebastian looked away. Because talk of a daughter reminded him of his own daughter? Probably. Most definitely not because he didn't like the idea of Melina having a child with someone else. He'd made it clear he didn't care. Sometimes she had to keep reminding herself of that.

After the waiter took their orders and served their wine, she took a fortifying drink, then said, "I need to ask you something."

He shrugged, hands wide to indicate permission.

"Are you married?" She was a little late asking. It should have been out of her mouth before the invitation to dance that night at the Starlite—certainly before her acceptance of his invitation to go home with him. But Lynda had told her that his wife had left him years earlier, and she'd assumed at some point there'd been a divorce, and . . .

His expression turned dark, though not with anger. Embarrassment, maybe. Wounded feelings. "Do you think I would have taken you home with me if I were still married?"

"Men do it all the time."

"I don't. You should know that."

"How? How could I possibly know something that personal about you?"

"You were with me practically every minute for four days and nights."

"And I never suspected you were using me. I never

had a clue you were planning to dump me. I never guessed you were no better than Rico."

"Stop comparing me to him," he said sharply. "I wasn't unfaithful to you. I didn't betray you. We had an affair and I ended it badly, but that doesn't make me like him."

She drank more wine. "But *I* didn't know it was an affair. I thought it was a relationship. I thought we had potential—a future. You knew I wanted more, you knew I thought it was more, and you didn't tell me. You took what you wanted and you ended it badly and to hell with me. If you don't like being ranked with Rico, sorry, but from where I sit, you're two of a kind." She finished her wine and signaled the waiter, then went on. "So answer my question. Are you married?"

"No," he replied sullenly. "Not for a year or so."

"Then what was with the wedding ring when you dumped me?"

Before he could answer, the waiter arrived. "Another glass of wine, ma'am?"

She considered it a moment. In their short acquaintance, she'd already had one hangover because of Sebastian, and it had been a doozy. She didn't think he was worth a second. "No, thank you. Iced tea, please." Then she turned a questioning gaze on Sebastian. "Well?"

After a moment he shook his head. He wouldn't or couldn't answer. Not that it really mattered. Nothing he said would change anything. He'd been a rat and she deserved better.

But, damn it, she still wanted him.

But she would get over it. She would, she would, she would.

The silence stretched out. They ate their salads, neither speaking. Melina glanced around the dining room, seeing every table filled with people having a better time than they were. The exception was a table across the room, where another couple sat, very much like them, not speaking or even looking at each other. The couple was pathetic, and she couldn't bear to have people look at them and think the same thing.

"See those people over there?" she asked, resorting to a game she played from time to time.

Sebastian nodded.

"Their affair is on its last dying gasps. See—she looks disappointed. He just looks annoyed."

He looked at them a long time, then shook his head. "Maybe he's disappointed, too, and she just can't see it."

"Nope. He's the one ending it. He thinks she wants too much."

"More than he can give."

"More than he *wants* to give. There's a difference."

The waiter served their food, then left them alone again. Sebastian had ordered boring spaghetti and meatballs. Her own entrée was mushroom-stuffed ravioli in a delicate sun-dried tomato sauce that made her sigh happily with no more than its aroma.

"Maybe he *wants* to give her more," Sebastian said, "and he just doesn't know how. Or maybe he's already made one hell of an error in judgment that he almost didn't recover from and he can't risk making another."

Melina looked at him. And maybe they weren't talking about the strangers across the room any longer. Maybe they never had been. "What was his error in judgment?"

"He trusted someone—loved someone—who left him."

"Why?"

He shrugged. "Who knows why women leave?"

"There's usually a reason. Was she unhappy? Did she want something he couldn't give her? Was there another man?"

"Your guesses are as good as anyone's," he said, tight-lipped. "Probably better than mine."

"Didn't he ask her?"

"She didn't give him a chance. He went home one day—" For a long time he fell quiet, so long that she was convinced there would be no more sharing of past traumas that evening. Then he looked at her, his gaze intense, shadowed, bitter. "I went home one day, and she was gone. She took everything she could fit into her van, cleaned out our bank accounts, and disappeared. The only things she left behind were her wedding and engagement rings . . . and Chrissy."

"And you didn't know . . . ?"

He shook his head. "We'd been talking about having another baby. When I left the house that morning, she'd kissed me and told me she loved me. We'd made love the night before. I didn't have a damn clue."

"How long had you been married?"

"We'd celebrated our eleventh anniversary in New York City a few weeks before."

What would cause a woman to walk out on eleven years of marriage without a word to her husband? Obviously Diana Knight had been unhappy. Happily married women planning to have a baby didn't abandon well-loved husbands and daughters. Maybe Sebastian had been too thickheaded to see that something was wrong. Maybe as long as *he* was happy, that was all that had mattered. Or maybe Diana was a damn good liar.

"Did the police consider the possibility of foul play?"

"For about five minutes. But she'd had lunch with her mother that day. She gave Ramona an early birthday present—because she couldn't wait, she'd said. After lunch, she and Chrissy went to the bank, where she cleaned out our accounts and told the teller, a friend of hers, that she wasn't going to be around for a while. From there she went to my mom's and asked if she could leave Chrissy there while she took care of a few things. Before she left, she told Mom how lucky she was to have such a good mother-in-law."

Definitely not the actions of a woman forced to leave against her will. She'd said goodbye to her mother, her mother-in-law, her friend, and, presumably, her daughter, but not her husband. Because *he* was the reason she was leaving? Because a better offer had come along?

"Did she work outside the house?" Melina asked.

Sebastian shook his head. "Not then. But that was her choice. She'd wanted to stay home when Chrissy was born, and I was making enough money that it wasn't a problem."

"Was your shop at home then?"

"No. I had a place in town. I didn't renovate the barn until after she left, so I could be home with Chrissy."

So he was away at work all day, and Diana was free to play. She told him what she knew he wanted to hear, and kept him satisfied enough that he never questioned what she did or how she truly felt. He never suspected that her needs and desires no longer matched his.

"Did anyone else leave town around that time—maybe a few months before or after?"

He scowled at her. "You think she was having an affair?"

"I think something made her want to no longer be

your wife or Chrissy's mother. In my experience, it's generally a lover who's responsible for changes like that. Besides . . ." She managed a cool smile. "Would you rather believe she left you because she was having an affair with another man? Or because she simply didn't want you anymore?" She knew from personal experience that while both were heartbreakers, the former was easier on the ego. She hadn't been *enough* for Sebastian—pretty enough, sexy enough, smart enough, Diana-enough. At least with Rico, she'd had the dubious satisfaction of knowing he wanted her. He just wanted every other woman in the world, too.

"No," he said, his tone somewhat grudging, but also challenging, as if proving her wrong. "No one else left town around that time."

That didn't mean there hadn't been another man. Melina knew too well that people who wanted to have affairs were going to manage no matter how difficult it might be. She also knew how thoroughly some people covered their tracks.

Frankly, though, she couldn't imagine choosing another man over Sebastian. He wasn't the most polished lover she'd ever had, and was far from the most experienced. He tended to be fairly plainspoken and had only a passing acquaintance with the notion of charming a woman. But *she'd* been ready and willing to give up other men forever for a lifetime with him, and she would have counted herself grateful for each and every day.

And Diana, apparently, had been just as ready and willing to give him up for a lifetime. *Why* was a puzzle that Melina might try to solve in her spare time.

The waiter took their plates away, then brought the dessert tray. She ordered zabaglione with fresh berries.

Sebastian settled for coffee. As she spooned up a bite of sweet custard, she casually, carelessly, said, "It must have hurt."

When his gaze cut sharply to her, she gestured toward the couple across the room. The woman was nibbling at the same dessert, and the man was gazing restlessly into a cup of coffee. He looked as if he'd rather be anyplace else. She looked as if she'd rather be home crying. "When his wife left him. He must have felt unwanted, unworthy, bewildered, and cheated . . . but it doesn't justify what he's done to her."

This time Sebastian didn't play along. He leaned close to her, his voice pitched low. "You came to me that night looking for sex, and you got it. How does that make me the bad guy?"

"*You* were looking for sex! *I* wanted—" Possibilities. Romance. The potential for happily-ever-after. She'd wanted *him*—not his body, not just sex, but all of him. His smiles, his heart, his love. And he hadn't even offered his affection.

He watched her, waited for her to finish. She stared back at him, feeling as if the tension inside her might explode if it wound one notch tighter. The truth was, their affair *had* been about sex. He hadn't offered possibilities, romance, or happily-ever-after. He'd offered the use of his body in exchange for the use of hers, and then he'd given her the kiss-off—nothing more, nothing less. She'd broken her own heart by indulging in foolish fantasies and stupid dreams—fantasies and dreams that he'd had no part of.

Swallowing hard, she pushed the remainder of her dessert away. "You're right," she said quietly, reasonably. "It *was* about sex. It was all I asked for and all you gave.

Excuse me. I'm going to the ladies' room before we leave."

SEBASTIAN WATCHED HER WALK ACROSS THE ROOM, moving with self-assured sexual grace, her red dress clinging to every curve, and he felt an odd emptiness in his gut. He'd wanted her to admit that he wasn't scum of the earth, that what he'd done was selfish and inconsiderate but neither terrible nor unforgivable, and she had, more or less.

It was all about sex. They'd both wanted it, and they'd both gotten it. Period. End of affair.

But now that she'd admitted it, he felt empty. As if he'd lost something sweet and special that he couldn't afford to lose. Maybe he hadn't been ready for a relationship with her, but it had done him good believing she thought him worthy of one. It had eased a lot of his hurt that this incredibly beautiful, sensual woman thought he deserved her time, attention, and affection.

But now she was agreeing that he didn't. It was just a sexual thing. Any man in the bar would have served as well. If he hadn't been there, or if he'd turned her down, she would have chosen someone else without a minute's regret.

Now the regret was his.

ALANNA AWAKENED WITH AN ACHE IN HER NECK and a cramp in her side. Her mouth tasted nasty, her hair was dirty enough to take on a life of its own, but as she looked out the window, none of that mattered. They were in Providence!

"Morning."

She glanced at Cheyenne, holding the envelope containing Berry's last letter in one hand and studying a map braced across the steering wheel. "Where'd you get my letter?"

Cheyenne nodded, and Alanna looked at the backpack between them, unzipped and gaping open.

"You had no right—"

"I didn't open it. I'm just trying to figure out where she lives." She marked a place on the map, then tossed the letter back. "How long since you've seen her?"

"How long since you've seen your mom?" Alanna snapped back, but right away she wished she hadn't. The look in Cheyenne's eyes was so sad, like she might cry at any time.

"A long time."

Alanna rubbed her nose with the back of her hand. "I haven't seen mine in five or six months. She writes pretty often, though."

"You think your aunt's told her you're coming?"

"Maybe. Probably." Alanna really hadn't thought about it, but after the police, Berry would be the first person Emilie would call.

"This guy that's your dad . . . he must be pretty awful."

Alanna wanted to say yes, he was horrible and she hated him, but truth was, she'd thought he was a nice enough guy until she'd found out who he really was. Like, he didn't talk down to her or treat her like she was a kid or nothing. So instead of lying, she said, "Not really."

"Of course he is. He didn't want you, and he lied to you. What kind of dad does stuff like that?" Cheyenne shrugged. "Maybe he was in jail or in rehab. Maybe he had to choose between being a doper and a father, and he chose the drugs."

Stubbornly Alanna shook her head. She'd seen enough of her mother's drug-addict boyfriends to know that Ben Foster was different. He had to be, or Aunt Emilie and Uncle Nathan wouldn't let him come around, and Aunt Emilie had been planning to do just that. She'd invited him to their house last Sunday, so they could tell her the truth about him together. That he was a liar. And her father.

"Why do you think he's come now?" Cheyenne asked. "Just to meet you?"

"I guess."

"He came all the way from—where?"

"Atlanta."

"All the way from Atlanta, Georgia, just to meet you. That's a long way, for someone who's a liar and can't be trusted."

"I know what you're doing," Alanna said sarcastically. "You're trying to make me say that maybe he had reasons for not wanting to have anything to do with me before now, like maybe he didn't know or it took him this long to find us on account of Berry always making us move and us not living with her anymore, but it's not gonna work. He *lied* to me. It was all just lies, and I don't care about his reasons. I hate him, and I don't need a father, anyway. I've got my uncle Nathan."

"Maybe your father needs a daughter," Cheyenne said.

Alanna didn't care if Ben Foster was all alone in the world and didn't have anyone to worry about him or miss him when he was gone or to spend Christmas and Thanksgiving with him. She didn't care about him at all.

"Where's *your* father?" she demanded. "Why doesn't *he* need a daughter?"

It was quiet for a moment while Cheyenne folded the map, then tossed it on the dashboard. Then, in a real normal voice, like she was talking about the weather, she said, "My father is dead. He was coming to see us three years ago, and his plane crashed."

"I . . . I'm sorry." Alanna felt so bad that when Caleb poked her on the shoulder from the backseat, she didn't even say anything to him.

Cheyenne looked in the rearview mirror and saw that he was awake. "Why don't you wake the squirt, Caleb? There's a pancake place down the street. We can clean up a little and get some breakfast, then see if we can find Alanna's mother."

She got out of the car to wait, and Alanna got out, too, going to stand in front of her. "I really am sorry."

"It's okay." Cheyenne slid her arm around Alanna's shoulder. "I don't mind talking about my dad. I did at first. I was mad at him for dying, 'cause if he hadn't divorced my mom, he would've still been living with us and he wouldn't have been on that plane. But he didn't make the plane crash. He didn't *want* to die. And after a while, it started not to hurt so much."

"What's wrong with us? None of our mothers wanted us. Your dad's dead. Caleb's dad is dead, too. And mine—"

"Yours is back home, hoping for the chance to be a real father. And Chrissy's got her dad and grandparents. Caleb's got his new family, and you've got your aunt and uncle. There's nothing wrong with any of you."

"You know . . ." Alanna drew a line in the dirt with

the toe of her sneaker. "You can go home with us. Aunt Emilie and Uncle Nathan just bought a big house with plenty of bedrooms. You could have one. They wouldn't mind."

For a moment, Cheyenne looked like her stomach hurt or something. Her face got kinda spotty red, and her eyes got wet. Then she grinned and looked okay again. "Yeah, and I bet they really appreciate you offering a room to every stray you come across. Come on, Caleb, Chrissy. Let's get moving." She started walking, and Caleb and Chrissy ran to catch up.

Maybe Emilie and Nathan wouldn't want to take her in, Alanna admitted. After all, they already had four kids, and they wanted another couple of babies of their own. Maybe Dr. J.D. would want her. Since Grandpa Bud had moved out, they had an extra room . . . but Caleb and Trey had been counting on getting it for their own, since they'd been sharing with Jacob and Noah. Or maybe . . .

Well, maybe *someone* in Bethlehem wouldn't mind having another kid for a while. All she had to do when they got back was ask.

Chapter Eight

PROVIDENCE WAS A WELCOME SIGHT EARLY Thursday afternoon. Sebastian exited the interstate and filled the gas tank while Melina bought a map and placed a call to the police department. By the time he paid for the gas, she'd finished her call and was waiting by the truck, stretching out the kinks after the long drive. Her arms were raised high over her head, pulling her shirt high enough to reveal a broad strip of smooth brown skin, and her jeans rode an inch or two below her waist, clinging to the curve of her hips and the long lean muscles of her thighs. With her heavy black curls falling down her back, she looked wild, wicked. A Gypsy in blue jeans.

He'd bought a Diet Coke and a bottle of water while he was inside the station, intending to give one to her. But after that display, he needed to keep them both for himself—one for his parched throat, the other to cool the heat she'd just kicked up into the fires-of-hell range.

She lowered her arms as he approached and pushed her sunglasses up on her head. "I talked to a Detective Santiago with the Providence PD. Berry's no longer at the address we have for her. She was evicted last week for nonpayment of the rent, and she didn't leave a forwarding address. The super doesn't have a clue where she's gone. There are no utility accounts in her name, no telephone. She's not in any of the local jails, hospitals, or rehab clinics. As far as they can tell, she's pretty much disappeared."

"Are the police watching the apartment in case the kids show up?"

She gave him a look that said he should know better. "They don't have the manpower for that. I hate to break this to you, but the cops aren't actively looking for the kids. After all, it's not like they're criminals. If they happen to come across the children in the course of their duties, they'll take them into custody. Otherwise, finding them is up to us."

It was a logical response, but not a very encouraging one. Still, it didn't stop him from asking his next question. "Are you meeting with Detective Santiago?"

"Probably later. Right now we're going to knock on doors." She nodded toward the two bottles. "Is one of those for me?"

He held them out, and she reached automatically for the Diet Coke, drew back, chose the water, then drew back again.

"Why don't you take both of them?" he asked dryly. "What does it matter if I die of thirst as long as you aren't forced to choose?"

Giving him a chastening look, she took the Diet Coke, then climbed into the truck. Once he settled behind the wheel, she gave him directions to Berry Dalton's former address.

He'd expected a poor part of town. He'd even had some idea what that meant from watching too much TV. Still, it was disconcerting to find himself in the middle of it.

The apartment complex was made up of shabby two-story brick buildings, with about twenty apartments per building and at least ten buildings. The parking lots were small and looked more like salvage yards, and the yellowed grass was sheared off a fraction of an inch above the ground. Huge patches of bare earth showed where the kids played and where reckless drivers took shortcuts from parking lots to street.

"The place looks abandoned," he remarked as he parked at the curb.

"It does, doesn't it? But it's not. Cheap housing is hard to find in the city." Melina glanced at her notes before sliding them into her bag. "There's Building C. We need Apartment 2. That end."

Each set of two apartments was fronted by steps leading to a stoop, and each stoop led to three doors. The outside doors opened directly into the ground-floor apartments, and the center doorway led into a stairwell that provided access to two second-floor units. Even in the middle of the day, the stairs leading to Numbers 1 and 2 were dark, sinister places that reeked of garbage and urine.

Once upon a time, there had been a doorbell attached to the jamb on Number 2, but all that remained was a wire and one screw. Melina knocked, careful not to rap hard enough to make the rotted wood give way as it had in half a dozen other places. Inside, the blare of a television went silent. A moment later the blinds shifted as someone looked out. "What do you want?"

She turned toward the muffled shout. "Hi. I'm looking for Berry Dalton. Is she home?"

A pair of eyes narrowed, then disappeared as the blinds were released. A moment later came the sound of locks being opened, then the door opened a few inches. A round distrustful face peered out at them. "I don't know no Berry Dalton."

"Really? This is the address she gave me. As of last week, she was here."

"Maybe. As of *this* week, she isn't."

"And you don't have any idea where she's gone?"

"I told you, I don't know her."

The woman moved to close the door, but Melina blocked it. "Has anyone else been by asking for her?"

"The po-lice came by. I told 'em the same thing I told you."

"And that's it? No kids? 'Cause I heard Berry's little girl was looking for her, too."

"No kids. Just the po-lice. Now I'm missing my shows—"

"Can I give you my card? If some kids do come by, would you call me, please?" She offered the business card, but for a long time it seemed as if the woman wasn't going to take it.

Finally she did, squinting to look at it. "You expect me to call all the way to Buffalo, New York, just to say some stranger's kid showed up?"

Melina smiled as if the woman didn't sound totally disbelieving. "Collect, of course. Oh, and did I mention there would be a small reward in it for you?"

"How small?"

"A hundred bucks."

The woman subjected Melina to an intense scrutiny, then muttered, "Looks like you could do better than a lousy hundred bucks."

Sebastian bit back the urge to up the ante, certain it wouldn't go over well with Melina, who merely smiled at the woman's greed. "A hundred bucks for a phone call that won't take two minutes of your time . . . Who else is lining up to offer you money like that?"

"Yeah, yeah," she grumbled. "If they come around, I'll call. I'm missing my shows. Go away." She closed the door with some force, and Melina moved aside to Number 1's door, where she went through the same spiel with a woman who was only slightly friendlier than the first. After learning nothing, she drew a deep breath and started up the stairs. "Wonder if they get a break on their rent for having to use these stairs? Can you imagine coming in here alone at midnight?"

"Not if my life depended on it." The higher they climbed, the worse the stench got, and once they reached the landing, he swore he heard the skittering sound of rats below.

There was no answer at either apartment, though he couldn't shake the feeling that they were being watched the entire time. In the dim light, Melina scrawled a note on the backs of two business cards—*Call collect, please. Reward for info*—and wedged them between each door and its frame, then they beat a hasty retreat back into the sunshine.

"Why don't you give them your cell phone number?" he asked as they headed for the next set of units.

"There are people in my office whom I pay to do nothing but talk on the phone. They know the questions to ask, and *they* have my cell number. They'll pass along anything important to me."

Her knocks brought answers at three of the next four apartments, though without much information. One woman said Berry had talked about going home, wherever that was. Another thought she'd moved in with her boyfriend, and no, she didn't know his name or where he lived, and as for what he did for a living . . . The woman had laughed. He did what most worthless, no-good sons of bitches did—got drunk, got high, and got laid.

"It's hard to imagine this is Emilie's sister we're talking about," Sebastian remarked as they trudged down yet another flight of stairs. "I don't understand how two sisters could be so totally different."

"Two sisters who weren't raised together," Melina reminded him.

"You think it would be different if they had been? Berry would be a better person, or maybe Emilie would be worse?"

"Probably not. Emilie's the stronger of the two. From what I understand, Berry came out of the foster care system with some serious emotional problems. Then there's the drugs. It doesn't matter how strong you are, how capable, how intelligent, or how much you're loved. You let the illicit wonders of the pharmaceutical world get hold of you, and you're screwed. Most people who are as deeply ensnared as Berry is don't ever escape."

Stopping at the bottom of the steps at the opposite end of the building from where they'd started, he watched her climb to the top, then patiently knock at the door on the left. "Why do you do this?"

"Do what?"

"Work at a job where you spend your time dealing with the dregs of society."

The look she gave him was tinged with mocking. "Spoken like a bona fide member of America's mostly white, comfortably upper middle-class society."

"What would you call them?" he challenged, stung by her sarcasm.

"How about the tired, the poor, the huddled masses yearning to be free?"

"You think Berry Dalton is 'yearning to be free'? If she didn't want to live like this, she would do something about it. She *chooses* this life. She chose it over her sister, her children, her job, her health, her freedom. She doesn't *want* to be comfortably upper middle class."

Scowling, she turned her back on him as the door opened an inch or two. From his vantage point he could see one thin, dark leg, a pair of dirty shorts, and, wrapped around the doorknob, a grimy hand about the size of Chrissy's. Melina crouched to the child's level. "Hi. Is your mom home?"

The dark-eyed girl shook her head.

"How about your dad?"

Another shake.

"Are you here alone?"

"What do you want?" An older girl, maybe ten or twelve, pulled the little one behind her and eyed them distrustfully. "You the cops? My mama already told you, we don't know where my dad is."

"No, we're not the police. I'm looking for the woman—"

The girl closed the door and locked it. Undaunted, Melina raised her voice to carry through the door. "I'm looking for the woman who moved out of Number 2 last week. I'm leaving my card in the door. If you or your mother know anything about her, please call me."

After trying the last three apartments, she came to the edge of the stoop and stared down at him as she picked up the conversation where they'd left it. "You think it's that easy, Sebastian? You *choose* to do or be something, and, boom, it happens? Are you really that naïve?"

"I'm not naïve."

Ignoring the steps, she jumped to the ground and set off around the end of the building. "Naïve, narrow-minded, sanctimonious. Which would you prefer?"

"I'm *not*—"

Around the corner, she stopped so suddenly that he almost ran into her, and she spun around to poke him in the chest. "Berry didn't *choose* to live in a place like this, or to lose custody of her kids, or to have a steady stream of worthless sons of bitches in her life. Fifteen or twenty years ago, someone—most likely a boyfriend—talked her into having a beer or two, most likely so he could get in her pants. And she discovered that drinking made life a little better. It took the edge off the hurt, let her forget for a while, and so she drank more.

"Then someone else—probably another boyfriend—coaxed her into sharing a joint with him, or maybe a line of coke, and that *really* took the edge off the hurt. She wanted that peace, that oblivion, and then she needed it, and then she couldn't live without it. It became the most important thing in her life—more important than her sister, her freedom, or even her kids. It's not that she *won't* stop using. She *can't,* no more than you and I can stop breathing. Not without a miracle. And in case you haven't noticed, miracles are in short supply around here. So is hope. Faith. Trust. Opportunity."

His face burning, Sebastian watched her spin around and walk off. Part of him wanted to go back to the truck and wait there. Another part felt as if he should catch up and apologize to her—and to the two girls in that apartment and everyone else who had opened their doors to them. And part of him, he was ashamed to admit, still thought free will played a bigger role in these lives than she gave it credit for.

When he did finally catch up to her, she was standing outside a squat building in the center of the complex. A faded sign on the door read Office and security grates covered the windows. A tall fence blocked off a square of grass, apparently for the super's personal use. A rusty gas grill and a couple of cheap lawn chairs sat on a concrete patio where steel bars protected sliding glass doors that led into the apartment. No security for the tenants who, however much rent they paid, were being overcharged, but plenty for the super, he thought sourly.

The door to the office was locked. As Melina turned from trying it, a woman approached from the direction they'd just come. "Hey, I was just looking for you," she called, her voice gravelly. She sounded tough and looked tougher. "What're you doing, bothering the tenants? Didn't you see the No Solicitors sign?"

"We're just asking a few questions."

"Not around here, you don't. Get on out of here."

"Sure," Melina said with a friendly smile, surprising Sebastian. "Not a problem. Before we leave, though, do you happen to have the nonemergency number for the Providence Police Department? I left it back in the car."

The super looked suspiciously at the cell phone Melina had taken from her pocket and now held, finger poised over the keypad. "What do you want the police for?"

"I just need to tell Detective Santiago that you don't want us here. She can go ahead and send in half a dozen uniformed officers and let them ask the questions instead."

The woman was torn, clearly wanting to throw them off the property and just as clearly not wanting cops all over the place. She wavered, then her features settled into a grim expression. "Hell, I don't care what you do."

Melina's smile brightened. "Thank you. We really do appreciate your cooperation. By the way, have you remembered anything about Berry Dalton since you spoke with Detective Santiago?"

"Like I told her, like I told that girl this morning, Berry Dalton packed up and left about a week ago. She owes three months' back rent, and d'ya think I'm gonna see a penny of it? Of course not. She's probably not even in the state anymore."

Sebastian's nerves went taut, and he could tell by nothing more than the way she stood that Melina was excited, too. "What girl?"

"I don't know. Some girl came around here this morning asking about Berry. Kinda pretty, black hair, blond roots. Said something about being Berry's daughter or something. I would've thought Berry was too young to have a kid that old, but, hell, babies have babies every day, and Lord knows, if Berry could find trouble to get into, she would've done it."

Anne. And if Anne was here, then Chrissy and the others—

"Were there three other kids with her—two girls and a boy?"

The super shook her head. "She was by herself. Real friendly kid. Headed off that way when I told her Berry was gone."

Sebastian and Melina both looked in the direction she gestured. There was a parking lot, another apartment building, and, beyond that, a few blocks of businesses.

"Thanks a lot," Melina said. "If you remember anything else . . ." She handed her a business card, then started to leave.

"What makes you think Berry's left the state?" Sebastian asked.

Keys in the lock, the super paused, then shrugged. "When she found out we were gonna evict her, she came over and paid some of what she owed. Said she was tired of Providence anyway. She said there was about forty states out there she'd never seen, and it was time to see some of 'em."

"Did you tell the girl that this morning?"

"Nope. Didn't think of it. But I gave her the box."

"What box?"

She gave a heavy sigh, as if she couldn't bear to waste one more minute. "A box of pictures and stuff. Berry left it behind, and it wasn't worth three months' rent to me. I can't store all my own junk, and I sure don't have room for someone else's. So I gave it to the girl. She seemed real pleased to get it."

"Did you tell Detective Santiago about the box?" Melina asked.

"Nope. I hadn't had time to go through it yet, and what with her being evicted and all, it rightly belonged to us." She gestured impatiently toward the door. "Can I go now?"

"Sure. Thanks."

They were halfway to his truck when Melina spoke. "Good catch on the leaving-the-state bit. I let that one slide by."

It was foolish to feel pleasure at her comment, but he did. It helped ease the lingering embarrassment that she thought he was naïve, narrow-minded, and sanctimonious—and that he'd given her good reason to think it.

He didn't respond, though. Instead, as he settled in the front seat and started the engine, he asked, "How far do you think the kids will pursue this? If they can't find Berry, or if they find out she's left the city, will they keep trying?"

"Unless they're getting better information than we are, they wouldn't have a clue where to go from here. Right now I think it's still an adventure for them. They've got money, and they've got Anne. They're not going hungry. They may be sleeping in the car, but, except for Chrissy, they've all slept in worse places. When the novelty wears off, when they get homesick enough, when they face the fact that they're not going to be able to find Berry, they'll want to go home."

Because he knew she couldn't answer, he didn't ask how long that would take. Truth was, it didn't matter. He wanted it over *now.* He wanted his daughter back. In two more days it would be a week since he'd seen her, and that was too damn long.

Without awaiting instructions, he drove toward the business district. It was shabby and rundown—well suited for the neighborhood. The streets were in poor repair, the stop lights blinked continuously, and trash littered the gutters.

When he started to park in the middle of the third

block, Melina touched his arm. "Just drive around a bit, okay?"

Her hand felt good on his arm, her skin soft, her fingers warm. He wondered how long she would leave it there if he didn't move, then gave himself a mental chewing-out for behaving like an idiot. It was just a touch. People touched each other all the time. Only a pathetic fool would make it mean something.

"You watch the left side of the street, and I'll take the right," she said, drawing away as he pulled back into traffic. "We're looking for a white car, most likely with out-of-state tags, and a teenage girl, slender, pretty, black hair, blond roots."

His gaze constantly scanning, he drove block after block, focusing first on the main street, then crisscrossing back and forth. "I'd never realized how many cars on the road are white or red," he remarked while he waited for traffic to clear at an intersection.

"Uh-huh. Probably half the agency's cars are one or the other—and five to ten years or older. Don't want to catch anyone's attention."

"Like you did Sunday?" At her curious look, he added, "The baseball bat?"

"Oh, yeah. I was distracted and got careless."

"Distracted by what?"

Melina thought back to those few moments before she'd realized she'd made a potentially deadly mistake. Keeping her gaze directed out the side window, she said, "I was thinking about what bastards men are and what a risk women take when they love them." Before he could point out that it worked both ways, she went on. "Keep in mind that I'd just gotten dumped a few days earlier, so under the rules of dating, I wasn't required to be fair. Here was my client, who *loved* this man. She'd given him thirteen years of her life, had let him be the father of her *children,* and there he was, in a cheap motel doing the horizontal mambo with a waitress from his favorite bar. I mean, how unfair is that?"

Unfair, but no more unfair than what Diana had done to him, she admitted. After getting some perspective the night before on their affair—and her dumping—from his point of view, she could see that.

"I'm surprised your job hasn't made you cynical."

"Like your divorce made you?" She stole a glance and saw the muscle in his jaw tighten. "I see lots of unfaithful people, that's true. But I also deal with thieves, computer hackers, industrial spies, con artists—even the occasional murderer. Just because I catch an accountant who's robbing his clients blind doesn't mean all accountants are crooks. I know better than to make sweeping generalizations." Though she did recall making a comment to the cop who'd investigated Sunday's incident to the effect that *all* men were bastards. Under the circumstances, though, she'd been entitled.

Since they'd pretty thoroughly covered the area, she suggested he park so they could get out and do what they'd spent the past few days doing—showing pictures, asking questions, tacking up flyers.

Before leaving the truck, though, she returned to a question he'd asked earlier. "I do this job because I can make a difference. I've put together cases that send career criminals to prison. I proved that a man murdered his wife—and that a woman murdered her boyfriend. I've stopped con artists who prey on senior citizens, and I've tracked down fathers who will do damn near anything to avoid paying support for the children they helped bring into this world. I've also reunited mothers with the children they were forced to give up for adoption, and I've located missing heirs.

"Yes, we handle sleazy divorce cases, but we've also ensured that people who break up their marriages don't walk away scot-free while their spouses and children pay the cost. And yes, it brings me into contact with a lot of lowlifes, but it also reminds me every day how fortunate I am to have a family who loves me, a place to sleep, food to eat, and hope, because that's more than a lot of people will ever have."

When she took a breath, she saw he was watching her, his expression inscrutable. For a moment, she chafed under his study, then she grabbed her bag and opened the door. "Come on. We've got a lot of ground to cover."

They started at the end of the block closest to the apartment complex and worked in tandem. She took every other business while Sebastian took the ones in between, and together they taped up posters. Half the people they spoke to didn't want to be bothered, and the other half couldn't have cared less. Though she found it frustrating, she also understood. In a neighborhood like this, being too observant or too chatty was a good way to shorten your life span.

They'd gone up one side of the commercial district and down the other until they were only half a block from where they started. As Sebastian went into a secondhand clothing shop, Melina passed to the next business. At one time the word *Antiques* had been painted across the plate glass in flowing gold script. More recently someone had painted over it with the words *Flee Market*. Bad penmanship, bad spelling, or a warped sense of humor? she wondered as she pushed the door open.

Though there was no bell, a black woman appeared from the back room as if on cue. She wasn't beautiful—her face showed too much character for that—but there was a commanding sense of authority about her that made Melina want to straighten her spine, lift her chin, and spit out a snappy *yes, ma'am* and *no, ma'am*. She wore a flowing tunic and pants in a striking African pattern, and a turban of the same fabric wound around her head, emphasizing her exotic features.

"Tell me what you're looking for, and perhaps I can help you find it."

Presumably she was referring to the merchandise that crammed the shelves and floor, but it was as good a lead-in as Melina had ever gotten. She pulled a flyer and a business card from her bag and looked at the woman. Though Melina topped five feet nine inches, she had to tilt her head back to meet the woman's gaze, thanks to her own above-average height and impossibly high heels. "My name is Melina Dimitris, and I'm—"

"It's a pleasure to meet you. I'm Norma."

Switching the papers to her left hand, Melina accepted her outstretched hand. Her shake was surprisingly strong. "I'm searching for three children who have run away. They were in this area this morning, and I was wondering if you'd seen them."

Norma took the flyer and wandered to a desk at the back of the shop. There she perched a pair of half-glasses on her nose, tortoiseshell frames painted across the top with, appropriately, a small parade of bespectacled tortoises. She studied the pictures through the glasses, then over them, before shaking her head. "Sorry. I haven't seen them today."

"They're traveling with another girl, about seventeen,

black hair with blond roots. Her name is something-Anne. Dianne, Marianne, Lee Anne? Have you seen her?"

"Black hair . . . Badly cut? Multiple earrings in each ear?"

"Could be."

Norma removed the glasses, folded them, and tapped the frames thoughtfully against her chin. "I took my morning break at the diner down the block this morning, and a girl matching that description came in to buy four cups of orange juice and four apple-wheat muffins. It very well might have been her."

Keeping her smile in place, Melina ground her teeth. She'd spoken to the waitress at the diner not fifteen minutes ago, and the woman hadn't admitted to seeing a thing.

"I don't know where she went when she left the diner. She simply walked down the street, and I didn't pay any further attention."

"You paid more attention than anyone else we've spoken to today."

"We? Oh, yes, Sebastian. Where is he?"

Melina stopped in the process of digging the tape from her bag. "How do you know his name?" Was she lying? Had she seen the kids, possibly even talked to them, and gotten his name from Chrissy?

The smile that spread across Norma's face was warm and sincere, with just a bit of chiding for the speed with which Melina's suspicion had been aroused. "We don't get many visits from people like you and Sebastian. Naturally we're going to talk about it."

People like what? Melina wanted to ask. A private investigator and a father searching for his daughter? More likely, outsiders—reasonably affluent white outsiders. But she answered Norma's question instead of asking her own. "He's next door, asking the same questions I am."

"He won't learn anything there. Tyeisha's like those three little monkeys. She sees nothing, hears nothing, says nothing. It's a wise policy around here."

"But one you don't feel the need to adhere to."

Norma's laughter was unrestrained. "There's no one on these streets who can harm me. I'm the guardian around here. I look out for them all."

Melina wasn't the least bit tempted to write her off as boastful. She had little doubt the woman could quell the toughest punk with little more than a look. In another time, in another place, she would have been a queen, earning respect, inspiring fear. Even in this time and place, she wasn't a woman to trifle with. "Well, if you see these kids, look out for them, will you? And give me a call?"

Norma accepted the business card she offered, then walked with her to the door. "They'll be safe. They're in good hands."

"You mean Anne's?"

"Yes, hers, too."

"Can I . . . ?" When Melina pulled out the tape and gestured toward the window, Norma waved her to go ahead. "Thanks for your help," she said as she taped the flyer to the window next to the door.

"Have faith, Melina. In yourself, in the children, and especially in him."

Melina followed her gaze outside to where Sebastian waited on the sidewalk. He looked tired but determined. Worry lines bracketed his eyes and mouth, and the muscle in his jaw was clenched. She would offer him comfort if she knew how to do it in a way that wouldn't cause her more pain, but she didn't have a clue.

She turned back. "I have plenty—"

The room was empty.

"Norma?"

It was eighty feet to the back room, without a single display tall enough to hide the woman. Melina took a few steps down the main aisle. "Norma? Where did you . . . ?"

Only silence greeted her.

With a shiver creeping up her spine, she headed for the door. There she took one lingering look over her shoulder before leaving the shop. "Weird," she muttered.

As they walked to the next storefront, Sebastian told her what Tyeisha had said—exactly what Norma had predicted—and she told him about the juice and apple-wheat muffins. They both fell silent as they faced their last stop. One plate-glass window was broken in spite of the steel grate that stretched across the front, and a dusty Gone Out of Business sign hung askew on the door.

"What now?"

"We find a motel, have a good dinner, and make a plan of action for tomorrow." She paused on the curb, looking back at the flea market. Movement at the back caught her attention, and she looked closer before abruptly spinning around. When she walked through the door, an out-of-tune bell announced her entry.

A woman at the back was sweeping the old tile floor. Without missing a stroke, she called, "Go ahead and look around. If you need anything, holler."

"I just wanted to ask another question of Norma."

That stopped the sweeping. "Okay, I give up. Who's Norma?"

"The woman who was just here. She works here."

"Ain't no Norma workin' here, honey. Just me, and my name's Rochelle."

"But—"

The bell rang again as Sebastian came inside. He stopped halfway between her and the door.

Bewildered, Melina looked from him to the woman. "She's tall, black, exotic—wears a turban. Her name is Norma and she's very imposing."

Not at all bewildered—or particularly caring—Rochelle shook her head. "I don't know who you're talking about, hon. I'm the only black woman around here, and I'm neither tall nor exotic." She followed the last with a great laugh. Her skin was as light as Norma's was night-dark, and she was as round as Norma was tall. As for exotic . . . she looked like somebody's mother, soft and cuddly and perfect for snuggling up to, crying on, or drawing comfort from.

"But she was just . . . I was just talking . . . She told me to have faith."

Rochelle gave her a long steady look before she started sweeping again. "I've never seen you or her before, but it sounds like good advice to me. I'd take it if I was you. Now, I hate to be rude, but it's closing time. If you're not shopping, I'd appreciate it if you'd move on so I can lock up."

"Not a problem," Melina said dazedly. "Thank you for your time."

"What was that about?" Sebastian asked as soon as they were outside, but she merely shook her head. *Have faith,* Norma had said, and she did, at least in herself. She hadn't hallucinated that entire conversation. Whatever had just happened there, she knew beyond a doubt she'd talked to *someone* and that someone had talked back.

And Rochelle was right. Norma had given good advice. And she intended to follow it.

At least, part of it.

NIGHT HAD FALLEN SEVERAL HOURS AGO, AND THANKfully, the temperature had fallen a few degrees, too. Not that Sophy minded the hot days of summer, but unrelenting heat was hard on people with few physical comforts, like the children asleep in the car below.

"Not as hard as a cold north wind and nothing but a blanket of snow for warmth," Norma pointed out.

Sophy gave her a look, then gazed down again. The three guardians sat on the roof of an abandoned warehouse surrounded by blocks of other ugly warehouses, some in use, most not. At first glance, it didn't seem to be an ideal part of town for four vulnerable children, but Cheyenne could have chosen worse places to park for the night. Other than an occasional late-arriving truck, there was virtually no traffic. The police came through only when they got a call, and with everything buttoned up tight, those calls generally didn't come until morning. Even the troublemakers who roamed the streets at all hours stayed out of this area. After all, there was no one to harass, nothing to steal without putting some effort into it.

The Cavalier was parked in the shadows between the building and a six-foot-high chain-link fence, and the kids were fast asleep. "What do you think they dream of?" Sophy asked.

"Alanna wants to find her mother and go home," Norma announced in her usual decisive tone.

"And Chrissy misses her dog and her daddy, though not necessarily in that order," Gloria said.

"And Caleb dreams of home—" Sophy looked at the other two, and they all added in unison, "And Alanna."

No one tried to guess what Cheyenne dreamed of. Sophy wasn't even sure the girl remembered how to dream.

"I wish we could just tell Melina and Sebastian where the children are." That was Gloria again. "I know we can't," she hurried on before Norma could say anything. "We can help, we can encourage, we can even give nudges in the right direction, but we can't resolve the situation for them. But I wish . . ."

Truthfully, Sophy did, too. It was never easy sitting back and doing nothing—well, little—but it was doubly hard with the children. They belonged at home with their families, including Cheyenne, who hadn't been a part of a family for so long that she claimed she'd forgotten what it was like. She remembered, all right. It just hurt too badly to admit it.

"What will happen to her when this is over?" Sophy murmured, not realizing she'd spoken aloud until the other two looked at her. Not that she needed to speak aloud for them to hear.

"Cheyenne?" Norma shrugged. "We'll have to wait and see."

Of all the things guardians did, that was one of the toughest. Maybe the children would find a place for her. Maybe she'd gather the courage to go home and face her mother again, and maybe her mother would find the strength to make the right choice when it came to her daughter and her husband. And maybe—

With a sigh, Sophy cut herself off. No use in worrying about next week's problems when this week's were still there, requiring their attention. All she could do was what Norma had told Melina that afternoon—have faith. And, of course, she did.

But it couldn't hurt to send a few extra prayers drifting up to heaven, could it?

Chapter Nine

Once again Alanna sprawled at an angle in the front seat of the car, her legs resting on top of Cheyenne's, who lay in almost the same position. Everyone was asleep but her, and Chrissy was snoring the way Josie did whenever she had a cold. Alanna had pretended for a while that the noise was keeping her awake, but it wasn't true. It was the ache inside her. She was homesick for the room she shared with her little sister, for Josie and Brendan and Michael, her aunt and uncle, her own bed, clean clothes, and regular baths.

She never should have left home. She wasn't going to find her mother. They didn't even know where to look. Just like she'd done a thousand times, Berry had picked up and moved on, and just like always, she'd left something behind. A couple of times it had been Alanna, Josie, and Brendan. This time it was just a shoe box of pictures and letters, mostly from Emilie, though there were a few from a woman she'd never heard of.

Emmaline Bodine. She lived in Atlanta, and she was Ben Foster's grandmother. That made her Alanna's great-grandmother, Cheyenne had said, but Alanna had pretended to ignore her.

She'd never had grandparents before. Berry and Emilie's mother had died a long time ago, and their father had given them to the state because he didn't want to raise them himself. They didn't even know if he was still alive. And since she'd never had a father, there'd never been anyone on his side, either.

Until now.

She wondered what Emmaline Bodine was like. Was she tall and thin, short and fat? Did she act old and walk bent over with a cane, or was she like Miss Corinna and Miss Agatha? Did she bake and crochet and think food solved everything? And what did she think of Ben Foster?

Sliding up in the seat, she reached for the shoe box and lifted it into her lap. She and Caleb and Chrissy had been waiting in the car, parked in an alley behind a drugstore, while Cheyenne went to Berry's old apartment. She'd been practically running when she came back, excited about the box. It had almost made up for the disappointment of not getting to see her mom.

Now she removed the lid and took out the picture on top. The moon was bright enough to make out the figures—Berry and Ben—but not to see their faces. That was all right. She'd stared at it long enough this afternoon to memorize all the details. They were real young, like kids themselves, and Berry had been really, really happy. Just-out-of-rehab happy, when she swore she would never use drugs again and she really wanted to mean it but was afraid it wasn't true, and, of course, it wasn't.

She'd been hanging on to Ben like he might try to run away, and he'd looked like maybe he would.

Before long, he'd left her and she'd left Georgia. It seemed she'd never settled down since. Alanna had been born in Tennessee, Josie in Virginia, and Brendan in Pennsylvania. They'd been in Connecticut the first time they'd had to live in a shelter, in Kentucky the first time Berry had abandoned them, and in Massachusetts when Emilie had come to live with them.

That was when their lives had finally changed. They'd still been poor, but they'd known *nothing* would take Emilie away from them. For four years now she'd mothered them, and for three Nathan had been their father, and for the first time in their lives, they'd felt safe.

And Ben thought he could make up for all that just by showing up in Bethlehem. Well, he was wrong. When she'd needed a father and a family, he hadn't been around, and now that he wanted a daughter, she wasn't gonna be around, either. She wasn't ever going to forgive him, and there was nothing anyone could do about that.

With a sigh, she returned the photograph to the box, then slid it back onto the floorboard. She scrunched up in what little room she had, her head resting on the car door, and gazed at the sky.

She was about to doze off when suddenly she blinked, rubbed her eyes, and stared at the sky. For a second, she'd thought she'd seen a falling star, except instead of falling down, it had been shooting *up* into the sky. But falling stars couldn't fall up. It was just her eyes playing tricks on her.

But there was another one, a bright streak of light racing up into the sky, and it looked like it had come from the roof of the building beside them. The higher it climbed, the longer it got, until it broke up into a million tiny bits of light that shimmered in the night, then disappeared.

As she stared up at the sky, a feeling of warmth came over her—not summertime warmth, but everything's-going-to-be-all-right warmth that came from the inside out. She smiled, pillowed her hands beneath her cheek, whispered her bedtime prayers, and immediately drifted off to sleep.

NORMA GAVE SOPHY A WRY LOOK. "YOU NEVER could settle for sending up prayers like everyone else, could you? You have to get fancy."

Hugging her knees to her chest, Sophy smiled. "I like to give them a little boost. And all over the city, people are resting a little easier now. There's nothing wrong with that, now is there?"

SATURDAY MARKED A FULL WEEK SINCE SEBASTIAN had seen Chrissy, and it stirred an actual ache inside him. As far as he could tell, they were no closer to finding her and the other kids than they'd been back in Bethlehem the past Sunday. Presumably, they were in the same city now, but that was just a guess. They hadn't seen or heard anything about the kids since Melina's mysterious woman had told her about the muffins Thursday afternoon. For all they knew, the kids could have headed off to anyplace Berry had lived and might want to go back to or anyplace she'd never lived and might want to see. Hell, that only covered the whole damn world.

And he and Melina were still covering Providence.

They'd spent Friday and most of Saturday visiting shelters, walking the streets, and driving. They'd met up with Detective Santiago, who'd introduced them to a staggering number of runaways, homeless kids, and prostitutes. They'd all acted so tough and seemed so vulnerable. He'd wanted to take every one of them home to his mother to clean up, fatten up, straighten up, and love. Seeing all those kids up close had been one of the hardest things he'd ever done.

"You okay?"

He glanced at Melina. When the sun had gone down, they'd gotten back in the truck to drive around again. She sat opposite him, shoes off, feet braced on the dashboard. The position pulled her jeans snug over the curve of her bottom, the muscles in her thighs, the bend of her knees. Her hair was pulled up and threaded through the back of the baseball cap she wore. Between that and her skintight tank top, she looked about eighteen years old . . . and sexy as hell.

Feeling about twice his own age, he sighed heavily. "Don't ever have kids. They can break your heart."

"I'm going to have at least three, maybe more. As soon as I find the right guy."

That made him swallow hard. He'd never taken the time to consider whether she was the maternal type. If pressed for an answer off the top of his head, he would have said no, she enjoyed life, men, and adventure too much to ever settle down and do the mom bit. Apparently he'd been wrong. "And what constitutes the right guy?"

She didn't glance at him but kept her gaze on the scene outside the window. He was getting to know the more disreputable areas of Providence as well as he knew his own hometown. Melina insisted the kids would stick to the sort of neighborhood where Berry Dalton was likely to live, and it made sense. In a better part of town, four kids sleeping in a parked car wouldn't go unnoticed by either the residents or the police. Over here, a few runaway kids blended right in. Over here, everyone was running from something or other.

"The right guy," she repeated after a moment. "I always thought I'd know him when I met him—you know, instinct. But I finally learned that's a crock. I mean, I thought Rico the rat was the one. He was handsome and charming, he loved kids, he loved me, he was one of the good guys, and he was generous—with his time, his money, and most of all his body. *Damn* generous. And then there was you—" Abruptly she broke off, and a flush colored her cheeks. "Well, obviously, my instincts can't be trusted. So I guess I'll have to approach it logically—make a list of what I want, find suitable candidates, and choose from one of them. Sounds kind of unemotional, I know, but Lynda tells me it worked beautifully for Tom Flynn."

Sebastian deliberately kept to himself, but even so, he'd met Tom Flynn, the number two man at McKinney Industries in Bethlehem. When Flynn had accomplished everything else in his career plan, he'd decided it was time to marry, and so he'd done exactly what Melina had said, and before long, he'd been happily married to Holly McBride, owner of McBride Inn. According to some, watching him pursue and win the Woman Least Likely to Marry had been the town's best entertainment in years.

Damned if he wanted to be around while Melina went through the same process.

And damned if he appreciated being lumped in with

Rico *again,* or being held up as proof that her instincts were faulty. He *could* have been the one, if things had been different. If he hadn't spent so much time mourning Diana. Under the right circumstances, he and Melina together wasn't outside the realm of possibility. They could be damn good. He couldn't imagine anyone who'd make a better wife and, Diana's opinion notwithstanding, he could be—had been—a damn good husband. And if she wanted to have kids . . . well, hell, he had one, no waiting, who was in serious need of a mother.

But circumstances hadn't been right when they'd gotten together, and he'd screwed up any chance that they ever could be. And none of it could possibly matter anyway as long as Chrissy was missing.

"Do you plan to ever get married again?"

Seeing flashing lights ahead, he gripped the steering wheel and the muscles in his stomach knotted. He'd come to hate the sight of an ambulance in the blocks where Melina thought the kids were—to fear driving past and seeing a familiar little body with brown curls being worked on or, worse, given up on.

He slowed to little more than a crawl. The emergency lights belonged to a police car and an ambulance, and the people receiving treatment on the sidewalk were adults, a man and a woman, yelling obscenities at each other even as the paramedics patched them up.

"Another domestic dispute. Amazing the way some couples show their affection for each other," Melina said sarcastically. "Park over there. We'll get some coffee and people-watch for a while."

He turned onto a side street and parked in the first empty space. They went into the diner on the corner and took seats in a booth at the front. A burly man in soiled whites brought them coffee and menus. Sebastian stirred sugar and cream into the coffee, then left it and the menu untouched as he stared outside.

"You never answered my question. You ever gonna get married again?"

Thinking of the couple they'd just seen screaming insults at each other, of Berry Dalton and all the men who'd used her, of his own misery in the years since Diana had left, he scowled at her. "Do I look like an idiot?"

"You had one bad experience. That's hardly a reason to write off any future attempts at trying again."

Four years of sorrow, mourning, guilt, anger, and bitterness, and she managed to condense it into a practically harmless phrase—one bad experience. Instead of saying something sarcastic or snide, he turned to the window again.

"What if Diana came back?"

In spite of the fact that the diner was about ten degrees warmer than outside, the thought of his ex-wife coming home sent a shiver through him. For years that was what he'd wanted—*all* he'd wanted. He would have forgiven anything, everything, would have pretended the past four years hadn't happened, just to have her back again. Now the idea left him cold.

When had that happened? What had changed his mind? His affair with Melina? Chrissy's running away? A combination of the two, maybe.

"No," he said flatly. "*Especially* not if Diana came back."

He wasn't sure, but he might have seen a bit of relief flash through her dark eyes. He might have felt it loosen the tension knotted in his chest.

"So you intend to live out the next fifty years of your

life alone, having sex with strangers and otherwise being pretty much a hermit, all because your wife left you."

The life she described sounded so damn pathetic that he wanted to argue with her, but he couldn't. He *was* pretty much a hermit. Until he'd hired Ben Foster and Sophy Jones to work in his business, the only person he saw most days was Chrissy. He'd dropped his friends, had cut way back on the time he spent with his family, and did rely pretty much on anonymous sex with strangers to satisfy those needs. Melina had been the only real exception to that rule in four years.

"You make it sound as if a casual acquaintance just picked up and moved away," he said with a scowl. "It was more than that."

"Of course it was more than that. She was your wife, the mother of your child. You loved her, and she left you, and she broke your heart . . . *four years* ago. It's past time to face it like an adult and move on. It's *way* past time to stop letting it determine how you live your life."

"You don't—You can't possibly—Did I ask for your advice?"

She grinned. "P.I.s are like bartenders. We listen to your problems, we tell you what to do to set them right, and sometimes we help."

He managed to continue scowling in spite of her grin. "I didn't volunteer to confide in you, I don't want your advice, and I don't want your help in anything but finding my daughter. You want to fix someone's love life, work on your own. For a beautiful woman, you're not having much luck."

"That's because I keep falling for losers," she said cheerfully, then immediately, before he could take exception to being called a loser, asked, "Do you really think I'm beautiful?"

His answer came grudgingly. "Didn't I tell you so a dozen times when we were together?"

Her pleasant expression shifted into a cool, distancing smile. "Yes, you did, but under the circumstances, you'll have to pardon me if I have trouble separating your truths from your lies."

"Damn it, Melina—"

Her gaze narrowing, she leaned forward to rap on the glass. Half the people outside turned to look, but she ignored them. "Hey, wait a minute!" she shouted. Jumping to her feet, she slung her bag over her shoulder and bolted out the door.

Had she seen the kids or someone matching Anne's description? Bewildered—and hopeful—Sebastian dropped some money on the table and went after her. She was more than a block ahead of him by the time he cleared the kids hanging out on the corner. As she crossed to the opposite side of the street, he started running, dodging people and cars. He couldn't tell which of the people up ahead she was chasing—no one seemed to be in a particular hurry—but then he saw a woman turn off the sidewalk in the middle of the next block. She looked back once, then disappeared through a gate.

When he reached the gate, Melina was standing in front of it, fingers wrapped around the rusted iron, looking frustrated and annoyed. "Damn it," she muttered, giving it a jerk that made it tremble on its hinges.

He grabbed her arm and swung her around. "What the hell are you doing running off like that?"

"I saw Norma!"

"Norma . . . from the flea market?"

"Yes!"

"So what? You've already talked to her!"

"I wanted to talk to her again!" She jerked her arm and, when he let go, returned to the gate to peer inside. A tall iron fence sat on top of a low brick wall, and behind it was a park that took up the entire block. It wasn't well lit, but over Melina's head, he could see sidewalks, parched grass, and benches, as well as some kind of monument in the center.

"From back there it looked like she turned in here," he said.

"She did."

"But the gate's locked."

She gave it a kick that rattled the lock. "It is."

"But how—"

She checked the lock, measured the space between iron rods with her fingers spread wide, then stepped back and looked at it as if studying how difficult it would be to climb over. Then she shook her head. "I *saw* her go through here."

That was impossible. But she certainly hadn't gone past this point—he'd been watching, and Melina had been mere yards behind her—and a look around showed no sign of her, in or outside the park. She'd gone *somewhere* . . . but through a locked gate? Vanished into thin air?

"This is ridiculous," she said impatiently. "People don't just disappear." She walked to the curb, looked long and hard to the right and across the street, then back to the left. "Damn it," she muttered again, then turned to glare at him. "What the hell were you doing grabbing me like that?"

"It seemed the best way to get your attention."

"You want my attention?" She folded her arms across her chest. "You've got it."

"You can't just run off like that at night in a dangerous neighborhood."

"I *have* a gun."

"So do half the people on this street!"

"Yeah, well, mine's probably bigger."

He would grab a handful of her shirt . . . if there was enough to grab. He settled for curving his fingers around the waistband of her jeans and yanking her up close. The move caught her unprepared and off balance, and as she grabbed for something to steady herself—him—he snatched the bag from her shoulder and tossed it to the ground. "Where's your gun now, Melina?" he asked softly, bending close so his breath brushed her temple.

"Damn it, Sebastian—!"

When she struggled to free herself, he moved her a few feet until the fence was at her back.

"Let me go!"

Taking two steps, he brought the front of his body into contact with hers, then took one more, pushing her harder against the fence. Though she wriggled, he easily caught both her hands behind her, the fingers of his right hand encircling both slender wrists. "How are you going to defend yourself now?"

Her eyes flashed with fury and her voice was taut, cold with it. "If you don't let me go right now, I swear, you're going to be the sorriest bastard that ever *hobbled* this earth!"

Having a pretty good idea what she intended, he wedged his knee between hers, then forced her legs apart and stepped in even closer. The muscles in her thighs clenched powerfully against him, but she couldn't shut him out, couldn't push him back or—probably her greatest disappointment—bring her knee up into his groin. She was helpless, and so furious that her entire body trembled . . . and he was aroused. The heat of her body against his, the familiar feel of her legs around him, the need and hunger that the mere touch of her stirred . . . Aw, hell, he was hard and horny and liable to self-combust right there if he didn't back off.

He tried to let go of her but couldn't, tried to step away but couldn't do that, either. And then it was too late because his erection came into contact with her belly and her eyes widened as she caught her breath in a startled gasp. The curses she'd been spitting out stopped, and she stared at him.

Her mouth worked several times before she got any words out. "You are a first-class bastard," she whispered.

"I know," he whispered back. He wanted to move away, to put about five hundred miles between them, but not as much as he wanted to move closer, to strengthen the ache by rubbing against her, to make it unbearable by sliding inside her.

She continued to stare at him, her breaths shallow, her breasts brushing his chest with each inhalation. "So what is it that turns you on?" She still whispered. "The adrenaline? The power? Having a woman merciless against your demands?"

He could joke, or he could lie. Either would be easier and smarter than telling the truth, but he chose the truth anyway. "You, Melina. *You* turn me on."

He bent his head closer and she didn't flinch or turn away. With that small encouragement, he brought his mouth to hers. She gave a small whimper of protest, then opened her mouth to him. He slid his tongue inside . . .

and an instant later, pain exploded through him. His left knee gave way, and he staggered back, knee throbbing, his tongue on fire, his right thumb damn near dislocated. Her timing had been perfect—at the same time she'd bitten his tongue, she'd brought her heel down on the back of his kneecap, forcing the joint forward, and then had taken advantage of his pain to wrench both hands free of his.

She straightened, brushed her palms together, replaced her bag over her shoulder, and smiled smugly. "Don't mess with me, Sebastian," she said pleasantly. "I could break you in two."

He sank down on the ledge where the brick wall extended past the iron fence and bent to rub his knee. The position was damn awkward, though, because he was still stone hard. "You didn't have to bite my tongue," he said sourly, wincing at both the pain from speaking and the distorted sound of his words.

"Call me funny, but you stick something in my mouth, I'm liable to bite it. Be grateful it was *just* your tongue." She slapped him on the back. Bent over the way he was, it practically knocked him off the ledge. "You ready to head back?"

"If I can walk." He sat up, tested his knee, then carefully stood. It was sore, but there wasn't any serious damage—though he had little doubt if she'd wanted to break something, she would have.

She started toward the diner and the pickup, but he stood there a moment, staring at the locked gate. When she turned back a few yards away, he looked at her. "This Norma . . . when you saw her, she was walking past the diner?"

She nodded.

"And you ran out of the diner and didn't stop running until you got here?"

She nodded again. "Why?"

"When I saw the woman who turned in here, she was walking at a normal pace. She didn't have more than a fifteen- or twenty-second head start, and you're pretty fast. How the hell did she get up here ahead of you without running?"

She looked at him for a long time, her expression as confused as it had been after her first encounter with Norma. Weird, she'd said at the time.

Damn weird.

IT WAS THE MIDDLE OF THE NIGHT, AND MELINA WAS having trouble sleeping. She'd made pages and pages of case notes, checked in with Lynda and Ben, watched TV, and read for a while. Her eyes had gotten so weary she couldn't see straight, so she'd shut off the lights and crawled into bed, and suddenly she was wide awake. Judging by the sounds coming from next door, Sebastian was as restless as she was. At least, she hoped that was the reason he was still awake.

She tried all her tricks to doze off, but when the digital clock on the bedside table rolled over to three-thirty, she threw back the sheet with a sigh and sat up. Shoving her feet into house slippers, she got up, pulled on a terry robe to cover the tank and shorts she slept in, and left the room.

Ten minutes later she was back with a bucket of ice, two cans of Diet Coke, and two candy bars. Balancing everything in her arms, she listened at the connecting door, heard a mutter from the next room, and knocked.

After a moment's hesitation, Sebastian called, "It's open." He sounded grumpy, and she couldn't really blame him if he was. The past week had been a stressful one, and after the incident outside the park . . .

She opened the door but didn't step through. Only the lamp nearest the front door was on inside his room, but it cast enough light for her to see that he was lying in bed, pillows behind his back and covers pulled to his waist, and that he wasn't wearing anything, at least from there up. It gave more than enough light to see that his hair was tousled and he looked handsome and somehow vulnerable and still sexier than any man she knew, and she knew all the way to her toes that she'd made a mistake in coming to his room. She also knew she couldn't retreat to save her life . . . or her heart.

With the remote he shut off the television that had apparently been muted anyway, and then he just looked at her.

A trickle of condensation ran down her arm and soaked into her robe, reminding her of the items she carried. "I come in peace," she said, aiming for teasing and failing. Taking a deep breath, she forced herself over the threshold and to the bedside table, where she set down each gift as she spoke. "Ice for your knee. Chocolate because it makes everything feel better. Coke to wash the chocolate down. And"—she dug in the pocket of her robe and came out with a pill bottle—"an anti-inflammatory for whatever ails you. It's over-the-counter, but it's good stuff."

He looked from the offerings to her, his expression unchanging. "I don't like chocolate," he said at last, "and I'm not really thirsty, and little blue pills aren't going to do a damn thing for the part of me that's most inflamed . . . but I appreciate the thought."

She felt like crying, and didn't know why. With a lump growing in her throat, she nodded brightly, then turned to go back to her room. She'd made it as far as the door when he spoke again.

"Melina . . ." His voice was husky, the tone intense. "You didn't ask what would make me feel better."

She tried to speak, cleared her throat, then tried again. "What—what would make you feel better?"

"You." His gaze seared her. "Just you."

She stood utterly motionless. There was no doubt exactly what he was talking about. She could see it on his face, could feel the sizzle deep inside herself, couldn't miss the proof of his erection underneath the thin sheet. Only a week and a half ago, he'd broken her heart, and he wasn't offering to put it back together. He was offering sex. Not love or marriage, not even sex on a long-term basis. Just right now. The same thing he'd offered before.

But before she'd misunderstood. This time she knew. This time if she got hurt, she would have only herself to blame.

She fingered the belt that secured her robe at her waist. She was great with casual sex—at least, she had been before Sebastian, and she could be again. She was even prepared for it. Like any modern single woman, she packed condoms right alongside her shampoo, toothbrush, and makeup. She was covered for pregnancy and disease. All she had to do was make certain she didn't let her emotions blind her to reality. Sexual passion was not the same as romantic passion. Physical need had nothing to do with emotional desire. Lust wasn't love.

Yeah, she could do this.

Slowly she loosened the knot in the belt and let the robe slide from her shoulders as she walked to the bed in her own room. She left the robe there, took a handful of condoms from her bag, turned off the light, and—sure, she could do this—returned to Sebastian's room.

Walking to the bed, she opened her hand and dropped a half-dozen plastic packets. One landed on his lap. The rest fell to the mattress on either side of him. "I would warn you how incredibly fortunate you are to be in such good shape," she said, placing one knee on the bed beside him, injecting a light note into her voice that she didn't really feel. "Because when I finish with a man in bed, he's weak and limp. But since you've already had the pleasure of my body, you know from experience how lucky you are."

She swung her other leg over and settled carefully over his thighs. His arousal tented the sheet between them, hot, throbbing, and made her ache to have him inside her.

"And I do mean lucky in more ways than one, big boy," she purred, leaning forward to brush her mouth along his jaw. His skin was warm and stubbled with beard that gave him a slightly disreputable and intimidating look. She wasn't intimidated, though. She was accustomed to *doing* the intimidating, one way or another.

When she would have brought her hands to his chest, he caught hold of her wrists and used them to hold her close, but not too close. "No games, Melina, okay? Just you and me."

For a moment she was still. She wasn't sure she knew how to have just sex without a certain amount of role playing. It was a way to stay in control, to keep her emotions locked up and make certain she was caught up in the right act. But he looked so damn sincere . . . vulnerable . . . sinfully sweet . . . that she gave in. "All right," she whispered, and she freed her hands, cupped them to his face, and kissed him gently, hungrily, nibbling at his lower lip, sliding her tongue between his lips, welcoming his tongue into her mouth.

Kissing was such a simple process that she was amazed at all the variations possible. She'd had sweet kisses, innocent ones, chaste, hungry, brutal, lusty. This one was . . . incredible. Passionate, gentle, greedy, tentative, and arousing—oh, hell, yes, arousing. It heated her blood, curled her toes, and sent all manner of need swirling through her body, and yet it was so sweet it brought tears to her eyes. It made her feel wanted and needed and impossibly secure. For the all-too-short moments it lasted, it made her feel loved.

His hands rested above her knees, warming her skin, then slid slowly to her hips, where the thin cotton of her shorts provided no protection against the power and strength of his touch. He slid her forward until his erection nestled between her thighs, almost where she wanted him, close enough to feed the sharp, raw edges of her need, and then he continued his journey along her body. Catching the hem of her tank top with his fingers, he peeled it up to her neck and left it to her to discard while he stroked her breasts with long, lazy, tormenting touches.

She ended the kiss to yank the shirt over her head, then groaned as his mouth closed around her nipple. He had the most talented mouth, she'd told him in their time together, and he'd willingly proven it again and again, leaving her in a dazed, bedazzled, boneless heap. She felt herself already wanting to collapse against him, to declare herself his, to do with as he pleased.

Abruptly, he lifted her and kicked the sheet away. She shimmied out of her shorts while he ripped open a packet, then unrolled a condom over his penis. With every nerve in her body tingling and the emptiness in her belly aching for him, she tried to help, tangling her fingers with his, brushing them over swollen flesh, paying attention to areas he neglected, but she succeeded only in making him groan an obscenity aloud and twitch convulsively. He grabbed both her hands in one of his, finished his task, and then suddenly he was there, pressing against her, pushing inside her. His arousal was hot, satiny, steely, and as impressive as the rest of his body. He filled her with one long, hard stroke that made her muscles clench, then relax in welcome. While her body stretched to accommodate him, he stabbed his fingers into her hair and brought her mouth to his for a greedy, hard kiss. She responded in kind.

"You're a wicked woman," he murmured, thrusting against her in a tautly controlled rhythm.

Her mouth curved in a smile. "I was just trying to help."

"You almost made me come before I even got inside you."

"That's all right. I brought plenty of condoms. You could have come again." She knew that from experience.

He combed her hair back from her face, then touched his fingertips to her cheek as if touching something fragile and treasured. "You are so beautiful."

Truth or a lie, caught up in the heat of the moment? She didn't care. When he looked at her like that, touched her like that, she *felt* beautiful.

Bracing herself on his chest, she sat up and made his hand fall away. The position allowed her to take him an inch deeper, an inch tighter, and allowed him to touch her . . . oh, hell, yes, deep inside, in that very special spot. Her muscles clenched spasmodically, shivers rippled across her skin, and she caught her breath at the incredible sensation.

"Do that again," she demanded, and he thrust into her once more, deeper, harder, and all the ache, all the heat, pooled between her thighs. "Again," she said, but this time it was a plea, and this time he did it over and over, driving into her with such power, tightening her need, her muscles, all her hunger, until breath-stealing pleasure became exquisite pain, until wanting turned to need turned to torment. With a cry, she stiffened against him, her back arched, her body quivering, and for an eternity she was helpless, voiceless, aware of the sensation about to burst free but powerless to bring it on.

Finally, she came with an intensity that caused her vision to go dark, that exploded in bright flashes in her head, that robbed her of speech but enhanced her other senses practically beyond bearing. A heartbeat later, through the rushing in her ears, she heard Sebastian's groan and was dimly aware of his own orgasm, followed after some time by a low and heartfelt curse.

"Sweet damnation."

She couldn't find the breath to echo it.

After a while he lifted her to lie beside him, disposed of the condom, then pulled the sheet over them. She settled on her stomach, exhausted, already half-asleep when he stretched out against her. Stroking her hair back, he pressed a kiss to her shoulder. "Melina?" His tone was wary, cautious.

All too aware that this was where he intended to make the this-doesn't-change-anything speech, she kept her eyes shut and smiled sweetly in his direction. "I know.

It was just sex. No more, no less, no discussion. We both understand." Fumbling blindly, she found his hand and pressed a kiss to his palm. "Good night, Sebastian. Sleep tight."

SEBASTIAN WATCHED HER, LISTENING TO THE SLOW, deep rhythm of her breathing that signaled she was asleep. *Just sex. No more, no less.* Her words stirred a regret deep inside him, because that was nowhere near what he'd been about to say.

I was wrong.

I didn't give us a chance.

Let's try again and see if we can do it right this time. For real. Forever.

It was too little, he guessed.

And way too late.

Chapter Ten

On Sunday Sebastian awakened several hours later than his days normally started, which seemed fair, since he'd also awakened with a woman, which wasn't normal for him, either.

He lay on his side, one arm pillowing both his and Melina's heads, the other draped over her middle, and his right leg bent over hers, bringing her bottom in snug contact with his groin. His eyes damn near crossed at the sensation of her soft warm flesh against his . . . but he wasn't protesting, as long as she woke up before too long.

This would be day eight of their futile search—another day without Chrissy, another day with Melina. There was a small part of him that wondered if he wouldn't be better off at home—especially after what had happened in this bed a few hours ago—but he couldn't bring himself to leave. At home all he would do was wait and worry. At least here he felt as if he were doing *something.*

At least here he got to spend time with Melina. He didn't think that was ever going to happen again back in Bethlehem.

He sighed heavily, and her hair tickled his nose. It smelled of some exotic blend of fragrances and hung in heavy curls that could trap a man's hands in a thick black web. Unfortunately they couldn't hold him there.

"Sebastian?" She spoke in a sleepy voice, barely getting all the sounds into his name.

"Hmm."

Looking over her shoulder, she brought her mouth close to his ear and murmured a vulgar request. If he hadn't already been aroused, that brash, blunt phrase, followed by a prim and proper *please,* would have gotten him there. Since he *was* already aroused, he bit back a groan, took a moment to locate a condom, then slid inside her from behind. The fit was snug—amazing how her slender body was perfectly designed for a man of his size—and felt incredible. He could stay there forever, and told her so.

It brought a throaty laugh from her, along with a slow, torturous clenching of her body where it sheathed his. He wanted to remain unaffected, but his hips bucked against hers. When she did it again, a shudder shot through him. The third time he paid her back by stroking between her thighs and thoroughly waking her.

"No fair!" she gasped.

"All's fair—" He didn't finish—*in love and war.* This was neither. This was just sex. Exactly what he wanted, right?

Flipping her onto her stomach, he settled them both on their knees. She stretched like a cat, arms above her head, lowering her face and chest to the mattress, long and lean and sinuous. For a moment he remained still inside her, stroking the length of her spine, her narrow waist, the graceful curve of her hips. Then she looked over her shoulder, smiled her sweetest, most innocent smile, and repeated her earlier request, and he complied.

When they'd both come, when he was lying on his back trying to catch his breath and control the shudders ricocheting through him, she rose from the bed. "You're an amazing man, Sebastian," she said, pulling on the T-shirt he'd worn the day before, then searching for her clothes. She found her shorts at the foot of the bed, her tank top on the floor near the night table. One house shoe made a lump under the sheet, and to reach the other, she had to drop to her knees and stretch under the bed. Sitting up again, she shoved a handful of hair from her face, then smiled at him. "Do you plan to stay in bed all day?"

"I thought about it," he lied. "You know, I have this knee injury . . ."

She studied him for a minute, then slyly shook her head. "You didn't do what you just did with a knee injury."

"What *we* just did," he corrected her.

She just looked at him a moment, then stood up without responding, her arms filled with clothes. "Come on, get up. Sex always makes me hungry. I'm going to jump in the shower, then we'll get some breakfast, then hit the streets again."

This wasn't going to be as easy as it should have been, he thought, watching her saunter into the next room. Maybe that was the reason he'd never slept with the same woman twice until Melina—because he'd known instinctively sex was easier when you didn't know anything about the woman to make it personal. But he knew plenty about Melina, starting with the fact that if she made one more reference to *sex,* he wasn't going to be responsible for his actions.

Long after she disappeared into her room and the shower came on in her bathroom, he stood up and took a few tentative steps. His knee was tender, but nothing he couldn't hide, and his right thumb hurt like hell, but there wasn't much else on the body easier to give up use of for a day or two. All in all, he'd survived his run-in with her little the worse for wear . . . and look what he'd gotten as an apology. That was well worth it at twice the price.

He'd just gotten out of the shower and started to towel off when she called, "Hey, can you hear me? Emilie Bishop says her sister likes flea markets—you know, the big open-air free-for-alls where one man's trash is another man's treasure? And the desk clerk says there's one every Sunday about a mile from the apartments where she used to live."

"You think she might show up there?"

"I don't know if she's even still in the state. But Emilie says she used to drag the kids to these things all the time. It was cheap entertainment." She popped her head around the corner, where she was doing her makeup at his sink. She wasn't the least bit shy about looking, and when he sought some modesty behind the towel, she merely smiled. "Too late. I have a photographic memory." Then she returned to the subject. "If Emilie remembered Berry's fondness for flea markets, maybe Alanna did, too. I know it's a long shot, but . . ."

It was the only shot they had.

She went back to the mirror, and he knotted the towel

around his waist before leaving the bathroom to get dressed. "What else does Berry like to do?"

"The same thing her neighbor said about her men—get drunk, get high, and get laid. The kids are too young to check out bars, unless Anne looks a lot older than she is, and I'm hoping they're too smart to check out men or drug dealers. But that's coming up on our list."

Sebastian was sitting on the bed, one shoe on, the other in his hand. As far as he knew, he'd never met a drug dealer in his life. He was damn sure Chrissy had never had any contact with one, and he resented like hell that Berry Dalton might change that.

"Cheer up," Melina said, watching his reflection in the mirror. "If we have to question bartenders, dealers, and other scum of the earth, Detective Santiago will do it with me. You'll stay here."

"Like hell I will." He shoved his foot into the shoe and yanked the strings into a bow, then went to stand indecently close behind her. "You're not going off someplace dangerous without me."

Her dark eyes turned hazy, and suddenly she looked overly warm in the terry robe. "Didn't we have this discussion last night?" she asked, her voice husky. "Didn't I prove I can take care of myself?"

"Only because you distracted me." He bent his head, nuzzled her hair from her neck, and murmured into her ear, "You made me think you wanted me."

She leaned heavily against him, eyes closed. "I did want you," she whispered. "Really, I did. It was a toss-up whether to let you keep kissing me or to prove my point."

"So I lost to your ego."

"Aw, that's not the way to look at it." She smiled at

him in the mirror once more. "You lost to my years of experience, my superior intellect, and my feminine wiles. My ego was just a small part of it."

With a wry shake of his head, he let her go and turned to pull a shirt on. He thought, for an instant before he turned away, he saw hunger and regret cross her face. He refused to think about it, though, instead concentrating on picking up his dirty laundry. "Hurry up," he said over his shoulder as he stuffed the clothes into a mesh bag. "You know sex makes me hungry. Let's get moving."

CHEYENNE PICKED UP A JELLY DOUGHNUT—CHRISSY'S favorite—and went to sit beside her on the park bench. "What's up? You look kinda down."

Chrissy took the doughnut, poked her finger in the middle, then sucked off the jelly before giving a sigh that was way too big for such a little girl. "All we done so far is look for Lannie's mom. No one's even tried to find mine 'cept me, and all I can do is look. Even that's kinda hard 'cause sometimes I can't r'member what she looks like."

Cheyenne remembered Alanna saying something about Chrissy thinking her mom was in Providence but she wasn't. Now she brushed back a strand of Chrissy's curls, anchoring it behind her ear. "Do you have an address for your mom?"

"No."

"Do you have a phone number?"

Her bottom lip poked out. "No."

"Do you know her name?"

"Diana Knight."

"Okay. While we're out today, we'll find a phone

book and look for her name, all right? But if it's not there . . . I don't know what else to do."

Chrissy's eyes got bigger and rounder until she burst into tears. "I know she's here! My grandma said so, and Grandma would never lie! I *know* she's here!"

Cheyenne handed the doughnut and its napkin to Alanna on the next bench—they couldn't throw good food away—and lifted Chrissy onto her lap. "Don't cry. Come on, dry your eyes and tell me exactly what your grandma told you."

Chrissy wiped her eyes on her sleeve a couple of times and started to do the same with her nose until Cheyenne stuck a napkin in her face. She blew her nose, then crumpled the napkin. "She didn't tell me. She told my aunt Shauna, but she wouldn't lie to her, either, 'cause Shauna's her only little girl."

"Okay, so tell me what she told Shauna."

"She said there's a special place for mothers like mine and Lannie's and Caleb's. And if Lannie's mama is here in Providence, then that means ours is, too. Caleb don't care, but I do. I want to see my mama. I want to take her home and s'prise Daddy."

Cheyenne looked over her head at the other kids. Caleb rolled his eyes, and Alanna just shrugged.

"All I can do is look in the phone book, Chrissy. Sometimes . . . sometimes mothers can be hard to find. Sometimes they don't want to be found. It doesn't have anything to do with you. There are other reasons, but I know she loves you." Cheyenne took a moment to silently apologize for the lie.

"If I can't see my mama, then I want my daddy. I want to go home! I want to see Sundance and Grandma and

Aunt Shauna, and I'm s'posed to be campin' with the Brownies this weekend!"

Cheyenne rocked her from side to side. "Hey, you've been camping with us all week. It's been kinda fun, hasn't it? And you're gonna go home soon, I promise."

"I want to go home, too," Caleb announced. He gave Alanna a wary look when he said it, like he was afraid of her reaction, but when she didn't say anything and kept staring at the ground, he stood up. "My parents, Chrissy's dad, your aunt and uncle—everyone's worried about us. They're scared and upset and they want us back and . . . we want to go back. We're never gonna find your mom, Alanna. We don't even know where to look. You know sooner or later she'll settle down someplace, just like she always does when she pulls this stunt, and she'll write you and Josie and Brendan and let you know where she's living, and you can talk to her then. But until then . . . we need to go home. You can talk to your father—"

"He's not my father!"

"Yes, he is! You know your uncle would never let him come around without proving that he is who he says! Your mom's got pictures of him in that shoe box! She's got letters from his grandmother! He's your father, Alanna, whether you want him to be or not!" Caleb dragged his fingers through his hair, then gave her a pleading look. He looked about five years old, Cheyenne thought—and about fifty. "Let's go home. Don't you miss your family? Aren't you tired of sleeping in the car? Don't you want to see your new room in your new house and unpack all your stuff?"

Her lower lip quivered with the tears that glinted in her eyes. "I want to see my mom."

"Well, you know what, Lannie? We don't always get what we want, do we?" He waited a moment, then held out his hand. "Come on, Chrissy. I'll push you on the swing."

Her own tears forgotten that quick, Chrissy slid off Cheyenne's lap, slid her hand into Caleb's, then trotted off in the direction of the playground.

Cheyenne threw the trash in the nearby garbage can, then bagged up the remaining doughnuts before she sat down beside Alanna. When she didn't say anything, Alanna glared at her. "What? I guess you want to go home, too?"

"I don't have a home to go, remember?"

"Yeah. Sorry." She sniffled. "What will you do when we go back?"

Cheyenne had been wondering the same thing. It was hard to believe it had only been a week since she'd offered them a ride. An entire week that she hadn't been lonely, that she'd had someone besides herself to worry about, that she'd felt like she'd mattered. Maybe the kids hadn't wanted her, but they'd needed her, and that was more than she could say for anyone else in a long, long time.

She was going to be lonely without them. It would be almost as bad as when she'd first left home.

But she didn't say any of that. She just smiled. "I'll be fine. I'll find someplace."

"You can stay in Bethlehem."

Alanna had told her that before. She didn't take her any more seriously now than she had then. She was just a kid. She didn't understand what it was like to truly not be wanted by anyone. She didn't see that if Cheyenne's own mother didn't want her around, then no one else would, either.

"Hey, I'll be fine," she said cheerfully. "Don't worry. But, Alanna . . . You *are* gonna have to go home real soon. We're almost out of money. There's no way I can take you back—the car's not gonna make it that far—and there's not enough money for gas. When we're broke, you're gonna have to call home and let them come get you. And that'll probably be in another day or two . . . *if* we're careful. Okay?"

For a long time Alanna's expression was so bleak that Cheyenne wanted to cry for her. Then slowly, looking as if she'd lost everything, she nodded. Cheyenne slid her arm around her shoulders. "Don't give up yet. We've still got this flea market to check out. And today I feel lucky, so let's get going."

FLEA MARKETS APPEALED TO MELINA ON SEVERAL levels. The only thing she loved better than shopping was buying at a bargain, and she was utterly fascinated by the things available for purchase. "Can you imagine actually taking the time to make an entire landscape out of *butterfly wings*?" she asked, both astonished and repulsed as she walked away from the picture in question.

Sebastian gave her a dry look. "Not your taste, huh?"

"It's just plain weird."

"How about a naked fertility goddess carved from a six-foot-tall log?" he asked, gesturing toward the figure at a booth ahead.

She gave him her best wicked grin. "I'm the only naked goddess allowed in my apartment, and I'm not ready to be fertile. I've still got to find the right guy."

He looked away, but not before she saw the muscle in his jaw twitch and the grim look that shadowed his eyes.

If she didn't know better, she would think he was just a bit jealous of her intention to find some guy to fall in love and have kids with. But she did know better. He wasn't interested in anything but her body—not marriage, not love, certainly not happily-ever-after. She had proof of that in the ache around her heart.

But that was all right. They were doing things right this time—just having an affair. They both understood the rules and had the same expectations of great sex and nothing else. Then, when she got back to Buffalo, it was going to be husband-hunting with a vengeance. In her job, she'd found hundreds of people who didn't want to be found. The right man for her would be no problem.

But until then, she was certainly going to enjoy the wrong one.

They'd been at the flea market, set up in a rather shabby park, for about three hours. They'd walked up and down the aisles together and separately, had studied both vendors and shoppers, shown their flyers, and asked their questions. She'd eaten a hot dog from a vendor whose cart was shaped like a bun and laughed when Sebastian warily said no, thanks. She'd been fed olives, feta, and kalamarakia, or squid, practically before she had teeth, she boasted. She could stomach anything.

Stopping at a display of earrings, she was considering a pair of dangling geometric shapes that would surely get tangled in her hair when one of a dozen voices nearby caught her attention. The accent was *so* not-from-around-there that it stood out from the others, and the words . . .

Her gaze swiftly found the girl, and her heart rate doubled. Pretty, black hair with blond roots, bad cut, multiple earrings—Norma and the apartment super had nailed the description. It was most definitely Anne. She wore short overalls with a T-shirt underneath and an expensive brand of tennis shoes that had seen better days, and she was showing a photograph to the vendor in the next booth.

Melina edged in that direction, her gaze scanning the area for any sign of the kids. Either Anne had left them at the car, or they'd split up, as she and Sebastian had done earlier. Either way, she would turn them over. Melina had no doubt about that.

The vendor handed the picture back to the girl, and she sighed, then headed for the next booth. Melina blocked her way. "Looking for someone?"

"Yeah. Have you seen her?"

She handed over the photo, and Melina took a quick glance at it. It was several years old, but there was no doubt it was Berry Dalton, probably fresh out of rehab. Alcoholic dopers didn't look so good any other time. "Nope, haven't seen her. But since you showed me your picture, how about if I show you mine?"

She pulled one of the flyers from her bag and stuck it in front of Anne. The girl paled, her eyes widened, and she actually stammered. "N-n-no, I h-hav-haven't s-s-seen—" Without finishing, she spun around and started running.

"Sebastian!" Melina yelled as she tore off after her. "Anne, wait up!"

Behind her she heard Sebastian call her name, but she didn't slow her stride or look back. Though Anne had gotten a head start, Melina was a good six inches taller, and all of it was in her legs. The girl was good at dodging around people and cutting through booths, but Melina was faster and could clear in an easy leap much of what Anne had to go around.

They were almost at the front edge of the flea market and headed for the parking lot. Knowing it would be easy to lose the girl among all those acres of cars, Melina dove for her, bringing her to the ground ten feet from the gate. People scattered out of their way as Anne fought furiously to free herself, but Melina had both arms locked around her knees and was slowly working her way up to pin the kid's shoulders to the ground.

She had succeeded in flipping the girl onto her back when an attack came from behind. Keeping one knee on Anne's chest, she straightened to glare at the pint-sized kid battering her with both fists, shrieking, "Let her go! Lannie, Caleb, help, a bad woman's got Cheyenne! Let go! Let go!"

"Knock it off, Christina, or I'll tell your father," Melina said sharply.

Chrissy's response was comical. One moment, her face was screwed up, looking for all the world like a brown-haired Shirley Temple in a pout. In the next, she recognized Melina, and her eyes grew to the size of saucers, her mouth opened wide, and she stared in astonishment. "You're—you're—*Where's my daddy?"*

"Melina!" Sebastian pushed through the crowd that had gathered. "Are you all—"

"Daddy!" Chrissy's squeal of delight hurt Melina's ears, then she launched herself into his arms. "I knowed you would come, I did! Jus' today I said 'I miss my daddy. I wanna see 'im,' and here you are! I knowed it!"

He forgot all about Melina and whether she was all

right. He hugged his daughter tightly, kissing her face, murmuring to her, and Melina was pretty sure she saw tears in his eyes before he turned away. She felt a little teary herself, though for totally different reasons.

As the crowd dispersed, a soft throat-clearing noise in front of her called her attention back from the Knights. Alanna Dalton and Caleb Brown-Grayson were standing there, both solemnly gazing down at her. It was Alanna who'd cleared her throat and who now spoke. "Would you please get your knee off our friend so she can breathe?" she asked politely.

Melina glanced down at Anne, sprawled on her back, her cheeks red from the exertion of running, her face otherwise pale, and she slowly stood up. She offered Anne a hand up, too, then brushed dirt and grass from the girl's back.

"I know you," Alanna went on. "You're Miss Barone's friend."

Melina was tempted to reply in kind: *And you're Miss Barone's soon-to-be-stepdaughter.* Instead, she simply nodded.

"This is Caleb. And this is our friend Cheyenne. She brought us here and took care of us. You really shouldn't have tackled her."

"But since you did, it was a pretty good one," Caleb said. "You're fast."

"I track people down for a living. I have to be fast." She offered her hand to Cheyenne. "Melina Dimitris."

Warily Cheyenne shook hands with her. "I didn't mean to run. It was just . . ."

"Instinct." The girl had good ones. Living the way she did, she needed them. Melina looked from one kid to the next, then took a deep breath and wiped the sweat from her forehead. "We've been looking for you guys," she said sternly.

"So now you found us," Alanna said with a disdainful sniff. "We were gonna call home in a few days anyway."

As if that diminished the fact that she'd found them? Melina thought with her own disdainful sniff before echoing, "A few days? Do you have any idea how long *a few days* is when you're worried sick? Your aunt and uncle, your brother and sister, Ben—*everyone's* been scared to death that something's happened to you! How could you put them through that?"

Alanna's lower lip poked out in a scowl. "Nothing happened," she muttered, defiance sharp in her voice . . . and contrition shadowing her eyes.

"And for that you can thank your lucky stars. Your guardian angels have certainly been looking out for you." Melina gestured for the kids to head for the entrance. "Let's get Chrissy and her dad and go someplace where we can talk."

Sebastian and Chrissy were standing just outside the gate, and she was chattering nonstop, telling him all about her adventures. Despite the fact that her clothes were wrinkled and she needed a head-to-toe dunking in a tub full of soapy water, she looked like a favored little princess in his arms, and he looked . . .

Happy. Melina had never seen him looking truly happy. It pleased her and saddened her, because *she* couldn't bring him that kind of pure contentment.

Once they were outside the gate, Cheyenne started dragging her feet. "Well . . . sorry we didn't find your mom, Alanna. Next time you guys think about running away, *don't*. See ya, Chrissy."

"Aren't you going with us?" Alanna asked.

Cheyenne shook her head. "You're going home. I think I'll stick around here a while."

She was smiling as she spoke, but Melina caught the faint tremble of her lower lip and saw the dampness in her eyes that she tried to hide with a pair of sunglasses. Sliding her own sunglasses into place, Melina hooked her arm through the girl's. "Come on. We'll pick up some clothes, then go back to the motel. Everyone can shower and clean up, then we'll go out for a steak dinner and decide what happens next."

"I don't want—"

Alanna took her other arm. "Come on, Cheyenne. Let's just do what they say. It's easier than arguing."

Melina grinned confidently. "I *love* smart children."

At Sebastian's pickup, Chrissy and Alanna got in the cab with him. Melina volunteered to ride in back with Cheyenne and Caleb. Their first stop was a variety store, where they bought new clothes for the kids from the skin out. While waiting outside the ladies' dressing room, Melina used her cell phone to call Lynda's house.

When Ben answered, she couldn't stop a brash grin from forming. "Hey, darlin'. Who's the absolute, all-time, number one best P.I. in all the world?"

"You found them?"

"We found them, and they're fine. Once we get them cleaned up and fed, we'll bring them home. Can you spread the word?"

He sounded choked up when he responded. "Sure. I'll call Emilie. You're incredible, Melina."

"Aw, all my men tell me that." She turned and saw Sebastian and Caleb standing a few feet away. The boy was holding an armful of clothing, and Sebastian was looking at her as if . . . she didn't know what. Was that regret in his eyes, because he'd given in and slept with her one lousy night before he would have been rid of her? Was he afraid that she would want something from him now that Chrissy was back—that she wouldn't stick to the just-sex agreement? Well, she would put his mind at ease about that.

"I can rent a car and drive the kids back," she went on, turning her back on Sebastian once more, "or we can fly. It's up to the families. Why don't you or Lyn find out what they want and let me know? Thanks, darlin'." She disconnected, plastered on a smile, then turned around again. "Want to toss those in the cart?" she asked, gesturing to the shopping cart that held her bag.

Caleb complied, then went to sit on a bench nearby. After a moment, Sebastian approached her, but he didn't touch her. Of course not. They were in the middle of a store. Caleb was ten feet away. The girls might burst out of the flimsy dressing rooms any second now. And things had changed. "I want to thank you—"

It was the first time he'd spoken to her since Chrissy had leaped into his arms, and he sounded so awkward. So I-wish-last-night-had-never-happened. He was making *her* wish last night had never happened, too, because she'd been wrong. She couldn't have a strictly sexual relationship with a man she'd dreamed of marrying. A man who was obviously regretting the woman in his arms last night now that his precious daughter was back in them today.

"It's no big deal," she said carelessly. "I was just doing my job. Lynda will pay me well for it."

"It's a big deal to me. Chrissy is the most important person in my life. Not being able to see her, not knowing where she was . . . I can't imagine anything worse."

Her pleasant, untroubled expression was starting to feel brittle, and her jaw was beginning to hurt from clenching so tightly. She didn't begrudge him one ounce of emotion for his daughter, but she couldn't help but wonder why he couldn't save just a little of it for her or—since he'd made it clear he couldn't—why in hell she still wanted it.

"Well, you've got her back," she said cheerily. "Tonight or tomorrow she'll be home where she belongs." *Everyone* would be home where they belonged . . . except her and Cheyenne. She had a home but no place to truly belong, and Cheyenne didn't have either.

Melina might not be able to help herself, but she could help Cheyenne, if the girl was interested.

As if on cue, the three girls came out of the dressing rooms, and together they headed for the checkout. From there it was a quick ride back to the motel, showers and clean clothes, and calls home. While the last two in the showers were finishing up, Melina got her own call from Bethlehem. Ross McKinney, Lynda's boss, was sending one of the corporate jets to pick them up. They would be back in Bethlehem before sunset.

"What about your pickup?" she asked Sebastian.

He was expertly brushing Chrissy's curls—yet another good reason not to look at her. "Chrissy and I are going to drive back. We'll take a couple of days, make a few stops along the way."

In other words, *she* could get back, finish her business, and return to Buffalo before they arrived in Bethlehem. She felt cold inside. "I think that's a good idea," she replied. "In fact, you could go ahead and leave now if you wanted. The kids and I will get some food, then catch a cab to the airport."

He gave her a narrow-eyed look. "I can take you."

"Nah. Riding in the back of the truck is dangerous and probably illegal. Once is okay. Beyond that . . . I'd rather take a cab."

"Well . . ." His expression was hard and wary. She couldn't blame him for being suspicious, considering that she'd begun daydreaming about weddings and babies after the first time they made lov—had sex. He was probably having a hard time believing she was not only ready to let him go but eager to see the last of him.

And she really needed him to believe it. She couldn't handle gratitude, regret, relief, or a drawn-out goodbye. If he was going, she just wanted him gone.

"If you're sure that's what you want . . ."

She gave a nod for emphasis, then went into her own room and closed the door behind her. Cheyenne sat on the bed, lacing her tennis shoes. Though the black and blond hair didn't work for Melina, she really was a pretty girl—as sweet and innocent-looking as any kid should be—and sadder than any kid should be, too.

"I have a proposition for you," Melina said, taking a seat at the head of the bed. "If you want to go home, I'll pay your way." When the girl's blue eyes clouded over and her lower lip began to tremble again, she quickly went on. "If you can't go home or don't want to, you're welcome to go back to Buffalo with me. I'll find you a place to live and a family to live with. I'll even give you a job if you promise to go back to school in the fall."

They were big promises, but she knew she could deliver. Her folks had two empty bedrooms and her mother was always looking for someone to fuss over, and so were her aunts. In fact, if the Greek family existed that couldn't make room for one more person, she'd never met them.

If nothing else, though she wasn't looking to hone her mothering skills on a girl half her age, she wouldn't mind a roommate for a while. It wasn't as if there were a man in her life to object.

"I can't go home," Cheyenne whispered.

Though she wanted to know why, Melina didn't press. It would all come out in good time. "Okay. On the way to the airport, we'll clean out your car, and we'll make arrangements this week to sell it or get it to Buffalo. And when we get on that plane this evening, you'll be with us. Okay?"

For a long time Cheyenne sat in silence, the air about her both hopeful and fearful. Was she afraid to believe she was finally getting off the streets? Hoping someone would care about her, knowing no one had before? Then she smiled, blinked away a tear, and nodded. "Okay."

And then she burst into tears.

WHEN MELINA HAD SAID THEY WERE FLYING back, Cheyenne had expected a regular commercial plane, with cramped seats and little bags of pretzels. She'd flown on one once the summer before her father died, going to spend a week's vacation with him, and she hadn't liked it at all. Since his plane crash, she'd never wanted to get on a plane again.

But this was no commercial airliner. It was a private jet, and it was too cool for words. The carpet was thicker than some mattresses she'd slept on, and the seats were leather and big enough to curl up in. There was a bathroom with plenty of room to move around and a shower, and a *bedroom*. The kitchen had a refrigerator, freezer, and microwave, and was stocked with food and drinks and real dishes and silverware.

"Wow," Caleb said, and Alanna's eyes were big. Cheyenne felt as if her own eyes might pop out of her head. Any minute now she was gonna wake up and find she was sacked out in the front seat of her car, parked in a poor part of town where nobody would pay her any mind, and such luxury was no more than a dream.

"Is this your plane?" she asked Melina as she sat down on the sofa and, mimicking the woman, fastened her seat belt.

"It belongs to our neighbor," Alanna said. "The McKinneys live down the street, and they've got a dog named Buddy and a little girl named Rachel and a helicopter and another plane, too. They're rich."

She said it the same matter-of-fact way Cheyenne would have said Melina was pretty or Chrissy's dad was big. People who owned planes were more than rich. They were, like, millionaires or something.

The pilot came back to check on them, then went back to the cockpit and started the engines. They taxied out and took off, smooth as could be, but before they were very high off the ground, Melina turned green. Gagging, she jerked off her seat belt and ran to the bathroom.

Cheyenne looked at Alanna and Caleb, who both shrugged, then looked out the windows. After a moment, she got up, took a bottle of water from the refrigerator, and went to knock on the bathroom door. "Can I come in?"

"Sure."

Melina was leaning against the counter, looking pale and shaky, and her face was damp with sweat. Cheyenne gave her the water, then wet a washcloth and offered it. "You get airsick?"

"Never have before." Melina wiped her face, then rubbed her stomach with one hand. "I did eat a hot dog at the flea market."

"Are you crazy? Hot dogs aren't good for you no matter where you get them, but especially places like that. Even the kids knew better."

"Hey, I'm Greek. I'm adventurous and I have a cast-iron stomach." She smiled weakly. "What are you?"

"Nothin'."

The plane dipped, and Melina bumped against her on purpose. "Sure you are. Your people came from somewhere. What's your last name?"

Cheyenne couldn't count the number of times she'd refused to answer that question in the past eight months. She thought about not answering, but Melina was a private detective. She could find out anything. "Bujold," she mumbled.

"Cheyenne Bujold?" She bumped her again, poking her elbow into Cheyenne's ribs.

"Julianne," she mumbled again, then corrected herself. "Julie actually."

"Julie Bujold. So you've got some French blood. How'd you become Cheyenne?"

"It was a nickname when I—when I had . . . a family. I was kind of quiet and kept to myself, and instead of Julianne, my—my dad called me Shy Anne." Telling it made her stomach hurt, and she tried to shake it off. "He's dead now, and my mom got married again, and her new husband . . . he doesn't want me around." She shrugged like it was no big deal, but it was. Maybe because Melina was being so nice, or because she'd seen Chrissy's dad practically cry when he held her, but right then it was a *really* big deal, and it hurt.

"I'm sorry."

"I don't want to talk about it. Are you gonna puke again?"

Melina's voice got real dry. "I don't think so."

"Then maybe you could leave, 'cause I gotta pee." She held the door open, and Melina walked out. To cover the lump in her throat, Cheyenne called after her, "As old as you are, you should know better than to eat hot dogs from a man who pushes a cart shaped like a giant bun."

"If you want to get any older, child, you should know better than to make references to my age. I caught you back there at the flea market, didn't I?"

"Only 'cause I wasn't really trying." Cheyenne—No, she could go back to her real name now—Julie closed the bathroom door and locked it, then stared at herself in the mirror. She didn't look any different than she had the day before or any day before that, but if Melina could be trusted, she was different today. As of today, she was no longer homeless. Maybe. *If* Melina could be trusted. *If* she could find someone who owed her a big enough favor that they'd take Julie in. *If* she could fit into a family again. Those were real big *ifs.*

Not that it mattered. Buffalo was a big city. If Melina was lying or nobody wanted her, she could always find a job. She could sleep in a park or maybe find a shelter, and make enough money to buy a bus ticket south. By the time cold weather rolled around, she could be in Florida. Closing her eyes, she imagined herself on a beach, the sand warm underneath her, the sun bright and hot overhead. The breeze would rustle through the palm trees, and the waves would lap against the shore. It would be like living on vacation.

She hoped Melina wasn't lying—hoped she could stay

someplace not too far from Alanna and the others and go to school this fall. She hoped she could live with someone who would kind of watch out for her and maybe notice if she didn't come home or if something happened to her, and she thought it would be awfully nice to know every morning where she was going to sleep that night and whether she was going to get to eat.

But if it didn't happen . . . it wouldn't break her heart. That had already been taken care of.

Chapter Eleven

THE AIRPORT NEAREST BETHLEHEM WAS FORTY-FIVE miles away in Howland. The jet landed there, and they transferred their belongings to the helicopter that waited. Twenty minutes later, they were landing on the helo pad at McKinney Industries. Alanna and Caleb climbed out first and disappeared into their families' arms.

As the rotors wound down, Melina looked at the girl across from her. "You wanna be Julie or Cheyenne from now on?"

"Julie."

"You ready to get out?"

Julie hesitated, then picked up Melina's ball cap to cover her shaggy, two-tone hair. Then, with a shrug, she said, "Yeah."

It seemed about a third of the town had gathered on the M.I. lawn and the atmosphere was definitely one of relieved celebration. Melina slung her bag over her shoulder, took her suitcase, and headed into the crowd.

Finding Lynda was easy since, at six feet, she was taller than every woman and many of the men around. Melina hugged her, then Ben, then smiled a greeting at Sophy Jones. She'd first met the young woman when she was working for Ben on the repairs at Lynda's house, then had seen more of her when both she and Ben had gone to work for Sebastian.

"Guys, this is Julie Bujold," Melina said, drawing the girl up beside her. "She took care of the kids while they were gone and kept them out of trouble."

"Kind of like a guardian angel," Sophy said with a grin. The words made Julie blush and look awkwardly at her feet.

"Everyone's been invited over to Miss Corinna's for a thank-God-we-found-them party," Lynda announced. "Do you want to go?"

Melina gazed at the crowd of people and thought about Sebastian and his quiet reunion with Chrissy and how quickly things had changed between him and her, and suddenly she felt the urge to follow Julie's earlier lead and burst into tears. Fortunately, she was a big girl and knew better than to follow *all* her urges.

"Truthfully, guys, I'm kinda tired," she said with the same phony cheerfulness she'd displayed for Sebastian that afternoon. "I'd like to put on my pajamas, curl up with a bowl of ice cream, and have a quiet night. But you go ahead. Have fun. Introduce Julie to everybody."

"I'd rather stay with you," Julie blurted out. A predictable response for a girl whose nickname had been Shy Anne.

"I don't think this is the right time for me to start socializing with Alanna's family," Ben remarked dryly.

Lynda made it unanimous. "I'm not letting you guys go home without me."

"Every party needs a pooper," Sophy chided. "You guys go home and put on your jammies. *I* wouldn't pass up Miss Corinna's hospitality for anything. I'll tell you all about it at work tomorrow, Ben."

They were halfway to the parking lot and Ben's car when Alanna came running after them. She put considerable effort into ignoring Ben and focused narrowly on her friend. "Cheyenne! Aren't you coming with us? Aunt Emilie and Uncle Nathan have to meet you if I'm gonna ask 'em to—"

"You can't ask them that, Alanna," Julie said. "It's—it's too much. Look, don't worry. Everything'll be okay. Go home, tell 'em everything we did, and get settled in your new house. I'll see you tomorrow, okay?"

"Promise?"

"Yeah. I promise."

It sounded like a damn sincere promise from a kid whose personal experience with promises was mostly broken ones, Melina thought sadly. Then she caught a glimpse of the wistfulness on Ben's face as he watched Alanna return to her family, and the concern on Lynda's face, and she rubbed her temples wearily. *Everything* was making her sad tonight. She needed ice cream—fast.

They drove to Lynda's house high on a hill overlooking the town and spent the next hour eating hot fudge sundaes and watching *The X-Files.* Ben went to bed as soon as it was over, and Julie went soon after.

Wearing their pajamas—a tank top and plaid boxers for Melina, a tank and cotton bottoms for Lynda—they went outside and wandered across dew-damp grass to the small retaining wall at the front edge of the lawn. There they sat cross-legged on the stone and gazed out over the valley for long, still moments before Lynda finally spoke.

"What happened with Sebastian?"

Melina pretended to study the stars, but there was no avoiding Lynda when she wanted information. Not that she *had* to confide in her. She could tell her friend that it hurt too much to talk about him, that the pain was too fresh, and Lynda would respect that.

But Lynda had been her best friend for nearly half her life. She knew every secret Melina had ever had. She'd helped her get beyond Rico the rat. She knew about the way-out-of-character love-marriage-babies fantasies. She was the only one—besides Sebastian—who knew Melina had fallen head over heels in love with him in their four days and nights.

"It wasn't bad," she said at last. "For the first few days I was hating him. The next few I was trying to be indifferent to him. I was dealing with the anger and the heartache and the rejection. Then I actually began to enjoy him. And then . . ."

"And then?"

"Then he kissed me. And I had sex with him again. And again. And then we found the kids and he was so afraid I was going to expect something from him that he couldn't even look at me."

Lynda slid her arm around Melina's shoulders, and Melina just naturally rested her head on her friend's shoulder. Her mother had always held her like this whenever she'd gotten her feelings hurt or had a fight with a friend or a boyfriend. Livia had stroked her hair and told her all the soothing things she'd needed to hear, and then she'd pulled out the big guns in the making-things-better department—loukoumathes, cinnamon and honey fritters, or kourabiethes, shortbread cakes shaped like crescent moons. Getting over Rico had required multiple batches of each. She wasn't sure there was enough honey or shortbread in all of Greece to help her get over Sebastian.

"Life's not fair," she murmured.

"No, darlin', it's not."

"But it worked out for you and Ben. Maybe someday I'll get lucky, too."

"Of course you will."

"But not with Sebastian."

"Maybe not." After a moment, Lynda asked, "What are you going to do about Julie?"

Melina straightened and moved away. "I don't know. I promised I'd find her a home."

"Not many people have kept their promises to her, have they?"

"You picked up on that, huh?" Melina's sigh was blue. "Her father's dead, and her stepfather made her mother choose between them. She chose him, and Julie's been on her own ever since."

"Bitch."

"Yeah. Here I'm wanting to have a daughter so bad I can hardly stand it, and she's throwing hers away—and for a man, no less. I thought I'd go to their house, ring the doorbell, smack her mother when she answers, then leave again without a word."

"I'll go with you." Lynda got to her feet, and offered her hand. "Come on. Let's go to bed before we get maudlin."

They were back on the porch and about to go inside when Lynda stopped. "Thank you for finding the kids,

Melina. You're the best friend anyone could possibly ask for. One of these days Sebastian's going to realize what he's lost, and he's going to regret it for the rest of his life."

For the first time in hours Melina smiled a genuine smile. Call her petty, but it sounded good and fair and just. If he couldn't love her and live happily ever after with her, then overwhelming regret was a more than suitable substitute—one that would make her happy. And in the long run, being happy was all she really wanted, wasn't it?

IN HIS ENTIRE THIRTY-FIVE YEARS, SEBASTIAN HAD never been away from Bethlehem as long as he had on this search for Chrissy and her friends, and he was grateful as hell to get back. They got into town late Wednesday afternoon, had dinner with the whole Knight clan, then went home to sleep in their own beds for the first time in more than a week.

After tucking Chrissy into bed, he sat down beside her and picked up the photograph of Diana on the nightstand. The picture had been taken at a family get-together shortly before she'd left. He couldn't remember the occasion now—someone's birthday or maybe a holiday. She was smiling, though, as if she hadn't had a care in the world.

What had really happened with her? How could she have fooled everyone as thoroughly as she'd managed? Why had she left?

"Mama's not in Providence, is she?" Chrissy asked hesitantly.

"I don't think so."

"But Grandma said—" She sighed. "Maybe she just didn't know."

"You miss her, don't you?"

She nodded.

He'd given her the photograph because his mother had told him to. Other than that, he'd removed all sign of Diana from the house and from their lives. He'd never wanted to talk about her—because it hurt, because he was angry, because he resented the hell out of her. She'd left him to raise their daughter alone, and he'd be damned if he would let her still be a part of Chrissy's life.

But she was Chrissy's mother, and all the anger and resentment in the world couldn't change that.

He returned the frame to the night table, then turned to stretch out on the bed beside her. "I'm sorry your mother's gone, Chrissy, and I'm sorry you miss her. But it was wrong for you to run away. If you had any questions, you should have come to me."

She rubbed her nose with the back of her hand before giving a great sigh. "I know."

"I'm your dad. Taking care of problems is what I'm supposed to do." Gently he brushed a curl away from her cheek. "And answering questions . . . that's part of what I'm supposed to do, too. So if you have any questions . . ."

"About Mama?" She sounded wary, and he couldn't blame her. When she'd asked questions about Diana in the past, his responses, he was ashamed to admit, had been neither patient nor kind.

"About anything. I won't get mad. Promise."

Resting her head on his arm, she fiddled with a button on his shirt. "Do *you* miss her?"

His breathing was steady but shallow, thanks to the

muscles knotted in his stomach. This wasn't a conversation he wanted to have—at least, not until she was older. Thirty sounded about right. "I did for a long time," he admitted honestly. "I wanted her to come back home. I wanted to be a family again—you, your mom, and me."

"But now you don't?"

"I wish she was back in Bethlehem for you. I wish you could visit her and she could go to your stuff at school and at Brownies and at church. I wish you could talk to her every day, but . . . No, I don't want to be a family with her anymore." He felt guilty for saying it, much less to Chrissy, as if he'd somehow betrayed her, Diana, and himself, but he would have felt guiltier if he'd lied to her. He couldn't give her false hope. Who knew? Someday Diana might come back. Better that Chrissy understand the reality of the situation before it happened.

"You think she's got a new little girl?"

"I don't know, babe."

"You think maybe that's why she doesn't want us anymore? Because she's got a new family?"

"I think she loved you the best she could. And I think she left you with me because she knew how much I needed you. She was stronger than I was. She could get by without you even though she missed you a whole lot, but I couldn't have made it without you."

"But why did she leave? Caitlyn's mama and daddy got d'vorced and stayed right here. My mama didn't have to run away."

"I don't know, babe."

"And why doesn't she ever come back? Why doesn't she come see Grandma Franks?"

"I don't know."

Chrissy rubbed her nose with the back of one hand

again. "If all you can say is 'I don't know,' you're not much help, are you?" She tried to look stern, but her dark eyes were dancing.

"I know I love you."

"I love you, too, Daddy."

"And I know if you ever run away again, when I find you, I'll lock you in your room until you're fifty."

"Oh, Daddy, that's *old*. B'sides, I'm not ever runnin' away again. I missed the Brownie camp-out, and Grandpa didn't have anyone to go fishing with, and now I won't get a perfect atten'ance star in Sunday school, and you were sad." She wrapped her arms around his neck and kissed his chin. "But now you won't ever have to be sad again."

"No," he agreed. He lied.

He held her until she fell asleep, then eased from the bed. After tucking her pink stuffed cat into her arms, he turned off the lamp and left the bedroom. Sundance, their Irish setter, followed behind him.

Instead of returning downstairs, where the lights were still on and the television still played, he went into his bedroom. He didn't need the lamp to make his way around the bed to the front window. After thirty-some years in the room, every step was etched into his memory.

There was a nearly full moon overhead, surrounded by countless stars. He picked out the brightest one and wondered whether it looked the same to Melina in Buffalo. He wondered if she'd been glad to get home, if she missed him half as much as he missed her. When would she come back to Bethlehem to visit? Would she speak to him, act as if nothing had happened, or dismiss him as insignificant?

He'd hated leaving her and the kids at the motel in

Providence. He'd wanted to have dinner with them, take them to the airport, find some way to adequately thank her—not just for finding Chrissy, but for everything. And she'd wanted to be rid of him as quickly as possible. She hadn't even given him the chance to tell her goodbye without an audience. He hadn't even been able to give her one damn kiss.

Because she'd meant what she said. Saturday night had just been about sex. No strings, no possibilities, no commitment. A couple of great orgasms to cure whatever ailed them, and nothing more.

His sigh was loud and weary in the still room. With a whine, Sundance appeared beside him, sliding his head underneath Sebastian's hand. He scratched the dog's ears for a time, but it wasn't enough of a distraction. It couldn't stop him from wondering where Melina was and what she was doing. If his family knew anything about her, they hadn't bothered to mention it over dinner, and he hadn't found the nerve to ask. Was she still in Bethlehem, or had she already returned to Buffalo? He could call Lynda Barone and ask, but asking was too . . . pathetic. Lynda didn't seem too fond of him to start with, and Melina would have surely told her everything that happened. Pride was cold comfort, but it was better than no comfort at all.

He would wait until tomorrow, when Ben came to work. Ben would know where she was and how she felt, and he wouldn't make Sebastian ask.

Suddenly weary, he turned away from the window, stripped out of his clothes, and stretched out across the bed. He'd been sleeping alone for four years—had gotten used to having the entire bed and all the covers to himself. But a few nights with Melina had changed that. Five lousy nights—five amazing nights—and it looked as if he was going to have to learn sleeping alone all over.

Or get her back.

One would be hard, the other damn near impossible. The hell of it was, he didn't know which was which.

JUNE TURNED INTO JULY, THE SUMMER GOT HOTTER, and Melina grew more listless. She found it impossible to concentrate on much of anything, and so she just drifted with the status quo. She went to work but accomplished little. She gave a lot of thought to finding a home and a family for Julie, but after three weeks, she was no closer to actually doing anything. In fact, about all she'd done in those weeks was take Julie to the best colorist in Buffalo to get her hair back to its normal blond and buy her a new wardrobe. Everything else in her life was pretty much on hold, and she couldn't shake the uncharacteristic malaise to do something about it.

It was a Friday afternoon—Friday the thirteenth—and she was sitting at her desk, contemplating a nap, when her secretary buzzed. "Ms. Barone's on line 2."

"Thanks." Melina gazed at the flashing light and wished she'd told the woman no calls. She was too tired to deal with anyone who couldn't be easily brushed off—and that definitely included Lynda. But, with a sigh, she picked up the phone and faked her cheeriest greeting. "Hey, Lyn, how are you doing?"

"Oh, I'm fine, except for all the time I've spent wondering why my best friend has suddenly gone incommunicado on me."

"I haven't—"

"Returned my last couple calls. Accepted my last couple invitations. Answered my last dozen e-mails. What's up?"

"Nothing's up, Lyn." *Honestly.* In fact, she couldn't remember a time in her life when she'd ever been more down than she was at the moment, and she didn't like it one bit. She wasn't a moody person. Passionate, you bet. Exuberant, absolutely. Melancholy, no way, no how.

"Uh-huh. We missed you on the Fourth," Lynda remarked.

"Julie and I caught the fireworks in town."

"You would have enjoyed them more here."

Melina considered sarcastically pointing out that little Bethlehem couldn't possibly put on a fireworks show to compete with Buffalo's huge display, but she would probably be proven wrong. She and Julie had had to fight the crowds and ride shuttle buses where the fumes were enough to make a person sick, all so they could have a tiny patch of grass to watch the fireworks before they faced the crowds, buses, and fumes again to get back home.

In Bethlehem, they would have gone to the park early, spent the late afternoon and early evening hours visiting with friends and neighbors, eaten a wonderful picnic dinner prepared by Harry at the diner, watched the fireworks, then lazily, contentedly, made their way back home. They *would* have enjoyed it more.

"We also missed you the weekend after the Fourth," Lynda went on. "And the weekend after that."

"I've been busy," Melina said in her own defense. "And I've got some sort of stomach flu that I'm having trouble shaking. It makes me tired and queasy."

"And whiny and cranky?"

"I'm not—"

"Have you been to the doctor?"

"I don't need a doctor. I just need"—she paused to yawn—"rest. I'll be fine."

"Are you afraid to see a doctor?"

"Why would I be afraid?" Melina demanded.

"Oh, I don't know. Because he might tell you that you don't have the flu at all. That maybe you've developed a bad streak of yellow running down your back."

Melina's eyes widened and she stared openmouthed at the phone. "Did you—I can't believe—Are you calling me a *coward?*"

"If the feathers fit . . ."

"Jeez, some friend you are! And what have I done to deserve such an insult?"

"You've let Sebastian Knight scare you out of town. Ben and I are thinking maybe we should have our wedding someplace else so you can put your fears aside long enough to stand up as my maid of honor."

The idea of a wedding made Melina's stomach hurt, but she hid it. "You can have your wedding anywhere you damn well please, smarty pants, and I will be there, ready to dazzle all the men. And for all I care, Sebastian can be the damn best man and it won't bother me at all! That's how little he means to me!"

"Uh-huh. As if I'm going to believe that any more than I believe you've been too busy or too sick to come and see us."

"I *was* busy. I'd been out of town for a week, and I had to get caught up on everything."

"Uh-huh."

"I am so over him that it's not funny."

"Good."

"I don't even know if he's back from Providence yet. I

don't even *care*. I've got other things to fill my time." Like puking. Napping. Feeling blue.

"Uh-huh." After a moment, Lynda went on. "He is. Back, I mean. He and Chrissy got back the Wednesday after you guys did."

"So what? I don't even think about him."

"Right. How long has it been since you saw him?"

"Nineteen da—" Abruptly Melina broke off, wishing her friend was there to appreciate the full effect of her glare. "You're *not* funny."

"Oh, honey, I'm not trying to be funny. It's just . . . you don't usually kid yourself—you faced the truth about Rico head-on—but you're in denial big-time about Sebastian. Look, I'm not going to give you advice, but, sweetheart, you can't stay away from Bethlehem forever. Your best friend is here. Julie's friends are here."

"You act like the roads only run from here to there," Melina replied sourly. "They come this way, too, you know. Climb into Ben's fast hot car and let him show you what it can do. You'll be here before you know it."

"But that would solve only part of the problem. We would get to see you, but the kids wouldn't get to see Julie."

"I don't care what the kids want. Haven't they caused enough trouble already? If they're so eager to see her, let *them* make the effort to get together. And if they don't care enough to do it, then, hell, Julie's better off without them."

There was a long silence at the other end of the line, followed at last by a soft exhalation. "I know you're not going to appreciate this, but, hey, I'm five hours away and I'm not leaving town anytime soon, so there's not much you can do about it unless you get off your butt and come here. So here goes . . . You know, Melina, whether it's PMS, perimenopause, depression, self-pity, or plain old bad attitude, they make a magic pill for it. Go see your doctor. Or come see me. I'll feed you so much ice cream you'll forget to be cranky. What do you say?"

"I'll think about it," she said grudgingly.

"You know I love you. And if you're really, honestly sick, I'll come right now, and I'll even apologize for calling you a coward."

Melina rubbed her temples with one hand. "I'll be fine. I just need . . ." For the first time in her life she didn't know what she needed. "I'll call you in a day or two, okay?"

After hanging up, Melina asked her secretary to hold any other calls, then leaned back in her chair. Lynda was wrong. She was neither depressed nor drowning in self-pity. Though menopause wasn't unheard of at her age, she was sure that wasn't her problem, either, and as for PMS, how could she have that when her period wasn't due for . . .

Unable to remember, she removed the black-leather organizer from her briefcase and flipped it open to the previous month. Her gaze scanned the last week from left to right across two pages. Finding no little red *x* on any of the dates, she checked the week before, as well as the one after. Nothing. May had one on the twenty-ninth, April on the twenty-seventh, March on the thirtieth, but nothing in June. February's was the twenty-fourth, January's the twenty-sixth, but no matter how many times she looked, no date was marked in June.

Maybe she just hadn't written it in. She'd been awfully forgetful lately. She couldn't remember what she'd had for lunch yesterday or which clients she'd talked to in the office . . . but she knew practically to the minute how long it had been since she'd waved goodbye to Sebastian in Providence. She knew how many letters he hadn't written, how many phone calls he hadn't made. She knew too well how much moping she'd done and how many tears she hadn't let herself cry.

And she knew there was worse news coming. Knew she hadn't had her period, then forgotten it. Knew she couldn't be that lucky.

She was late.

The organizer fell from her nerveless fingers, but stayed open where she'd left it, the unmarked days of June mocking her. Oh, God, no period, all the nausea and vomiting, the moodiness, the *sex . . . !* No, no, it couldn't be. Life wasn't so unkind. She couldn't possibly be pr—preg— Hell, she couldn't even *think* the word!

She wasn't the sort to panic. She would stay calm, would handle this coolly and rationally, the way she handled any crisis . . . just as soon as she remembered how to breathe again. Feeling as if her lungs might explode at any moment, she leaned forward, head down, and gasped for what few tiny breaths she could manage.

That was how Mike Scott, her senior investigator, found her a few moments later. He slowly walked around the desk, two wingtips and the cuffed legs of a pair of custom-tailored trousers appearing in her line of vision, and stood there a moment before mildly saying, "This looks like a woman thing. I'll come back later."

She dragged in the first breath of substance she'd managed and sat up. Her face was warm from the blood that had rushed to her head, and her hair tumbled wildly. "I was just—just—" Unable to think of anything that might make the least bit of sense and unwilling to offer the truth, she shrugged. "What do you need?"

"I closed all the cases I could and wrote interim reports on the ones I couldn't." He laid a stack of folders on her desk. "In another ten minutes, I'm officially outta here."

"Out? Out where? Where are you going?"

"Vacation. Remember? Sailboat? Ocean? Maine?"

She stared at him blankly. "You told me about this?"

"It's been on the schedule since January. Man, Melina, that last case with the runaway kids really knocked you for a loop, didn't it? The way you're acting, a person would think the kids are still out there in danger instead of safe at home with their mamas and daddies. Get a grip on yourself."

Her scattered mind focused on one phrase—*mamas and daddies.* She wanted kids, she really did, but she'd wanted to do it the usual way. So many of her life choices had been unconventional, and that was fine in its place, but a baby needed a father, and in *her* family, the father really needed to be married to the mother before there even was a baby or, failing that, before the baby was born.

Too late on both counts, she thought grimly. She was already pregnant—though the idea hadn't even occurred to her until a few minutes ago, she was sure of it; she could feel it in her bones—and he'd already made it clear he didn't want her.

"Melina?"

Blankly she looked at Mike, watching her with morbid curiosity. For a moment she couldn't remember why he'd come in, then she saw the file folders. Interim reports, vacation, sailboat. "Have a good time, Mike," she said, coming near the normalcy she'd aimed for. "Remember to come back."

"Sure. I'll bring you a souvenir."

"Lobster," she said with a smile that covered the queasiness that instantly stirred in her stomach. "And lots of it." She walked him to the door, closed it behind him, then made a mad dash to the bathroom.

THE HOME PREGNANCY TESTS ADVERTISED THEMSELVES as foolproof, and Melina hoped they weren't just bragging. She'd bought one box each of three different brands, for a total of four tests, and had spread them all out on the bathroom counter so she wouldn't forget Saturday morning.

As if that were possible. She'd awakened before six o'clock, instantly alert, her stomach tied in knots. Though she knew Julie wouldn't be up for several more hours and wouldn't come into her room uninvited, she'd locked the bedroom door, then the bathroom door for good measure. She'd read through the instructions she'd practically memorized the night before, then gathered the four plastic strips and gotten down to business.

Three tests strips lay discarded in the trash. Holding her breath, she willed the fourth and final strip to change symbols, change colors, to dance in her hand singing, "No, no, no"—anything besides what the other three had done.

Her breath escaped in a great groan when it did exactly what the other three had done.

Sinking to the cold marble floor, she rested her arms on her knees and hid her face. She was pregnant. She'd known it yesterday, but she'd held on to the tiniest bit of hope that she was wrong. Now she'd lost even that. She'd been right. The tests were right. Of course, she would call her doctor Monday morning and make an appointment to pee in a cup for an official verdict, but it wouldn't change.

She was pregnant.

With Sebastian's baby.

In the shadowy space between her knees and chest, she smiled thinly. All he'd wanted was a four-night stand. All she'd wanted was everything. Looked as if they'd each gotten more—or less—than they'd expected.

Pregnant! It was such a mind-blowing thought. She was a single career woman who carried a gun and often dealt with violent people. She worked long hours and traveled a lot. She liked to party—liked men and sex and fun . . . at least, she had. This little development very well might change her opinion of the opposite sex.

So there would be no more dealing with violent offenders. No more twelve- or fourteen-hour days. Fewer out-of-town trips, fewer parties, most definitely fewer men.

And that was just while she was pregnant. After the baby was born, who knew what her life would be like?

When her butt had gone numb and her toes turned blue from contact with the stone floor, she stood up, washed her hands, then started to gather the tests' packaging from the counter. She didn't get far, though, before she was leaning closer to the mirror, staring at herself. She looked sickly, and her cheeks were pudgy from an extra pound or two. She'd attributed the former to unrequited love, though now she acknowledged that puking at odd hours of the day was an even better explanation. As for the weight, she'd thought she was spending way too much time lately with Ben & Jerry. It had never crossed her mind that it might be because she'd spent too much time last month with Sebastian.

An ache tightened her chest at the thought of him. Of course she had to tell him, and she didn't look forward to it. But he—and Lynda and Ben—were the only ones she would tell. With the family—Papa, Nikos, and Stavros in particular—it would be better to keep Sebastian's identity a secret.

They couldn't kill him if they didn't know who he was.

Suddenly she was stricken by the urge to cry, to wail and weep like the star of her own Greek tragedy. Since the best shoulder to cry on in this circumstance was in Bethlehem, that was where she should be, too.

Just as quickly as the Bug could get her there.

WITH THE SUN SHINING ON HER FACE, JULIE STRETCHED and tried to roll over, but something held her in place. Restlessly she fiddled with it, then realized it was a seat belt. For an instant she was confused—weren't her days of sleeping in a car over, at least for a while?—but then she remembered. Melina had dragged her out of bed at some unearthly hour, shoved some clothes into a bag, and stuffed her into the car. They were going to Bethlehem, she'd said grimly. *Sit back and enjoy the ride.*

She'd enjoyed it, all right. They were practically there, if the sun's straight-overhead position really did mean twelve o'clock, and she'd snoozed the entire way. That was what she got for staying up until three in the morning reading.

Straightening in the seat, she looked at Melina. Her hair was held by rubber bands, and dark glasses covered half her face. For the first time since they'd met, she didn't have music blasting from the radio while she sang along. In fact, also for the first time, she looked like she wasn't enjoying the trip at all, and the speedometer hovered within a mile or two of the speed limit.

There was definitely a problem when Melina Dimitris didn't exceed the speed limit.

"Is something wrong?" Julie yelled to be heard over the rushing wind.

"Nope."

"This trip was kinda last-minute, wasn't it?"

"Yep."

After another mile or two passed, she tried again. "Are we just staying for the weekend?"

"Don't know."

"Do they know we're coming?"

"Nope."

Giving up, Julie gazed out ahead where the road curved down the mountainside into the valley where Bethlehem lay. It was silly, considering she'd only been to the town once before, but looking at it down below . . . It was like coming home.

When they got into town, Melina drove straight to Alanna's house. Julie looked from the house to her. "I take it I'm getting out here?"

"Didn't you want to see Alanna?"

"Sure. I'm not complaining. I just— If you need to talk, I'd be happy to listen."

Finally Melina smiled. It was supposed to be reassuring, but Julie thought it just looked sad. "Thanks for the offer, but I'm fine. Have fun with Alanna. You can give me a call at Lynda's or on my cell phone if you need anything. I'll wait to make sure someone's home."

As Julie was getting out of the car, the screen door slammed, then Alanna came running across the yard. "Hey, Julie!" She skidded to a stop, then grinned. "I like your hair! You're so pretty!"

Self-consciously Julie touched her hair, then shrugged. "Thanks. Listen, do your aunt and uncle mind if I spend a little time with you?"

"Of course not. Come on."

With a wave to Melina, Julie followed the kid inside for a tour of the house. After talking for a while with her aunt and uncle, they wound up on the porch swing out front.

"We got a letter from my mom," Alanna said after a minute. "She's in San Francisco."

"So we were only three thousand miles short of finding her."

"Yeah. I wrote her back and told her about meeting *him,* and she called. She said he *is* my father, but I don't have to have anything to do with him if I don't want to, and I don't."

"Why not?"

"Because—" She looked like no one had asked her that before. "Because he's a bad father."

"You don't know that."

"He didn't want to be my dad back then, so he doesn't get to be now."

"Payback, huh?" Julie tucked one foot under her, but left the other on the floor to keep the swing moving. It would be a hot day if they were actually doing anything, but it was just about perfect for sitting on a swing in the shade and talking.

"What do you mean?" Alanna asked with a scowl.

"You're punishing him for what he did back then.

Maybe it makes you feel better right now, but in the long run, you're punishing yourself as well as him. You're keeping him from knowing what it's like to have you for a daughter, but you'll never know what it's like to have him for a father—and he could be a real good father."

"That's dumb."

Julie laughed. "I thought so, too, when my dad said it to me. I always hoped he and my mom would get married again, you see, so when she told us she was marrying my stepfather, I was kind of a brat about it. I was real hateful to him, and I never wanted to listen to him or include him in anything. Finally my dad told me even if my stepfather wasn't around, he and Mom were never gonna get back together. He said I had to give my stepfather a chance to be a second father to me, and I had to take the chance to be a daughter to him."

"But your stepdad didn't want you. He made your mom throw you out."

"Yeah," Julie agreed, smiling in spite of the old ache deep inside. "Dad was wrong. But I never would have known if I hadn't tried, and I'm glad I did. When they threw me out, I didn't have to wonder whether it was my own fault for being hateful. I knew I'd done everything I could, and that made it not hurt so bad."

Alanna stared at her a moment, then shook her head. "I don't care, and I never will." *So there,* she might as well have added.

Instead of pushing it, Julie changed the subject. "How's Caleb?"

Alanna's face turned pink. "He's okay. We both got grounded for running away."

"You should have."

"Yeah, we get grounded, and you get a new job."

"But I didn't run away. I *took care* of the runaways until they came home."

"I wish you would stay here. You'd like Bethlehem a lot. You could get a job, if you wanted, and go to school and have lots of friends and"—Alanna's voice became as wheedling as her smile—"and have me for sort of a sister if you'd just stay here."

"Oh, gee, how can I pass that up?" Julie teased, then went on. "No, you can't ask your aunt and uncle to let me live with them. They've got enough to take care of with the four of you."

"Miss Agatha always says the more, the merrier."

Before Julie could retort that she couldn't ask Miss Agatha, either, the screen door swung open and Alanna's uncle came out, ducking so the little boy on his shoulders would clear the frame. He was tall, real cute for an older guy, and nice, like he really did like people, even kids. But he wasn't as cute as Alanna's real dad, loyalty to Melina and her friends forced her to admit.

"Hey, guys, it's lunchtime. Load up in one of the cars and let's get some food."

"We always have lunch at Harry's on Saturday," Alanna explained as she led the way to his truck. "We'll ride with Uncle Nathan 'cause the boys always go with Aunt Emilie."

As soon as everyone was buckled in, they drove downtown to the crowded restaurant. Caleb and his whole family were already there, plus Alanna's best friends, Susan and Mai, and Mai's mother, and some others. It was like a big party for no reason, one they had every Saturday, and everyone made her feel like she belonged. It would be so cool to live in a place where people did things like that just for fun. Back home in Ohio, they'd celebrated birthdays and holidays and stuff, but she couldn't remember ever having a party just because it was Saturday.

Before lunch was over, Julie had to agree with Alanna about one thing. She did like Bethlehem.

And she wished she could stay there, too.

Chapter Twelve

INSTEAD OF GOING FROM THE BISHOP HOUSE TO Lynda's, Melina found herself driving around town. She passed City Park, where a bunch of mothers sat on benches talking while their kids played. A few blocks down the street, she saw two men, jogging through the neighborhood with babies in strollers. When she parked her car near the square and got out to walk away her blues, the first shop she passed was filled with kids' clothing, baby furniture, and toys.

It seemed fate was conspiring to keep her dilemma uppermost in her mind. She wanted to raise her face to the sky and shout out that she didn't need any damn reminders. She hadn't forgotten for one second of the twenty-two hours or so since yesterday's call from Lynda.

Bethlehem was a great town for walking. It was safer in the middle of the night than most cities were at high noon. The sidewalks were in good repair, and most drivers were more than happy to let pedestrians cross the street without trying to run them down. The place was almost too damn good to be believed.

But she'd been coming long enough to believe it. Before Lynda had moved there, she'd been only vaguely aware that the town existed. Since Lyn's move, Melina had been a regular visitor and had, on occasion, even found herself envying her friend. Smog, rush-hour traffic, high crime rate—not in Bethlehem. Road rage—only from an out-of-towner. With good schools, friendly neighbors, and a real sense of community, the town was a great place for families.

And in about eight months, Melina was going to have a family.

Her parents would be thrilled, once they got over the fact that there wouldn't be a wedding. Yaya Rosa loved both Melina and babies so much that she probably wouldn't care about the absence of a father. Cousin Antonia would smirk and whisper about Melina's wild ways, but the only ones who paid her any mind were idiots just like her, and she would *never* say anything to or about the baby or Melina would kick her ass. It had been a few years, but she'd done it before and she would have no qualms about doing it again.

Sebastian wouldn't be thrilled. Beyond that, she didn't have a clue how he *would* feel. True, he adored Chrissy, but he'd also adored her mother. He'd wanted to spend his entire life with Diana, when all he'd wanted to spend with Melina was four nights.

Maybe he wouldn't even want to acknowledge her child—in which case, she would kick his ass, too. Maybe he would grudgingly play dad on weekends and for a week in summer. Hell, maybe he wouldn't let his feelings for her get in the way and would actually be a good father.

She wouldn't know until she told him, and she couldn't begin to imagine how she would do that.

After covering a fair portion of Bethlehem on foot, she wound up back in front of the kids' store, gazing in the display window.

Before long she would need one of those cribs, and maybe a cradle for taking the baby to work with her. And one of those playpens that looked like nothing so much as a soft-sided cage. A high chair, a stroller, and one of those carrier things for taking the kid shopping or into restaurants. Plus a child-safety seat and a new car to put it in. She loved her Bug but no way was she going to transport her baby in it.

And a new place to live. Her apartment was only two bedrooms, and right now those rooms were taken. Even if she'd found a home for Julie by then, she would still need another room for a guest room.

Made weary by the thought of so much to do, she crossed the street to the square in a daze and sank down on the first park bench she came to. Time passed by unnoticed, until finally the object her gaze had fixed on slowly came into focus. It was a small wooden sign, gaily painted, that read For Rent. It stood in a patch of neatly tended lawn and referred to the house behind it.

The house was two stories tall and of no particular style. It was painted the palest of yellows, with shutters in dark green and a heavily carved wooden door. The porch was wide and deep, and every picket on the white fence across the front featured a heart-shaped cutout.

It was easy to imagine the family a hundred and fifty

years ago who'd decided to build their home right smack in the center of town. He had probably been a businessman, owner of the local mercantile or possibly president of the bank down the block. She had stayed home, of course, overseeing the servants who ran the household and raising the children who'd played in the lush side yard. She had probably been responsible for the heart cutouts on the fence, since that was such a—

"There you are!" Lynda sat down at the opposite end of the bench, blocking Melina's view of the house and interrupting her fantasy. Leaning forward, she hugged Melina tightly, then sat back. "You look like hell. You really are sick, aren't you?"

Melina smiled faintly. She hadn't been queasy all day, not even before she'd looked at that first positive test strip. It was as if now that the kid had gotten her attention, it—he—no, *she* was more than happy to settle down. "How'd you know I was in town?"

"Julie called. Said you were supposed to come to my house after you dropped her off at Alanna's, but when they left Harry's after lunch, she saw you sitting here looking lost. She was worried." Lynda's voice softened. "Frankly, Lina, so am I. I've never seen you like this. What's wrong?"

Melina supposed there were ways to ease into the announcement she had to make. She didn't feel like figuring them out. "I'm pregnant."

Lynda's smile was rare, one that involved every one of her features. "Oh, my gosh! Melina, that's wonder—Oh."

"Please don't say 'Oh.' Just say 'It's wonderful, great news, aren't you excited.' I've been saying enough 'Oh' for all of us."

"It is wonderful. It wasn't so long ago you were talking about how much you wanted kids, and look—you're *pregnant*! From your mouth to God's ear, as my mother would say."

"Yeah, well, God missed the part of the request involving a husband."

"Are you going to tell Sebastian?"

"Of course. How could I not?" He might be happier not knowing, but it wasn't her decision to make. He was as responsible as she was, and even if he chose to do nothing, he had a right to know. "Can you believe it, Lyn? *Me,* pregnant. You know what my nickname was in high school? Everready, because I was always prepared. I bought my first box of condoms when I was sixteen. I've probably bought more rubbers than most men because I liked sex and I wasn't going to trust some guy to protect me and I wasn't going to get pregnant until I was married and it was time. And here I am."

"I take it you're saying you and Sebastian used a condom every time. So . . . guess what, darlin'?" Lynda smiled gently. "It's time."

Panic welled inside Melina. "But I'm not ready!"

"Honey, this baby got here against the odds. By the time she puts in an appearance, you'll *be* ready." Then Lynda grinned. "You'd better be, because with that kind of determination, I suspect she's going to be a dark-eyed, curly-haired hellion just like her mother."

The image her words created made Melina feel all soft and funny inside. She needed to start thinking about names and doctors and what kind of birthing experience she wanted for her child. And there was the question of godparents—Lynda, of course, and Ben and Nikos and

Stavros. And of course Sebastian had family, too—a sister and three brothers who might want to play some role in their niece's or nephew's life even if he didn't.

"You've got that panicked look again."

Melina grasped Lynda's hand. "Promise me one thing. Have your wedding before I get fat. Wearing a bridesmaid's dress is bad enough, but wearing a fat bridesmaid's dress is out of the question."

Lynda laughed. "It's a deal. Now . . . come on. Let's go home before Ben comes out looking for both of us."

Melina let her pull her to her feet, but instead of heading for her car, she walked to the side of the square nearest the house. She was scribbling the phone number on the wooden sign in her checkbook when Lynda asked, "What's that for?"

She looked at the house again, her gaze starting at the shake shingles and ending at the heart cutouts in the picket fence, and then she looked at Lynda. "I have to buy so many things for the baby—clothes, diapers, pacifiers, a pony, a bike, cuddly things to sleep with. But first I'm getting that." She gestured toward the house, then turned and headed for her car.

DADDY, CAN I GO TO GRANDMA'S?"

Sebastian didn't look up from the door he was carving. The pattern was complicated and a more difficult design than he would choose on his own, but it wasn't his own. He was matching a door for a client in Albany who was restoring a two-hundred-year-old house, so he was giving it more than his usual care. "It's Tuesday. Isn't that Grandma's bridge day?"

"Grandma's not a bridge," she replied with a giggle.

"Maybe she's volunteering at the hospital."

"Nope, she's not. She's home all by herself 'cause Grandpa's gone fishing—and without me," she said in her most serious can-you-believe-it? voice. "And she's got cookie dough that needs baking. It's your favorite—oatmeal raisin."

"Oatmeal raisin is *your* favorite."

"Oh. Yeah. Can I go anyway? Please?"

"What if I've got plans this afternoon?" Plans to work—hard. It was the only thing that kept his mind from wandering too far away.

"All you're doing is working on an ugly door. It can wait while you take me to Grandma's. She said so."

"She did, huh? And what if I said your going over there could wait until I finished?"

"Daaaaddy. You been working on that door forever. You're never gonna be finished." She threw her hands up in the air, then settled them on her hips in an imitation of his mother. "This is the most boring summer I've ever had. *Pleeeaase* let me go to Grandmaaaa's."

He glanced at Ben in the far corner of the workshop, lucky enough to be wearing protective ear gear and using the belt sander, then at Sophy, who was doing a final sanding on a set of cabinet doors. She smiled at Chrissy's antics and lifted one shoulder in a shrug. "There's not much worse when you're seven years old than being bored, is there, Chrissy? Besides, it would do you good to get out."

Sebastian scowled at her. "I get out."

"In daylight? You're in here by sunup and you stay until sundown. It's not healthy."

"It's not my fault I have a lot of work to do."

"No one else is accepting all those jobs. If you're not

to blame, then who is?" she retorted good-naturedly. "Go on. Take the child to see her grandmother. Ben and I can take care of things here."

Chrissy was standing on his feet and hanging on to his middle, swinging back and forth and giving him her sweetest smile. "Please? Pretty please? With a cherry on top?"

"Okay." What could he say? He was a sucker for females with big eyes and curls . . . of any age.

"Oh, boy! See ya, Sophy!" Chrissy raced out of the converted barn, grabbed her backpack where it hung on a fence post, and headed for his truck.

"Whoa, kiddo. What's in the pack?"

She turned on another charming smile. "Just my stuffed cat. And some clean clothes in case these get dirty."

"And?"

"And some pajamas. In case Grandma needs me to spend the night."

"I don't know . . ."

She placed her hand in his and looked up at him, all serious. "Daddy, it's been a long time. I haven't spent the night with Grandma or Aunt Shauna or Gracie or anyone ever since we got back from looking for Mama. I won't runned off again. Cross my heart, hope to die, stick a needle in my eye."

Frowning at her rhyme, he said stiffly, "We'll see." Maybe it had been a long time—coming up on six weeks—but he wasn't ready to spend an entire night with her anywhere but down the hall. He wasn't sure he ever would be.

She chattered all the way into town—too much silence was never a problem with Chrissy. Once they reached his parents' house, he pulled into the drive and she leaned over and honked the horn.

"Hey, don't do that."

"This way Grandma will come out and you can go straight back home to your ugly old door. B'sides, I like honking the horn." She did it again for good measure.

His mother appeared on the porch, apron around her waist and a spot of flour on her nose. "Come on in, son," she called. "I've got fresh cookies, bread just out of the oven, and some roast beef left over from last night's dinner. I'll fix you the best sandwich you ever had."

"Thanks, Mom, but I've already eaten. You sure you want this little squirt for a whole afternoon?"

"And a whole night, too." His reluctance must have shown on his face, because she came down the steps. "I know how you feel, Sebastian, but you can't lock her up till she's grown."

"Why not?" he asked with a scowl.

"Because it's illegal. Your dad's gone fishing with the judge at his cabin up at the lake, and they won't be back until tomorrow evening, so it'll be just Chrissy and me. I promise, she won't even burp without my knowing it."

With a grin, Chrissy inhaled a deep breath, swallowed, then burped loudly. "How's that, Grandma?"

"Pretty good. But you're not supposed to do it in front of your daddy, remember?"

Sebastian frowned mildly. "You should be ashamed of yourself, teaching your grandkids to burp. Do you know how many times they've gotten in trouble because of you? And no one ever believes you taught them."

Hildy simply smiled, then returned to the question at hand. "Let her stay. I'll protect her with my life. And then, since you'll have the evening free, maybe you could do something fun, like go out on a date. I hear Leanne Wilson is available."

Yeah, fresh from an affair with a married man. Not that he blamed her for it. She was lonely and didn't get many chances to meet available men in the kids' clothing shop she owned, and the guy had been too practiced at hiding the wedding ring when he was out of town on business trips. Rat bastard.

For a moment he went still, thinking of the times Melina had used that phrase, remembering the time she'd called *him* that, and for that moment, the pain was intense. Gradually, though, it eased to a dull ache that never quite went away, even if he did manage to forget it at times.

"Please, Daddy," Chrissy said, then she and Hildy sang in unison, "Please, please, pleeeaase!"

"All right," he said grudgingly, and Chrissy gave him a sloppy kiss before diving out the window into her grandmother's arms.

"See ya, Daddy!" she called, waving as he backed into the street. "I'll call you tonight!"

His real concern, he admitted as he drove through town, wasn't Chrissy's safety. His mother *would* protect her with her life. He had no doubt about that. It was being alone. Having an entire evening in the house by himself. Too much time to think. To remember. To regret.

Maybe he *should* ask Leanne out—not on a date, but just to dinner. Two friends with nothing better to do, commiserating over their rotten luck in love. She could bring her little boy, so if they ran out of things to talk about, they could at least talk to him.

That decided, he turned at the square, intending to go halfway around the block to her shop and ask before he changed his mind. But getting around the block was easier said than done. A delivery van from a local furniture store was parked in the street, behind a van from an office supply store in Howland. The For Rent sign was gone from the yard in front of the Caldwell house, and three teams of men were carrying merchandise through the gate and inside while a tall, slender woman with wild black curls supervised from the porch. His gaze slid over her as he drove slowly past, then jerked back in stunned surprise. She looked enough like—

With the shriek of crumpling metal, the truck shuddered to a stop, throwing Sebastian forward until the seat belt caught. He blinked, looked at the car ahead, and came to the dazed realization that he was stopped because he'd rear-ended it. It took another moment for the black-and-white paint scheme and the light bar on the roof to register. Even then, all he could think about was the woman on the porch.

Looking over his shoulder, he saw that she was gone, presumably inside the house. Because she was a newcomer to Bethlehem who had a thousand things to do to settle in? Or because it *was* Melina and she had no desire to see—or be seen by—him?

Sheriff Ingles opened Sebastian's door. "You okay, son?"

Okay? Other than being numb all the way through, why wouldn't he be okay? Then he remembered the accident and nodded. "Yeah . . . I'm fine."

"You know, I've been driving that vehicle ever since I became sheriff of this county. The department budget being what it is, I'd kinda hoped to drive it a few more years." The sheriff took off his hat and wiped his forehead. "Might as well go ahead and get out your license, registration, and proof of insurance. One of Mitch's boys will be over here in a minute to take a report."

Sebastian removed his wallet from his hip pocket, added the registration and insurance card, and pressed it all into the sheriff's hands, then started away.

"Hey, son, where are you going? You gotta stay here and talk to the officer. *Sebastian—*"

Ignoring the sheriff's call and the curious looks from the deliverymen, he walked through the gate, took the steps three at a time, and went inside the house. Instinct led him through a large arched entry into what had once been a formal parlor but for years had served as office space, where uncertainty brought him to a sudden stop.

She sat behind a large desk, looking like a queen in the massive leather chair. Her spine was straight, her chin held high, and her mood was impossible to gauge. So cool. So dispassionate.

He wanted to wrap his arms around her, kiss her senseless, then carry her upstairs to try out the bed that was making its way up a piece at a time. To get down on his knees and beg her to give them another chance. To be cordial, polite, like the friends they'd never been.

Nah, he was right the first time. He wanted to hold her, kiss her, make love to her. For about fifty years, until the fever in his blood cooled to a manageable pitch.

"Hello, Sebastian."

Obviously she was opting for cordial and polite. What would she do if he kissed her anyway? If he showed her how damn much he'd missed her? If he curled her toes and uncurled her hair and foolishly, shamelessly, pleaded for whatever she might want to give him?

He didn't have the courage to find out.

"Melina." He managed to sound as cool as she did,

even though he was burning inside. "You rented this place?"

"That was my intent, but the woman made me an offer I couldn't refuse. It's mine, or will be Friday."

"You're going to live here?"

"For a time."

"And work here?"

Hands raised palms up to indicate the room, she shrugged.

"Why?"

It was the wrong question to ask. Her gaze chilled a few degrees and a nerve twitched in her jaw. "It's a free country. I can go wherever I want. But don't worry. I spent a lot of time in Bethlehem without ever laying eyes on you until a few months ago. Now that you know where I am, we won't ever have to have contact with each other except for the occasional accidental sighting."

"I didn't—"

Loud footsteps sounded in the hall behind him, then a uniformed cop came in, followed by the sheriff. "There you are," Ingles said. "Thought we were gonna have to put out an APB on you."

His gaze shifted to Melina, who chose that moment to stand up and come around the desk. She wore a sleeveless black dress that fitted like a second skin and revealed practically every inch of her incredible legs. With her heels, she was six feet of beautiful, sexy, willowy woman who made Sebastian's blood boil and left all three men speechless.

"Sheriff, I'm Melina Dimitris. We met in June on the missing children case. I'm not officially opening an office of Dimitris Investigations here in Bethlehem, but I will be working out of this office while I'm living here. If there's anything I can ever help you with, please don't hesitate to let me know."

After a moment, Ingles recovered enough to take the hand she offered. With a sly wink at Sebastian, he elbowed the cop in the ribs. "At least now we know the cause of the accident. Driving under the influence of a beautiful woman."

She smiled coolly. "Would you like to use my office to take your report? I'd be happy to turn it over to you."

When she strolled past, Sebastian caught a whiff of the elusive fragrance of her cologne and remembered how damn erotic it smelled when it was all she wore. His fingers remembered the hot silky texture of her skin, and his body recalled the hot, tight feel of her body clenching his, and suddenly he was having trouble breathing. His lungs were too tight, the air too heavy.

When he would have followed her to the back of the house, Sheriff Ingles stopped him. "It was mighty considerate of you to have your accident in front of the police station so James here wouldn't have to go far to investigate, but it's a bit on the rude side to make him go chasing you all over creation. Report first. Then you can go talk to your girlfriend."

Sebastian watched the door at the end of the hallway close, then wiped his hand over his forehead. Oh, man. He was about to spontaneously combust right there in Melina's office, and he hadn't even touched her yet. How in hell was he going to survive this move—*any* move—of hers?

MELINA BENT OVER THE KITCHEN COUNTER, RESTING her forehead on the cool granite, and worked at remembering how to breathe again. Maybe buying this house and living in this town hadn't been such a great idea. No matter that Lynda was so excited she could hardly stand it, or that Julie hadn't stopped smiling since Melina had told her. Forget that the house couldn't be more perfect if she'd built it herself, or that the idea of living on the square in a lovely little town suited her Melina-as-doting-mother image to a T.

The only way this could possibly work was if Sebastian cooperated and kept his distance . . . or fell in love with her. And, gee, since she didn't think the latter was ever going to happen, she'd damn well better pray for the former, or start packing up to head back to Buffalo.

Thankfully, the door from the hall into the kitchen creaked and gave her enough warning to stand up so straight her back ached. She pretended she'd been gazing out the window, watching Julie and Miss Corinna at work in the backyard.

Summoning her best unaffected smile, she glanced over her shoulder long enough to see that Sebastian stood a few feet inside the door. Then she looked out the window again. "Miss Corinna brought over a basket of 'thinnings.' I assume that's some sort of plants. At least, she and Julie seem to be planting them."

For a moment he remained so still that she might wonder if he'd left again if she couldn't *feel* his presence. Then finally he spoke. "Did you get our card?"

She swallowed a snort. If she counted all the letters he hadn't written, then she also had to acknowledge the card he had sent but shouldn't have. It was nothing—less than nothing. A store-bought thank-you card on which he hadn't even signed his name. His daughter had painstakingly penciled in the only personalization—*Thank you. Chrissy Knight and S. Knight*. Melina hadn't known whether she didn't know how to spell Sebastian or if she'd feared running out of space. As it was, the *ht* on *Knight* had run onto the back.

Maybe she would send *him* an impersonal, stranger-to-stranger card in eight months. *Congratulations! You're a father!* Then, if he protested, she could say "But didn't you get our card?"

She turned to face him, leaning against the counter in what she hoped was a casual pose. As long as he didn't guess she needed the support to give her weak knees some strength. . . . "Yes, I got your card. Such an effusive, heartwarming expression of thanks."

His eyes narrowed. "I tried to thank you at the motel in Providence, but you wouldn't let me."

Oh, yeah, he'd wanted to thank her . . . but he couldn't look her in the eye. He couldn't bring himself to touch her. "I didn't do it for your thanks."

"I know. You didn't do it for me at all. You told me." He warily circled the island, keeping the expanse of stone between them. "How long are you planning to stay here?"

"I don't know."

"A few months? A year? Forever?"

"I don't know," she repeated. "It's a simple answer. Maybe you can get your daughter to explain it to you when you get home." Then . . . "Does it matter?"

He opened his mouth twice, then closed it again. The second time he turned and walked out. The kitchen door creaked behind him, his boots echoed loudly in the hall, and then it was quiet.

Melina stood motionless a long time, then abruptly began rummaging through cabinets. She came up with what she wanted—a bottle of very expensive and very smooth sippin' whiskey—then, remembering, she returned it to its place. Instead she filled a glass with tap water and tossed it back.

"Well . . . I think that went well." Her voice sounded small in the empty kitchen. Okay, so maybe she should have made nice. And maybe she should have found some way to tell him about the baby right up front. When he'd asked why she'd moved there . . . it was the perfect opportunity. When he'd asked how long she was planning to stay . . . also a good chance.

But, still, it went okay. She didn't throw herself at him again. Didn't offer herself as a plaything to use however he wanted before discarding. Didn't pathetically beg for his affection.

It could have gone better. But it had been okay.

FOR A FIRST-TIME-SEEING-HER-AGAIN MEETING, IT had gone okay, Sebastian thought as he checked his truck. At least she hadn't bitten or kicked him, tried to unman him, or threatened him with her weapon. It was a start.

Though Lloyd from the garage was hooking up the sheriff's car to his wrecker, there wasn't much visible damage to Sebastian's truck. The bumper was dented and scraped, the grille broken, and one headlight would have to be replaced. He would take it in and have Lloyd look at it later, but at the moment, if it was drivable, he intended to drive.

The ticket the cop had given him crinkled in his pocket as he settled in the seat. He returned the sheriff's wave, ignored his call to watch out for beautiful women, and drove around the block. As he drove back along the other side of the square, though, he couldn't resist looking across at the Caldwell house. He couldn't help staring long and hard at Melina, standing on the porch again, hands resting on the railing.

He made the drive back home in record time, parking in front of the barn, where Ben and Sophy were taking their break in the shade of a tall maple. Holding a Coke in one hand, Ben walked over to examine the front end of the truck as Sebastian got out.

"You have a little run-in with an immovable object?"

"Yeah. The sheriff's car."

Ben winced.

"Why didn't you tell me?"

"Tell you what? That the sheriff was going to be out and about today?"

"That Melina had moved to Bethlehem."

Ben didn't bother to lie. The guilty look on his face wouldn't have let him get away with it, anyway. He glanced at Sophy—who, judging from her expression, had also known—then shrugged. "I figured you would find out soon enough. It's not like you two ever really were together or anything . . . except for those few days."

It was true, Sebastian acknowledged. They hadn't had even one real date. She'd picked him up in a bar, and they'd taken it from there. He'd used the occasion of their first date to clumsily end the affair by standing her up. But he'd gotten more involved with her than with any woman he'd ever officially dated, and he would like to get even more so . . . if they could just manage to carry on a civil conversation.

"If you hadn't found out on your own sooner or later, I would have told you," Ben said. "Did you see her?"

"Yeah."

He glanced at the truck's crumpled bumper. "Were you driving at the time?"

"Yeah."

There was a choked sound from Sophy, still sitting in the shade in an Adirondack chair Sebastian had made years earlier. He scowled at her and saw that she was trying to hold back a laugh. In spite of her efforts, the giggle burst free.

"I'm sorry," she said, though she clearly wasn't. "I was just thinking that it takes quite a woman to stop traffic. What did they cite as the cause of the accident—driving under the influence of a beautiful woman?"

Now Ben was smirking, too, but Sebastian just stared at her in annoyance. "How did you know— Never mind." Looked as if Bethlehem's grapevine was in top form today. He could just imagine Sheriff Ingles on the phone, saying with a hearty laugh, *And I said to young James, Well, at least now we know the cause of the accident. . . .* "Maybe you can sit around all afternoon, but I've got work to do."

They followed him into the shop, still in good spirits. Most likely everyone in town was in good spirits over the circumstances of his accident. Funny thing was, he didn't even care. The gossip when Diana had left had frustrated and shamed him, but he didn't give a damn what anyone was saying at the moment.

Except Melina.

It took a tremendous effort, but he was finally able to put her out of his mind and concentrate on work. He hardly noticed when Ben and Sophy called it quits at five o'clock, and he paid little attention to the setting sun. He ignored the aches in his back, shoulders, and arms the best he could, but when his fingers began to throb from gripping the chisel too long, he straightened, stretched . . . and saw her.

She was standing in the doorway, black hair and dress, bronzed skin, as dark as the night. Judging from the way she leaned against the jamb, she'd been there a while, just watching him. The thought made him swallow hard.

"Hi." It was all he could think of, all he trusted himself to say.

"Hi." She came farther into the room, not stopping until only the width of the old door separated them. She looked from it to the original, leaning against the wall, then ran her fingers lightly over a section of carving. "I saw Chrissy at the ice-cream shop with your mother, so I thought this might be a good time to . . . to talk to you."

She had come to the workshop one evening before, and they'd ended up making love against the wall. He didn't think that was what she had in mind tonight, and regretted it.

"Beautiful piece," she said, her attention on the door again. "But don't they make some kind of tool that will do all this carving in no time?"

"Sure. But then you can't say it's hand-carved. Besides . . ." Thinking of what they'd done that other night in there, and how long had it had taken, he huskily added, "Faster's not always better."

Her cheeks turned a faint rose, giving him a sense of bittersweet satisfaction.

When she spoke again, her voice was husky, too. "Do you prefer this part of the job over actually making the pieces?"

"I've made enough cabinets for every house in a fifty-mile radius. The construction's easy. Mindless. Carving and inlay are as much art as craft. It's more satisfying to say 'I made this' "—he gestured to an inlaid tabletop he'd finished a few weeks earlier—"than it is to say 'I made that.' " He bent his head toward the far wall, where stacks of cabinets were lined up awaiting pickup.

She nodded, then gazed around the room. She was restless this evening. Even when she stood still, she wasn't still. Her fingers were stroking the wood or she was shifting her weight from foot to foot. What did she want to say that made her so nervous? *Don't bother me again? Stay away from me, stay away from my house?*

The certainty that it was something along those lines made the muscles in his gut clench and led him to grasp for a delay. "Would you like something to drink?" The refrigerator in the corner was well stocked with soft drinks, water, and beer. He figured he'd be able to use a beer in another minute or two, and he'd rather not drink alone.

"No. No, thanks." She looked down at her hands as if she didn't know what to do with them, then clasped them tightly. Her red nails presented a vivid contrast against the black of her dress. "First . . . I didn't come here to ask anything of you. I make plenty of money. I've got lots of family and friends. I don't need anything else. I just think . . . well, some things are too important to keep secret. It doesn't change anything. I don't expect anything to be different. It's just . . . well, in the interests of full disclosure . . ."

"Full disclosure," he repeated. "Are you suing me or something?"

"Oh, no. Of course not. I'm not asking for anything, and I'm willing to be reasonable, so there's no need for legal action."

"I hear your words, but I don't have a clue what you're talking about," he said wryly.

She blinked, then frowned. "Oh, yes . . . well . . . that's next. I know this wasn't part of the plan. I mean, sure, I wanted it someday but not quite yet, but . . . It's a bit late to be thinking about that. But you know, nothing's a hundred percent foolproof—except, apparently, home pregnancy tests—but certainly not condoms. I mean, yeah, they run a two percent failure rate, but look at the odds. We have to be having sex *and* the condom has to fail at exactly the right time of the month, and considering how few times I've had sex in the past six months, it never should have happened, but—"

Sebastian felt as if his face had gone as pale as the white walls around them. He stared at her—tried to speak but couldn't find his voice for a time. Finally, a choked, panicked sound sputtered out. "Y-y-you're p-p-pregnant?"

Clamping her jaw shut, she nodded.

"And you're—you're sure it's *m-my* baby?"

A wounded look came into her eyes, and she whirled around and headed for the door.

"Melina, wait!" Instead of wasting time going around the long worktable, he slid across the top, then raced after her. He caught up with her ten feet from the car, catching her arm to stop her from escaping.

Her cheeks wet with tears, she smacked him on the chest with one fist. "You think I'm so damn easy that I don't even know who the father of my baby is?"

"No, of course not! I'm just so—"

"Skeptical?"

He caught her hand before she could land another blow, then pulled her in close, holding her securely where she could neither hit nor kick. "Surprised, Melina. I'm incredibly surprised."

Her bottom lip stuck out in a pout. "If it'll make you feel better, you can have a DNA test done after the baby's born to prove paternity."

"I don't need proof. I believe you. I swear." Grateful for the light mounted above the barn door that shone on her face, he gazed down at her, searching her face for some emotion besides distress, some evidence of how she felt about this surprise. It was difficult to tell when she was still pouting, still—for whatever reason—nervous. "When? When is the baby due?"

"Sometime in March."

"Chrissy was born in March. The twenty-first. Springtime." He grinned. He couldn't help it. "Wonder what she'll think of a new baby brother or sister for a birthday present. She used to ask for one all the time, as if I could go out and buy one the same way I bought her puppy. She'll be excited."

An oddly uncomfortable look came across Melina's face. "I doubt it'll make much difference to her," she said flatly. "It doesn't have to make a difference to anyone."

A baby not make a difference? Impossible. He and Diana had been married eight years before she'd agreed to have Chrissy, and she hadn't been open to even the discussion of a second one for three years after that. He'd waited a long, long time for another child, and it was going to make all the difference in the world in his life—in Melina's life, too. And since Chrissy would be part of their family . . .

Almost as if she'd read his mind, she stonily went on. "I told you, I'm not asking for anything. No money, no name, no support."

It took a moment for the meaning of her words to sink in. Stunned, he slowly released her, then took a step back, followed by another. "No name— You're planning to raise my baby alone?"

"I'm a single woman. That's what single women do."

In that instant his heart felt emptier than his arms. She didn't want him around. Didn't want him to be a part of their child's life. Didn't want a damn thing from him. "But this is *my* baby," he said numbly.

So? She didn't say the word aloud, but her shrug did. As far as she was concerned, he'd done his part. He'd provided the sperm, and now the rest was all hers. She expected him to walk away from her and his baby, to turn his back on his son or daughter, to deny Chrissy the chance to know her brother or sister, because it was what *she* wanted.

She really did think he was a rat bastard.

"No," he said.

The look of surprise on Melina's face would have been comical if the subject hadn't been so damn serious. "What do you mean, no?"

"Maybe you're willing to be reasonable, but I'm not. You're not throwing me out of my kid's life because it suits you."

She stared at him in dismay. "Look, I didn't *have* to tell you—"

"Then maybe you shouldn't have. But it's too late for second thoughts, isn't it?" He dragged his fingers through his hair. "I'm not going to be dismissed like some employee whose services you no longer need. This is *our* baby—not mine alone, certainly not yours to own. I fully intend to be an everyday part of her life whether you like it or not."

"And what if I move back to Buffalo?" she demanded sarcastically.

"I can do carpentry anywhere."

His words seemed to rob her of arguments for a moment; then she found her second wind. "I don't need you!"

He rubbed the tight, hurtful feeling centered in his chest. "No, you don't," he murmured. "You've made that clear. But kids need both parents, and you know it. You're not God, Melina. You can't keep me away from my own kid."

"I could make her hate you!" she hissed, venom in her eyes and her voice.

The pain shifted from his chest to his throat and made it impossible to swallow. "I'm sure you could. And I could sue you for custody. Who do you think the court would consider a better parent? The father who's lived in the same place his entire life, who has a stable home environment, another child he's raised, and works reasonable hours? Or the mother who carries a gun, works a dangerous job, has little experience with children, reacts with physical violence when provoked, and goes home with strangers she picks up in bars?"

She stared at him a long time, her gaze scorching. "I was wrong about you. You don't deserve a damn thing from me." She stalked to her car, then looked back. "Do me a favor, Sebastian—forget you ever knew me. Because I'm damn well going to forget you."

Her tires threw up a spray of gravel as she backed around his truck, then gunned the engine. Once the taillights had disappeared from sight, he raised his gaze to the heavens. "Okay, God, anything else up your sleeve? You wanna bring Diana home now? Maybe infest my workshop with a plague of termites? How about having Melina shoot me where I stand? Or would that be too easy for you?"

The only reply he got was a twinkling of brilliant stars.

"Poor Sebastian," Sophy said with a sigh.

"Poor Marina," Gloria disagreed.

"Poor *Melina*? This is all her fault."

"She's only reacting badly because he broke her heart."

"Well, he only broke her heart because he was afraid."

"But to threaten to sue for custody of their little girl—!" Gloria said disapprovingly.

"Oh, Sebastian would never try to take the baby from her mother, just like Melina would never try to keep him from being a father to her." Sophy had known them both long enough to know that for fact. Of course, she'd been doing this job long enough to know that when it came to love, fear, insecurity, and pride could be terrible hindrances.

"I fear we've got our work cut out for us this time," Gloria said, her sigh rustling like wind through the trees.

Sophy looked at her then and grinned broadly. "You say that every time."

"And isn't it true?"

It was. Humans were stubborn, hardheaded, and always thought they knew best. And Sebastian and Melina's relationship hadn't run smoothly from the start. They had a lot to overcome, but they had good reasons to overcome it.

They just needed a little help.

Chapter Thirteen

THE FLOWERS WERE ON THE FRONT PORCH WHEN Melina went outside Wednesday morning—a simple bouquet of daisies, carnations, baby's breath, and a few varieties she didn't know. They spilled out of a glass vase tucked inside a rusty metal pail, and they'd been dropped off recently enough that the water spilled on the steps hadn't yet evaporated. Part of her thought they were lovely and rustically charming and would look wonderful in the bay window in her office. Part of her eyed them suspiciously as if the original evil serpent might come crawling out.

"How pretty." Julie slipped past Melina and picked up the bucket. "No card. I wonder who it could be from. Let's see . . ." She tapped one finger against her chin. "Which one of us could possibly have an admirer who would bring us flowers anonymously? Hmm . . . I don't believe it's me, so that means it must be *you.*"

"It's too early in the morning to be so damn cheerful," Melina warned sourly.

"Early? It's eight o'clock. Of course, I wasn't up late crying my eyes out . . . or up early puking my guts out. You ever gonna tell me you're pregnant?"

Melina shoved a handful of unruly hair from her face to stare at the girl. "How long have you known?"

"I suspected it when you threw up on the plane coming back from Providence."

Before *she'd* suspected it. "What gave it away?"

"My mom used to turn that color of green when she was pregnant. And the condoms on the bed in the motel room made it pretty clear that you and Chrissy's dad were more than just P.I. and client."

A hot flush filled Melina's face and spread down her neck. "Oh, God, tell me those kids didn't see—"

"Nah. I hid 'em under the covers. So . . . you told the proud papa last night and he wasn't so proud. It's not like you *need* him. I mean, you've got money, and women raise kids all the time without fathers without any problem, and Lynda and Ben will help, and so will I."

For lack of anyplace else, Melina sat down on the step. Julie sat down, too, and set the bucket between them where the flowers perfumed every breath they took. "It's not like that," she said grudgingly. "I was all prepared for him to be appalled or angry, to blame me and to not want anything to do with the baby. And instead he—he wants to play daddy. He wants to be a father."

Julie's eyes opened wide and her mouth formed a circle in an imitation of cartoon outrage. "Why, that dirty rotten low-down pig! Imagine—wanting to take responsibility for his own child! What fantasy world does *he* live in?"

Melina breathed deeply of the flowers' scent, then

gave her a long, dry look. "It's a good thing I'm so tolerant, because you're *not* amusing."

"But you like me anyway," Julie said with a brash smile. Then she suddenly turned serious, reaching for Melina's hand and squeezing it tightly. "And you love him anyway, don't you?"

She loved him anyway, Melina silently acknowledged. And he didn't love her.

That was the problem.

AT THE TOP OF THE STEPS THURSDAY MORNING SHE found a foam cooler, packed with dry ice and a plastic tub of homemade strawberry ice cream. Julie brought two spoons from the kitchen, and they sat on the steps again and ate until their mouths were frozen and their stomachs full.

"I like his idea of breakfast," Julie remarked as she licked her spoon, then leaned back against the post.

"Oh, yeah, brilliant. I live three doors down from an ice-cream shop, I'm pregnant and gaining weight every time I breathe, and he brings ice cream, of all things." Melina repacked the dish in the cooler, then mimicked Julie's position.

"Yeah, I could tell by the way you wolfed it down you were really displeased."

Keeping her frown in place required some effort. "He didn't even buy gourmet ice cream."

"No, he made the best stuff I ever had. I didn't know ice cream could taste like that."

It had been awfully good, Melina admitted. Maybe if she filled the empty bowl with peaches and left it on the porch, he'd do it again.

"Are you gonna call him?"

"Nope."

"Why not?"

"In case you haven't noticed, I'm pouting. I'm also debating."

"What?"

"Everything." Once more she shoved her curls back. "I always knew I'd get pregnant, but I thought I'd be married and settled and it would be a time of celebration. Greeks love to celebrate. The impending birth of a baby is a wonderful thing in most Greek families. It's not supposed to be troubled and confusing."

She let her chin sink down to her chest, then blew her breath out loudly. "Don't grow up any more, Julie. Life just gets complicated, and it isn't fun anymore."

"Maybe . . . but it beats dying, doesn't it?"

WHERE THE PORCH TURNED THE CORNER TO RUN along the side of the house, there was a hexagonal-shaped bump-out, and that was where Melina found Friday morning's surprise—a pair of Adirondack chairs painted the same deep green as the shutters on the house. They were so new they hadn't yet collected even the lightest sprinkling of dust, and the finish was as smooth as glass.

"Ooh, pretty," Julie said, dropping into one and wiggling to test it out. "Having a guy who can build things can be pretty cool. What do you think?"

Melina lowered herself into the second chair, forcing her mouth into a noncommittal line. It was just some boards and nails and paint. For a craftsman as talented as Sebastian, it had probably been child's play—like catching a straying husband for her. He'd probably knocked them together on his break.

But she had to admit that for boards, nails, and paint, the chair was awfully comfortable. She didn't know how long she would be able to sit in it—correction: didn't know how long she'd be able to get up out of it—but at the moment it seemed a lovely place to pass a few lazy hours.

"Do you think it was a lucky guess that you needed some porch furniture, or . . . ?"

"Or?"

"Or do you think he's been out there somewhere watching and saw that we had to sit on the steps the last two mornings?"

Melina jerked upright and leaned forward to scan the square, the streets, and the sidewalks. When nothing grabbed her attention, she relaxed and leaned back again. When you were six five with shoulders as broad as a door, it was a little difficult to hide. "I think it was just a lucky guess," she said with a yawn, even though she'd been out of bed less than a half hour. "Lucky for us most of all."

SATURDAY MORNING MELINA GOT UP EARLY, PULLED on a robe over her pajamas, and slipped downstairs, but she wasn't early enough. A matching table and footstool had joined the chairs.

Sunday morning she was up before dawn. After a quick check with a flashlight revealed no new deliveries, she tucked herself into one of the chairs to wait.

It wasn't long before the pickup turned off Main, then pulled into a parking space next door. She sat utterly motionless as Sebastian got out, whistling tunelessly to himself, and came through the gate with a handful of what looked like sticks. As she watched, he crouched beside the flower bed not five feet in front of her and stuck them into the soil. Once he'd dealt with the last one, she turned on the flashlight and zapped him in the face. He looked guilty, trapped, and endearingly embarrassed.

Without a word, she shifted the beam to his feet, where he'd planted a half-dozen carved garden fairies. Perched on stakes of varying heights with their wings outstretched, they appeared to hover over the sleeping flowers. Even by flashlight, she could see they were amazingly detailed, and they made her throat clog.

She switched off the light, then murmured, "You may as well come up. I can offer you a great seat. Made by an expert craftsman."

For a moment he hesitated, then came onto the porch and sat down opposite her.

"Thank you for the gifts."

"You're welcome. I thought they might get me farther than the usual roses and chocolate."

"Aw, how many women have you given roses and chocolate to?"

"Just one, and it didn't seem to help. She left me anyway."

"After eleven years of marriage," she pointed out.

They fell silent for a long time, comfortable in the pre-sunrise gloom, before he spoke again. "About the other night . . . I would never call into question your ability to be a good mother. I couldn't have chosen a better mother for my child."

She tried to make her sniffle sound as if she were just

breathing and wasn't tearful. "So you want to be a father again."

"I always wanted at least three or four kids."

"No matter how many women it takes to get them."

"No, Melina. I wanted one wife, one mother for my kids. I didn't plan to be divorced, or to raise my daughter alone, or to stand back and watch while someone else raises my other child alone."

"Do you think I planned to be single and having my baby alone?" she asked stiffly. He wasn't the only one with dreams, and he certainly wasn't the only one who'd faced disappointment.

"We can fix that."

"How?" she asked without thinking, then a sudden dread started growing inside her. "Never mind. Forget I asked. Please don't—"

"We can get married," he said quietly, calmly, as if suggesting that they remedy hunger by going for breakfast or boredom by watching a movie. "That would solve all our problems, wouldn't it?"

Except one. The heart he'd just broken again. The pain in her chest was real enough to take away her breath, intense enough to send her running to a dark hideaway to wail, if she could manage to get to her feet. But she couldn't get up, couldn't move, couldn't do anything but stare at him and hope the hurt didn't show on her face.

When it became clear that he was actually waiting for an answer, she drew a breath and was surprised it didn't kill her. "People don't get married to solve problems."

"People get married for all kinds of reasons, Melina."

She shook her head. "Not Greeks. Greeks marry for love, for passion and romance and lifelong commitment."

"Well, we can't always get what we want, can we?" he asked, a sharp, cynical edge to his voice.

Swallowing hard, she kept her gasp inside, but she was no less stunned for that. She *knew* he didn't love her, *knew* he'd certainly never intended to be stuck with her for the rest of their lives, but did he have to be so obviously disappointed by the prospect? If he was prepared to make the sacrifice, couldn't he at least pretend he didn't find the idea offensive?

"So . . . you can't have what you want, but you can make do with me. Is that the way you see it, Sebastian? Because you're *wrong.* I don't settle for less. If I can't have something I want, then I do without until something better comes along. So you can take your gifts and your damn proposal, and you can go straight to hell!" Thankfully, her limbs decided to obey her brain's command—it would have ruined her exit completely if she'd been unable to stand—and she pushed herself out of the chair.

Before she took two steps, though, he was blocking her way. "Nothing better is coming along," he warned as he advanced on her, as she backed away. "There's not a man in town who will come near you when it means having to deal with me."

"No one even knows I know you beyond my finding your runaway daughter." A squeak of panic entered her voice as she bumped into the railing, with no further retreat possible. That didn't stop him from coming, though.

"I'll tell them you're carrying my baby."

"I'll deny it!"

His hands were hot on her hips when he lifted her onto the rail, and his arousal was even hotter when he moved between her thighs. She was achy, feverish, and wanted to cry, because with no more than that, her body was throbbing for him. Already she wanted him more than she'd ever wanted any man.

He slid his arms inside her robe and around her waist, then kissed her throat, her jaw, her cheek. "And who do you think they'll believe?" he whispered, his mouth brushing hers with every word. "The local hometown boy they've known all his life? Or the city girl with her scandalous dresses and wild hair and incredibly sexy body?"

Catching his face between her palms, she claimed his mouth and kissed him with every bit of unsatisfied hunger and need inside her. She stabbed her tongue into his mouth and threaded her fingers through his hair, wrapped her legs around his hips and rubbed against him frantically, whimpered helplessly.

His hands were underneath her tank top, sliding over her breasts, when suddenly they were lit up by a spotlight. Blinded, she hid her face against his chest. Cursing, he raised one arm to block the light. "What the hell— Damn it, Mitch."

The light shut off, though brilliant spots still danced on her eyes, and a chuckle came from the street. "Sorry, Sebastian. I just answered a prowler call a few blocks over and when I saw someone there in the shadows . . . You know, the sun's going to be up before long. You guys might want to take it inside. Nice to see you, Melina." With another laugh, he drove away.

Melina slowly raised her head, feeling awkward as hell. When Sebastian tenderly touched her cheek, she looked up to find him staring at her, all hard and intense. "Who do you think they'll believe?" he asked again in a taut voice.

He took a step back, and she missed his warmth unbearably. After lifting her to the floor, he took her hand and walked to the front door. She expected him to lead her inside. He made no move to do so, but just looked at her.

Nervously, she shuffled her feet, looked away, combed her hair back, then looked at him again. "Julie's spending the night with Alanna. She won't be home until after church." It was as close to an invitation as she could get.

"Maybe next time."

Not once in her life had a man turned her down. She couldn't resist glancing down, to see if he was still hard. He was, impressively so.

With one finger under her chin, he raised her gaze back to his face. He was smiling faintly. "Will you have dinner with me tonight?"

She should refuse, for the sake of her battered heart. Instead, she nodded—for the sake of her battered heart.

"I'll pick you up at seven." Bending, he kissed her sweetly, innocently, then walked away.

She leaned against the door for support and watched him drive by, lifting her hand in a wave she knew he couldn't see. When the sound of the truck's engine faded into the silence, she found the strength to walk as far as the top step and gazed up into the dawn sky, where only the brightest of stars was still visible. "I could use a little help down here," she whispered, then gave a tearful shake of her head. "It's not supposed to be this hard."

JULIE'S FATHER HAD LOVED JIGSAW PUZZLES. BACK WHEN he and her mom were still married, she'd griped because there was always a puzzle in progress on the dining table so they'd always had to eat on TV trays in the living room. When she'd quit griping, she had helped him put them together, and so had Julie. The first clue she'd had that something was wrong between her parents was when her mother had stopped helping, and then her father had put away the puzzles for good.

His favorite ones had been folk art villages with brightly colored houses, horse-drawn buggies, and a river drifting past. There was always a park with kids and a dog or two, and all the trees were thin trunks topped with round green shapes to represent the leaves.

Bethlehem could have been one of those villages a hundred years ago. It was the closest modern equivalent she'd ever seen.

She was wearing shorts and a T-shirt and no shoes, and was sprawled in one of the chairs Chrissy's dad had made for Melina. Alanna, dressed the same, sat in the other. It was the middle of a lazy, hot Sunday afternoon, and Julie couldn't remember the last time she'd felt so . . . *good.*

"What grade will you be in?" Alanna asked.

"I had to quit in my senior year. I should have graduated in May."

"The schools here are pretty good. I like 'em. You will, too."

"You think so?" Though she loved to read, Julie had never cared a whole lot about school until she'd quit. Then she'd missed it so much—her friends and teachers, even the classes themselves. But she had to admit, she was nervous about going to a new school in a few weeks where she didn't know anyone. She wanted the diploma, and she'd promised Melina she would go back, but it was gonna be scary in the beginning.

"My friend Mai has a sister in the tenth grade," Alanna

said. "And Trey's friend Bryan has a brother in the twelfth grade. Maybe you can meet 'em before school starts so you won't be a stranger."

"Maybe."

After a little bit of quiet, Alanna asked, "Have you told your mom where you are?"

"No. Melina thinks I should, in case she's worried, but I think if she was going to worry, she should've done it back when her husband threw me out."

"When we were gone, I missed Aunt Emilie and Uncle Nathan and Josie and Brendan and Michael so bad. I wanted to come home so much sometimes it hurt." Alanna's voice got soft and sad on the last few words. "Don't you miss your brothers and sister? Don't you miss your mom?"

"All the time. When I'm a little older, I'm going to see if I can visit the kids, or if they can come wherever I'm living."

"But not your mom."

Julie glanced at her. "I'll make you a deal. You talk to your dad, and I'll write my mom."

Alanna's scowl was automatic. "I don't want to talk to him."

"Look me in the eye and tell me you're not the least bit curious about him."

The brat did just that in a monotone voice.

"Liar. *I* like Ben."

"Yeah, well, he's not your father and he didn't run out on you."

"What do you think he should have done? Marry your mom just because she was pregnant?"

"Well . . . yeah."

"And then they would have fought all the time, and

they would've started to hate each other. Then they would have gotten a divorce and your mom would have dragged you all over, and he still never would have gotten to see you."

"Yeah, but at least he would have tried."

"He didn't have to marry your mom to try. He could have been a perfectly good father without getting married."

"But he wasn't."

"Because your mom disappeared as soon as they broke up. She didn't give him a chance, and she doesn't want you to give him a chance now. Why else would she tell you that you don't have to have anything to do with him if you don't want to?"

Instead of answering, Alanna stared across the street.

"And why would you listen to her about him when you say you don't care about anything else she says?"

"You're just taking his side because—because he's gonna marry Miss Barone and she's friends with Miss Melina."

"Maybe." Julie stretched her legs out until her feet bumped Alanna's on the footstool. "Or maybe because he's a nice guy who wants to apologize for what he did. Or maybe because I'd give anything in the world if my dad was still around. I know you love your uncle, and you should. But dads are special." She smiled sadly. "I miss my daddy more than I can say."

Alanna stared at her a moment, then shoved her feet into her sneakers and walked to the steps. "Get some paper and a pen," she said in a mean voice. "I'll be back to pick up that letter so I can be sure it gets mailed."

Julie watched her march down the sidewalk, through the gate, and across the street into the square. She walked straight up to a bench near the bandstand, where Ben Foster and Lynda Barone sat. After a moment, Lynda stood up and started toward the house. After another moment, Alanna took a seat where she'd sat.

The little brat. Julie hadn't even noticed that Ben and Lynda were in the square, but obviously Alanna had. She should probably get up and find paper and pen, because she had no doubt Alanna would come back, demanding the letter. It wouldn't take long to write. *Dear Mother, Miss the kids. Hate you. Julie.*

Lynda came up the steps, greeting her with a serene smile. She was the most beautiful, most elegant woman Julie had ever met. She was intimidated by her, but she tried to hide it. "Hi. Melina's inside."

"Is she busy?"

Julie shrugged. "If it's an odd hour, she's weeping. If it's an even hour, she's sleeping. If the sun's shining, she's happy, and if there's a cloud in the sky, she's mad."

As she opened the screen door, Lynda smiled. "One of these days when you're older, you'll develop respect for hormones."

Oh, she'd already done that, Julie thought as she settled in comfortably again. She'd learned to respect most things about life, from small disasters to great miracles.

Right now a couple of miracles would be awfully nice, if anyone up there was listening.

I ONLY CAME OVER HERE BECAUSE IT'S THE ONLY WAY to get Julie to let her family know where she is," Alanna announced.

"You must like her a lot," Ben said.

"She's like my big sister."

"You were lucky to find her."

"Miss Agatha says it was a miracle." She sat straight on the bench, gripping it with both hands, but she looked at him from the corner of her eye. "Do you believe in miracles?"

"Absolutely. My grandmother Emmaline believed life was made up of miracles."

"Emmaline Bodine. I read her letters."

"What letters?"

"To my mom. When I was a baby. Where does she live?"

He was quiet for so long that finally she turned a little on the bench to face him. He looked real sad, then tried to hide it when he saw she was looking at him. "She died this past spring. She was eighty-seven years old."

So she didn't have a great-grandmother after all. It didn't matter whether she was tall and thin or short and fat, or whether she walked with a cane and baked and crocheted, or what she thought of Ben Foster.

"Her greatest disappointment was that she never got to meet you," he went on. "She had a silver locket that she never took off, and she kept a baby picture of you in it. It had been in her family for a hundred and fifty years, and just before she died, she asked me to give it to you. I've got it at the house."

A hundred and fifty years of family. *Her* family had really only been around for three years. Before Uncle Nathan, before Aunt Emilie, they hadn't been a real family. If Berry had had her way, they still wouldn't be.

"Did you see her a lot?"

He grinned. "All the time. She raised me."

"Why?"

"My parents didn't care much about being parents."

"Kinda like my parents," she said deliberately.

It made his grin go away, and for a minute he looked real sorry. "Yeah, like your parents. Except where I had Emmaline, you had Emilie. Alanna, I'm sorry—"

"How old were you when you met my mom?"

"Nineteen."

Julie was only two years younger than that. It was weird thinking of her having a baby in two years. She was still just a kid herself . . . not that it mattered. Susan's mom was a nurse, and she said if you were old enough to have sex, you should be old enough to deal with the consequences. Though, really, when Mrs. Walker said that, Alanna hadn't liked thinking of herself as a consequence.

"I don't need you," she said flatly. "I've got Aunt Emilie and Uncle Nathan. I don't need another mother or father."

"I understand that."

"Then why are you here?"

"I came to deliver Emmaline's locket. I was going to leave it with Emilie to give to you, but . . . After I saw you, I wanted to meet you, and then I met Lynda, and . . ." He shrugged as he looked at her. "There's nothing for me in Atlanta. I only hear from my father when he's in trouble and needs money, and I see my mother maybe once a year. Emmaline was my only other family except for some distant relatives I barely know, and with her gone, there wasn't much point in staying."

Alanna knew a lot of people who had big families with aunts and uncles and cousins, but she knew a lot, too, who didn't have anybody that cared. She'd waited a long time to be a part of a real family, and she was never gonna let anything happen to it. Someday her children would have more relatives than they could count, and they would know and love every one of them.

Except their grandmother and their grandfather.

Which seemed kind of not fair.

But life wasn't fair. She'd figured that out a long time ago. If Ben Foster had wanted his grandchildren to know him, then he should have stuck around so his child would know him. There was no one else to blame.

"I gotta go," she said abruptly. She got as far as the sidewalk before he said her name.

"Alanna . . . Lynda and I are getting married soon. It would mean a lot if you'd come to the wedding."

She shrugged like maybe she would or maybe she wouldn't, then walked off. That was something she'd have to ask Aunt Emilie about. She could bring it up with Julie, but she already knew what her answer would be. *He's a nice guy, I like him, dads are special.* Easy for her to say, since she'd always known her dad, and when he'd left, it wasn't his choice. Her dad had always wanted her and always loved her. She couldn't judge Alanna's dad by her own.

On the other hand, their moms were pretty much the same.

"Well?" Julie said when Alanna sat back down in her chair.

She shrugged again. "Where's the letter?"

Julie picked up a pad from the table and handed it over. On the first page was her mom's name and address. On the second page, in hot-pink ink, she'd written, "Mother, If you're interested, I can be reached at this address and number. Give Alli, Matt, and Dex kisses for me and tell them I love them." It was signed "Julianne

Bujold," and had Melina's address and phone number underneath her name.

"Huh. I figured you'd write 'Dear Mom, Drop dead.' "

Julie smiled faintly. "That was my first draft."

"I'll mail this tomorrow."

"You should save your stamp. She won't care."

"Hey, I talked to *him*. Now you have to keep your end of the bargain."

"Mail it. It doesn't matter to me. Just don't expect her to acknowledge it."

"You never know."

But Julie just shrugged and looked stubborn, like she did know. And maybe she did. Hadn't Alanna known nothing would come of talking to Ben Foster? And hadn't she been right? It hadn't changed her mind one bit. She was just as sure as ever that she didn't want him in her life.

Though she *would* kinda like to know more about her great-grandmother Emmaline.

SUNDAY EVENING'S DINNER WAS, MELINA THOUGHT, oddly like a regular date. Sebastian picked her up at exactly seven o'clock for a leisurely stroll to McCauley's Steakhouse, one of the few date-worthy places in Bethlehem. They talked politely, almost like friends—most definitely not like former lovers and soon-to-be-parents. After dinner, they walked back to her house in the quiet warm night, but he stopped at the top of the steps.

Melina gave him a wry look, hoping it covered her disappointment. She knew it was certainly in their best interests that he not come one step closer, but she couldn't resist asking, "You don't want to come in?"

"I'd like to, but I won't."

"Why not?"

"I have to pick up Chrissy's from Mom's."

She didn't ask why Chrissy couldn't spend the night with his mother, as she'd done plenty of times before. Instead, she smiled coolly. "I haven't had many dates end at the door," she lied. "Is this where I tell you I had a nice time and you give me a chaste peck on the cheek?"

"Yeah, I guess so."

She leaned back against the door frame. "I had a nice time."

"So did I."

He closed the distance between them with a couple of easy, lazy steps, then brushed one finger across her cheek. The touch warmed her even as it sent a shiver down her spine. She made a conscious effort to look unaffected by such a simple caress, maybe even slightly bored, but doubted she came close to succeeding.

Bending closer, he brushed his lips over her hair, his breath feathering lightly across her forehead. She drew a deep, steadying breath, heavy with the mingled fragrances of soap, shampoo, and Sebastian, then resorted to short, shallow breaths through her mouth. It was too little, too late. His scents were seeping through her, embedding themselves in her very pores, creating a bone-deep need for *more.*

He was playing with her, seeing just how erotic he could make a chaste peck on the cheek. She knew that and didn't care. It felt too good, and she needed it too much.

Slowly he cupped his palms to her face, all warm

callused skin and hard strength, and he tilted her head back, brought his mouth within a millimeter of hers, heated her breath with his. She raised her hands to his wrists—to pull him closer . . . or stop him from retreating—and felt the rapid throb of his pulse beneath her fingertips. Tension and heat thrummed through him, and through her, too, creating an aching need deep inside.

Then he kissed her. His lips pursed against her cheek. One beat, two. A soft, sweet, innocent little smack.

He drew away slowly, as if he hated to give up the contact—first his palms, then his fingers, then he freed himself from her grip. "I'll call you," he said in a thick, husky whisper, and he walked away.

Melina's knees felt weak, and every nerve in her body was crying out in protest. In a rush of frustration, she wanted to yell after him: *Don't bother. Go to hell. Leave me alone.* But the best she could manage when she opened her mouth was a soft whimper of disappointment.

Achingly aroused from head to toe, she finally made it inside the house and upstairs to her room. She'd just sat down on the bed when Julie knocked at the open door. "Come in."

The obnoxious child was grinning as if she knew exactly how Melina had wanted the evening to end. "Do you know what time it is? Just what are you doing home at such an hour? It's not even nine-thirty."

"You're much too young to mother me," Melina said, scooting back to lean against the headboard and leaving room for Julie to sprawl at the foot of the bed.

"Sorry. It's what I do. You guys didn't fight again, did you?"

"No. He had to pick up Chrissy and get home."

"You gonna give in and marry him?"

Melina stared at her reflection in the mirror across the room. Was she as scared as the Melina in the mirror looked? She'd always had every intention of marrying, so why did the mere mention of marriage to Sebastian frighten her?

Because he didn't love her.

Because he never would have asked if not for the baby.

Because he saw it as his duty—the right thing to do—and she would never be anyone's duty. Her baby deserved more than a father who'd never wanted to be part of their family, and so did she.

"Sebastian doesn't want to marry me."

"Then why did he ask?" Julie shrugged at her sharp gaze. "I heard you talking to Lynda today, but I couldn't hear everything."

"He asked because I'm pregnant."

"People get married for worse reasons."

"Yeah, well, they also get married for better reasons."

Julie rolled onto her side, leaning her head on one hand. "If you married him, then you could be Chrissy's stepmom. She really needs one."

Melina mimicked her position. "And you could be her sister—sorta. Would you like that?"

"You mean . . ." Julie swallowed hard, then blinked. "You'd want me to still live with you if you got married?"

"Do you think I'd send you away?"

"My mom did. And you never said . . . I thought this was just temporary . . ."

With a wince, Melina covered her face with one hand. Somewhere along the line, she'd simply accepted that she didn't want Julie to live anywhere else, and she'd assumed the kid understood that. But how could Julie make such an assumption when her own mother *had* thrown her out?

"Okay, listen up," she said, brushing a strand of Julie's silky blond hair behind her ear. "We make a pretty good team, don't you think? I mean, we could find a traditional family to take you in, but I honestly don't think you'll find anyone who wants you more than I do. You and me and this baby are a family, and any man who doesn't want all three of us doesn't deserve even one of us. Okay?"

Smiling tearfully, Julie nodded.

"Now . . . if you'd rather have a more traditional family, I won't stand in your way. I'll find the best one out there. But—"

"No," Julie said hastily. "There's no place I'd rather be than here, with you."

They were sweet words and they took the edge off Melina's tender feelings. "Good. Because there's no place I'd rather you be."

Chapter Fourteen

AFTER THREE DATES IN ONE WEEK WITHOUT A single argument and without him saying something stupid or clumsy, Sebastian was beginning to think that he and Melina might be getting the hang of this dating stuff. Of course, they were doing it backward, she'd pointed out when he'd kissed her good night at the door Saturday evening. Most people dated first, then had sex, while they'd stopped having sex and then started dating.

Not that she'd stopped offering invitations. All three nights, walking away from her with nothing more than a kiss had been harder than anything a man should have to do. No one was making him go, she reminded him, but that wasn't entirely true. He wanted more than just sex, more than a few hours here and maybe an entire night there. He wanted to marry her, and he was pretty sure his chances were better if he didn't make love with her until it meant the same to both of them.

If he could last that long. She was the single most stubborn woman he'd ever known, and she was determined to be single when their baby was born.

The warm breeze floating through the pickup's open windows brought with it the sound of the school bell. It was the first day of the new school year, and at the bus stop that morning, he'd promised Chrissy he would pick her up after school and spend a little time doing whatever she wanted before taking her to his folks' house. She'd rolled her eyes and said, "Another date with Melina," in a long-suffering voice.

Then she'd sucker-punched him. "If you want her to be my new mama, it's okay with me, Daddy. I'd like to have a mama that's here all the time."

It was a good thing the bus had come when it did.

The elementary school kids spilled out of the building like ants fleeing a size-twelve shoe, while the middle school and high school kids took their time, too grown-up or maybe too cool to kick up their heels and run. Sebastian knew many of the children racing out—had gone to school with their parents, done work for them, or met them in the everyday course of life in a small town. He liked that connection. Liked knowing that Chrissy's first-grade teacher had also been his first-grade teacher. That there wasn't much she could get into at school, church, or anywhere else without someone letting him know. He liked that she was growing up with memories similar to his own.

He wanted his and Melina's child to do the same.

"Hi, Daddy!" Chrissy shoved her backpack through the open window, then opened the door and climbed in. Sitting on her knees, she leaned across to give him a kiss before plopping down in her seat. "I'm in Mr. Peterson's class, and guess what? Gracie's class is across the hall, and I got a list of stuff I have to have for class tomorrow, like pencils and paper and rulers and stuff. And you know what? We got a new kid. She's got red hair and big glasses, and her name is Kerry, only Kevin Madigan called her Scary and everyone laughed—but not me." She smiled prettily at him. "I was nice to her. I told her Kevin's just a dumb ole boy and you gotta be, like, thirty to care what boys say."

Maybe even older, Sebastian thought privately. Melina was thirty-four, and she wasn't showing much sign of mellowing where he was concerned. "What do you want to do?" he asked as he eased away from the curb and into traffic.

"First, I'm hungry."

"Hungry?" he teased. "You just ate lunch a few hours ago."

"Thinking and playing are hard work," she replied seriously. "Can we go to Harry's and get some ice cream and pie?"

"Yeah, we can do that."

It was just a few blocks to Main Street. He parked in front of the diner, then cast a longing look toward Melina's house, half-wishing she would be outside so he could invite her to join them. He was seeing her this evening—burgers and dancing at the Starlite with Ben and Lynda—but six-thirty seemed a whole lot more than three hours away.

Mid-afternoon in the diner was slow, but there never seemed to be a time when Harry and Maeve had no customers at all. Sebastian followed Chrissy through the door and to a stool at the counter. She liked the stools so she could swing her legs and spin around from time to time. He liked the booths because his legs were too long for the footrest running the length of the counter and his knees bumped the wood.

"How are you doing, Chrissy?" Maeve Carter wiped the counter with a damp cloth, though it was already clean. The waitress considered the diner as much hers as Harry's—after all, she'd worked there about as long as he had—and kept everything in perfect order.

"I'm fine. I just got out of school," Chrissy said. "What's the best pie today?"

"Oh, they're all good, hon—but don't tell Harry I said that. It might go to his head."

"I heard that," Harry called from the kitchen, his voice gruff.

Chrissy giggled. She'd been coming to Harry's all her life and was well aware that his bark was much worse than his bite. "I'd like cherry, please, warmed up in the microwave and cooled down with ice cream."

"Microwave?" Harry peered at her through the pass-through. "There's no microwave in my kitchen, and I'll nuke anyone who says otherwise."

With another giggle, Chrissy leaned forward to see him better. "I got Mr. Peterson at school. He's the best teacher in my grade."

"Well, now, that's reason to celebrate. I think that calls for two scoops of ice cream, doesn't it?"

She bobbed her head enthusiastically.

"What about you, Sebastian?" Maeve asked. "Pie? Coffee? Maybe a piece of baklava?"

He followed her gesture to the glass dome covering a plate filled with puffy, golden-brown triangles of pastry. "Baklava?"

"It's a Greek dessert. Melina was craving it last week,

and she challenged Harry to see if he could make it as well as her mother does. Here, try it."

He took a bite off the piece she served him. It was flaky, nutty, and tasted of honey and cloves. "Good."

"Do you like Greek food as much as you like Greek girls?" Maeve asked slyly.

He felt the tips of his ears warm. "I've never had much Greek food." But if it would help convince Melina to marry him, he would become the most accomplished connoisseur of Greek food the Western world had ever seen.

"But you do like Greek girls . . . or, at least, one in particular." Maeve's smile was broad and vastly amused. "That Melina's quite a looker, isn't she? And nice . . . I liked her from the first time I saw her."

So did he.

Beside him, Chrissy was spinning in slow circles, extending her legs where she could, tucking them under when space required it. "She's pregnant," she announced matter-of-factly before circling once more. "That means she's gonna have a baby."

Sebastian turned to stare at her. Maeve was wide-eyed, too, and it seemed every conversation in the diner had quieted. Stopping her rotations, Chrissy looked up innocently. "Well, Grandma said. She went to the baby shop to get something for someone, and Melina had got a baby bed and a stroller and a high chair and a car seat and a baby bathtub and a pretty little pink dress with matching booties. And Grandma said she must be pregnant, and Aunt Shauna said who's the daddy. And then cartoons came back on so I didn't listen no more."

Sebastian's face was burning, and his palms had gotten sweaty. Was everyone really staring at him, or was it just

Maeve and Harry? And had they really guessed who the daddy was just now, or were they still getting to that point?

Oh, no. They were there. Maeve distracted Chrissy by serving her pie and ice cream, then gestured to Sebastian to move one seat away from her. When he reluctantly did so, the waitress rested one hand on her hip and fixed her gaze on him. "Are you going to marry that girl?"

She whispered, but her voice must have carried to every customer in the place, because when Sebastian glanced around, they were all watching. He looked back, swallowed convulsively, then tried to breathe. "I— This isn't— I shouldn't—"

"Well? It's a simple enough question. If you're that baby's father, it ought to be a simple enough answer," Maeve declared.

He looked blankly from her to Harry, then back again, then shook his head. "Nothing's as simple as it ought to be with Melina. She's—"

"A foreigner," old Homer, who generally spent his days gossiping at the hardware store, put in as he took a seat at the end of the counter.

Sebastian glanced at him impatiently. "She's not a foreigner. She was born in New York, just like the rest of us."

"Born of foreigners," Homer added, nodding for emphasis.

"Not a foreigner," Homer's buddy said. "But she's a women's libber. Has a good job, makes a lot of money, and thinks she don't need a man for much of anything."

"That's not a women's libber," someone else—a woman—said. "It's a smart woman. You think she should give up that good job and all that money to wash your clothes, cook your meals, and keep your house?"

The old man turned and winked. "Gal as pretty as that one is? I'd die a mighty happy man if she would."

Sebastian looked at Chrissy, apparently absorbed with her dessert, but appearances could be deceiving. It seemed she heard a lot of things when no one thought she was listening. "Knock it off," he said with a pointed look in her direction.

"Don't like to be teased 'bout your lady friend, huh?" Homer asked.

"There are little ears around," Maeve said, giving the old men a stern look. "You go back to your table and mind your own business or I'll start charging rent on those chairs you've been occupying all afternoon."

Laughing, the two men did as she said, but that didn't mean Sebastian was in the clear. "We'll continue this conversation later," she said with a meaningful look. "And you'd better have some satisfactory answers. You can't just abandon that poor girl. Your mama and daddy raised you better than that. Heavens, *I* raised you better than that."

"Poor girl," Sebastian snorted. "That's like calling an alligator a misunderstood lizard. That girl can chew all of us up and spit us out without even breaking a sweat."

Maeve studied him for a moment, then grinned. "Well, she's sure done *some*thing to you. You know . . . it's been awfully quiet around here since Tom Flynn went a-courtin'. We could use a little spectacle."

Chrissy looked up, ice cream dripping down her chin. "What's a spectacle?"

"It's a sight, hon." Maeve grabbed a napkin and cleaned Chrissy's face. "It's something to see."

Courting Melina was exactly what he was trying to do, with a small measure of success so far, but he hadn't wanted an audience. He had too much at stake—his future, his love, his family, his baby. If he failed . . .

His mother was a big believer in positive thinking. The only needlework project she'd ever completed hung on the kitchen wall and read "Whether you think you can, or you think you can't, you're right." Saying *I'll never pass this class* or *I'm not good enough to make the team* had earned him, Shauna, and their brothers an admonishment. Even saying *I can't, I'll never,* or *I'll fail* in her house risked the prospect of creating a self-fulfilling prophecy, she believed.

So he wouldn't consider the possibility of failure.

Their baby was too important.

Melina was too important.

THE STARLITE LOUNGE WAS ABOUT AS CLOSE TO A honky-tonk as Melina cared to get. The burgers were greasy and good, the music loud, and the patrons out to have a good time. In her tight jeans and tighter top, she fit right in with the other women in the joint, all of them looking like Lynda's poor wrong-side-of-the-tracks cousins. It was amazing—the innate ability her friend had to make attractive women fade into the woodwork. Except Melina. She was too bold and brash to fade.

After two Diet Cokes, she excused herself to go to the ladies' room. Lynda followed behind. "I'm surprised you can breathe in that outfit," Lynda remarked once they entered the hallway that led to the bathrooms and conversation became less difficult.

"Breathing's not important, darlin'. Looking good is." Once they reached the ladies' room, Melina locked herself in a stall. "Of course, the jeans weren't this tight a month ago. I figure another day or two, and I'll never be able to wear them again."

"Honey, I think you passed that point already," Lynda replied from the next stall.

Once she'd taken care of business, Melina washed her hands, then started to lift a hand to her hair. After studying herself in the mirror, she let it go untouched.

"Can't improve on perfection, huh?" Lynda asked dryly as she ran a comb through her own black hair. Melina had envied her sleek, manageable hair from the day they'd met, but at some time in the past ten years, she'd not only accepted but come to like her curls. Of course, she thought with a wicked grin, it didn't hurt that men liked them, too.

"There must be something to this pregnancy business," Lynda remarked as she reapplied her lipstick. "I've never seen you look so good. You're actually glowing."

"Yeah, there's something to it. Endless trips to the bathroom, mood swings, cravings, throwing up . . ."

"And that's different for you . . . how?"

"Smarty pants." Melina made an obscene gesture, then dug in her bag for her own lipstick. She'd just started to apply it when the door swung open and a slinky blonde sashayed in. Oh, great. The blonde was probably the one person in Bethlehem Lynda would rather never see again. Her name was Kelli, and she was single, available, and didn't like to take no for an answer—much like Melina in her younger days, but with less class. When Ben had first come to town, Kelli had set her sights for him. She'd missed, and resented it like hell.

When she recognized them, she sniffed, lifted her head, and turned away in a snub. Lynda coolly pretended she hadn't seen the woman. That was her style. Melina stopped in front of the stall door and raised her voice. "Hey, Kelli, how ya doin'?"

That was *her* style.

Linking her arm through Melina's, Lynda drew her out of the bathroom. "How's it going with Sebastian?"

"It's going . . ." Melina stopped abruptly. She'd been about to say *fine.* While she might lie to her parents, to Julie, and even, on occasion, to herself, she never lied to Lynda. "It's . . . going."

"Has he brought up the subject of marriage again?"

"No."

"How do you feel about that?"

Melina came to a stop, looking left, where a broad doorway led back into the bar and to Sebastian and Ben, then right, where double doors led outside. She pulled Lynda in that direction, out into the warm night, and sat down on the stone wall that formed sorry-looking planters against the front of the building. "I'm relieved."

"Really."

"Don't I look it?" She forced a smile, lips apart and teeth clenched together. "Don't I sound it?"

"Nope. Sorry, darlin', you don't."

She let her smile turn upside down into the frown that felt more comfortable. "I was relieved at first. I *so* didn't want him to ask—at least, not the way he did. I thought there was no possible way I could spend time with him if he kept suggesting that we get married, that it was the solution to our *problems.*" Feeling frustrated all over again, she lifted her hair off her neck, then let it drop again. "I want *romance,* Lynda! I want a man who loves me, who can't live without me, who wakes up in the middle of the night and thinks how lucky he is to have me there beside him. I want someone whose day is better just because I'm in it, who could get by without me if he had to but doesn't see any earthly reason why he should. I want what you have! And instead I get problem-solving."

"Maybe that's not what he meant. Maybe he's just not particularly romantic. Some men aren't. Some men have problems dealing with their emotions."

Melina snorted before glumly replying, "He had no problem telling me he wasn't interested in seeing me again after our infamous four days and nights together."

"Yes, he did. He didn't tell you *anything,* remember? Not until you showed up at his house and forced the issue. Even then, all he said was standing you up seemed the easiest way."

She had been so hurt, Melina remembered. Up until that point, the most painful thing she'd ever done was examine the evidence her own employees had stumbled across documenting Rico the rat's numerous affairs while he was engaged to her, but that hadn't compared to Sebastian's betrayal. Maybe it was because she'd known Rico for years and hadn't had a whole lot of illusions left about him, while with Sebastian she'd really had nothing *but* illusions. He'd been her fantasy, a dream come true—her Knight in shining armor, her warped sense of humor chimed in. Whatever the explanation, her heart had broken more thoroughly that night than she had believed possible.

"But you know what, Melina? Having a way with words, being charming and sentimental, saying 'I love you' and sounding as if he means it . . . that doesn't make it true, and it certainly doesn't make a man better husband material. Look at Rico. *He* had a way with words. He was the best at romantic gestures. He told you he loved you on your first date, and damned if he didn't make it sound like God's honest truth. And he could charm the pants off any woman within a ten-mile radius. He sure charmed 'em off you often enough."

"And half of our female clients." Melina could joke about it now. Back then, though, if two of her biggest and burliest investigators hadn't forcibly restrained her, there was no telling what she would have done to him. Torn him apart limb by limb. To quote an old movie, turned him from a rooster into a hen with one shot. Made him sorry he'd ever lived.

"So Rico was a first-class romancer and would have made a rotten husband," Melina said. "And some guys are lousy at the romance, yet make wonderful husbands. And some are lousy at both."

Lynda shook her head with feigned impatience—at least, Melina hoped it was feigned. "You're determined to be difficult, aren't you?"

The temptation to let her believe just that was strong, but instead Melina sighed heavily. "I'm not being difficult. I'm . . ."

When she didn't go on, Lynda finished for her. "Scared?"

How long had it been, Melina wondered, since she'd been scared of anything? Oh, sure, she had those adrenaline rushes when some nutcase came after her with a baseball bat or pulled a gun on her, but to be really, truly afraid . . . She couldn't remember the last time.

"What if he never loves me?" she asked, hating the plaintive note in her voice but unable to disguise it with anything less weak. "What if someday he decides that having a child isn't reason enough to be married? What if he waits until I can't live without him, and I wake up in the middle of the night and think how lucky I am to have him there beside me, and my days are so much better because he's in them, and then he ends it again?"

"And what if he doesn't?"

"But what if he does?" She shook her head. "I can't take that chance."

"Everyone takes that chance, Melina. There are no guarantees. Love is a gamble. Marriage is a risk. You think I'm absolutely certain Ben will be there beside me in forty years? I think so. I dearly hope so. But I can't know it beyond a doubt."

"But you know he loves you, don't you?"

Lynda couldn't argue that with her. That was the single biggest difference between their situations. She'd known before Ben proposed to her that he loved her at least as much as she loved him. And Melina knew just as completely that Sebastian didn't love her at all.

Because she *couldn't* argue any further, Lynda's only response was to slide her arm around Melina's shoulders and squeeze her tightly.

They sat like that for a moment, until a group of young women passed by on the way from the parking lot to the bar. One, a petite, wholesome-looking blonde, glanced at them, then did a double-take. "I'll meet you inside," she called after her friends, then approached them. "Excuse me. You're Melina Dimitris, aren't you?"

"Yes, I am." Seeking her usual self-assurance, Melina straightened, then slid to her feet.

The woman startled her with an enthusiastic hug. "I'm so glad to meet you! I've seen you around town a few times and figured we would meet eventually—in a town like Bethlehem, it's kind of hard to avoid. But when I heard the news today . . . This is so great! We'd pretty much figured Sebastian was never going to get over

Diana enough to get seriously involved with another woman, but he fooled us. Mom is so excited. Weird, huh, to be excited that your son was careless enough to get his girlfriend pregnant, but, hey, after everything he's been through, Mom's just happy he's *got* a girlfriend."

Melina stared at her, feeling a chill in spite of the warm evening temperature. "What did you say?"

The woman blinked, then laughed. "Sorry. My family's been telling me since I was a kid that I talk too much. Umm, let's start over. Hi, I'm Shauna Knight, Sebastian's sister. Your future sister-in-law. Welcome to the family."

She stuck out her hand, and Melina numbly shook it. "You—you—He *told* you?"

"About the baby?" Shauna laughed again. "No, not yet. Mom told me a few days ago that you were pregnant, but neither of us found out until this afternoon that it's Sebastian's baby. I heard it from Granny Sara. She heard it from Sadie, who's a dispatcher at the police department, and Sadie got it from Virginia at the grocery store, who heard it from . . . oh, I forget. Bethlehem has a very efficient grapevine."

"You mean everyone in town knows?" Melina didn't know whether to be horrified that her private life had become public or annoyed with herself for not being prepared for it to happen.

"Pretty much anybody who's interested," Shauna replied. "Has Mom gotten in touch with you yet? She's planning a family dinner this weekend to introduce you to everyone. Hope you're used to large gatherings. There'll be a crowd there."

A woman at the door called her name, and Shauna waved. "Guess I'd better get inside. We'll talk more this weekend—and this time I'll actually give you a chance to get a word in. See you."

The night seemed still and quiet once she'd gone inside. Melina remained where she was, motionless, stunned. An awful lot of *something* was building inside her—anger, frustration, fear, hurt, helplessness. She felt as if she might explode at any second, leaving behind nothing but a seething mass of excess emotion and a few scraps of stressed-to-the-max denim on the ground.

Behind her Lynda cleared her throat. "I'd better get back inside before Kelli tries to replace me in Ben's affections."

The only response Melina offered was a nod as she continued to stare at nothing. She felt Lynda's fingertips brush her arm, heard the sound of footsteps walking away, then the blast of music as the door opened, then closed, behind her friend. She heard voices and laughter from inside, distant traffic, and the crunch of gravel in the parking lot, but she wasn't aware that she wasn't alone until strong arms slid around her middle from behind.

Her first impulse was to take defensive action. An instant later she realized it was Sebastian, and her new first impulse was to lean back against him. She barely managed to resist it.

"Did the smoke and the noise get to you?" he asked.

She'd come outside so she and Lynda could talk, but now that she'd breathed fresh air for a bit, she didn't want to go back in, so she nodded.

"You want to go home?"

She nodded again.

He tucked her against his side, then they headed for his pickup. The eight or ten blocks to her house passed in silence, but she knew it was only a temporary reprieve. Sure enough, when he parked in front of her house, he turned off the engine, then looked at her. "What's wrong, Melina?"

For a moment she considered retreating inside the house and locking the door on him, but that wouldn't accomplish anything. Instead she turned to lean against the door and gazed at him. "Why did you tell your mother I'm pregnant?" *And how could you not tell her that you're the father?*

That was the worst part of Shauna's little surprise—that he'd seen fit to share *her* secret, but not his own. Was he ashamed? Breaking it to his mom in stages? Putting off the worst part until it could no longer be avoided?

Even in the dim light, she could see the guilt in his expression. He rubbed his hand over the curve of the steering wheel, then dragged in a loud breath. "I didn't tell Mom. I didn't tell anyone . . . exactly."

"Then how did it get all over town?" She would deal with that *exactly* later.

He hesitated. "Chrissy."

"You told *Chrissy*?"

He shook his head. "Mom did."

"Who told your mother?"

"Apparently, she was in the baby shop the day you bought a bunch of stuff for the baby, and she assumed that you were pregnant. She mentioned it to Shauna, and Chrissy overheard and announced it at Harry's today after school. Maeve put two and two together and . . ." He shrugged uncomfortably.

Melina let his strong profile go blurry and stared at the nearest vehicle, parked a dozen spaces away. Harry's was gossip central. Spend enough time there, and a person could hear every rumor, current, recent, and some that were ages old. If it was talked about at the diner, it would soon be all over the county.

"I'm sorry, Melina," Sebastian said. "I didn't mean— How do you know my mother knows?"

"I met your sister while Lynda and I were outside the bar. She's thrilled at the prospect of being an aunt again."

"Shauna loves kids. She teaches first grade—" Suddenly his gaze sharpened as the implication of her words sank in. It wasn't just her pregnancy that had become common knowledge, but also his part in it. "Oh, hell. Mom's gonna kill me."

"I don't know. Shauna said she's tickled pink that you've managed to get a girlfriend, considering that your family thought you were still carrying a torch for Diana." That bothered her, too, Melina realized. He'd been divorced for more than a year, and had been involved with her in one way or another for three months, and yet his family thought he was still in love with his ex-wife. It had made her wonder if he was. If that was the reason he'd wanted nothing more than sex from *her.*

And what if he was, and he caught Melina in a weak moment and she agreed to marry him, and then Diana came back? Getting dumped because he didn't want her had been bad enough. Getting dumped because he wanted his ex-wife more would be unbearable.

"Come here," he said gruffly, then lifted her sideways onto his lap. It was a snug fit between the steering wheel and his body, but she didn't mind. With his arm circling her shoulders and his fingers twined with hers, it was really very comfortable . . . and comforting. "First, my sister talks too much and should be ignored most of the time. Second, I'm over Diana. She was a part of my life for a lot of years, and she's my daughter's mother, but . . . I don't have any feelings for her. I'm not carrying a torch for her or anyone else."

With a handful of words, he took the comfort right out of their embrace. He had loved Diana for years, had married her and happily—deliberately—had a child with her. If he could dismiss her so easily, how much easier would he find it to dismiss Melina, whom he'd never loved or wanted to marry?

Feeling weepy and hurt, she pushed against him in an effort to free herself. It wasn't easy, but she managed to slide back into her seat, grab her purse from the floorboard, and open the door. "You should tell that to your family, not me," she said hastily. *Maybe they'll care.*

Hoping he would take the hint and leave, she got out of the truck and started toward the gate. He got there before her, though, and swung it open. She smiled faintly, then hurried up the steps to the porch. "I had a nice time," she said politely as she unlocked the door. It wasn't a complete lie. Until her conversations outside with Lynda and Shauna Knight, she *had* enjoyed herself. Her only regret was that she hadn't gotten one slow dance with Sebastian before she'd lost her pleasure in the evening.

"Aren't you going to invite me in?"

She stared down at her feet. "Uh . . . I—I'm kind of tired. I seem to need a lot of sleep these days. And I know you want to pick up Chrissy and get her to bed in plenty of time for school tomorrow."

"Do I at least get to kiss you good night?"

Her pride wanted to say no. The woman in her couldn't. "Sure." She could handle a kiss, especially when she craved it with every cell in her body.

He slid her purse strap from her shoulder and hung it on the doorknob, then took her hand and led her along the porch.

"Where are we going?"

"Too much light and too little privacy. I'd rather not risk an audience." He turned the corner, then went to the end of the porch, where a set of broad steps led into the side yard. It was darker there, protected from the street by distance, from the business next door by a windowless stone wall, and from the neighbors in back by a tall fence. The only way anyone would see them there was to come looking for them.

After seating her on the top step, he sat a few steps lower and turned to face her. Melina gestured to the distance between them. "This is silly. This isn't a good-night kiss."

"Sure, it is. It's called foreplay."

"Uh-uh. I *know* foreplay, and this ain't it."

"You're so impatient. Sometimes the best part of something can be the anticipation."

"Okay. I'll anticipate. But don't blame me if I fall asleep while I'm waiting."

His only response was a chuckle.

It was a beautiful night. The air was balmy, the sky a blanket of black velvet with millions of twinkling stars. A faint breeze brought the fragrance of flowers and the hint of dampness from the sprinklers belonging to the house behind hers. From her own house she could hear the music Julie preferred over the television, and around them were all the usual quiet-night-in-Bethlehem noises.

Nearer she could hear the steady sound of Sebastian's breathing. Though she'd done it only five times, lying in bed in his arms and listening to that soft regular cadence had quickly become one of her favorite things. He was so big and strong, and she'd felt so protected. As long as he was there, his body hard and warm, his breathing so regular, nothing could go wrong.

She wondered if their baby felt the same way about her. Could she hear her mother's steady heartbeat and feel her smooth respirations and know that she was safe?

Melina hoped so.

With a soft sigh, she broke the silence. "Your mother's planning a dinner this weekend to introduce me to the family. They seem to think that we're getting—that I'm the newest—"

"Of course they think we're getting married." He spoke calmly, as if it were the most natural thing in the world. She wished she shared his belief at the same time she wanted to smack him for his smugness.

"And why is that so obvious?"

"Because that's what you do when you're going to have a baby."

So simple, old-fashioned, and sweet, in a way. And so damn stupid. "No, Sebastian, that's what you did fifty years ago, when it mattered. Women have babies without getting married all the time. No one cares."

"I care. My family cares, and I imagine yours does, too. And the baby will care, when she's older."

"She'll have two parents who love her"—*if not each other*—"and that's all that will matter to her."

"And you speak from what experience?" he asked stubbornly. "I'm the single parent here. I think my expertise counts for more than your guesses."

"I'm the expert in self-defense here. I think you'll accept that no one's opinion has more value to me than my own, or you'll be walking and talking funny when you leave here."

He enfolded her hand in his, then moved to his knees and caught her other hand, too. "Aw, you wouldn't hurt me, especially there. If you did, we might have to delay the honeymoon, and I don't think you want that any more than I do."

He nudged her knee, and she grudgingly—well, sort of—moved her foot to the outside. When he nudged her other knee, she moved that one, too, and he moved between her thighs. Just that action started a tingle deep inside her, and she cleared her throat to hide it. "You want a honeymoon? Great. Let's have one. We'll skip the tiresome wedding, the formal clothes, and all the hassle, and get right to the good part. We can start right now, in fact."

With a grin, he shook his head. He was so close she could feel his breath on her skin. Such a little thing, yet it kicked her heart rate up a few notches and raised her temperature another degree. "If you get your honeymoon now, how will I ever get my marriage?"

"You're not getting it anyway, so you might as well accept the consolation prize."

He brushed his mouth across her jaw, then down her throat to the vee where her shirt buttoned. The first button slid free easily. So did the second and the third. As she felt the warm evening air on her skin, she let her eyes drift shut, then gave a small gasp when his tongue touched her midriff, just below the single hook that fastened her crimson lace bra.

"Maybe I'll change your mind," he murmured.

As she shook her head, a falling sensation came over

her. His hands were on her shoulders, the heat of his body full-length along hers, and she realized he was laying her back on the scuffed white boards of the porch floor. With pleasure and need coursing through her entire body, she sighed and let him arrange her where he wanted.

"Papa says I'm the most stubborn child the Dimitris and Emanuelides families have ever produced. I'm hot-tempered and hardheaded, and I *never* do anything I don't want."

"I hope our daughter is just like you. It'll serve you right." He pulled her shirt from her jeans, undid the last two buttons, then folded back the edges so she was exposed to the night air and his gaze.

He laid his callus-roughened hands on her middle, spanning her from side to side, then rubbed upward, from waistband to bra. The occasional kisses he left on her skin were hot, wet, gentle bites that left her aching for more. When he unfastened her bra, she caught her breath, and when he leaned closer to take her nipple into his mouth, she forgot all about breathing. Arching her back against him, she gave a low, purely pleasured moan, then combed her fingers into his hair, urging him to suckle harder. The strong, steady pull of his mouth did funny things to her insides and made her greedy for all of him. It had been so long, and she was so hot. . . .

Bracing his hands on either side of her head, he stretched out on top of her, close enough she could feel his weight, but not so close that she bore all of it. He took her mouth with his, stabbed his tongue inside, and began moving against her, rubbing his arousal hard against her, creating a friction over two layers of tight denim that both tormented and pleased. Her mind went hazy as the need consumed her, made her match his rhythm, and drew a helpless whimper from her.

"Please, Sebastian . . ."

"Marry me."

"I want you . . . need you . . . Come inside me now."

"Marry me," he repeated stubbornly as she wrapped her legs around his hips, pulling him closer still. Kissing her greedily, he moved to the side, slid one arm under her head to better claim her mouth, and used his free hand to stroke her, caress her breasts, tease her nipples, tickle around her belly button. Her muscles tightened as he undid the button on her jeans, and they knotted even more when he pulled the zipper slowly to its end.

She reached for the button and zipper of his jeans, but he gently moved her hand away. "Let me," he whispered, his words a hot promise against her jaw.

With his erection pressed solidly against her thigh, he slid his fingers, just the tips, inside her jeans. For a moment, they were motionless, curved protectively over the beginning swell of her abdomen, then they eased lower, underneath the elastic band of her panties, sliding beneath crimson silk and lace, gliding to that heated, moist place where she needed him most. When one finger rubbed against her, she gasped. When it slid inside her, she cried out, but he muffled it with his kiss.

It was incredible—the sheer pleasure his talented fingers delivered, the risk of getting caught, the long time unfulfilled. The throbbing spread through her entire body as he stroked her in just the right way, with just the right pressure. Her nerves were tingling, her muscles clenching, her hips lifting to meet his every touch. Her climax was building, hot, relentless, making her tremble in anticipation, when unexpectedly the pressure eased.

"Will you marry me, Melina?"

"Wh—*Please* . . . I need . . ."

"I know what you need, darlin', and I'll give it to you when you give me the right answer."

"An-answer?" she gasped. "You can't be ser— Damn it, Sebastian, please . . . !"

"Just say yes, darlin', and I'll finish." As if to prove he spoke in good faith, he drew his finger over her in one long, slow stroke that made her shudder, then did it again, and then waited.

"Yes!" she whispered. "Oh, please, yes! Now . . ."

With a low chuckle, he kissed her once more as his fingers resumed their magic play. For one endless moment, he tormented her with the sweetest pain imaginable, then when she was certain she could bear no more, he ended it, letting her climax sweep over her with bone-melting intensity. His kiss was as fierce as her orgasm, blocking her cries as they subsided into purrs of satisfaction.

She couldn't think, couldn't move. If her mother and Yaya Rosa appeared in front of her at that very instant, she couldn't find the energy or the shame to cover herself. She was without virtue . . . and she loved it.

After a time, her eyes fluttered open of their own accord, and she saw Sebastian lying beside her, grinning in that incredibly egotistical way men got after making a woman come. When she got her breath, she would remind him that she could exhibit the same skill and power over him. Better yet, she would show him.

Then they would see who grinned biggest.

"You are a wicked man," she announced when she found her voice.

"Not me. I've never been wicked a day in my life."

"No, you save it for the night." She smiled seductively at him. "Now it's your turn."

Before she could move, he'd rolled over, balancing on his knees, straddling her hips. She watched, more than a little bewildered, as he fastened her jeans, then her bra, then started buttoning her shirt. Finally she laid her hands over his, stopping him. "I want to make love to you."

"Thank you, but I'll wait."

"For what?" Her gaze narrowed at his bland expression. "I told you, there's not going to be a honeymoon. You can't hold me to what I said a minute ago. It was blackmail. I was under duress."

He made a dismissive gesture. "That was just to get you accustomed to saying yes."

She stared at him a moment, then burst out laughing. "Anyone who knows me knows I have no problem saying yes to men. I've been doing it since I was sixteen. In fact, it's common knowledge that I really need to practice saying no."

Now it was his turn to stare. In the dim light, she couldn't read his expression clearly, though she could tell he'd gotten very serious—maybe even angry. He moved off her, brushed off his clothes, then pulled her to her feet with one hand. Suddenly she felt awkward and embarrassed, and she didn't even know why.

"I . . ." She didn't know what she wanted to say, which was all right, because he didn't wait around to hear it. Instead, without a word, he headed for the front porch. She hastily finished buttoning her blouse as she followed him. "Hey!" Catching his arm at the corner, she pulled him around. "What's wrong?"

He didn't say anything. He didn't even look at her.

"*What?* You didn't know I was easy? Did you think

you were the first stranger I'd ever picked up in a bar?" Her laughter was supposed to sound reckless. Instead, it merely sounded forced. "Surprise, Sebastian. You're not my first, my tenth, or even my twentieth. I've been with more men than you can imagine. I like men, remember? I like sex. I like sex with you—but that doesn't mean I'll ever agree to marry you."

He glared at her. "I don't give a damn how many men you've been with in the past. All I care about is the one you're going to be with in the future—me. And anyone who thinks you're easy is out of his mind. You're the most impossible woman I've ever met. And you'll marry me. You can do it voluntarily, or I'll drag you bound and gagged before the preacher, but you *will* marry me."

"When hell freezes over," she muttered, and he grinned a truly wicked grin as he bent close to murmur in a silken voice.

"Better grab a coat, darlin'. I feel a chill coming on."

Chapter Fifteen

IT TOOK A WHILE OF AIMLESS DRIVING THROUGH Bethlehem's darkened streets for the erection-that-wouldn't-quit to go away, making it all right for Sebastian to go to his parents' house and face his mother and daughter. He parked behind his father's pickup and had just reached the porch steps when the front door opened and his dad stepped out.

"Thought I heard your truck," James said. "Wasn't easy to tell with all the chattering going on in there."

"Who's here besides Chrissy?"

"Both your grandmothers and your brother's wife." James fished a cigar from his shirt pocket and lit it, sending the bittersweet scent of tobacco into the air. He removed another from his pocket and offered it to Sebastian. "You ever learn to smoke?"

"Nope."

"A good cigar on a quiet evening is one of the great pleasures in life. I've been smoking one a day for as long as I can remember, and you know, your mother still won't let me smoke 'em in the house." After returning the unlit cigar to his pocket, he slapped Sebastian on the back. "Come and go for a walk with me, son. It's been a long time since we've talked."

Though he really would have preferred to just pick up Chrissy and head home, Sebastian fell into step at his father's side. They crossed the street and headed in the direction of the nursing home where Grandma Sara had lived ever since Grandpa had died. Not that she needed nursing. She was frail, as anyone her age would be, but his mother insisted Sara would outlive them all.

"You know there's talk going around town," James said after a while.

"So I've heard."

"Is it true?"

"Yes."

"What are you going to do about it?"

He thought of the time he'd just spent with Melina on her porch. If he wasn't careful, he could still feel her against him—could still taste her, smell her, want her. "I'm trying to convince her we should get married, but . . . she's not easily persuaded."

"A mite stubborn, is she?"

Sebastian snorted. *"Mighty* stubborn is more like it."

"Your mother's planning a party to welcome her into the family. You have any opinions about that?"

"Tell her to welcome away. Maybe it'll nudge Melina in the right direction." Obviously she didn't feel he alone was worth giving up single motherhood for, but maybe his family could make a difference. She came from a large, loving family, so maybe his large, loving family could provide an incentive he apparently couldn't.

A block passed in silence before his father spoke again. "You love this girl?"

Sebastian could count on one hand the number of times his father had brought up an emotional subject with him—when each of his grandfathers had died, when he'd announced he was marrying Diana, when Chrissy had been born, and when Diana had left him. Virtually every conversation they'd ever had centered on more mundane subjects, and for the most part, both of them preferred it that way.

That was why he gave the simplest answer. He didn't say Melina was all he could think about, or that he needed her in his life, or that he couldn't imagine living without her. He didn't mention that he'd offered to leave Bethlehem, if that was what it took to be with her, or that he wanted to go home to her every night for the rest of his life, or that the fear of losing her was so great at times that it tightened his chest and choked the breath right out of him. All he said was the plain and simple answer to the question, and for his father, he knew, it was enough.

"Yeah, I love her."

"Good. Love isn't vital for a marriage to be successful, but it sure makes it a lot easier. So . . . when is the baby due?"

"March."

"And when are you getting married?"

"Soon as she says yes."

"You know, it would break your grandmothers' hearts to see their great-grandbaby come into this world without its mama married to its daddy."

"It wouldn't do wonders for mine," Sebastian said dryly. "I'm doing the best I can, Dad."

He just didn't know if it would be enough.

In silent agreement, when they reached the hospital, they turned and started back. After a time, his father said, "I heard the Millers are planning to renovate that big old house of his mother's and put it on the market. They're gonna give you a call about doing some of the work. It's a great old house. You ever been inside?"

Sebastian shook his head, and his father launched into a description of turn-of-the-century opulence. Sebastian murmured in all the right places, but his mind was on another old house, equally as grand but on a smaller scale, in the middle of town. The fact that he hadn't cared much about where they lived had been one of Diana's chief complaints during their marriage. A master carpenter should live in a better example of workmanship than the old farmhouse, she'd believed. The house was still of little importance as far as he was concerned, but he found himself wanting to live in that yellow house on the square.

But, hell, he'd be happy to live in a tent if Melina lived in it, too.

As they approached his folks' house, his father returned once more to the subject of Melina. "What does this girl think of Chrissy?"

"Honestly, I don't know. She likes kids, though, and Chrissy informed me this morning that it was okay with her if we got married."

"Don't you think you ought to get the two of them together sometime to see how they get along?"

"Probably."

"And don't you think you should tell Chrissy about the baby before someone else does?"

"Yeah, I guess so." That was something he hadn't

really considered. In his life before Melina, the chances of his having another child had been somewhere between slim to none. His sex life had been practically nonexistent—once here, another time there. If he'd ever thought he might get over Diana and find someone new, he would have assumed they'd be married long before a baby became a remote possibility.

"Come on in and let the women fuss over you a bit," James said, popping a breath mint into his mouth as if it could disguise the smell of cigar smoke that clung to him.

If anyone knew how to fuss, it was Sebastian's mother and grandmothers. By the time he got Chrissy and made it out the door again, he felt as if he'd been through an expert inquisition. And he still had to talk to Chrissy when they got home.

He managed to put it off while she bathed and got settled in bed. Then she scooted to one side of the bed and patted the mattress. "Lie down and tell me a story."

"All right." He stretched out beside her, and she snuggled close, one hand curled around her pink cat, the other around a handful of his T-shirt.

"You smell funny." She sniffed loudly, then giggled. "Like a girl. Like Melina. Did you kiss her?" Fluttering her lashes, she made kissy noises before giggling again.

"Yes, I did. You wanna make something of it?" he teased.

"Do you think she's pretty?"

"Yes."

"Are you gonna marry her?"

"I'd like to."

"And have babies with her?"

"Yeah, that, too."

"She's not as pretty as my mama."

Sebastian didn't respond to that. Diana had certainly been lovely in a blue-eyed-blond-haired-cheerleader sort of way, but Melina . . . She was the most beautiful woman he'd ever seen.

"But she's a pretty good private d'tective. D'ya think she could find Mama?"

He suppressed a wince as his chest tightened. If Chrissy was still harboring hopes that Diana could come home and live with them again . . . "I don't know, babe. Maybe she could."

"D'ya think she could bring Mama back like she did Lannie and Caleb and Julie?"

"Lannie and Caleb came back because they're just kids and this is their home, and Julie came because there was no place else for her to go. But your mom . . . She's a grown woman, Chrissy. She gets to decide for herself where she wants to live. No one can make her come back here."

Chrissy abruptly veered off on another tangent. "If you marry Melina, does that mean Julie's gonna be my sister?"

"If you want her to be. Sort of."

"Good. I like Julie. Will her baby be my brother or sister, too?"

Sebastian swallowed. "Yeah. Even . . . even if I don't marry her, you'll still be her baby's sister because . . . because I'm her baby's father. Do you understand?"

Chrissy solemnly shook her head.

He swore he felt beads of sweat popping out on his forehead. "You were made by your mama and me, right? And that baby was made by Melina and me. Okay?"

"How?"

"How?" he echoed gruffly.

"What did you do to make a baby?" Scrunching up her eyes, she rubbed her nose with the back of her hand. "Kasey Hudson says babies come from kissing, and her daddy's a doctor, but Josie Dalton says they do not. Aunt Shauna says there's books for kids that explain. Grandpa says I don't need to know till I'm thirty, and Grandma says I should ask you."

Nothing like passing the buck. Maybe he could put her off until he convinced Melina to marry him, and then it would be her place as mother to provide an explanation, wouldn't it? "When did you get so interested in where babies come from?"

"I dunno. Will this baby look like me?"

"Maybe." He thought Chrissy was beautiful, but she took after the Knights, so he was hoping this one looked like her mother, all dark and wild and full of life. Then they could work on having one who looked like both of them, to tie the family together.

"So I'll get a big sister and a baby sister or brother at the same time. Someone to be the boss of, and someone to be the boss of me." She grinned. "Okay. Hey, did you know Gracie's cat had kittens? Her mom says we need one or three or four to help keep the mice away. I told her we don't have mice, but she said we need 'em anyways. Can we?"

"Sure," Sebastian said absently, amazed at how easily she could switch gears and make decisions.

Her eyes brightened, and she threw her arms around his neck. "Really? We can? Thank you, Daddy! I already picked out names for 'em. Coco and CeCe and Tiffany and Melvin and—"

"Whoa, kiddo. No more than two, okay?" Then he did a double-take. "Melvin?"

She bobbed her head. "Isn't that a good name for a boy kitten? We'll pick 'em up before school tomorrow, okay? And they can sleep in here with me, and we'll get 'em two little milk dishes and two little food dishes and two little water—"

"We'll talk about this tomorrow, babe." He kissed her forehead, then slid to his feet. "I love you."

"I love you, too." She snuggled deeper under the covers and sighed. "A new mom, two new sisters, and two new kittens. That's pretty good for not being my birthday or Christmas or anything."

Sebastian turned off the lights and went to his room, with Sundance on his heels. There he stretched across the bed in the dark, reached for the phone on the night table, and dialed Melina's number from memory. "Do you miss me?" he asked when she said hello.

There was a moment's silence, then a sullen, "No."

"Liar."

"Hey, you had your chance. You could have left Chrissy at your mom's for a few more hours."

"Or you could quit being so stubborn. We could have been married two weeks ago and I could be making love with you every night instead of sleeping alone and missing you."

"There's a whole lot more to being married than sex," she pointed out sarcastically.

"No kidding. Let's see, I was married for eleven years, and you . . . oh, yeah. You've never been married."

"I've never killed anyone, either, but I know it's wrong."

"What's so wrong about getting married?"

"Wrong question. Ask me what's wrong about marrying you."

A twinge of pain knotted his gut. He wasn't up to hearing one more time how all she wanted from him was sex. It hurt too damn much. Instead he changed the subject. "I told Chrissy about the baby tonight."

"Told her what?"

"That she's going to have a brother or sister."

He expected an outburst: *You did what?* He got a long silence, followed by a grudging response. "I suppose it had to be done sooner or later."

Ask me how she took it, he silently urged, but when she remained frustratingly quiet, he went on. "My family wants to get together Saturday evening at Mom and Dad's. Is that okay with you?"

"Sure. But if you don't explain to them that we're not getting married, I will."

"You don't *explain* things to the Knight women. They're pretty hardheaded. You should fit right in."

"I'll take that as a compliment."

"I meant it as one," he retorted. "Will you and Julie have dinner with Chrissy and me tomorrow?"

"Why include the kids?"

"If we're all going to live together someday, it might help if we all spend some time together."

Her heavy sigh suggested his words annoyed her even if she wasn't going to argue the point with him again. "What if I would rather see you alone?"

"We'll arrange for that, too. We'll see you at six." He was close to hanging up when he heard her speak his name. Quickly he brought the phone back to his ear. "Yeah?"

"I *do* miss you."

Her admission, however unwillingly given, sent a rush of warmth through him and made him smile. "I know. See you tomorrow."

After being on her own for so long, Julie was used to being the newcomer with no ties, no friends. Usually it didn't bother her at all . . . well, except on holidays. And Mother's Day had gotten her pretty down. And on Father's Day, she'd been all upset. But usually she was okay with it.

At Bethlehem High School, being the odd one out was tougher. It seemed everyone knew each other, and it didn't help that she was older than most of the other seniors. None of them knew it, but she did, and that was all that mattered. It made her feel self-conscious and lonely, but she hid it from Melina when she got home Wednesday afternoon.

Melina was sitting at her desk, the computer turned on and papers spread across the work surface. The phone was propped between her ear and shoulder, and she was saying *uh-huh* every few moments.

Julie set her book bag down, got two Diet Cokes from the kitchen, then came back and slid one across to Melina before settling in the armchair on the opposite side of the desk.

"Thanks," Melina said when she got off the phone. "How was school?"

"It was fine."

"Did you meet some kids?"

"Yes."

"Do you like your teachers?"

"Most of them. Are you practicing sounding motherly?"

"Maybe, smarty pants. Did I succeed?"

"Yeah, you did." There had been a time when her mother had asked about school and friends, and been truly interested in the answers. But if she thought about that long enough right now, it would hurt, so she pushed it out of her mind. "Are we still going to dinner with Sebastian and Chrissy?"

"Yep."

"You know, I can stay here with Chrissy and order pizza, and you guys can go out alone."

"The idea is for the four of us to spend time together." A scowl settled over Melina's features, matching the tone of her voice. "If all of us are going to live together, he says, it might be nice if we spend some time together."

"Are we going to live together?"

Melina didn't have an easy answer. She opened her mouth, then closed it, then dragged her fingers through her hair. She looked troubled and sounded sad. "I don't know. Sebastian and I met early in the summer and had a . . ."

"A fling," Julie suggested.

"Right. I thought it was more. He made it very clear it was much less. He didn't want to see me again, and if Chrissy hadn't run away, he wouldn't have. When we left Providence, it was over between us. He didn't have any place in his life for me. But then I found out I was pregnant, and now he has this ridiculous idea that he has to marry me for the baby's sake."

"You think that's the only reason?"

Melina's smile was wobbly. "Honey, I *know* that's the only reason."

"I don't know," Julie said, shaking her head. "It's not like people care anymore if a kid's parents are married. And he can be a father without marrying you. And let's face it—you tend to give him a hard time. There's gotta be more that keeps him coming back than just duty. Like"—she grinned—"your sparkling wit. Your sweet disposition. Your generous nature."

"Brat," Melina said, tossing a clothing catalog at her as the phone rang. She picked up the receiver, said, "This is Melina Dimitris," in a businesslike voice, then said, "May I ask who's calling?"

A strange look came over her face, and she put the call on hold before looking at Julie. "It's for you. It's . . . your mother."

Julie stared at the receiver. For so long she'd dreamed about her mother tracking her down, sparing no effort to find her, to apologize and ask her to go home. After five or six months on her own, she'd pretty much given up dreaming, but once in a while, something reminded her of the way things used to be, and she dreamed again for a bit.

This last time it had been the letter. When she'd given it to Alanna to mail, she'd told herself nothing would come of it . . . but there'd been a little tiny hope that her mother might have regretted her choice. She'd even wondered what she would do if her mom wanted her back—if this time *she* would have to make a choice between a blood relative and someone she'd come to love.

Oh, God, she didn't want to have to choose between her mother, Alli, Matt, and Dex, and Melina, Alanna, and everyone in Bethlehem.

"Do you want me to go out?" Melina asked as she pressed the phone into Julie's hand.

"No. Stay." Her arm was shaking, so Julie braced it on the desk and nodded for Melina to take the call off hold. "Hello," she said, and her voice shook, too.

"It's me, Julie. I got your letter. How are you?"

She closed her eyes, remembering countless other times she'd listened to her mother's voice. Telling bedtime stories. Singing while she did housework. Laughing with her father. Fighting with her father. Telling her she had to leave because her husband didn't want her around. She'd thrown her daughter out of the house on her seventeenth birthday to make it—or not—on her own, and she could ask *How are you?*

"I'm fine," Julie replied, feeling choked.

"So . . . you're living in New York."

"Yeah."

"How long have you been there?"

"A couple months."

"You like it?"

Her fingers tightened around the phone. She wanted to stomp her feet, throw something, or scream what did it matter whether she liked the place when it was the only place on earth where she was welcome! But instead she bit the inside of her lip and said, "Yeah, it's fine."

"This Melinda person . . . who is she?"

"Melina. She's a private investigator."

There was that quick-to-side-against-her tone to her mother's voice that she hated. "You in trouble?"

Yes, I've been in trouble ever since you threw me out with a beat-up car, my clothes, and a few hundred bucks! "No. She was looking for some kids who had run away from home, and they were with me. She brought me back with them."

"So you're living with her."

"Yeah."

"That's nice. So . . . things have been okay."

"Yeah, they're okay . . . now that I don't have to live in my car or worry about having enough food to eat."

For a long time her mother was quiet, then she sighed like she did when she was pretending *she* was the victim of unreasonable people. "You're angry. I understand that, and I don't blame you. I know the past year hasn't been easy on you . . . but, Julie, you have to realize that it hasn't been any easier for me."

"Really. You had a place to live. You didn't have to worry about freezing to death when it was cold, or someone *stealing* your home when you went to work, or going hungry, or getting murdered for your coat. But it was just as tough for you. Yeah, right, Mom."

"Look, I did the best I could. I'm sorry it wasn't good enough for you."

She made it sound as if Julie had made *so* many demands. She'd wanted to live in her house with her family. Was that asking so much? Her daddy had *paid* for that house, and he'd done it for his wife and his kids—*not* for his wife's no-good husband and whichever kids *he* decided should live there. She'd had a right to be there!

But knowing her mother obviously didn't agree, she changed the subject. "Are the kids there? Let me talk to Alli."

"They're gone to the store for school supplies with their dad."

Her face flamed red hot as outrage raced over her. "He's *not* their dad! How can you call him that? Their dad is dead, and no one can ever replace him, especially that—that bastard!"

"You watch your mouth, Julianne. I won't tolerate your disrespect."

Tears filled Julie's eyes and clogged her throat. The first time she'd spoken to her mother in almost ten months, and all the woman could do was heap pity on herself and defend a man who wasn't worthy of the name. There was no *I'm sorry.* No *I miss you.* No *Please come home.*

No *I love you.*

"Why'd you call, Mom?" she demanded. "To make yourself feel better? So you can pretend you're a good mother? You're not. You're an *awful* mother. I'm just sorry I couldn't take the kids with me when I left because no mother at all would be better than one like you! For God's sake, I'm your *daughter!* Doesn't that mean anything to you?"

Her voice broke then and the tears began falling. She hardly noticed when Melina took the phone from her, said something sharp, and hung up, then wrapped her arms around her. Somehow they both wound up on the floor, and Julie held on to her and sobbed the way she did the day her mom had pushed her out the door and locked it behind her.

"It's okay, Julie," Melina whispered, rocking her back and forth. "It'll be okay, honey. Go ahead and let it all out, darlin'. Everything will be all right."

IT TOOK A TREMENDOUS AMOUNT OF EFFORT FOR Melina to get herself and Julie ready for dinner that evening. First she had to talk the girl into going. After that damn phone call, all Julie had wanted to do was curl up on her bed and cry inconsolably. Cold compresses, eyedrops, and a heavy hand with the makeup covered the most obvious signs of distress, but even dressed up, made up, and ready to go, she still looked fragile, as if a wrong word might shatter her.

But they managed to be ready on time—well, only ten minutes late. "And we're beautiful, too," Melina announced as they walked arm in arm down the stairs.

Julie giggled. "There's no shortage of vanity in this house, is there?"

Melina stopped her in front of the ornate mirror that hung in the hallway. "No vanity, darlin'. Just a simple acknowledgment of the truth. Look at those faces. Absolute feminine perfection."

She watched Julie study their reflections for a long moment, saw the sadness in her blue eyes, and once again her anger flared. For a nickel, she'd go to Ohio and—well, she didn't know what she would do when she got there, but it wouldn't be pretty. The former Mrs. Bujold would be sorry she'd ever made Melina's acquaintance, and she would be damn sorry she'd ever abandoned her daughter.

After collecting their bags, they headed for the door. When Sebastian and Chrissy had arrived a few minutes before six, Melina had raised Julie's bedroom window and called down to them to come inside and get comfortable. He had called back that they would wait on the porch. They found him sitting in one of the two chairs, with Chrissy on his lap. She scrambled to her feet when she saw them, gave Julie a hug, then walked right up to Melina.

"Hi," she said softly, her gaze settled somewhere around Melina's middle. "My name's Christina Diana

Knight, but ever'one calls me Chrissy, and I'm seven years old."

Puzzled because certainly Chrissy knew she remembered her, Melina imitated the girl's murmur and replied, "I know that."

Chrissy glanced at her, then lowered her head and her voice. "I'm in second grade, in Mr. Peterson's class, and I got two new kittens today. I learned to swim this summer, and I like to go fishin' and camping, and I got a dog named Sundance that's an Irish'etter, and my favorite color is pink. See?" She twirled around to show off her pastel top and hot-pink jeans, as well as pink print sneakers, then comically smacked her forehead with one palm. "I bet you can't see, can you? On account of it's dark in there."

She was talking to the baby, Melina realized, and felt a sudden urge to cry again. Feeling Sebastian's gaze on her, she looked up to find him watching them with a tenderness that made her ache. She wanted to fling herself into his arms . . . or run away and hide where he could never find her. He was getting too close, becoming too important. He could break her heart with no more than a look.

More importantly, he could break her baby's heart.

Finally Chrissy turned her attention to Melina. "Does all she do is sleep in there?"

"Pretty much. When she gets bigger, she'll start moving and kicking."

"Can I feel?"

"Well, there's nothing to feel right now, but . . . sure."

The girl's touch was so gentle Melina hardly felt it. After a moment, she patted Melina's stomach twice, then backed away and giggled. "Is it for sure a girl?"

"No, not for sure." Though she hoped so. She wanted

a little girl who would learn to cook at Yaya Livia's side, who would look just like a perfect little angel with the sweetest smile, and outpitch, outrun, and outclimb every boy in the county. She wanted a daughter who could take care of herself, run any business, and still bring a man to his knees with no more than a smile.

Though a little boy would be nice, too, she thought with another glance at Sebastian. One with his father's dark eyes and quiet strength and that wicked smile to make the girls swoon.

"What're you gonna name it?"

"I'm not sure. If it's a girl, I thought maybe Alyssa."

"What if it's a boy?"

"It's tradition among Greeks to name the first son after his father's father. What is your grandfather's name?"

"Daddy's daddy is Grandpa James."

James Dimitris . . . or James Knight. Not bad.

Of course, the same tradition applied to the first daughter and the father's mother, but she had no intention of naming her sweet little girl Hildred, Hildy, or any variation thereof. But James, Jim, Jay . . . she could live with any one of those.

Chrissy turned back to Julie, automatically slipping her hand in the older girl's. "Wanna hear about my kittens? There's two of 'em, and their names are Tiffany and Melvin, and they're so cute . . ."

As they wandered down the steps, Sebastian came closer to Melina. He had an intent look in his eyes that meant he was either going to kiss her or propose to her. She stalled by following the kids to the top of the steps. "Tiffany and Melvin?"

"I know. I voted for Coco and CeCe, but she insisted

they were Tiffany and Melvin." Catching her hand, he pulled her back and into his arms. "Don't I get a kiss?"

"There are people around."

He didn't look to see if there truly were. After all, it was Bethlehem, and there was always someone about except in the night. And sometimes even then, she thought, remembering when Mitch Walker had spotlighted them necking on the porch.

"I'm not talking about stripping you naked and having my way with you right here right now," he teased. "Just a kiss. Surely a man can give one kiss to the woman he's going to marry without shocking anyone."

"I'm not going to marry you," she murmured even as his mouth brushed across hers.

It was one kiss. Sweet. Gentle. Warm. One kiss that trembled on the verge of becoming wicked, hot, and greedy, that made her weak and hungry, that promised everything but left her empty and aching.

When he ended the kiss, he touched his lips to her cheek, her forehead, her hair, then held her close. Leaning against him, drawing strength from him, she hesitantly raised her gaze to his. "Are you ever going to have sex with me again?"

He shook his head. "But once we're married, I'll make love to you whenever you want."

She wasn't proud to admit that she could be tempted for nothing more than that. But if having a baby was a lousy reason to get married, how much worse a reason was regular sex?

Marriage was too difficult a proposition to base on anything less than wholehearted, soul-deep love. They couldn't lay the burden of making a marriage work on an innocent child not yet born, and couldn't count on passion and lust to last. Love and everything that came with it—respect, friendship, commitment, devotion . . . that was what her parents had, what Yaya Rosa had shared with Papous George and Yaya and Papous Emanuelides with each other. She would shame the family and herself if she settled for one bit less.

Thankfully her stomach chose that moment to rumble as if some wicked imp resided inside. Sebastian gave her a wry look, and she responded with an innocent smile. "I believe my child is hungry. Shall we go?"

Chapter Sixteen

SATURDAY EVENING WAS ABOUT AS GOOD COOKOUT weather as Bethlehem ever had. The temperature was in the low seventies when Sebastian pulled to the curb half a block down the street from his parents' house. Chrissy was already there—she'd spent most of the day with her grandmother—and he had Melina and Julie with him. Neither appeared particularly thrilled to be there.

Melina was looking at the houses on her right. "Which one is your folks?"

"Down there on the corner." He pointed ahead and to the left, where at least twenty-five people were already gathered.

"All these cars belong to your relatives?"

"Pretty much." If he thought she might be impressed by the fact that they filled the driveway and went halfway down the block in all four directions, he was wrong.

She sniffed smugly. "This is nothing. The Dimitrises have more people than this for a simple Sunday dinner."

"Then you won't have any problem dealing with such a small bunch." Sebastian got out, and so did Julie, but Melina didn't move. He gave her a taunting grin. "What's the matter, sweetheart? Chicken?"

"No." She slid across the bench seat, under the steering wheel, and to the ground. It was quite a sight, with her tight black dress sliding even higher on the thigh than it normally went, with her mile-long legs and three-inch sandals displayed for his appreciation. When she was on her feet, she tugged the hem of her dress an inch or two lower, then shrugged into the shirt she'd brought to camouflage the fact that the dress stretched tighter than usual over her stomach. The shirt's fit was as loose as the dress was snug, and it was made from a sheer black fabric that draped over her breasts and clung to the curve of her bottom when she tied the tails in a knot at her hips.

"Do me a favor, darlin'," he said, leaning close so his voice wouldn't carry to Julie. "Wear that shirt on our wedding night . . . and nothing else."

She frowned at him. "Do all these people know I'm pregnant?"

"I imagine so."

"Do they all know you're the father?"

"If they know one, they know the other. And if they don't, they'll find out real quick. Why?"

"Just considering whether I should disabuse them of the notion that we're getting married individually or as a group. It would be quicker to just climb up on that table and announce it to everyone at once, but it might be more effective one-on-one."

The muscles in Sebastian's jaw tightened, but his grin

didn't waver. "You can deny it until you're blue in the face, but no one's gonna believe you."

"We'll see." Giving him a devilish smile, she left him and Julie standing on the curb and strolled—sauntered—no, sashayed—into the crowd as if she'd known them all her life.

He watched admiringly until his female relatives blocked her from view, then glanced at the girl beside him. "Tell me, Julie. Do you think I have a chance?"

"She's not crazy about this idea of getting married just because she's pregnant."

"Yeah, she's made that clear."

"But as long as she continues to see you, you've got a chance . . . and six and a half months to change her mind."

And he might need every minute of it.

"Come on," he said, his mood grimmer than it had been a few moments ago. "I'll introduce you to some of the kids."

Once he'd taken care of that and said his hellos, he got a Coke from the cooler, found a back-porch pillar to lean against, and watched Melina. She was sitting in a padded lawn chair, with his mother on one side, his grandmothers on the other, and a fair number of the other women in the family gathered around. Did she have any clue, he wondered, how well she fit in? How natural and right it was for her to be there?

Did she care?

He wandered around a while and talked to a few relatives and a few old friends before returning to the porch for another drink. He'd just popped the top on the can when his mother's voice came from behind him.

"There you are. Carry this for me, will you?"

Turning, he saw Hildy balancing a tray of hamburger patties while closing the back door. He took the tray, then followed her to the gas grill at the edge of the porch. "Think you have enough meat here?" he asked dryly.

She glanced at the teetering stacks of patties and frowned. "There's more inside if we need it. I'd rather cook too much than too little. I don't want anyone to go away hungry."

"Has anyone *ever* gone away hungry after a meal at your house?"

"Not to my knowledge, and I don't intend for it to happen tonight."

"I thought Dad was in charge of grilling."

She brandished a pancake turner at him. "Hush your mouth. You know how he grills hamburgers—they're burned on the outside and raw inside. I told your brothers to distract him this evening. If you see him coming this way, head him off."

"Yes, ma'am."

She placed eight or ten patties on the grill, then glanced at him. "I like your girl."

His gaze automatically returned to Melina. Chrissy was sitting on her lap now, and they were laughing. They looked natural and right, too, but maybe it was an illusion. Maybe he just wanted them all to be a family so badly that he was seeing it where it didn't exist.

Maybe it would never exist.

"There seems to be a little confusion, though, about when you two are getting married. Your father said soon. She said never."

His jaw clenched again, and a chill snaked down his spine. How many times had she told him the same thing? So why did this time feel worse? Why did this insistence make a dent in the determination that had kept him going up till now? Maybe because all the other rejections had been private, but this time she'd brought his family into it, just as she'd promised she would. All those other proposals and rejections had been something of a game, but telling *him* she wouldn't have him was one thing. Telling his family she didn't want him was another.

Maybe it was time to take her seriously. To accept that she had no desire to marry him. To use the next six and a half months to prepare himself for being a part-time father to their baby. For seeing Melina and knowing he couldn't have her. For knowing they would never be a family.

Truth was, if they couldn't be a family, he didn't want to be anything. Not friends, not even polite acquaintances. He wanted everything . . . or nothing.

"Sebastian?"

He looked at his mother, who was watching him closely.

She gestured toward the party. "Your grandmother's calling. The ladies want you to join them."

Ten minutes ago he would have been happy to sit with Melina and listen to her charm his grandmothers, or vice versa. At the moment, though, he'd sooner be trapped with his great-uncle Boren, who could send a person into a coma with his monotone voice and his endlessly meandering stories-without-a-point.

"Go on now." Hildy nudged him with her elbow, and he reluctantly headed toward the all-female group, hoping for whoever Boren's current captive audience was to escape so he could take his place. He had no such luck, though.

He bent to kiss his grandmothers' cheeks and got a kiss from Chrissy before she skipped off.

"Have a seat," Grandma Sara urged.

He made a point of looking around. "No chairs."

"You can sit with Melina," Grandma Hildred said with a sly grin. "There's plenty of room. Lift up, Melina, and let him slide in there with you."

The only way he and Melina could both fit in that chair was with her on his lap, and that was the last place he wanted her when she was wearing that skimpy little dress—at least, when they had an audience. "Thanks, but I'll stand."

"Suit yourself." Hildred glanced at the people around them, then made a shooing motion. "You all take your chairs and go off and talk among yourselves. Sara and I have things to discuss with the kids."

Everyone obeyed without question. Of course, it rarely occurred to anyone to disobey the two old women.

"I understand you've bought the Caldwell house," Sara began. "Are you going to live there, or out at the farm?"

"I thought I'd stay at my house and Sebastian could stay at his," Melina said evenly.

"The farmhouse has plenty of room," Sara said. "But the Caldwell house is so lovely, and right there on the square. You'd have a front-row seat for all the goings-on in town."

"It'd be awfully convenient for the Christmas Eve service," Hildred added.

"And the Fourth of July parade."

"To say nothing of the summer band concerts."

"And, of course, Sebastian's workshop is at the farm, so it's not as if he would be abandoning it."

"What about your business?" Hildred asked.

"My office is in Buffalo, but I've been working out of

the Cald—out of my house since I moved here. I'll probably continue to do so."

"What do you think of that?" The old lady directed the question to Sebastian, who shrugged.

"It's her business, Grandma. She can do what she wants with it."

"But that other one was a full-time wife and mother."

"You can say her name. It was Diana," he said, feeling a twinge of impatience. "And what does she have to do with anything?"

Sara shook her finger at Melina in warning. "We don't much approve of divorce. That's what's wrong with the institution of marriage today. There's no shame in divorce, so there's no reason to make the marriage work. You change your mind, you get a divorce. Have a fight, get a divorce. See someone you might like better, get a—"

Hildred silenced her with a hand on her arm. "We get the picture, Sara. Now how about babies?"

Melina was smiling, either sincerely enjoying herself or doing a hell of a job pretending. "I won't be making any decision on having more babies until I pop this one out. Who knows? I might be a real weenie about the labor and delivery part."

Hildred's eyes glazed over. "I remember giving birth to Sebastian's mother. Twenty—"

Sara butted in in the resigned voice of someone who'd heard the story plenty of times before. So had Sebastian, but he wouldn't dare interrupt or finish it for them. "Twenty-four hours in labor, and she like to have killed her husband when it was over. Didn't let him forget it for two years."

"Not for two full years." Hildred nodded in agreement. "Of course, back then, husbands weren't allowed in the delivery room and mothers were put to sleep through the worst of it."

"Yes, back then things were done *right*. Why, these days they let just about anyone wander in—your husband, your kids, your parents and friends. My father would have passed out cold at the mere thought of being in the room when I gave birth."

"So would mine," Melina said.

"Is this the first grandbaby for your folks?" Sara asked.

"Yes, ma'am, it is."

"They must be so excited. Well, except for the part about your not being married yet."

"Actually . . ." Melina glanced at Sebastian, and he was surprised to see that her cheeks were a faint bronze. "I haven't told them yet. I want to do it in person, and I haven't had a chance . . ."

The two old ladies exchanged looks. "Haven't told them yet?"

"Complete strangers know, but your own mother and father don't?"

"Well . . . I didn't tell the complete strangers, either," Melina said in her defense.

"Why, you're just determined to do everything all out of order, aren't you?" Hildred asked while Sara tsked and shook her head.

"Okay," Sebastian said. "You've monopolized her enough. I'd like to introduce her to a few other people if you don't mind."

"Yeah, like your father," Sara said. "And your brothers and your sister-in-law."

"Plus your aunts and uncles and cousins," Hildred added. "And I don't suppose you've met any of her family, either, have you? Why, your grandfather had to ask my father for my hand before he was allowed to ask me. And here you've already got her pregnant without the families any the wiser."

He pulled Melina to her feet and led her away from his grandmothers—not that that stopped them from clucking their tongues and continuing the conversation without them.

"They don't mean any harm," Melina said after a moment.

"Of course they don't. They're just bossy old busybodies."

She swatted his arm playfully. "Don't talk about your grandmothers that way." Then, her voice more serious, she asked, "What's wrong? You seem . . ." She shrugged, and the sheer fabric of her shirt rippled. She was damn sexy in the dress alone, but it was funny how adding a shirt—one he could see through, no less—upped the impact about a thousand times. It offered tantalizing glimpses of what was underneath and made him want to peel it off . . . slowly. Her dress would be next to go, along with whatever she wore underneath it—which couldn't be very damn much—and then he would sink inside her and . . .

Under her watchful gaze, he gave himself a mental shake. "Nothing's wrong."

"Except I'm having a better time with your family than you are. Why?"

"Illusion," he murmured, fingering her shirtsleeve. "It's all illusion."

She looked puzzled, as if she might press for more of an answer, but luckily his mother chose that moment to announce that dinner was ready. They sat down to eat at a table with twenty relatives, so there was no privacy for conversation, and he kept it that way until long after the sun set. Finally, with all the food put away and the youngest of the kids settling down on blankets or laps to sleep, he caught Melina hiding a yawn of her own and seized the excuse to leave the party.

With Chrissy spending the night with his parents and Julie going to a party in town with his cousin Rick's daughter, Courtney, it was just the two of them returning to the old house on the square. They sat down at the end of the porch, their feet propped side by side on the stool, and Melina gave a heavy sigh. "I like your family."

"Did you think you wouldn't?"

"I wondered," she admitted honestly. "You have to admit, it would complicate things if I didn't like them or they didn't like me. . . . Did they?"

"They hugged you, kissed you, and made plans to see you again. What do you think?"

She smiled smugly. "I think they were impressed by your good taste. Your grandmothers are a hoot. Wait until they get together with Yaya Rosa."

"And why would they ever do that?" he asked stiffly. He could think of only two reasons for her eighty-year-old grandmother to make the trip to Bethlehem—for a wedding or, possibly, the baby's birth. Since Melina kept insisting there wouldn't be a wedding . . .

"I don't know." After a moment of uncomfortable silence, she asked, "What's wrong, Sebastian? You've been in a mood all evening. Did I behave inappropriately? Was someone offended by the way I'm dressed? Did some relative not like me as much as Diana?"

"Nothing's wrong."

"You made a comment earlier about something being an illusion. What did you mean?"

He shrugged, but she wasn't about to be put off so easily. Moving fluidly, she shifted from the chair to the footstool, sitting where he had little choice but to look at her. Of course, looking at her was the easy part. Touching her, holding her, loving her—those were hard.

"What did you mean?"

"I was talking about your shirt."

"Oh, yeah, right. This shirt always brings men down and makes them moody."

He managed a sort of smile. "I'm not moody."

"Take it from a woman who has PMS with a vengeance every month like clockwork—well, under normal circumstances. This is moody." She hesitated. "Did someone say something to you?"

"Like what?"

"Oh, I don't know. 'She looks like a tramp. Are you sure it's your baby?' Or 'She's not like us. Can't you claim the baby's not yours?' "

He hooked his fingers around hers. "They would never say anything like that."

"But . . . ?"

"I just realized . . ." The time for games was past. He wanted a commitment from her. A future. A family. He wanted to see her every day, to spend every night beside her. He wanted to know that he was as important to her as she was to him, worthy of her respect, her friendship, and her devotion, if not her love. He wanted to claim her as *his*—his wife, the mother of his children, the better part of his heart. He wanted to marry her.

Or forget her.

Never issue an ultimatum you aren't prepared to live with. It was good advice. There was no way in hell he was prepared to live without Melina . . . and no way he could go on the way they were. There wasn't even a suitable name for the relationship he had with her. Boyfriend? Too juvenile. Lover? Implied an emotional connection she was missing. Significant other? Too dopey and not necessarily true. Friend? Maybe.

But he had friends. He didn't need another.

"You just realized what?"

"We've turned something serious and important into a joke. I ask you to marry me, and you say no. As long as I don't accept that you really mean it, I can still believe that someday you'll say yes, and as long as you keep saying no, you think someday it'll sink in and I'll quit asking." The next words stuck in his throat, and he had to take a breath before he could get them out. "I guess I just realized that 'someday' is today. No more joking, no more pressure. I'll ask once more, and whatever your answer is, I'll accept it. So . . . last time, darlin'. Think long and hard before you answer, because I won't ask again."

He used a car driving past as reason to delay, when really he needed the time to summon his nerve and prepare for the worst, because that was really all he could expect. She'd told him no a dozen times, but he'd wanted it so much and hoped so much . . .

When he looked back at her, she was watching him, her expression calm and steady. Not regretful, as in Sorry-I'm-going-to-break-your-heart. Certainly not anticipatory, as in Surprise-yes-yes-I'll-marry-you.

He thought about doing something hokey, like getting down on one knee, then settled for taking both her hands in his. "Will you marry me, Melina?"

In that first instant, she looked relieved. Wish as he might, there was no mistaking it. She was relieved that he wasn't going to bring up the subject of marriage again, and that gave him her answer. A cold, empty space formed in his gut as a sense of futility underlaid with sorrow seeped through him. He would give damn near anything to take back the words, to avoid having to see that look on her face and know the reason behind it, but better to face it now than later. Later would be too painful . . . though right now was painful enough.

She moved to sit astride his lap, bracing her hands on the chair back on either side of his head. "I thought you were going to say you'd realized you were still in love with Diana or something, in which case I would have to hurt you badly." She brushed her mouth along his jaw in a seductive gesture. "No, I won't marry you, but I *will* seduce you right out of your socks if you'll give me a chance." Without waiting for his response, she shifted her hips against him and let her features settle in a sexy pout. "It's been so long, and I still look pretty damn good out of my clothes—but trust me, darlin', that's gonna change before long."

In a husky imitation of a western drawl that would make him laugh if he didn't hurt so damn bad, she asked, "Whaddaya say, cowboy? You wanna saddle up and take this filly for a ride?"

He gazed at her for a long time. The right thing—the smart thing—would be to make some excuse, tell her goodbye, and walk away. But he knew he could no more do that than he could sprout wings and fly. Besides, wasn't it only fair, after the times he'd said no—the times he'd wanted to wait until it meant something more than just sex to her—that he have one last time to remember her by?

As if he would ever forget her.

"Sebastian?" she prompted.

He brushed her hair back from her face, trying not to notice that his hand was unsteady, hoping she didn't notice, either. "I'm trying to remember whether a filly is any young female horse, or a female horse who's never been pregnant."

She shifted against him again as her mouth feathered across his. "Forget the damn horse, darlin', and take me to bed before I start begging."

Sliding his fingers into her hair, he held her still for a sudden, hard kiss. The instant the heat flared through him, he put her away, got to his feet, lifted her over his shoulder in a fireman's carry, and headed for the door.

"Sebastian!" she shrieked with a giggle as she tried frantically to tug the skirt down. "My dress is too short for this! Everyone can see my panties! Put me down!"

"Darlin', there's no one looking but me, and I intend to take those babies off with my teeth." He settled one hand over her bottom in a lazy caress, holding the fabric in place . . . or maybe easing it up an inch past indecent. Her giggles became a soft moan that cut through him, leaving raw hunger in its wake.

He could do this. She might have broken his heart and ended his chance of having a real family, but, yeah, he could do this.

IT WASN'T THE MOST COMFORTABLE POSITION FOR BEING carried to bed—though Melina certainly had a good view of faded denim stretched over Sebastian's tight butt and muscular thighs—but the getting-put-down once they reached her bedroom . . . that was worth the blood-rush to her face and her hair falling wildly. Hands on her hips, he slid her down one slow inch at a time, bringing the front of her body into intimate contact with the front of his. By the time her feet reached the floor, she was hot and tingling all over, and he was hard. Impressively so.

By silent agreement, they each dealt with their own clothes . . . more or less. She tossed her shirt across the footboard of the bed, kicked off her shoes, unzipped her dress and shimmied out of it, then peeled off her green silk panties, all in the time it took him to remove his shoes and undo half the buttons on his shirt. Of course, that was because he was watching her with an appreciative look that warmed her all the way to her toes.

"Need some help?" she asked, reaching for the button at the waistband of his jeans.

"Aw, you just want to get into my pants," he teased.

"Gee, how'd you guess?" His shirttail brushed against her knuckles as he pulled it loose from his jeans, then slid out of it. Distracted by the sight of all that naked skin and muscle right before her eyes, she fumbled over the button, then drew the zipper down as she leaned forward and left a line of hot, wet kisses across his chest. When her teeth grazed his nipple, he groaned, and when her fingers slid inside his jeans and wrapped around him, he did it again.

"Damn, Melina, let me finish—" He sucked in his breath as she caressed him, long and slow.

"Remember the other night on the porch?" she murmured. "When you tortured and tormented and blackmailed me before you let me finish?" With her free hand, she pulled his head down for a hard, fierce kiss, and with pleasure she made him groan again, made him shudder convulsively. "What is it they say about turnabout?"

His eyes were closed, his forehead dotted with sweat, and his muscles were clenched tightly, including his jaw—as if he couldn't speak without making some incredibly erotic sound. Just looking at him, so obviously aroused practically beyond enduring, and knowing she was responsible fed her own need, tightened her own muscles. Then, suddenly, his hands were on her, carefully removing her hand from his crotch, holding her at arm's length while he hastily shucked the rest of his clothes, then lifting her back onto the bed as he filled her with one long, sure stroke.

His body pressed her into the mattress, warm, heavy, comforting. As he braced himself above her on his elbows, he grinned that seriously wicked grin. "Turnabout's fair play . . . and, oh, baby, am I gonna have fun playing with you."

Then he proceeded to prove his boast.

Much to her delight.

THE DOOR WAS CLOSED, THE LIGHTS OFF. NINE jasmine-scented candles burned on the dressing table, the triple mirror reflecting their light into infinity. Overhead, the ceiling fan slowly turned, its blades creating just enough of a breeze to make the candles' flames dance crazily and to cool the sweat that made Melina's skin slick. She lay on her back, weak, lazy all the way down to her toes, unable to do anything but stroke Sebastian's hair where his head rested on her abdomen.

"So this is what they mean by 'complete and utter satisfaction,' " she remarked in a voice made hoarse by too many whimpers, groans, pleas, and cries.

"Hmm."

"When people around here say you're good with your hands, they don't have a clue, do they?" He'd brought her more pleasure in one night than all the other men she'd ever been with combined. Of course, she hadn't been in love with any of those other men except Rico the rat, and the love she'd felt for him was nothing compared to what she felt for Sebastian.

Maybe it was even enough to build a marriage on. So what if he didn't love her? If he never would have proposed or even seen her again if not for the baby? He was fond of her—she was sure of that—and grateful for her help in finding Chrissy. He was responsible, dependable, reliable, and he treated her better without loving her than Rico ever had. He was handsome, thoughtful, an incredible lover, and a wonderful father, and he *wanted* this baby—enough to take her and Julie to get it. Maybe all that was more important than love.

Or maybe all that didn't matter without love. The baby was his biggest concern—the only reason he was in her bed at that moment or in her life at all. There was no law that said he had to marry her to give their child his name—Melina had no objection to that—and he could be the best father in the world without living in the same house or taking on the burden of another marriage that would surely, eventually fail. He would meet someone and fall in love. She would fixate on what she was missing and grow bitter. Their baby would grow up and away, and leave them with no reason to be together.

He would break her heart.

And it wasn't just *her* heart she had to think about. There was the baby, who would be caught in the middle, and Julie, who'd already lost too many people she cared about.

So what was she supposed to do? Keep seeing him, fall deeper and deeper in love with him, and hope that someday he would come to love her, too? Or should she end the relationship now, before he became an integral part of her self, before Julie learned to love him, before the baby came to accept the two of them together as right and normal? Before she lost any hope at all of surviving without him?

She'd never been so torn in her life.

"What time is Julie due home?"

"Midnight."

Sebastian moved to lie beside her, then curved his hand protectively over her belly. "Too bad she doesn't know Courtney well enough to spend the night with her."

"Would you spend the night here if she did? And shock everyone in town when they see your truck parked out front in the morning?"

His laughter was a vivid contrast to the sleepy, lazy tone of his voice. "I've got news for you, baby. They already know we've been exchanging a hell of a lot more than good-night kisses on the porch."

Rolling onto her side, she gazed into his dark eyes. "You don't have to leave just because Julie's coming home."

"I'm not going anywhere yet, darlin'."

She studied him a moment to make sure he meant it, then sat up. "Unfortunately, I am. This child is no bigger than a wish, but she's already figured out that pushing on my bladder is the best way to get me up and moving." She slid from the bed, acutely aware of his gaze on her, grabbed his shirt to use for a robe, then went down the hall to the bathroom. The white cotton shirt was so soft and smelled so enticingly of sunshine and Sebastian that when she returned to bed, she left it on, then curled up next to him, where he naturally fitted her against him.

"You're incredible, Sebastian," she murmured sleepily.

"So are you, darlin'." He pressed a kiss to her forehead. "So are you."

LISTENING TO THE EVEN SOUND OF HER BREATHING, Sebastian tried once more to let go of her, to get out of bed, get dressed, and go. It was hard, damn hard, when all he wanted to do was spend the rest of his life right there, but finally he managed. He got dressed, debated reclaiming his shirt from her, then decided what the hell. He was going straight home, and he didn't want to risk waking her.

Finding a blanket folded over the footboard, he spread it over her, blew out the candles, then returned to the bed to give her a light kiss.

"G'night," she mumbled, then burrowed deeper into the pillow and started snoring softly.

"Goodbye," he whispered.

Moving quietly, he left the room and went downstairs. He was just reaching for the doorknob when the door abruptly swung open. He jerked back to avoid getting hit, and Julie gave a startled cry, quickly regained her composure, and gave him a long, dry look.

"Forgetting something, aren't you?"

She was young enough to be his daughter— Mentally he shied away from a line of thought too painful at the moment. She was barely half his age—that was better— and by anyone's standards, he was decent, yet he knew from the heat in his face that he was blushing. "Melina fell asleep wearing my shirt, and I—I didn't want to wake her."

"Uh-huh."

"Did you have a good time at the party?"

"Yeah, I did. It was fun."

"Yeah, well, uh . . . I'll see you."

"Sure." She closed the door behind him, and he heard the lock click as he started down the steps. It sounded so . . . hard. So final.

Maybe because it was.

MELINA AWAKENED SUNDAY MORNING WITH THE scent of Sebastian on her skin and all around her. She showered and dressed and rousted Julie from bed for a quick walk to Harry's, where she ate quite possibly the biggest breakfast she'd ever had. She was still torn between the options for her relationship with Sebastian—marry him or dump him for her own good—so she'd decided that for now she would put off making a decision until later. Now that he wasn't going to pressure her anymore to marry him—more importantly, now that he was going to make love with her—she was going to just go along and enjoy, and worry about the consequences later. Yes, it was the coward's way out, but what could she say?

When they got back home, she sat down at her desk while Julie went to the family room at the back of the house, and she dialed Sebastian's number. After three rings, the answering machine picked up, and she listened to his voice on tape, sounding self-conscious. *You've reached Sebastian and Chrissy Knight. At the sound of the tone, leave a message and your number, and we'll get back to you.*

She smiled faintly as the machine beeped. "Hi,

Sebastian, it's me. I just wanted to say . . . well, nothing, really. I just wanted . . . Aw, hell, I hate machines. I mean, heck. Sorry about that. Does Chrissy ever listen to these messages?" She cleared her throat. "Let's try this again. Hi, it's Melina. Call me, will you?"

She tried again a few hours later, and a few hours after that, and a few more hours later. In between she and Julie cleaned house and did laundry. They walked to the store and bought groceries, then walked to the ice-cream shop three doors down for a double-dip cone.

Each armed with a cone big enough for three, they were walking back to the house when she saw Sebastian and Chrissy sitting on the bandstand steps. A surge of warmth filled her, and she was about to suggest they detour that way when she realized they weren't alone. Leanne Wilson, who owned the baby shop, and her little boy were with them. The kids were playing, and Sebastian and Leanne were polishing off their own ice-cream cones.

It was perfectly innocent, she told herself as she nervously, embarrassedly, looked away. Sebastian had come into town to pick up Chrissy after church, and they'd probably had dinner with his parents, then stopped for a treat on the way home and ran into Leanne and her son. Simple. Innocent. Nothing to make the nerves in her stomach clench. From her job and her own experience, she knew the kind of men who two-timed the women in their lives, and Sebastian wasn't the type.

Which didn't change the fact that after making mad, passionate love to her the night before, he'd taken Chrissy to the ice-cream parlor right by her house and hadn't stopped by to say hello or to ask her and Julie to join them.

Back at the house, instead of surrendering to the part

of her that wanted to hide inside and watch him through the curtains, she sat down in one of the Adirondack chairs, propped her feet on the railing, and leisurely ate her ice cream without tasting a bite.

He never looked her way.

Julie was content to sit quietly with her, although when Sebastian, Leanne, and the kids left the square together, she broke the silence. "What's the deal with that?"

Melina forced a careless shrug. "I'm sure they've known each other for years."

"Yeah, well, still . . ."

Yeah, Melina agreed with a chill of trepidation. *Still . . .*

Chapter Seventeen

MELINA DIDN'T CALL SEBASTIAN AGAIN THAT day. Instead she moped around the house, replaying every moment of the previous night over and over in her mind. He'd been behaving perfectly normally when they arrived at the cookout. It was later, when his grandmothers had summoned him over, that she'd noticed his mood had changed. Had someone said something to him before then? Compared her unfavorably to Diana? Found fault with her? Judged her as undeserving of him and Chrissy? He'd denied it, proposed to her, made love to her, then left her—and apparently he was having second thoughts about coming back.

Why?

She waited near the phone all day Monday for him to call. When four o'clock rolled around without a peep from him, she left a message on his machine, inviting him and Chrissy to dinner at seven. She set the table for four, cooked the meal, and even baked a cake for dessert, and when seven o'clock arrived and they didn't, she put away the extra dishes without a word of explanation to Julie and wondered what the hell was going on.

Her first impulse was to cry, stomp her feet, and throw things—preferably at him. Her second was to tell him to go to hell, that she didn't need him, and neither did her baby. She kept both in check for the time being.

Tuesday passed without a call, too. And Wednesday, Thursday, and Friday.

That evening found her sitting on the porch, watching the rain that had started a few hours earlier. Julie had gone to a pep rally that kicked off every new school year with Courtney, who'd assured them a little bit of rain wouldn't hinder the fun, and then they were having a sleepover at a friend's house. Melina had called Lynda to commiserate, but she and Ben had been on their way out the door to have dinner with the Bishops and Alanna. Father-and-daughter relationship was still rocky, but progressing, Lyn had announced, and Melina had made appropriate responses.

Next she'd considered calling her mother, but she couldn't tell Livia anything without telling her everything, and there was no way she was going to break the news of the impending birth of their first grandchild over the phone. So she'd nixed that plan.

She felt so alone. Everyone had places to go, things to do, and people to be with except her. The only person she really wanted to be with *didn't* want to be with her. It was time to face the fear that had been lingering in the back of her mind all week.

Sebastian had dumped her.

Again.

The fear morphed into an ache in her chest and a lump that lodged in her throat, and it brought tears to her eyes that she impatiently dashed away. She wasn't a weak woman. She didn't cry over men. Her motto was get drunk, get mad, and get even.

Of course, being pregnant, she couldn't get drunk. She was too hurt to get mad. And how did she get even with a man who apparently didn't care nearly as much for her as she'd thought? The only thing she had that Sebastian wanted was her baby, but damned if she would use her own child as a means of punishment.

So all she could do was hurt.

Ducking her head, she covered her eyes with one hand and willed the tears to go away. There was no sense crying over what she couldn't have. She still had more than a lot of people dreamed of—a successful business, good friends, a wonderful family, a lovely home, financial security, her health, and her baby. She'd been so blessed that it shouldn't matter if Sebastian didn't want to be part of the picture.

But it did.

"Isn't it a lovely evening?"

The call came from the sidewalk. She looked up to see a woman standing at the gate, bareheaded in the rain. Though Melina couldn't place her, there was something familiar about her. Maybe she was one of the Knight friends and relatives she'd met last weekend, or another of the countless friendly residents of Bethlehem.

"Yes, it is," Melina answered weakly, not caring that it was a lie. The only thing lovely about the evening was that the rain matched her mood, as if the heavens were shedding the tears she couldn't let herself cry.

"Do you mind if I join you?" The woman waited, one

hand on the gate. "You look as if you could use a little company."

"Sure. Come on in."

The woman paused at the top of the steps, gave herself a shake, then sat down in the other chair. "What a comfortable chair. Sebastian Knight's handiwork, isn't it?" Without waiting for a response, she gestured toward Melina. "And so is your blue mood, isn't it?"

That wasn't such a big guess, since apparently everyone in Bethlehem knew everything about everyone else. Melina extended her hand. "I'm—"

"Marina Dimitris." The woman's grin was smug. "I know who you are."

"It's Melina," she corrected her.

"Of course it is. Isn't that what I just said?" The woman shook her hand. "I'm Gloria."

Melina felt a curious sensation, as if the name Gloria should mean something—as if the *woman* should mean something—but try as she might, she couldn't recall where she might know her from. In the weeks she'd lived in Bethlehem, to say nothing of the months she'd been visiting Lynda there, she'd been to dozens of celebrations of every sort and met hundreds of people. Quite possibly they hadn't even spoken wherever they'd met, beyond a *Hi, how are you*.

"How's the little one?" Gloria asked with a nod toward Melina's middle.

"There truly are no secrets in this town, are there?" Melina asked wryly.

"Not from me. It's my business to know everything."

"It's my business, too. I'm a private investigator. What do you do?"

"Oh, I like to say I'm in the business of futures."

Futures? The stock market? Melina gave her a quick scan, taking in her rather dowdy pants and top and sensible shoes of the sort Yaya Rosa wore. She didn't look like any investment counselor Melina had ever seen . . . though, to be fair, other than her own stockbroker, the only ones she'd had contact with were the subjects of investigations—unfaithful husbands, deadbeat dads, and sticky-fingered thieves. Losers, the lot of them. Like most men. One of these days she would realize she was better off without one. It would save her from having to divorce him or shoot him.

But because that day hadn't arrived yet, she redirected her attention to Gloria's question. "The little one is fine, and so am I. Like the song says, my future's so bright, I have to wear shades."

"I don't know that song."

"A lot of people don't." She brought her feet up into the seat, rested her chin on her hand, and sighed.

"He hasn't called you back, has he?" Gloria asked sympathetically. "And he didn't stop to see you when he brought Chrissy into town earlier, did he? Even though he drove right past."

Just what she needed to know. "Did you come to depress me even more? I'm just curious, because if that's the case, let me tell you, I'm down enough. I don't need to be kicked, too."

"Why, I would never kick you, Melinda! Well, maybe figuratively, but never literally. What kind of guardian would do that?"

"Guardian? I thought you said you were a stockbroker."

"A stock—" Suddenly Gloria burst into laughter that sounded like ice crystals pinging off glass. Though Melina didn't understand the reason for it, it lightened her mood a degree or two, and for that she was grateful.

"Yes, of course," Gloria went on. "I told you I deal in futures, and you— Can I ask you a personal question?"

"Nothing's stopped you yet."

"Are you just going to give up? Are you going to let your and Sebastian's fears keep you apart? Do you intend to deny your baby a family just because neither of you has the courage to offer the other your heart?"

Pain stabbed through Melina, making her huddle a little tighter. "My baby has a family. She's got me and Julie, Lynda and Ben, Mama and Papa and Yaya Rosa, and all the Dimitrises and Emanuelideses, and she'll have her father and his family. I would never stand between her and the Knights." Her voice began to tremble as she went on. "And as far as offering my heart, why on earth would I do that again when he's made it painfully clear that he doesn't want it?"

"Because you love him, and you're going to love him as long as you live."

"Oh, God, now there's a depressing thought."

"You don't mean that."

"Don't bet money on it, Gloria. You'd lose. I fell in love with the bastard, and I'll damn well learn to fall out of it."

The older woman tsked—whether over her language or her stubborn insistence, Melina didn't know or care. "So you *are* just giving up. The most stubborn child the Dimitris and Emanuelides families have ever produced, and you're giving in without a whimper. Ah, your Yaya Rosa would be so disappointed."

Melina gave her a sharp, suspicious look. "What do you know about Yaya Rosa?"

"I told you, child—it's my business to know everything. Rosa never gave up and she never gave in. She left her home and her parents when she was but a girl to come with her husband to a strange country, to make a better life for herself and her family, and she succeeded against the odds. Now the odds merely *seem* to be against her favorite granddaughter, the one most like Rosa herself, and what does she do? She folds. Gives in. Curls up like a little baby and feels sorry for herself. Go ahead, *koukla mou*. Wallow in your self-pity while your one best chance at love slips away because you're afraid."

Koukla mou. It was a sweet endearment, meaning "my baby"—one her grandmother often used—but there was nothing sweet about it coming out of this stranger's mouth in that taunting tone. Melina jumped to her feet, kicking the footstool back in the process, and glared down at the woman. "Look, lady, I don't know who the hell you are, but you don't know me, and you don't know what I feel or why I do a damn thing. Maybe this is a new concept to you people, but my private life is *private*. The last thing I need is some stranger inviting herself in to criticize things she knows nothing about. Now kindly get the hell off my property before I call the police and have you arrested for trespassing."

Anger was vibrating through Melina as she stalked toward the door, intending to lock herself inside . . . or maybe come back with her pistol or her pepper spray and put the fear of God into the woman. Her nerve was contempti—

"The fear of God. Good one." That light, tinkling laugh came again, rippling through the air before fading.

Startled by the words, Melina whirled around to demand an explanation of the woman, but the chair was empty. So was the yard and the sidewalk out front. Her bare feet making little noise on the floorboards, Melina walked to the end of the porch and peered around the corner and into the backyard. Empty, too.

Gloria was gone.

Melina rubbed her arms as a chill swept over her. She never would have believed the older woman could move so quickly or so quietly . . . but what was the other option? That she'd disappeared into thin air? People just didn't do that. Couldn't do that.

Shouldn't do it. Though Norma had done it in Providence . . . twice.

Slowly she returned to the door, twisting the knob, but she didn't push it open or go inside. Instead she looked back at the empty chairs. Gloria was right. Yaya Rosa *would* be disappointed in her, and ashamed, too. Her entire future was on the line here, and what had she done? Surrendered. Given up and given in. She hadn't even asked for an explanation. She could just see herself in twenty years, when her baby had grown into a beautiful young woman asking, "What went wrong between you and Papa, Mama?" And she would shake her head sorrowfully and say, "I don't know. *I never asked.*"

Damn well not likely.

If Sebastian didn't love her, fine. If he didn't want her, okay. Either one would break her heart, but she could accept it.

But damned if she wasn't going to make him tell her so face to face.

SEBASTIAN SAT AT THE WORKTABLE IN THE SHOP, WITH only the lights directly above the table on and the stereo playing softly, barely audible over the rain falling on the tin roof. It was a sound he usually found soothing, but not at the moment. About the only thing that soothed him lately was the dreams he had of Melina whenever he managed to sleep. They were both a blessing and a curse, though, because he always woke up and had to leave them behind.

He hadn't heard from her since Monday afternoon's call. *Why don't you and Chrissy come for dinner?* she'd asked. *I'll cook. Hey, I'll even bake for you. I don't make that offer often. We'll eat about seven, but you guys can come over whenever you're ready. See you.* He'd listened to the message ten times or more before erasing it, and when seven o'clock had come, he'd been sitting at the bar in the Five Pines Lounge, staring down a bottle of whiskey.

She hadn't called again.

Deliberately he forced himself to focus on the piece he'd been working on all week. The carving was his own design—a border of hearts circling an oak tree with an umbrellalike canopy of leaves and, underneath it, a teddy bear, a quilt, and a rocking chair—and it was almost finished. All that was left, besides a little detail work, was the bottom segment of the hearts border. But something was missing. He hadn't figured out what yet—some small element that would make it the perfect piece he wanted it to be.

It had to be perfect. It was for his baby.

His back was aching and his hand cramping when he laid the knife aside and stood up to stretch. Closing his eyes, he bent his head side to side, then rolled his shoulders to ease the taut muscles there. When he opened his eyes again, he saw a figure just inside the door and gave a start before recognizing Sophy. "I didn't hear— What are you doing here?"

She gestured toward her slicker, hanging on a hook inside the door. "The rain's not going to stop for a few days, so I came to pick up my jacket."

"The forecast says sunny and warm tomorrow."

"Yeah? Well, trust me—it's going to rain until Monday. Why are you working so late?"

"Chrissy went to a birthday slumber party at a friend's house, and—" And he'd had nothing else to do. No one to talk to. No one to spend the evening with. Nothing to occupy him but painful memories and his own misery. But instead of detailing for her how pathetic he was, he shrugged instead.

"You should have called Melina. Julie's spending the night at your cousin Courtney's house, so she's alone tonight, too."

He didn't say anything. He hadn't told Ben and Sophy that it was over between him and Melina. Ben, he suspected, knew something was up. Of course, he was living with Melina's best friend. Sophy, apparently, didn't have a clue, and he just wasn't up to giving her one that evening. She would hear something soon enough.

Though he wished she would take her jacket and leave, instead she came over and leaned on the table across from him. "Your carving is lovely."

"Thanks."

"Melina will be touched."

He didn't even try to deny that she was the other reason he wanted it to be perfect. Maybe he couldn't be a part of her life, but this gift for their baby would always be there.

"When's the wedding?"

He'd just laid the blade against the wood, intending to start the series of hearts that would complete the ring, but her question made his fingers clench. Carefully he laid the knife down again and looked up at her. It looked as if he was going to give her more than a clue. "There's not going to be a wedding."

"Why not?"

"Melina doesn't want to marry me. She's never wanted to marry me. All she wanted was an affair, and I can't settle for just that, so . . . it's over."

"How do you know she doesn't want to marry you?"

"Let's see . . . the time she said all she wanted from me was sex was the first hint. Oh, and then there were the dozen times I proposed and she said no." He felt the bleakness creep into his expression. "Trust me. She made it very clear."

"I don't know. I think maybe she didn't want to get married just because of the baby. Maybe she didn't want to be part of a package deal. Maybe she's always dreamed about marrying for love."

"I'm sure she has. Unfortunately, she . . ." His jaw tightened. "She doesn't love me." Though there'd been a time when she had thought she did, back in those first four days and nights they'd been together. He had liked her thinking so, even though he'd known it wasn't true, even though he'd had no place for her in his life at that time.

Back then she'd thought she loved him, and he hadn't wanted her to. Now he *knew* he loved her, and she didn't want him. The irony didn't amuse him.

"How do you know she doesn't love you?"

He dragged his fingers through his hair. "For God's sake, Sophy—"

"No, for *your* sake, and Melina's and the baby's. How do you *know* she doesn't love you?"

"She told me so!"

"She actually said *I don't love you?*"

Wishing she would go away and leave him alone, he sighed impatiently. "No, she didn't actually say it. Look, Sophy, I appreciate your concern, but—"

"But you'd rather be alone in your misery. But every day you spend alone mourning what you don't have is one more day you've lost with Melina. Life is too short to waste even one of those days."

"I *can't* be with her. It's too hard knowing—"

"Thinking."

"—she doesn't want the same thing I do. It—" Embarrassed that he was admitting such weakness to a girl little more than half his age, he looked away and lowered his voice. "It hurts too damn much."

"What did you do to try to convince her to marry you? Besides proposing a dozen times."

"Everything."

She smiled. "I've found over the years that a man's idea of *everything* often differs from a woman's."

Yeah, like she'd lived so damn many years. He didn't know how old she was, but he figured twenty or so. Definitely not a day over twenty-two, not with that face.

"Thank you," she said.

He was bewildered. "For what?"

She made a dismissive gesture, then drew a tall stool to the worktable and sat down. "Okay, did you spend time with her?"

He didn't want to talk about Melina anymore—he hadn't been kidding about the hurt—but maybe if he humored Sophy, he would be rid of her that much quicker. Besides, truthfully . . . it was kind of nice that she cared enough to badger. When Diana had left him and he'd told his family and friends to leave him alone, they had, and he'd gotten so damn lonely it had almost killed him. "As much as I could."

"Did you treat her with respect and affection?"

"Yeah. For the most part." They'd had some rocky times, but he figured his behavior had been better than decent most of the time.

"Did you tell her she's beautiful?"

"Yes." And one night when he'd told her so, she'd questioned him. *Do you really think I'm beautiful?* Because she hadn't believed him all the other times he'd told her. Because he'd used her and hurt her.

Would it matter to her that he regretted all the mistakes, all the wounded feelings, and the disappointments? Would she think better of him if she knew he would go back and undo the hurts if it was possible?

"Did you apologize when you should?"

"Yeah. Usually."

"Did you criticize the way she looks?"

He scowled at Sophy. "She looks incredible. Why would I criticize that?"

"Hey, some men are jealous. They don't want their women dressing in a manner that makes other men look at them."

"Men look at Melina no matter how she's dressed because she's beautiful. You think I'm petty enough to hold that against her?"

"Okay. So . . . did you nag her about quitting her job or letting the big strong men take care of business for her?"

Remembering that night he'd kissed her outside the park in Providence, when she'd kicked him, bitten him, and practically broken his hand, he smiled wryly. "I haven't met the big strong man who could take care of her. She's the most capable woman I've ever known."

"Hmm. You treated her as an intelligent, capable human being who also happened to be the most important woman in your life. You were affectionate and considerate, and treated her respectfully. And, of course, you told her you loved her. That covers just about everything. I don't know—" She broke off, and her gaze narrowed. "What?"

He shifted uncomfortably. "What do you mean, what?"

"You did tell her you loved her, didn't you?"

The heat started at his ears and spread through his face. It made his collar suddenly feel tighter and made his voice hoarse when he replied. "I, uh . . . no."

She stared at him, mouth open. "But . . . you *do* love her."

Finding the mud on the toe of his shoe most interesting, he rubbed it off on the floor, then broke the little clods into powder before finally meeting her gaze again. "More than anything."

"So why haven't you told her?"

"Because she just wanted— She didn't even want—" He broke off and walked to the window to stare out. The rain was coming down harder, creating one hell of a racket on the tin overhead. It fell in sheets that obscured his view, with only a dim glow from the lights inside the house showing its location. He'd lived in that house for thirty-five years, but it hadn't been a home for the past four. It never would be again if he didn't make things right with Melina.

He turned away from the window and began putting away the tools left on the bench against the wall, keeping his back to Sophy. It was easier to talk that way. "Diana was my first real girlfriend. We started dating in high school, and we got married not long after she graduated. It seemed we'd been together forever, and I thought we always would be. Then she left. It came right out of the blue. I had no idea she was unhappy or that she wanted something more or something else. One day my life was normal and happy and satisfying, and the next . . . I thought I'd never quit hurting, missing her, loving her."

It would have been easier if he'd had some hint something was wrong, if she'd been short-tempered or moody. But, no, things had been the same as ever, only more so. Her mood had been sunnier than usual. She'd been willing to consider having a second child. She'd said *I love you* a little more often, with a little more passion.

And then she'd disappeared and left him devastated. If she'd had the courage to face him, if she'd said *I don't love you anymore, I want someone else, I want something else,* he still would have been devastated, but . . . he . . . could . . . have . . .

The realization came slowly that those were exactly the things he hadn't said to Melina. No explanation, no apology, nothing.

Oh, God, she was right. He *was* a rat bastard.

He needed a moment to get his thoughts together again, to remember where he'd been going with the conversation. His voice was only as loud as necessary to be heard over the rain. "There were occasional women after Diana, but never the same one twice. Until Melina. She was so . . ." Beautiful. Passionate. Vibrant. So emotionally alive when he'd been dead for so long.

For a long time he stood motionless, unable to focus

his gaze on the work he was doing, unable to gather his thoughts. Finally he turned to face Sophy, to tell her he couldn't continue this conversation.

She was gone.

His gaze swept the room, but there was no mistake. The jacket she'd come for was gone from its hook and the door stood open, letting in the sweet fragrance of cool summer rain. He was alone.

Feeling lonely and too damn melancholy, he went to close the door, then hesitated. Headlights shone through the rain from a vehicle parked beside his truck. Sophy's ride? he wondered. But there was no sign of Sophy and, from what he could see, no one in the vehicle.

Just someone standing beside the driver's door.

Someone who looked as forlorn as he felt.

Someone with a mass of black curls, with legs a mile long.

Someone who was everything he'd ever needed in his life.

A dozen halting steps took him through the door and into the rain. Water soaked his hair and his clothes, seeped into his shoes, and sluiced down his face, but he hardly noticed. He wondered where Sophy had gone but didn't bother to look—wondered what had brought Melina out but didn't question his good fortune. He just stood in the rain and stared.

When he stopped moving, she started, coming to stand a few feet in front of him. She was little more than an arm's length away, but it seemed like a million miles. She wore a bright yellow slicker with an electric blue lining, zipped up to her neck and completely covering whatever she wore underneath it. In deference to the weather, she wore sneakers instead of the usual heels, but in defiance of the weather, the jacket's hood hung down her back. She smelled of the rain that glistened on her hair and her face, and of jasmine and a scent that was purely Melina, and he wanted her in his life more desperately at that moment than he'd ever wanted anything.

Minute after minute ticked past in silence. Finally he said, "I was just talking about you."

"To whom?"

"Sophy. She came to pick up . . ." Forgetting what she'd come for, he let the words trail off.

"What were you telling her?"

"That you were beautiful. Full of passion. Warm-hearted and hot-blooded. Lustful and sensual and sexual, and frankly, you scared the hell out of me." Abruptly he gestured toward the workshop. "You want to go inside?"

She gave a shake of her head, and water sprinkled from the ends of her hair. "I came to tell you something. It'll just take a moment."

Sebastian swallowed hard and rubbed one hand absently across his chest. She was looking at him, God help him, in exactly the same way he knew he was looking at her. As if she was hungry for the sight of him. As if she could memorize every feature if she just looked long enough, hard enough. As if she'd missed him, and loved him, and wanted him back in her life.

For a moment she lifted her gaze to the night sky, eyes closed against the rain. Then she drew a deep breath, opened her eyes once again, and focused on him. "I'm not a weak person. I don't cry over men. I don't surrender just because the odds are against me. I don't give in, and I never, ever give up. I'm Yaya Rosa's favorite granddaughter, and I've got a stubborn streak to be proud of, and I'm not going to slink off into a corner and spend the rest of my life wondering what went wrong between us."

She looked bedraggled, drenched, and damn near drowned, but she still managed to pull off a dignified air, even with the hurt that turned her dark eyes as liquid as the rain. "I know you don't love me. You made it clear that if not for the baby, you wouldn't be involved with me at all. And that's all right. Of course, I wish you loved me with all your heart, but either it happens or it doesn't. I can't hold it against you because it didn't happen for you. But I *can* hold it against you that you could treat me the way you did, could make love to me the way you did, then walk away without a word. I deserve better than that. At the very least, I deserve a goodbye."

Finally she took a deep breath, signaling that she was finished. Now it was his turn to respond, to offer an explanation or an excuse, anything that would allow her to leave, put him out of her heart as well as her mind, and live her life without him. Fall in love with someone else. Make love, babies, and a future with someone else.

As she'd told him before, *When hell freezes over.*

"Well?" she asked. "Don't you have anything to say?"

He wiped his hand across his face, giving the rain a new path to drip down. He had so many things to say that he didn't know where to start. He chose the most important point in her little speech. "How do you know I don't love you?"

Clearly she thought the question was cruel, in bad taste, or both. Her eyes widened into exotic dark circles and her jaw dropped open in dismay. Before she could come up with any arguments, though, he went on.

"Is it because I treated you badly and used you only for

sex and never wanted to spend time with you? Because I kept you secret from my family and refused to let you spend time with my little girl? Or is it only because I never told you so? How do you *know,* Melina?"

Her mouth worked before she could get any words out. "Of course you didn't— But you never said—"

"No, I didn't. But not saying something doesn't make it so. You never told me that you loved our baby from the moment you became aware of her existence, but it's true, isn't it? And I never needed to hear you say the words to know that you love Lynda better than a sister and Julie like a daughter, but you do. And you love me, too, even though you never said so. Don't you?"

He half expected her to deny it, or to ignore the question altogether, and it was clear from the panic in her expression that she was considering that action herself. Then she took a couple deep breaths, slid one hand down so it rested on their baby, as if the contact gave her courage, and she quietly admitted, "Yes, I love you."

He'd heard the words hundreds of times before. Diana had offered them freely, easily—maybe too easily, considering the way she'd left. Certainly she had said them at times when she obviously didn't mean them. But this time they were different. Healing. Gratifying. Satisfying.

"You want to know what went wrong between us, Melina?" he asked softly. "We were both afraid. We'd been hurt—by Rico and Diana, by each other—and neither of us wanted it to happen again. So you pretended you just wanted sex, and I pretended I wanted to marry you only for the baby's sake, and neither of us had the courage to risk getting our hearts broken again. And in the end, that's exactly what we wound up doing."

"So you're saying we're both cowards."

A raindrop slid down her cheek to her jaw, where he caught it on his fingertip and wiped it away. "Me more than you. I hadn't found the courage yet to go to you and beg for another chance. I hadn't even decided I deserved another chance, then I looked out the door and there you were . . ."

For the first time since she'd arrived, a ghost of a smile touched her lips. "My mama didn't raise a coward."

"No. She raised a beautiful, capable, strong, intelligent woman."

"Don't forget stubborn."

He smiled, too. "How could I forget?"

Just as quickly as the lighter moment had come, it was gone, and her expression turned serious again. "So . . . what do we do now?"

"First I tell you how incredibly sorry I am for everything I did wrong."

She moved a step closer. "And then?"

"I tell you I love you more than I thought I was capable of loving anyone." She took one more step, and he swallowed hard. "Then I ask you one more time to marry me, except this time I do it the right way."

"And what is that?"

He slid his hands into her hair and gently tilted her head back so the light over the barn door illuminated her face. "I love you, Melina. I know I can live without you, but God help me, I don't want to. When I wake up in the middle of the night, I want to feel you beside me, and when I can't be with you, I want to know you're missing me the way I miss you. I want to raise our daughters with you and spoil our grandbabies, and when I die, I want to know that every minute of my life was richer because you were in it. Will you marry me?"

For a moment she stared at him, lower lip trembling, then she sniffed. "That's so sweet. And then what?"

"And then you"—*please, God*—"say yes." He waited expectantly. And waited. Though his chest was tight and air was difficult to come by, he managed a crooked smile. "Have mercy on me, darlin'. Don't make me beg."

"But you would, wouldn't you?"

"In a heartbeat."

She smiled smugly, then wrapped her arms around his neck. "Yes, yes, yes, *agape mou,* my love. And then you kiss me, and then do we get the celebratory lovemaking?"

"Sweetheart, I thought you'd never ask." Instead of kissing her, though, or carrying her inside or, hell, just lowering her to the ground, he hugged her, holding her close, breathing her scent, and letting all the tension and loneliness and heartache ease away. For the first time he could recall, he felt completely at peace.

Then her lips brushed his throat, and the heat of her body began warming his from the outside in. When she pressed against him, his own body responded, and when finally he kissed her, he swore he heard the sizzle and pop as the rain hitting them turned to steam. Lifting her into his arms, he headed for the house, where he intended to spend the rest of the night showing her what he'd finally found the courage to put into words.

They were halfway there when she laid her hand gently against his cheek and asked one more question. "And then what, Sebastian?"

He gazed at her, and for a moment his heart was too full for words. Then he swallowed over the lump in his throat and said in a husky voice, "And then we get married."

"And we live happily ever after."

"Of course," he agreed.

Was there any other way for a love story to end?

IN THE QUIET OF THE SHOP, THE LIGHTS ILLUMINATED the work-in-progress on the table like a spotlight. It was the end of a cradle, made by a master craftsman for his second beloved child. Carved into the hard oak was a circle of hearts, and inside that was an intricately detailed oak tree, a rocking chair, a quilt, and a teddy bear. Across the bottom, where a segment of hearts was missing, a simple phrase flowed in graceful script.

Agape mou.

My love.

And it was perfect.